One Last Thing Before You Go

CAROLINE FRANK

ONE LAST THING BEFORE YOU GO

CAROLINE FRANK

CONTENT WARNINGS

- Sexual Content
- Loss of Parents (off-page)
- Infertility
- PCOS
- Endometriosis
- Divorce (off-page)

A NOTE FROM THE AUTHOR

Hi there! The following book touches upon subjects like infertility due to PCOS and endometriosis. While having PCOS and/or endometriosis does not mean a person is automatically unable to have children in general, some people with this diagnosis cannot.

PCOS and endometriosis affect millions of women everywhere, but each case is different, and different doctors choose to take different avenues according to what they believe is best. In Lottie's case I used my own health journey —for the most part—to tell her story. Lottie is a worst case scenario kinda girl.

CHAPTER ONE

LOTTIE

I use the lemon twist in my martini to absentmindedly swirl the contents of my glass. The dim overhead lighting of the bar bounces off the tiny shards of ice floating in the vermouth and vodka, casting tiny rainbows in my drink in a way that fascinates me, but not enough to distract me.

Sighing, I drop my head in my hands, messing up my already mussed curtain bangs.

I'm sad. Of course I'm sad—I just came from a funeral, for god's sake. But I can't help the way my mind wanders to the potential consequences of Walter's death. And just as it does, just as I begin to consider how I'll have to adjust it to get my life back to what it used to be, to move back to New York, find myself another job, and leave this small town (for good this time), another wave of grief crashes over me—followed quickly by one of guilt. Today is supposed to be about Walter, and I'm here freaking out about what his death will mean for *my* future?

I scoff, disgusted with myself, before tossing back what remains of my favorite cocktail, silently toasting to my fallen boss, friend, and mentor. The alcohol burns my throat on the way down morphing my expression into a grimace, but it's okay. *I deserve the pain.*

In a practiced motion, I raise my hand slightly and flag down my favorite bartender. "Can I get another?" I ask Alejandro.

"No problem; I got you." He nods sympathetically and walks away with my empty glass.

"*Holy shit.* How'd you do that?" The sound of a disbelieving voice—deep, smooth like butter—pulls me from my dark thoughts. I swivel in my barstool to face the person responsible for preventing me from diving into a downward spiral—*thank god.* "I've been standing here for legit ten minutes, and he hasn't so much as looked in my direction. Yet one wave from you, and you've got the bartender at your feet."

He scratches the stubble on his square jaw as he stares down at me with a tired, yet excited gaze and a lopsided smile so adorable it knocks the breath out of me. From his disheveled hair and dark under-eyes, it's obvious this man hasn't been having the best day either. But even so—even looking like he hasn't slept in days—with just one glance I can tell there's a lightness to him that has my heart beating faster. The stranger towers over me, running his fingers through his dark brown hair. The worn leather jacket he wears covers the wide expanse of his back, moving with every single one of his muscles, making it seem like it was almost custom-tailored to his body.

A deep instinct, left dormant for several years, seems to awaken inside, shaking me to the core. It's been a while since I've wanted to *be* with anyone—I mean, what's the point?—but one word from this man, and suddenly my body doesn't care about anything that's happened, everything I've been through. It doesn't care that we made a vow a couple of years back to never date again.

It's not like I lost my sex drive since my divorce—that definitely isn't it. I have a nice collection of, *ahem*, helpers in my top bedside drawer that are on regular rotation. I even gave my favorite one a name (Henry Cavill, of course, because how could I not). But it's been a long time since I've been with a real man.

Since leaving New York several years ago, I've been on a few dates—most of which were because I was forced into them by my siblings as a result of their fear of me dying alone. The last one was such a mismatch I actually stood up in the middle of dinner, walked away, and Venmoed him for my half of the bill (even though I most certainly could not afford it). That's when I made the call to never date again. Since then, I've been focusing most of my efforts on getting the hell out of this town again. Focusing on saving up enough money to go back to New York. Easier said than done, though, since I destroyed my career, my personal life, and my finances. But I don't want to think about that now.

Alas, we persist. Kind of.

So, not a good idea to pursue him. Plus, he looks way younger than me.

Still, I'm human, so I stare at the man, completely dumbstruck because I *think* from the way he's looking at me that he might be into me? Thankfully, I recover quickly and slap on a poker face.

Emboldened mostly by the vodka, I say, "It's all about who you know," with an air of self-confidence I one-hundred percent do not feel. "And you don't really look like you're from around here." I allow myself to give him a conspicuous once-over to make my point.

He snorts and places what looks like a camera bag on the bar before taking the stool beside me. "Definitely not," he says, as if insulted by the idea.

I should be a little more protective of my small hometown, but I don't blame his derisiveness—I know exactly what he means. All I ever wanted growing up was to get the hell out of Ceres Cove—which I managed to do. It's the staying away part I failed at. Though it wasn't really *entirely* my fault, was it? All because I... Anyway, I didn't have any other choice but to come back.

"Just passing through," the stranger continues, but doesn't elaborate.

Though we're a small beach town that does get a surprisingly significant influx of tourists during the warmer months, we rarely see out-of-towners in the off-season. Needless to say, this man's arrival into town is bound to make a splash in the local rumor mill.

With a heartbreaking smile, he removes his leather jacket and sets it on the stool beside him before pushing the sleeves of his shirt up his arms. I have to stifle a groan when my eyes flicker down to check out his forearms because... well, *forearms.* Muscular and sprinkled lightly with hair, the hint of a tattoo peeks from underneath the sleeve of his shirt on his right arm. Up until this very second, I didn't know I had a thing for tattoos, but I suddenly find myself *needing* to run my fingers over the lines of ink.

Jesus.

It doesn't help that the navy waffle henley he's wearing is fitted enough that it shows off every single one of his muscles, stretching over defined pecs, strong biceps. Not too tight—just right. My mind wanders to all the different ways in which I could get him to take off that shirt. To find out whether it's the only tattoo he has or whether there are more.

Phew. Okay. Calm down, crazy.

"To be fair," the stranger starts, pulling me back to the present as he looks me over slowly in a way that heats my skin, "you don't seem to be from around here either."

I smirk because I suppose to the untrained eye, it would be a safe assumption to make. But my black pencil skirt with the slightly snagged hem, yellowed white silk blouse, and worn designer heels tell a different story. They'd tell you I had another life before coming back to Ceres Cove, and that now that it's over, these clothes are all I have left of it.

Before I can reply to the stranger, Alejandro slides a fresh vodka martini in front of me and I thank him with a smile. From the corner of my eye, I watch the stranger attempt to order a drink, only for the world's most overprotective bartender to shoot him a glare and walk away.

"What's a guy gotta do to get a beer around here?" He sighs.

I burst out laughing, surprising us both. A wide grin spreads across his face as he watches me, glacier eyes brightening even in the darkened bar. "Sorry, sorry," I say, slowly coming down. "I don't mean to make fun of you."

He smiles and shakes his head. "If your laugh didn't make you ten times more beautiful than you already are, I'd be slightly offended."

My breath catches at the way his words fall over me, the look on his face as his gaze bounces from my eyes to my lips and back again. Not wanting to get caught up in whatever the hell just happened, I look down at my martini and whisper, "That was a terrible pick-up line."

Normally, I would cringe if a guy I'd just met said something like that to me. But something about the way he carries himself, the way he looks at me, tells me he meant what he said. When our eyes meet once again, I feel as though the air has been sucked out of the bar, and I know he can feel it too. He fidgets in his seat, his smile dropping just enough for me to notice as he stares down at me with surprising affection.

"It wasn't a line. I'd bet my life that you don't give those smiles away easily. So thank you for that."

An unfamiliar tightness builds in my chest as I'm suddenly at a loss for words.

What the hell is wrong with me? I'm not usually like this, discombobulated and tongue-tied. I mean, it's not the first time a hot man talks to me, for god's sake.

We're quiet for a moment—my eyes on my drink, his eyes on me. We're not touching, but it's as if I can feel every inch of his body, the heat of it, all over mine. And I'm not completely sure that I hate it.

Alejandro, misinterpreting my discomfort from the other

end of the bar, walks over. "Everything okay over here?" he asks, glaring at the hot stranger before looking back at me.

Ignoring him, I ask the stranger "Can I get you a drink?"

He smiles broadly, sitting up straight. His lopsided grin is heart-melting; it forces me to thank the universe for the barstool beneath me, holding me up despite my weakened knees. "You gonna buy me a drink?"

"No, I mean—"

He laughs softly. "I know what you meant. Yes, I'd love that. Thank you."

I nod emphatically at Alejandro, who doesn't look too happy about the flirting going on right under his nose—especially given tonight's circumstances. He holds my gaze for a moment, frustrated, before rolling his eyes and turning to my new friend. "Well?" he asks, impatient.

The stranger stifles a laugh and orders an IPA, which is delivered promptly with a menacing glare.

"Damn. I don't think he likes me very much." We laugh softly as Alejandro walks away.

I take a sip of my martini and shrug. "He's just protective of me. Brothers can be that way sometimes."

"Your brother?" A wide grin spreads across his face, somehow delighted by this piece of information.

I nod with a smile. "It's just been a weird day, and he's looking out for me."

"I can see how you'd inspire protective instincts in some-one." He takes a sip from his beer. The stranger's eyes close briefly as if savoring every second of it that he can, the way someone would after having a long day.

"We don't even know each other and you're already making assumptions about me?"

He laughs and nods. "You're right. So, let's get to know each other, then." He leans forward and sticks his hand out, his grin wider still. "The name's Knox."

I stare down at his outstretched hand and say nothing.

"This is where you give me your name, Pretty Girl."

"*Pretty Girl?*" I snort, but can't help the goofy grin on my face. The way he smiles, the way his voice wraps around something in my chest, somehow brightens the darkness inside me.

"Carlota. *Lottie*," I say, reaching out to shake his hand. The second we make contact, my smile falls and gaze drops to where we're joined, skin buzzing. I suddenly feel warm and safe, and want to lean into him, inhale the wave of leather and citrus crashing over me. Our hands linger for a moment, relishing in the new comfort. I miss it as soon as we let go.

Through my lashes, I look up at Knox, his eyes widened like he can't believe what he felt, either.

"Hello, Carlota-Lottie," he says softly after clearing his throat once. "It's nice to meet you."

CHAPTER TWO

KNOX

This girl is amazing.

We've been talking for what feels like hours, and I never want to stop. These past couple of days have been a rollercoaster—I don't really know how to feel about everything that's happened—but she seems to have become the bright spot in the darkness in just a matter of minutes.

It's hard to tell since she's sitting down, but she looks to be on the tall side. Her dark-brown hair is wild, reaching all the way down to her waist in wide curls, wispy bangs falling over large, dark eyes that seem to reach something deep inside me, taking hold.

I'm trying really hard not to objectify her—especially after finding out how cool she is—but *damn*. I can tell from the way she's dressed that she's going for a professional look, but her skirt is cut so well, hugging every single one of her curves, and the shirt's buttons are unopened enough that it's making my imagination run wild. It's almost obscene.

She looks to be in her mid-thirties—older than me. But none of that shit matters, at the end of the day.

And it isn't just that she's gorgeous—because she is. No, she's also sarcastic and witty and spicy and has made me feel more alive in the past several minutes than I've felt in a while.

I've been trying to play it cool, to not seem too overeager or intense, but the low light coming from overhead does nothing to help my case. The soft beams reflect off her hair, showing hints of red undertones, shining on her like a spotlight, making sure she's all I see. I wanna pull out my camera and capture them—capture *her* and this moment. But I don't think she would take too kindly to a stranger asking for a photo. We're surrounded by people, but I barely acknowledge their existence. In just a few minutes, she's become the center of everything, and I'm wrapped up in every single word that comes out of her mouth.

Lottie unconsciously flips her hair over her shoulder as she discusses the advantages and disadvantages of living in a small town, and it's got her fired up in an adorable yet fierce way. Like a tiny, feral kitten.

"I'm not saying living in a small town is horrible," she clarifies, "but there's just no comparison to living in a metropolitan area. I mean, you have so much more access to everything. And most of the bigger cities have fantastic public transportation, which small towns don't. You need a car to get around, and having a car is really expensive. Have you seen the price of gas these days?"

I laugh at how inexplicably passionate she feels about

small-town life. "Seems like you have strong feelings about the topic."

She nods with a blush and a grin. "A bit of an understatement."

"Then why are you still living here? Why not get out, then?"

Her face falls, and I suddenly regret asking the question. She's so beautiful when she smiles, and I'm pretty sure I was right when I told her I bet she didn't give those away easily. I don't want to do anything to risk losing the privilege of seeing it again.

"Sorry, I didn't mean to—"

"No, you're fine. My being here is... It's temporary. I hope."

"Gotcha," I say, shooting her an encouraging smile.

She clears her throat and takes a sip of her martini.

What I wouldn't give to be that martini glass right about now...

"What about you? What brings you to our lovely beach town in the off season? You here visiting someone or something?"

Not wanting to get into it, I say, "Or something." I force a grin, hoping it comes off more coy and less serial killer. I'm not about to let my emotional baggage ruin what's looking to be an amazing night. At least considering the circumstances. "Visiting family. Kinda."

I could tell her the truth... But honestly, that's just gonna depress us both, and I'm done letting my father live rent free in my head. He doesn't deserve it.

Lottie raises a quizzical eyebrow. "What *kind of* family?" She presses her lips together, trying not to smile.

I can't help my laugh or the giddy, ridiculous way I feel. "Is that your lame attempt at double-checking whether I'm single or not? Checking whether I have a wife or something?" I casually take a sip of my beer, but my stomach is in knots. I actually like this girl. It's the first time in a really long time that I feel this sort of connection with anyone—maybe even *ever*.

She smirks and shrugs, blushing. "Or something."

A huge grin spreads across my face. "Well, I am, for the record. Single, I mean. No wife. No girlfriend. No partner. Free as a bird." I smile, and she laughs again tipping her head back in a way that makes my abs tighten.

"That laugh... Every time it's like it bursts through you. Like you're surprised by it because you don't do it often." Which of course, makes me smile even harder. I get to make her laugh, and already it feels like a privilege.

Lottie's eyes widen, like I've caught her in the act of something she never wanted anyone to know.

"Sorry, it's just..." I sigh, shaking my head.

"You're... observant." She purses her lips, studying me.

"It's my job to be. I'm a photojournalist. Freelance."

"Ah. That explains the camera bag, then." Her lips quirk just a bit.

I laugh softly. "Yup. And what do you do?"

She takes another sip in an attempt to hide a grimace, but I catch it. "I'm going to be honest with you, Knox. I'm not exactly in the best place, professionally speaking. Or personally. Or... Screw it, I'll be the first to say it: I'm a goddamn mess right now. So I don't want tonight to be about that. For the first time in a while I'm having fun, and there's no way I'm going to let my mess of a life get in the way. So, does it matter? What I do, I mean?"

I sit up straighter in my seat, surprised by her honesty.

"Wow. I… appreciate your honesty. So many people nowadays whitewash their lives, showing people only what's on the surface." And here's this woman—this smart, funny, beautiful woman—a stranger I only just met in a bar admitting that her life isn't perfect, but she doesn't want tonight to feel like it. She doesn't want it to darken this. She's not telling me *why* it isn't perfect, but at least she isn't lying about it, she isn't giving me some bullshit highlight reel.

"It's refreshing to see someone be vulnerable and real," I tell her. And maybe that's the allure of being with a stranger. Of being able to act and speak without a filter, without fear of being judged. Because you're never going to see each other again, so why the hell not?

And it's what I need tonight, too. I need to be with someone I like but don't know. I need to not think about it all. I need to be able to connect without feeling tied down.

"Thanks, I guess?" She huffs once. "I will volunteer *one* thing about work though: I get unlimited access to Post-Its, so there's that."

I smile broadly. "Oh, yeah? You got a thing for Post-its, Pretty Girl?"

"Definitely. I don't know what I would do without them." Lottie laughs in spite of herself, and I wanna kiss her. "They're the way to my heart."

"Good to know. Gotta keep that in mind for the future." I

tap the side of my head with my index finger and smirk, watching her blush.

As we laugh, I unconsciously move my hand that was resting on the bar closer to hers, fingertips less than an inch apart. Our eyes meet briefly, filled with a sudden need, one that I've felt building since I first saw her. My lower stomach tightens and I decide to go for it; to move my hand and cover hers with it, our fingers interlacing. It's a ballsy move, I know. I mean, I've known this woman for less than a night, but something about it feels right.

"Work is dumb," she says, her voice shaky. "Let's pretend we're both unemployed, yeah? Sound good?"

I smile broadly at her and bring her hand to my lips. "I mean, I work freelance, so it's basically the same thing, isn't it?"

At that, she laughs even harder than before, her face glowing, the previous lightness returning. My chest tightens and I can't help but panic slightly. Yes, I might need a stranger just for tonight, but suddenly the thought of never seeing her again doesn't sound great.

Shit.

With my other hand, I reach out, push her long bangs away from her eyes, and smile tenderly at her. Something inside me shifts, my heart beating like a loud drum in a quick beat.

"Can I—" I hesitate, frowning. "Can I take you out to dinner?"

"I... Right now?" I nod, heart racing as I wait impatiently for her to think it over. "Sure," she murmurs after some thought.

An unfamiliar feeling radiates through me, something a little like hope. And for the first time in a long time, I feel a little less lonely.

"I used to come here all the time on Sundays with my parents and siblings," Lottie volunteers as we walk into the family restaurant next door. "It's a bit run down these days, though."

I hadn't noticed. I've been too busy staring at her ass, at the way her hips sway side to side in that tight skirt as the hostess walks us to our booth.

When we settle into our seats, a sudden wave of nerves crashes over me. "Hey," I say, my heart racing.

She smirks at my awkwardness, gingerly placing her napkin in her lap. "Hey."

Her lips look soft and pink, and her skin is flushed. I hope to god it's a reaction to what I feel happening between the two of us tonight, and not just the two martinis she had at the bar.

An awkward silence settles between us as we wait for the waitress, and I hate this moment for us. Wracking my brain to get rid of this horrible vacuum before it ruins an otherwise amazing night, I try for a bad joke to break the ice: "There's something I should tell you before we let the night go on further," I start, voice deadpan. "I tell *a lot* of dad jokes."

She presses her lips together, trying not to smile. "Oh, yeah?"

"Yeah," I nod seriously. "But I don't have any kids. I'm a *faux Pa.*"

She blinks at me for a few seconds. "*Wow.* I cannot believe you just said that."

I burst out laughing at my own joke, loving the way she smiles while muttering "You're such a loser" under her breath.

"So, what's good here?" I ask, ignoring Lottie's comment. I flip through the worn menu with plastic covers, trying to act as casual as possible. She's so quiet, I have to sneak a peek at her. Thankfully, I catch her looking at me with a smile on her face.

"Will you quit staring at me like that?" she asks, but her voice is light.

"Sorry." I feel my cheeks heat.

"You're cute when you're awkward, you know that?"

I exhale slowly. "I guess I'm suddenly a little nervous." I fidget with the fork on the table, overcome with a wave of insecurity, of fear that this thing we're doing is going to go wrong and I'll never see her again.

Which is dumb, right? I mean, I don't even live here. What am I doing? This is sure to be a one-night thing. It's what I *wanted* when I first spoke to her. What I thought I wanted not more than twenty minutes ago. *Maybe* I could've stretched this out by a couple of days depending on how long I stay in town. And that's *if* she lets me see her again.

"I feel like I'm fucking this up." *In so many different ways.*

Lottie looks up from her menu and smiles. She reaches

out to place a hand on mine, stopping my movements. "Hey. I don't know about you, but I'm having a really good time."

I drop my menu on the table and place my other hand directly on hers, creating a Lottie hand sandwich. "Yeah. I'm having a pretty great time, too."

She pulls her hand free, but not before shooting me a wink. I reach out and pull it back in mine but accidentally knock over the fake candle votive and tiny vase of flowers instead.

"You're kind of a mess, aren't you?" She smirks, fixing the arrangement in the center of the table.

"Me?" I ask in mock outrage, pointing at myself. "What are you talking about? Are you saying you're not impressed by my suaveness?"

She snorts, not unkindly, and takes a sip of her water. "Super suave, Casanova. It's part of why I'm so attracted to you."

"Oh?" I smile, dropping the act and sitting up in my seat. "You're attracted to me?"

Her eyes widen. "Uh, I only meant that—" she stammers. "I—"

"No, no. You're attracted to me, it's cool," I say, getting a kick out of watching her scramble for words. I try to control it, but something in my chest swells and a shit-eating grin spreads across my face because she's into me. This amazing, smart, hot as hell woman is into me. I feel like a fucking love-struck teenager.

"You're not allowed to take it back now. You're attracted to me."

Lottie looks me straight in the eye. "I'm—I don't know. I

told you. I'm having a good time," she says with a shrug, and takes a sip of her water, avoiding my gaze.

"Yeah, you mentioned that." I smile fondly at her and reach out, taking her hand once again, keeping it in mine this time. I don't feel like letting go of this girl any time soon.

Lottie stares down at our joined hands on the table and blushes. "I don't do this often. Or at all, if I'm being honest," she whispers, as if revealing her deepest darkest secret.

"Go on dates with strangers you met less than two hours ago?"

"Go on dates. Period."

A little in love with the fact that I'm an exception, I give her hands an encouraging squeeze.

"Lottie?" I ask.

"Yes, Knox?" She presses her lips together to keep from laughing at the sudden intensity I feel in my expression, but I'm not trying to be funny.

"Lottie, I *really* wanna kiss you right now," I say in all seriousness. "Can I?"

She takes another sip of water and looks in every direction but mine before settling her gaze on my lips. Finally, she says, "Okay."

CHAPTER THREE
LOTTIE

"I don't know why you're suddenly obsessing over this," I tell Jenn as I stretch onto my tiptoes to reach the top row of the shelf. I slide a collection of Shakespeare's sonnets in between more books that we'll never sell, and walk over to the counter, avoiding eye contact. "Not a big deal by any means."

"Are you kidding me?!" She throws her hands in the air in frustration, her face the picture of the dramatic. "It's a *huge* deal! *Massive*." I roll my eyes and scoff, but that doesn't stop her. "Poppy Goodwin said you were *glowing* when she saw you guys at the bar. Absolutely *glowing*," she says, slamming her hands on the counter by the register. I continue to make myself busy, trying not to think of the way Knox's smile made me feel; the way his boyish grin made my heart jump in my chest, my core tighten. "And Lizzie McCalister—*Lizzie-freakingMcCalister!*—told me she sat you guys down for dinner at *Mamma's*. For *dinner*, Lottie. You had dinner with the guy. And you're telling me it wasn't a big deal? When was the last time you went on a date with someone? Like an honest-to-god date."

Damn this small town life.

"Never. *Ne-ver.*"

"That is categorically false. I've been on tons of dates. It's just been a while." Which is a bit of an understatement, but whatever.

"A while," she says, voice flat, brow raised, hands on her hips.

With a sigh, I admit, "Three years."

Jenn scoffs and follows me around the store as I ready it for our meeting with Walter's lawyer, her red-haired space buns bouncing with every step. Nervously, I rearrange some books here and there, making sure everything is clean and organized before our meeting. Suddenly, I feel a sharp pain in my pelvic area, followed by a steady throbbing that leaves me gasping for air. I try to inhale, to breathe through it and act natural, but it takes a minute for me to be able to speak again, praying the entire time that Jenn doesn't notice or bring it up.

Keep going, keep going.

When I can speak again, I face her head-on, fighting through the pain: "And anyway, this wasn't a date. *Date* implies that there was some sort of planning involved. Premeditation. I just met a nice man, we got to talking, I got hungry, and he took me to dinner. It was nothing more," I lie. But I'm not about to prove her right and give this girl ammo to question me further. "And can we stop talking about my personal life, please? I'm your boss. This isn't appropriate."

She snorts—the idea of boundaries hilarious to her,

apparently. "You went on a *date* and you expect me not to say anything about it? You're going to pretend like it's super whatever and nothing new when you and I *both* know that you haven't shared a meal with another man in *years*."

"How would you even know? You're basically a *child*, Jenn," I tease.

"Excuse me, *ma'am*." I wince. Such a low blow. "But this is a small town, in case you haven't noticed. People talk. And I am nineteen years old. *Of age*. I know stuff."

"You're giving me a migraine," I lie taking the very familiar bottle of naproxen out from behind the register. She grimaces as I pop two pills with a sip from the water bottle I keep hidden back here, because we both know she's not the reason I need them now.

Stupid uterus.

I cannot *wait* to get rid of it. *Just two more weeks until my hysterectomy.*

"C'mon." Her tone turns gentler, and I can tell it's to get my mind off the pain she knows I'm currently battling with. "Tell me about it. I love this for you."

"Stop," I plead, not wanting to dwell on it. The truth is, my mind has been jumbled ever since that night. I had never felt a connection so quickly or as strong as I did with Knox— not even with my ex-husband, Finn, on our best days. And yes, I let Knox take me to dinner. And yes, I did feel like I was glowing around him—or at least something akin to it. But he was just a transient late-night companion I will never see again.

I try to push the sadness I feel at that little factoid out of my head and heart as soon as it pops up. There's no reason I should feel this attached to a man I spent less than twelve hours with.

And yet...

"*Please* tell me you went home with him. Poppy said the man was gorgeous. Are you seeing him again? Is he from around here? Because Lizzie said she's never seen him in town."

"I hate everyone," I mutter.

Bringing the heels of my hands to my eyes, I push my reading glasses up over my nose, willing Jenn to disappear. I don't want to think about that night anymore—but it's all I've been able to do. It was amazing, in every way possible. The conversation, the chemistry—in *and* out of bed. Because, *yes*, I did go home with him (or at least to his hotel), and *yes*, I did have the best sex of my life. But as soon as I snuck out of his room at the crack of dawn, it was over. It's time I move on —something that hasn't been particularly easy given the aforementioned chemistry and sex and just general gorgeousness of said man and how quickly this story has spread all through town.

"Jenn, I'm trying to move past this man, not relive every second with him." At least not in public—I save the steamier parts for when I'm alone.

"*Trying?* Does that mean what I think it means?" Her grin is giant and a bit mischievous, the excitement she feels for me having potentially found someone making her jump in place. It would be extremely adorable if she weren't so annoying right now.

"Listen, I'm not judging. I'm all for you exploring your sexuality and hooking up whenever you want with whomever you want. You know, feminism et cetera et cetera. God knows you deserve it—*especially* after the last few years you've had. When I think of everything you've had to go through—"

"*Jennifer*," I snap. There are few things I hate more than whenever people bring up the failed state of my existence. "I said stop. This is my personal life. You are my employee. It isn't appropriate."

She crosses her arms in front of her chest. "It's giving denial, Lottie. You know it's a big deal, or you wouldn't be this upset. I'm just saying it's a good thing."

I go back to impatiently tidying things that don't need tidying annoyed because Jenn is right: it *was* a big deal. I never go on dates. Flirt with the occasional tourist passing through town? *Maybe.* But go out for an actual meal with someone? Talk to them outside of the darkness of the one and only bar in town? Nope.

So, though I can blame her for putting her nose where it shouldn't be—because, since when is it okay for my Gen-Z bookseller to talk about my sex life so freely with me?—I can't blame her for being shocked by my behavior. Especially when I can't believe it myself.

"Let's just finish getting things ready for when the lawyer gets here, okay?" I say, my voice softer now.

Jenn nods once. Pouting, she grabs a spray bottle of Windex and a rag, and proceeds to wipe down the display cases. "When's he due?"

I check my phone for the time. "Any second now."

The shop had remained closed in observance of Walter's death for the past three days, but his lawyer had made contact at the funeral, asked us to meet him here today. When Walter passed away, I was so nervous about what would happen to the store—not just to me as an employee. But knowing that he put his affairs in order settled some of the panic. *Of course* Walter had prepared for any scenario. It's the type of man he was.

As if right on cue, the bells over the shop door chime and a short man in a taupe suit and cowboy boots walks in. In his hand, a leather suitcase; on his head, a cream Stetson.

Where the hell does this guy think he is? Because it definitely is not in a microscopic beach town in Maine in the middle of spring.

His eyes bounce around the shop until they land on mine. "Miss Veracruz?" I nod and he sticks his hand out, which I shake. "Leroy Jones. Lawyer to the estate of the late Doctor Walter Adams."

"*Doctor* Walter Adams?"

The short man smiles. "Ph.D. He used to be a professor."

"Walter was a professor?" I ask, a bit awestruck. "I've—I *had*—worked for him for several years and never knew."

"Really? He was pretty well-known in the academic field when he was younger. Wrote lots of books."

"Walter wrote *books*?" Jenn bursts out.

"Textbooks, mostly. Comparative Literature, I think," the lawyer clarifies, as if it should make it any less impressive. "You must be Miss Roberts?" Leroy shakes her hand with a toothy grin. He places his suitcase on the counter, laughing softly. "I guess you didn't know Doctor Adams as well as you thought you did."

"He wasn't an easy man to get to know," Jenn mumbles.

In all honesty, there wasn't much I really knew about Walter. Sure, I knew how he liked his coffee and how much he hated music. I knew he was as stubborn as he was brilliant. And I knew he had an immense passion for classic literature and was constantly frustrated by people who did not share the same interest. He was a man of few words with a watered-down Scottish accent. An outsider who showed up in town almost ten years ago and kept mostly to himself. No friends, no family—nothing but this bookstore.

He was also the only person in town who never commented on my life or the choices I made. Given the size of Ceres Cove and its main collective hobby being gossip, I'm sure he'd heard how my life imploded in slow motion, but he was kind enough to never bring it up.

Probably because he didn't really care, to be honest.

It was what I liked the most about him. He didn't care about all the noise. None of it ever mattered to him. Walter was all about his books and his quiet life and he owned it.

But still, a professor? Who wrote books? *Text*books? I had no idea.

"No," I whisper. "I guess I didn't know him as well as I thought I did."

So we both had past lives, old friend.

A pit forms in my stomach—*there's that guilt again.* This man took me in, gave me hope when I crawled back to town in tatters, and I realize now that I barely knew him.

I am a *horrible* person.

"Anyway, we'll get started once Mr Riddick arrives," Leroy says, breaking through my thoughts.

"Mr Riddick?" Jenn asks.

"Yes." He checks his watch. "He texted saying he would be a few minutes late, but—"

"I don't understand. Who's Mr Riddick, exactly?" I ask, my head still spinning with the new information.

The bells above the front door jingle again, but I keep my eyes on Mr. Jones.

"So sorry, sir. But the shop's closed until further notice," I hear Jenn say to the incoming customer.

"Oh. I'm actually here to meet someone?"

My entire body freezes, a shot of adrenaline coursing through it as my mind tries to process the sound of the man's voice. The last time I heard it was when he groaned my name in a dark room, his lips to my ear, and...

I know that voice. I know who it belongs to. I know what it sounds like when he laughs at his own jokes, when he breathes my name on a sigh. I know what it sounds like when he groans in pleasure, when he begs for more, his body under mine. I know it perfectly because I've been replaying it in my head for the past three days.

Trying my best to catch my breath, I turn towards the door, bracing myself to face the man I've been dying to see, yet also hoping to never meet again.

Just like that night, I'm surprised by the immediate attraction I feel. Even more so now, since I *know* how great of a guy he is and what hides beneath that black henley and faded jeans.

It's like a high-speed montage of the other night flashes before my eyes, blinding me, throwing me completely off balance. It leaves me breathless, my body heating everywhere he touched it, my mind running through all the things he said.

At first, he doesn't seem to notice me as his eyes scan the bookstore with skepticism. But as soon as Knox's gaze lands on me, a slow, broad smile spreads across his face, my knees weakening.

"Hey, Pretty Girl."

"Knox," I breathe. "Wh—What are you doing here? How did you know I was here?" My mind races with fantasies of him hunting me down, of him needing to find me after I left him in the middle of the night. Surprised, I stop myself from running through movie-like scenarios, because *what the actual fuck, Lottie?*

"So you *were* hiding from me, then? Is that why you snuck outta my room without saying goodbye the other night?" His tone is light, but I can tell there's something deeper behind his playful words. "I didn't even get to take you out for breakfast."

Jenn chokes on a laugh, but I ignore her.

"You—You're here... How did you—"

"You two know each other, then?" Jenn snickers, eyes bouncing between us. I shoot her a glare, because it's painfully obvious we do. She presses her lips together, stifling a laugh.

"That's it," I whisper at her. "You're getting nothing but opening shifts from now on."

Her back straightens and she sobers up. *Marginally.*

"Oh, yeah," Knox grins. "Lottie and I go *way* back."

My cheeks redden beneath my wire-rimmed glasses, and suddenly I am *very* conscious of the way I look. My dark bangs hang in front of my face, hair piled up high in a messy "I haven't washed my hair in three days" way. I look down to check out my outfit and grimace, wondering why the hell I decided to go with a plaid green skirt that, though cute, hasn't fit right for a couple of years. That, combined with the oversized olive cardigan over my shoulders has certainly shifted me into librarian status—and *not* the sexy kind. But oversized tops are a need for me, unless I want people to mistake being bloated for being six months pregnant.

Oh, the irony of endometriosis and PCOS. I get to look pregnant even though it's not a possibility. At least it never happened for me.

Meanwhile, Knox looks like an artsy, edgy Greek god with that leather jacket and camera bag strapped across his wide chest.

"Fantastic, then! This should make things easier. Let's get down to business." Leroy claps his hands once, choosing to ignore the obvious sexual tension. Either that or he's completely oblivious to it. But from his surprising no-nonsense demeanor, I'd gather it's the former.

"To business? Are you here for the same meeting we are?" I frown, so confused.

"I guess so? You *are* Walter's lawyer, aren't you?" he asks Leroy.

"Obviously. So, shall we? As executor of Doctor Adams's estate, it is my responsibility to carry out the provisions set forth in his last will and testament. I've asked you three here because he chose to leave you each with something."

Jenn and I glance at each other in confusion. "Like, he left us money?" Jenn asks.

I frown, my heart growing a few sizes in my chest. For all his stoicism and occasional coldness, Walter did care—always in his own way.

"Doctor Adams did leave you both something, but, ah, it is not in the way of cash, per se."

Mr. Jones pulls out a folder from the suitcase resting next to the register while I continue to try and process the fact that *Knox is here*. He's *here*. How???

Knox and I gaze anxiously at each other, both completely at a loss for words as we wait to hear more.

The lawyer flips through his things before pulling out a document. From my vantage point, I can see it is no longer than three paragraphs. Concise, of few words, but filled with meaning—just like Walter.

"*Brevity is the soul of wit, Lottie,*" he always liked to tell me. Shakespeare, of course.

As Mr. Jones reads the will aloud, I watch Knox from the corner of my eye. A part of me is happy to run into him again, while another wishes he would have never come back into my life—even for this brief moment.

That night with Knox, though incredible, was an indulgence. Nothing more than a moment of weakness. I was grieving and... and... Yes, *grief*. That's all it was.

But even now, as I watch Knox, I know I can't put it all on

that. Maybe losing Walter, my quiet champion, did bring down my walls. But it's clear Knox and I share something we simply cannot have. This connection that just—

His eyes lock on mine, smirking because he caught me staring. I want to look away, but I can't. His ice-blue eyes are hypnotizing, holding me like they did that night as we talked into the early morning in between kisses and sex.

God, I'm so insensitive. I should be sad. I should be listening to the lawyer. I should be mourning Walter and thinking about how this whole thing is awful. Instead, all I can think about is how incredible that night was and wondering what the hell he's doing here and how long he'll stay in town and—*oh my god*—what if it's permanent, what if—

"...And as for my bookstore, *Adams's Books*, I leave five percent to Miss Jennifer Evelyn Roberts—"

My head snaps up to Leroy, a gasp bursting through Jenn's lips.

"—thirty-five percent to Miss Carlota Elisa Veracruz—"

"Oh my god." My hand flies to my mouth.

"—and sixty percent to my son, Lennox Riddick Adams."

"*Son?*" Jenn and I burst out simultaneously.

CHAPTER FOUR
KNOX

A blanket of shock and silence falls over us. I'm not sure whether it lasts just a few seconds, but it feels like hours.

Eventually, I clear my throat, pulling at my collar. "So, we're sharing the store? How's that going to work?" I ask Leroy, ignoring the women's question. Truthfully, I'm also trying to process the fact that Lottie knew my dad *and* that she was close enough to be left in his will.

Because the Walter I knew was pretty much heartless.

But how is this real? How is it that the woman I've been fucking dying to see for three days is suddenly here, standing in front of me, like one of those movies my mom loves to watch? Did we seriously just inherit a part of my father's bookstore together? I already found it weird that he'd even considered leaving me something small, let alone his entire business. It'd be an understatement to say I was surprised. And now to hear he called me his *son* in a legal document?

I'm shocked. To be honest, I half expected the old man to leave a directive to burn all his shit to the ground before having anything to do with me again—even after death.

"You're his *son?*" Lottie asks, her wide eyes turned on me, now. "I—Walter never said he had a *son.*"

I snort and shake my head. I try to play it cool, but I can't lie to myself. A microscopic part of me feels a bit of a sting. "Of course he didn't."

At my reaction, she recovers, guilt clear on her face. "To be fair, you'd be hard-pressed to talk to Walter about anything other than books."

"Don't worry about it. I know exactly the type of man he was. I'd venture to guess you were much closer to him than I ever was." Lottie frowns, her lips pursed in defensiveness. "*Obviously,* since you guys made it into his will, too. Although, the fact that I'm also in it doesn't say much about you in the end."

"Well, to answer your original question, Mr Riddick, the three of you can do whatever you want with the bookstore." Lottie, Jenn, and I stare at each other for a moment. "You can rent it, renovate it and keep it going, or just keep running it as is. Or even sell it. You can do anything you want with it. As partners, of course. You need to decide together."

"Sell it?" Lottie gasps. "What? I—"

But I just scratch my head, shaken. I didn't expect to have to inherit anything when I came here, let alone have to share it with my one-night stand (and the best sex of my life) and someone who doesn't look to be a day over twenty. Though I'm really not hating the fact that the universe has brought me and Lottie back together. I just wish the circumstances were better.

"Did he leave a note?" I ask.

Lottie snorts. "He wouldn't do that. Walter would've thought it too cliché or something. Probably hoped his actions spoke louder than words—even from beyond the grave," she says with the confidence of someone who knew him well and the fondness of someone who loved him. And I realize that this woman—this woman I've been dreaming of for days—might've actually known my father far better than I'd ever hoped to.

"No, I'm sorry." Leroy shoots me a sympathetic look. "I know you and your dad had your issues, but—"

"He wasn't my dad."

"Are... Are you sure? He was pretty positive he was your father."

"Oh, he was definitely my biological father. Just, not my dad. I don't think a man like that deserves that title, to be honest."

"*A man like that?* A man like *what*, exactly?" Jenn asks, spine straightening into a protective stance.

Lottie puts a hand on Jenn's shoulder, pulling her back gently. "Jenn," she whispers, shaking her head at her.

I must've somehow slipped into a parallel universe or something. Because... Are they sticking up for him? Like... Did these people actually *like* the guy?

"Well, in any case, he left sixty percent of the store to you, Mr. Riddick. Plus, the loft upstairs and any remaining funds in his bank account, which... isn't much, if we're being honest. But you do need to do something about it."

"I don't even live here." I shrug, frustrated. Though I have never been more confused about something in my life, I appreciate Walter's generosity. Especially considering how we left things the last time we spoke—but what was the guy thinking? "I'm a freelance photographer who travels the world for a living. It's not like I got a ton of flexibility, here. I'm not exactly in a position to stay in one place and manage a business. I wouldn't even know where to start."

"I believe it was Doctor Adams's intention for you all to use Miss Veracruz's experience to renovate it, perhaps—"

"What?" Lottie cuts him off. "Walter *hated* my ideas. He always put them down. Told me it wasn't 'the right time.'"

"I don't know about that. It's certainly not what he said at our last meeting. He spoke very highly of you. Maybe when he referred to it not being the right time he meant, well... not in *his* time, but yours."

Her laugh is hollow, humorless. A far cry from the one that filled me with light the night we spent together. "This has to be a joke, right?"

"No, Miss Veracruz. But of course, like I said, it's up to you three to determine the best course of action. Actually, as per Doctor Adams's request, I've set up a meeting for you three with a business manager for tomorrow at four here in the store. I hope that's okay. If you should have any problems, here is my business card." I take one in a fog, my mind still trying to catch up with everything.

I glance over at Lottie and watch as she stares out the window, looking lost. I want to go over to her, the feeling almost overpowering. So I clutch my hands together to keep from reaching out.

"Right..." I sigh, still dumbstruck.

I gotta get out of here. Fast.

For the first time since hearing the news, Jenn speaks up: "Just out of curiosity... How long ago did he prepare this... this will?"

Leroy smiles fondly at her, as if understanding the meaning behind her question. "Last week, Miss Roberts. Just two days prior to his death."

Jenn's face crumbles, tears streaming freely down her cheeks.

Lottie takes her small frame in her arms, running her hands in soothing motions up and down her back. "Hey, it's okay. It's okay."

"It's... It's a pretty big coincidence," she says between sobs.

"Not really." Leroy sighs. "He'd been diagnosed a while back. He knew it was just a matter of time."

My stomach drops. "Diagnosis? Didn't he die of a heart attack?"

"Yes. I'm the one who found him. I even rode with him in the back of the ambulance," Lottie says, Jenn still in her arms.

Walter was sick? And Lottie was the one who found him?

My head spins as I attempt to catch up, trying to make sense out of everything.

I keep my eyes on her as Leroy speaks. "Ah, not quite. He had been sick for a while. The heart attack, I assume, was due to the strain the lung cancer had put on his body, perhaps." Lottie's breath catches. Meanwhile, I feel this sudden *need* to scream. "Doctor Adams called me right after his diagnosis months ago, but urgently had me change his final will a few days prior to his death to include Miss Roberts."

"I knew it," she whispers.

Their voices fade into the background like a faint buzzing as I go through an out-of body experience.

Walter knew he was going to die months ago and didn't make contact? I don't know how I should feel. We didn't have a relationship, but... He knew he was dying. He knew he was fucking dying and he couldn't pick up the damn phone once and tell me so? He'd rather have died without speaking another word to his *son* than meet me half way after *one* stupid argument years ago?

Rage. It buzzes through my skin, courses through my veins, coats my entire body in bitterness, and heats me all over.

Fucking Walter.

"Anyway. These are for the loft upstairs. I believe there is point of access through the store and one through the back of the building. Miss Veracruz will be able to show you the way." He pulls a set of keys from his briefcase.

"I—I've never actually been inside, but yes, I can take you," she says, her voice small. I turn to look at her—to *really* look at her—and realize her eyes are bloodshot, her brows pulled together, and she's gnawing on her lip as if trying really hard not to cry.

Again, I have to stop myself from comforting her—which is insane, right? I mean, it was *my* father who died. Not hers. *I* should be the sad one. *I* should be devastated. Instead, all I am is enraged.

"Perfect. Here you go, then. Pleasure doing business with you." With that, he drops the keys into my palm, gathers his things, and leaves the three of us completely dumbfounded.

CHAPTER FIVE

LOTTIE

Once Leroy leaves, it's Jenn who breaks the awkward silence: "I'm Jenn, by the way. I'm a bookseller here." She sticks out her hand, which Knox takes with a small smile on his face. "It's nice to meet you, Lennox."

"Please. Call me Knox. We're officially business partners now." He shrugs, eyes gentle and kind.

Jenn's eyes widen as she wipes her nose with the back of her hand. "*Whoa,*" she gasps.

"You're right."

Knox laughs softly before shooting a smile in my direction.

Oh my god. Oh my *god*. So not only is Knox standing here, but thanks to Walter's insane generosity—or is it just plain eccentricity?—now we're all stuck in this shit storm of a situation.

I'm torn down the middle, completely conflicted. On the one hand, the guy I've been daydreaming about is standing in front of me after I left him behind in the middle of the night like some kind of slutty, mid-thirties, modern Cinderella. On the other, I cannot have him here. I cannot allow these feelings—whatever they may be—to develop. Forget about the fact that I promised myself never to go there again *on principle*. He's also *way* too young.

No. *Nope.*

"Jesus."

Another painful pause.

"I'm sorry for getting so upset back there, by the way," Jenn murmurs. "I think Lottie would agree with me in saying that Walter was *way* misunderstood—the guy really had zero rizz." *Rizz? Really?* "Still, his generosity... Thinking of including us in this... It's kinda overwhelming."

"I gotta admit that I had a different experience with him growing up. But I'm happy he had a positive impact on other people's lives," Knox says, without a drop of sarcasm.

"He... He caught me crying behind the stacks about a week before he died. I haven't told anyone, but I got into college in December—early decision—and the deadline for the deposit is coming up in a couple of months, but I just don't have the cash." Jenn shrugs, sniffles. "I guess this was his way of helping out."

"You got into college?" I breathe, a wide smile spreading across my face. "Jenny! Congrats!"

"Ew. Don't call me Jenny—I've already told you a million times."

I laugh softly, wrapping my arms around her, squeezing her tight once before releasing her. *Teenagers.*

"It's just state. I'm not going to a fancy school like you

did." She shrugs, cheeks red. I nearly fall over in surprise. Jenn, blushing? Unheard of.

"But I thought you said that academia was a fascist institution and that the previous generations before yours were all brainwashed into thinking a degree will secure financial success, when in reality it has done the complete opposite to an entire generation, leaving them crippled and suffocated for the rest of their lives due to unnecessary debt?" *She's really not wrong about the securing financial success bit.*

"I still think all those things are true, don't get me wrong. But I do need a degree to become a nurse so… there it is. Plus, I might've also said that because I didn't get anywhere last year. But I reapplied and… I got in." Her smile is wide and hopeful and I can't help the way I pull her into my arms once more.

"That's amazing. I mean, I have so many questions. Like, nursing?" Jenn is amazing, but she does not scream *caregiver*. "But so proud!"

She laughs and gently pushes me away. "So… I guess we should talk logistics?" she asks, surprising me with her sudden take-charge attitude. She's oozing initiative, which is wildly concerning. This girl has been known to stand by while a *literal fire* started in our office that one time the toaster went crazy. Love her to death, but no. Jenn is not what you'd call a "self-starter."

"Well, I guess we just go to this meeting Leroy organized for us with the business manager. We can't really do much now, can we?"

"Are we opening the store to the public for the time being or…?" Jenn hesitates. She and Knox look back at me, unsure. I mull it over, thinking about what Walter would've wanted. But I already know the answer: he wouldn't even have bothered to close the day of his funeral, let alone the days following. He would've said grieving over him for more than a day —or even at all—was a waste of time. There is no doubt in my mind that Walter would've prioritized practicality over emotion.

"I can't imagine the store being open without Walter... But he also would've wanted us to stay open. At least until we figure this whole thing out."

Knox nods thoughtfully. "Okay. I trust your judgement. Plus, it wouldn't hurt for the store to keep making money, right?"

Jenn snorts and I have to press my lips together to keep from laughing. Knox has a lot to learn about the store's success—or lack thereof. Because Ceres Cove isn't exactly known for its voracious appetite for reading—at least when it comes to the kinds of books the store sells. Foot traffic has historically been a bit... *slow*. Honestly, the fact that Walter has been able to keep the doors open this long has always been a mystery to me. Sure, I've never had full access to our accounting, but I'm not stupid. With how little we sell in a week, there's no way we should've remained open this long.

It's no use worrying Knox with this piece of lovely info yet, though. He clearly has a lot to process—we all do—and now just isn't the time.

"*Right*," I say, stretching out the word. "So, let's open up for regular business hours starting tomorrow. Meet with the business manager, and then figure everything out based off of what they say." I turn to Knox, trying to keep a wall up between us when I ask, "Is that okay with you?"

But now that the serious business is out of the way, he's back to looking at me with *almost* the same amusement as before. I guess some excitement was bound to dull given everything. It's not every day your estranged father leaves you his bookstore after his death to share with your one-night stand and a nineteen-year-old firecracker, now, is it?

"Yeah, that's great." Knox smiles. "Now there's just the question of the apartment. D'you mind showing me where it is?" He takes a step closer, his scent filling my nostrils, weakening my knees. For a moment there, I sway. Jenn, the little traitor, stifles a giggle.

"Of course, Lottie will take you," she tells him. "Meanwhile, I'll just head out. Leave you two alone to... catch up. See you guys tomorrow."

She winks in my direction behind Knox's back while I restrain the urge to murder her.

I attempt to swallow the knot in my throat, and nod once. "Okay. Let me show you around, then."

"You weren't at the funeral," I point out as we climb the stairs to the loft, the steps creaking under our weight.

"Couldn't make it in time. I'd just made it to town from an assignment in South America when I met you at the bar."

"Mmm," is all I can manage as I try to keep my focus on

taking the stairs one step at a time, and not on the delicious man behind me.

"This place is…"

"Old?" I finish his sentence, smiling.

He lets out a soft laugh. "Yes."

"It just needs some TLC." I shrug casually, keeping my eyes in front of me. "Be careful with the stairs; they're super narrow. You definitely can't have two people go side-by-side."

He laughs, deeper this time. "I can't say that I mind it right now, actually."

I stop briefly to consider his words, looking over my shoulder at him only to catch his eyes on my ass. "Were you just—?"

"No," he says too quickly. That trickster grin is back, ice-blue eyes warming every inch of my body. I glare at him, hating the effect he has on me. Jesus, why does he have to be so… So… *Hot.*

God, Lottie. What the hell is wrong with you? He was just blatantly staring at your *ass.* What kind of feminist are you? You should be angry. You should be yelling at him. Telling him to respect your body.

Except… We had *such* a good time when he was disrespecting it in bed. *Wink wink.*

I groan, rubbing my eyes under my glasses.

"You seem… conflicted." I hear the smugness in his voice, and I grow frustrated with the way his grin tugs at something beneath my ribs.

I look up at him, irritated. "Can we just focus?"

"Sure." But I narrow my eyes at him, holding his gaze until his smile falls. "I promise to keep my eyes on the steps."

Once we reach the landing, I stick my hand out palm up. "Keys."

He places them in my hand, his fingers grazing my skin with the lightest of touches, and I hate myself for the small gasp that escapes my lips.

I turn my back on him, fingers shaking as I try to fit the key in the lock.

"Are we going to talk about it?" He asks, his deep voice close to my ear, sending shivers down my spine. I can feel the heat radiating off his body, warming mine.

"Talk about what?" I try for my most innocent voice, but the shakiness betrays me. I pray to god, to Taylor Swift—to *anyone* who might hear me—to help me open this goddamn door as quickly as possible. Anything to avoid having this conversation right now.

"You know what. The amazing night we had. How you snuck out without so much as a goodbye. No way to contact you the next morning." His voice is low in my ear as I struggle with the lock of Walter's door.

Jeez, this key. What the hell is wrong with it? Maybe if I—

"Lottie."

I groan. "Fine. Let's talk about it in the cramped landing of your dead dad's—"

"*Walter's.*"

"—apartment." I place my hands on my hips and try not to let myself be hypnotized by the clear blue of his eyes, try not to notice the occasional shades of green near his pupils. "Why would you have needed to contact me again? It's fine. I knew it was a one-night stand, so there's no need to make a big deal about it. No hard feelings."

"There *were* hard feelings, Lottie. Mine," he says, staggered, the hurt in his voice sincere. His brows pull together, frown deep as his eyes scan my face. "I didn't like waking up in the early hours of the morning just to find you gone. It might've started off as a one-night stand, but you and I both know that they didn't stay that way the rest of the night, did they? After the night we had, I deserved better. We both did. Don't you think?"

"I—I—" I blow a puff of air through my lips and shake my head. "You're right. I'm sorry." Because of course it was a crappy thing to do, even if there's no way that night could've been as special to him as it was for me. Still, it's difficult to regret my actions when I find myself stumbling through my words like a thirteen-year-old talking to her crush.

His face visibly relaxes at my apology, but he waits for me to continue.

"I don't usually do that."

"Leave in the middle of the night?"

"No. I don't usually hook up with anyone. Ever. At least, I haven't in a while. I don't even date—I told you that night. And so when I woke up before you… It just didn't feel like a good idea to stick around."

His frown deepens. "Why? Because we hit it off? Because what happened between us that night was more than just—"

I hold a hand up to cut him off and squeeze my eyes shut. I don't want—*can't*—hear this. "I don't think—"

"Don't even *try* to deny you didn't feel what I did."

I look up at him, surprised to have been called out on my bullshit. Jesus, am I that obvious?

"It wasn't anything like that. It was because you don't live here, so why bother?" Which isn't even a complete lie. But for god's sake, what the hell else does he want from me? Sure, I liked him. *A lot.* But I have nothing to give. Nothing to offer. Why would I ever involve myself with someone knowing I would never be able to give them what they wanted only to end up hurting us both? Or at least, myself.

No, thanks. I'm done. Been there; done that. Read the book; saw the movie.

"It was just a one-night stand," I say through gritted teeth.

Something flashes across his face. But it only lasts a second before he gathers himself. "Still, don't you think I merited a goodbye?" Knox holds my eyes with his hurt ones.

He seems to be relatively okay that his estranged father died and left him a bunch of stuff in his will. But the fact that I Irish-exited the shit out of our night together has him crashing out? What is even happening?

Wanting to veer off this topic and into another one— literally any other than the one of us hooking up—I ask "Do you really think this is an appropriate conversation to have while we're about to go into your dead father's apartment? Aren't you the least bit upset about this?"

"No."

"Fantastic. I slept with a sociopath. Or is it a psychopath? I can never tell those two apart," I whisper, shaking my head.

Seeing the mild horror on my face, he replies, "Look. As one human to another, yes, I was sad to hear he passed. But

Walter and I hadn't spoken in years. About ten, actually. We didn't have a relationship, so he was basically a stranger to me."

"Ten years?" I breathe, sidetracked. As someone who lost her parents and misses them every day, I can't ever imagine myself reaching that point. I would've done anything to have my parents by my side as my world was crumbling down around me, leaning on them. "That's... a really long time."

"Yeah. So to answer your question, no, I'm not bothered enough by his death to forget about how you snuck off. I'm not bothered enough to forget about how amazing that night was. And no, I'm not bothered enough to not wonder what could've happened if you'd stayed." My breath catches as he tucks a strand of my hair behind my ear. "Is that okay? Or does it bother *you*?"

I seriously consider his question.

Walter just— And he *just— So shouldn't I...?*

I exhale. "Honestly? I feel like I should be slightly insulted? I feel oddly protective of your da—*father*. But I see your point. And... I'm sorry I fled in the dead of night like some criminal or something." The corners of his mouth twitch. "It wasn't nice and... I guess we both definitely deserved better."

"Cool. So... Can I take you out for dinner again?"

I sigh. "Knox..."

His face falls, shoulders slouching just a bit. "Really?"

"You're so young. And I'm... not."

"I'm not *young*," he spits the word out like it's dirty. "I'm twenty-seven."

Oh, god. Twenty-seven. *Seven years* younger than me. I

try to control my facial expressions, trying not to reveal the horror I feel at the fact that I slept with someone his age.

And how fantastic it was.

Jesus.

"Is that a problem?" He chuckles as I hold my face in my hands. "And you are not *not* young. Plus, I'm hardly a kid. I do my taxes all by myself and everything. I could do the shit out of your taxes, too, if you want." He grins, and I can't help the way I smile back.

"Crap," I whisper, my chest expanding.

I stare into his hopeful eyes for a moment, considering. I could go out for dinner with him. I really could. And then I could grow to like him and get attached and then he'll leave because he'll want things I can never give him.

Like I said: no, thanks.

"I think you and I had a fantastic night—I won't deny it," I start, trying to keep my voice as gentle and level as possible. "But we can't do this. This is complicated for a lot of reasons, and I don't do complicated. That okay?"

He sighs, resigned. "Fine. I understand. Or I guess I'll try to." And with that, he gently pushes me aside and finally manages to open the door.

"Holy…"

I try to look around him, but his broad shoulders block most of the doorway. When he finally takes a step into the apartment, I realize what we're *really* in for.

"Oh my god," I breathe.

What the hell was Walter up to?

CHAPTER SIX
LOTTIE

"Holy shit. This place looks like something straight out of *Hoarders*," Knox breathes, taking in the unexpected mess that is Walter's apartment.

"Except that instead of having a creepy collection of old school porcelain Madame Alexander dolls or something, it's just old books stacked high on every available surface," I add.

"The hell are Alexander dolls? Like Ken dolls?"

"*Madame* Alexander dolls. And trust me—you don't want to know." I shiver dramatically at the thought of the irksome porcelain dolls. "Just count your blessings that it's not something worse."

"Well, I wouldn't say that confidently. We've barely walked into the apartment. Who knows whether the old man has something else hidden in one of his closets."

I snort. "Walter wouldn't." But I do a mental double-take because I had *never* seen that man with a hair out of place, a shirt untucked, a piece of paper thrown on his desk. Walter was the picture of neatness, and this apartment... most definitely is *not*.

I laugh to myself.

"What? What is it?" Knox looks at me with a curious smile on his face.

"Nothing," I shake my head. "It's just, you think you know someone. And then... Well.

This." I sweep my hand in the air before dropping it. "And you."

"Me?"

"You." I nod, with a small laugh. "I didn't know you existed. This is like some movie."

He laughs once. "That was exactly my first thought."

I giggle at the absolute ridiculousness of the situation. "For real, though. A family member dies and suddenly this whole other secret family shows up, and all the things you believed to be true... aren't. It's insane."

"Is that what Walter was to you? Family?" he asks, quietly. All humor has been stripped away from his expression, replaced by a gravity I'm sure is rarely seen worn on Knox.

I take a beat as I think over his question before replying: "Kind of. My *kind-of*-chosen extra family member. The one who never gave me any shit about my personal life. He was the one who took me as I was. Am. Whatever."

He gazes at me with a curious expression in his eyes before leading the way through the loft. Treading carefully, Knox looks around at the small space—just big enough for one person and their gargantuan collection of books.

"Whoa," Knox breathes, bending down to take a closer look at some of the titles.

"I know."

I make my way to the bedroom area of the loft, to the perfectly made bed next to a large worker's table that takes up at least a quarter of the apartment floor plan. On it, is another book. This time, however, its cover is missing and it's secured to the table with two yellow C-clamps.

"What the..."

"It looks like he restored old books," Knox says quietly, picking up a bottle marked *Acid-Free Glue.* "Did you know about this?"

"I had no idea," I shake my head, taken aback by the increasingly unsettling feeling that I had no idea who Walter Adams was. *Doctor* Walter Adams, I mean. "We saw each other almost every day, but I guess..."

Knox picks up the other items one by one—a spool of waxed string, an upholstery needle, drill, some leather scraps —all while lost in thought.

I'm dying to ask how he's doing, whether he's okay. I want to—*need* to know how he is, need to make sure he isn't freaking out internally despite the several times he's told me he's fine, despite how unaffected he's seemed all day. I open my mouth, unable to bear it any longer—

—but stop myself just in time because, *Jesus Christ*, we are nothing more than one-nightstands to each other. And I guess business partners, too—an even bigger reason not to get involved, not to care, not to wonder whether he's okay or needs someone to talk to.

Distance.

We need emotional distance from each other.

I keep to one side of the loft while he explores the other, both of us in silence, and it isn't until I'm getting to the good stuff, snooping through an old box of photos and documents, that Knox calls my attention back to him.

"Holy shit, Lottie." I nearly shiver at the familiar way in which he says my name, the way his deep voice sinks into my bones. But then I reel it in because, again... dead boss and all.

I swear to god I'm going to hell. I just know it.

"What is it?"

"This book. I think this is a first edition *On the Road*." Knox's eyes widen as he holds the black book up.

I run over to him just as he opens the cover of my favorite Kerouac novel. "Stop! If it really is a first edition, you shouldn't be touching it without gloves. This book was published in the fifties or something, right? And it looks almost brand new. It must be worth a lot of money."

With wide eyes, Knox gently places the book onto the pile he must've found it on.

"Do you think—Do you think *all* of these are first editions?" he asks, his eyes scanning the apartment. "Holy shit, Lottie. Are all the books in the store first editions?"

"God, no. I mean, we do have older books that are locked in a display case to keep safe, but no one ever buys them—maybe the odd tourist in the summer. But they're not as valuable." I wonder idly how much the copy in his hands is worth and choose not to think too hard about it. "But it does make me wonder... Walter wasn't one to share much about his life"—obviously— "but he did mention going to rare book conventions and trade shows. I just never expected him to be an actual rebinder and trader of rare books."

"This is going to be fun." He scoffs, shaking his head.

I laugh softly, which makes him look at me.

"What?"

"I just... I want you to know that your father was actually a good guy. Even if he was grumpy at times. He—Well, he wasn't always like that. At least not with me. A little cold, yes. But never a dick."

And because he looks like he doesn't believe me, I go on: "When I came back to town, it wasn't under the best circumstances and... I guess by coming up to the loft, I thought I might be able to show you something, to prove to you that he was a good guy, deep down. Very misunderstood, but... Yeah. It's just all a mess. This apartment is a mess. This whole situation is a goddamn mess. Not exactly a reflection of the man I knew."

He nods thoughtfully. "I get what you wanted to do—and I appreciate it. But you don't need to worry. To be honest... I feel kinda relieved, him being impersonal one final time." He laughs, almost embarrassed. His words devastate me, heart aching for him. For Walter, too, for not being able to give his son the goodbye they *both* deserved. "This whole thing was a mystery to me. I kept wondering what made him change his mind enough to leave me everything. Well, *almost* everything." He smiles. "But now that I've seen this apartment, I know it was his final 'fuck you' to me."

"What do you mean?" I frown.

"Well, do you really think this whole thing is going to be easy? That cleaning this place up and figuring out what to do with the bookstore will be something I can wrap up in a week?"

He lifts a brow. "Nah. He's forcing me to stay in one place, to see this through, because he *knew* I wouldn't pass up this opportunity."

"What opportunity?" I'm so confused.

"The money selling the apartment would bring. The store, too, maybe."

Wait, what? Sell the store? But...

"I could use it all to buy some new equipment I desperately need. Finally go on a photo trip that I *want* to take and not one I was assigned to this time. All I have to do is extend my time here by who knows how long." He shrugs easily, and it hurts.

Does he not understand how special this place is? But then I process his words, and my heart jumps at the thought of Knox staying here for a few more days. I do my best to squash whatever type of hope or excitement I feel in that moment because that's just not me anymore.

Needless to say, I'm not too successful.

Nothing can happen, I try to remind myself. But I can't help the way my skin flushes and heat builds deep inside just at the thought of having him around for longer.

It's like he knows exactly what's going through my head, because his next words are: "Though spending time with you like this doesn't sound *too* terrible" Knox's lips quirk at the corners, stepping closer to me. The look in his eyes reignites what I lost the second I slipped out of the warmth of his hotel bed and into the cold night.

"We'll be working here together a lot. Side by side." He takes a step closer still, his voice low, eyes flickering down to my lips for a second too long before moving back to my eyes.

I swallow hard once, wanting desperately to take a step back—figuratively and literally. To put more of that much-needed space between us. But Knox is a wild predator, prowling toward me. I'm rooted to the spot, unable to move. Hints of citrus absolutely hypnotizing.

And I want nothing more than him. Nothing more than him *ever*.

"I-I guess so," I manage to stutter.

"So, since we'll be spending all this time together, maybe we *should* go out? Have dinner and get to know each other some more?"

The word *dinner* almost brings my daydreaming to a screeching, near-deafening halt. But then...

Then my brain fogs over as he pushes a stray strand of her behind my ears again, and I'm gone. Dead. Deceased. Someone call the morgue.

"You look cute in those glasses, by the way. Have I told you that yet? Kinda like a sexy teacher."

Something warm unfurls in my heart, making the heat build in my core. His pupils are blown, his breathing as ragged and fast as mine (*and when the hell did that happen, anyway?*). I can see his chest rise and fall, the pulse in his neck. All of a sudden, however, he frowns and pulls his hand away, taking a step back.

I feel his retreat like a punch to the gut.

"I really want to kiss you," he says, his voice rough. "But I'm not about to do it in my dead father's apartment five seconds after seeing you again. Even though I've spent every goddamn second of the last couple of days wondering where the hell you went."

I inhale sharply.

"You left in the middle of the night."

"I know."

"That's fucked up. It wasn't a nice thing to do."

I nod in agreement. And I know in that moment that I was no better than his father, leaving him alone without explanation, without another word. "I know."

"Don't do that again," Knox says in a commanding tone that runs all the way down my spine to my toes, electrifying me.

I want to ask whether he means for me not to do it with another man in general, or whether he's making the assumption that we'll get there again. But I don't, because I don't know which answer scares me the most. The idea of me wanting to hook up with another guy right now seems wildly unlikely. To be perfectly honest, I'm pretty sure if real-life Henry Cavill showed up, tossed me over his shoulder fireman-style, and threw me on a king-sized mattress to have his way with me I'd be wholly unimpressed. But if it were Knox... Well, it's exactly the excitement that starts to build at the thought alone that stops me in my tracks. Neither of those two sound appealing, though for different reasons, of course. I'd climb Knox like a tree right now if I weren't so freaked out.

For a moment, we simply stare into each other's eyes, the

air around us filling with the same odd electricity as before. Somehow, I manage to break away, keeping my gaze laser-focused on my boots.

"I should probably get out of here," I mutter, feeling my cheeks blush.

"You mean, before I make a move on you?" His laugh is gentle, rueful, almost.

I clear my throat, willing my feet to move. Unfortunately, it feels like they've been tied to the floor. Or turned into cinderblocks. Rendered immobile.

"Yes," I admit.

"Because this is my dead father's apartment?"

"Yes."

"And it feels kinda wrong?"

"Uh-huh."

"Hmm." He nods, looking disappointed. "Yeah, I can see how that doesn't look great. Plus, all these books... and the dust. Not exactly a turn-on is it?"

I want to laugh out loud, because the warmth coursing through my veins would say otherwise. Honestly, I don't think there's any environment right now you can stick me in that I wouldn't be crazy turned on by him. But he doesn't need to know that. Instead, I tell him, "No, it isn't. Although your dad would probably encourage us despite it all."

He laughs once, startled. "What? He would?"

"Yes." I laugh softly. "He never pressured me to date anyone, but he wanted me to be happy and have fun. Wanted me to find someone 'full of life' who could give that to me."

"Did he have someone in particular in mind for you?" He

grins, but I don't miss the brief tightness in his smile or the shift in his eyes.

"No, I don't think so. He wouldn't ever have even considered it. Walter wasn't playing matchmaker or anything. It was never his style to get involved." It was why he was the only person I allowed to make comments about my love life —because he rarely ever did.

"So, you're saying I don't have competition, then? That I'm your number one pick?" He smiles, his earlier tension forgotten, and I roll my eyes.

"The only reason you don't have competition is because you aren't even in the running," I tell him, trying not to let him get too cocky.

"C'mon. We both know that isn't true. We had an amazing night together."

"*Had* being the key word, here. And did we not just talk about this already? *Jesus.*"

"You gonna tell me you haven't thought about it since?"

"No," I reply too quickly, my cheeks heating—a dead giveaway.

Knox smiles—perfect teeth, warm, full lips. He takes a step closer. "You sure? Because I can't stop thinking about how soft your skin felt beneath my fingertips. The way your teeth bit into my shoulder when I pushed into you the first time. Or the way you called out my name when you came and came and came."

I gape at him, my breathing shallow. I'm trying so hard to hide how much this is really affecting me, but I'm tired. The past few days have been draining. Between Walter's death, my endo flare-up, and the fact that Knox and I are pretty much stuck together for the time being? It's disorienting. All of it is disorienting.

Knox takes another step closer, and once again I'm overwhelmed by his very presence, his scent fogging my head, dulling my other senses, and certainly clouding my judgment.

"You know what else I remember?" He asks, his voice low, face inches apart from mine. "I remember the way you pulled at my hair when you came. I remember thinking you were like honey on my tongue. I remember thinking I'd never tasted anything better."

A whimper escapes my lips, my eyes locked on his as I feel the warmth spread through every inch of my body.

A sharp inhale. "You can't—You can't just do that."

I feel the heat of his body against every line of mine. Or maybe that's me. Maybe I'm the one on fire. I want him, yes. But this is wrong for so many reasons. It's a no for *so. Many.*

Reasons. I just need to remind myself of them now.

"This is insane. It isn't happening." I keep my eyes closed as I speak, shaking my head. "We should stop." But I really don't want to.

He laughs softly. "Fine."

My eyes fly open, shoulders sagging. "Wow. You give up quickly." I scoff, equal parts relieved and disappointed.

"Give up?" He snorts. "No way. I haven't given up. I'm gonna show you that you're wrong. I'm gonna show you that this thing between us wasn't a one-night-stand. You're just not ready to see that yet, and it's okay. We have time."

But we don't. You're going to leave eventually. One way or another.

"I think you're delusional. And I think it's time I go home, leave you to deal with this by yourself."

Finally, I manage to muster the emotional fortitude to make my way to the door. But just as I'm about to pull it shut behind me, he calls out: "Alright, Pretty Girl. I'll win you over some other way."

CHAPTER SEVEN
LOTTIE

Six, seven, eight, nine—

"Morning," a cheerful voice breaks through my concentration, nearly making me jump out of my seat.

"Jesus Christ!" I yelp, hand flying to my chest, twenty-dollar bills spilling all over the desk.

"Whoa, you good?" Knox asks, brows raised.

"You scared me. What the hell are you doing here, anyway? Are you stalking me or something? Do I need to call the police?"

"Uh, I own part of this store? Plus, I live above it. And it looks to me like *I* should be the one calling the police. Are you robbing the place or something?" Knox surveys the piles of cash on the desk and the open safe behind Walter's leather desk chair, where I'm currently seated.

"Wait. You—? *What?* What the hell are you talking about you living here?" I just finished my first cup of coffee a few minutes ago, but I should've guessed after yesterday that today was going to be a two- to three-cup morning.

Knox's lopsided smile is back. "Did you suffer some sort of major head trauma or something between last night and this morning? Some temporary amnesia I don't know about?" His eyes widen in mock seriousness. "I'm *Knox*," he puts a hand to his chest, speaking slowly. "I inherited the apartment above and part of the store, remember?"

I reach for a Post-It block on the desk and throw it at him. He laughs, dodging it just in time.

"It just made financial sense to move in there while I'm in town, know what I mean? I do own it, after all."

Knox walks over to the coffee maker on the sideboard and picks out a random mug—his father's, though I'm sure he has no idea. It's simple—white with a blue handle.

"No fuss, Lottie. Not like yours," he would say. *"There's no need to express your every thought on cutesy mugs."*

I smile fondly to myself, remembering how much he teased me for mine: a black mug with a gold outline of a cat and the words, "You're stressing meowt" emblazoned on the front. Watching Walter huff in annoyance every time he saw me drinking from it was part of my morning entertainment.

Knox's voice brings me back to the present: "Plus, it means I get to see more of you." He smiles, making my heart jump in my chest.

"You're such a flirt," I try to hide my smile behind my mug.

"Yes," he nods, not a hint of shame in his voice. "But only with you. And I have a feeling I'll be a bit relentless, so... fair warning."

I snort and shake my head.

"Is this the only flavor you have?" He asks, going through the K-cups. "And just almond milk; no regular milk?"

Ignoring his questions, I go back to the topic at hand. "The fact that you own the apartment still doesn't explain why you're here."

"I just told you," he says, loading the coffee maker.

"Right but—"

He cuts me off, turning to look at me with his piercing blue eyes. "Listen, how about we cut to the 'too long, didn't read' version, okay? I spent the night upstairs because I didn't want to keep spending money on a shitty motel the next town over that screamed *Schitt's Creek*—no offense to the lovely hosts who run it—when I had a perfectly okay-ish apartment I could stay at for free."

I blink a few times at him. "But... that's Walter's apartment."

"Was. It's mine now." He says it so casually, my jaw drops slightly.

"So, you're just sleeping in his bed?" I ask, my voice dry.

"*My* bed, now. And don't worry. I changed the sheets." Knox smiles behind his mug before taking a sip. He closes his eyes and hums, the sound of it taking me back to that night.

I shake my head, not letting myself be dragged down to another daydream. "But... why?"

"Why did I change them? Because I didn't want to sleep in my dead father's sheets."

"No—" I sigh, exasperated. "I mean, why did you spend the night there. What's wrong with your hotel?"

"Did I not just say why? Money? Lumpy mattress? You

remember the mattress, don't you, Pretty Girl?" He smirks, his eyes bright. "Shit, is that why you ran off and didn't spend the night? The mattress was too lumpy?"

I roll my eyes, a deep blush spreading across my cheeks and neck, and pick up the cash to set it into a neat pile next to the ten dollar bills. "Okay, I'm done with this conversation now. I'm gonna go back to balancing the store safe, thank you very much," I say curtly.

He takes another sip and walks around to the other side of the desk, pulling the chair out and taking a seat across from me.

I stop counting the twenties for the second time, and sigh. "What are you doing?"

He grins his boyish grin, and I wonder if this guy is ever *not* happy. "Just sipping my coffee. That a problem?"

I continue to count, ignoring the way he watches my every move— ignoring the way he makes my skin tingle as his eyes roam over me. And absolutely ignoring the memory of every single thing he said last night before leaving Walter's apartment.

Once I'm done and the cash is locked up in the safe, he asks, "So what'd you do last night, Pretty Girl?"

I groan. "God, can you please stop calling me that? It's so cringey."

Knox rolls his eyes. "Okay, *Miss Veracruz*," he teases. "What did you do last night? Did you do anything fun? Pick up any other unsuspecting strangers at the local bar?"

"No." I glare at him, but he just sips his coffee, waiting for an answer.

Well, after having dinner with my brother, his wife, and their two girls, I spent the night in my apartment above the garage coming to the image of your tongue, flat against my clit, me screaming out your name, and pulling on your hair begging for more.

I don't mention it, obviously, since doing so would probably send some mixed signals.

"I watched a romcom," I say instead, an involuntary smirk spreading across my face.

"Oh, yeah? Which one?"

Jeez Louise. This man. "I'm going to need more coffee this morning," I mutter, my annoyance growing.

I get to my feet with my empty mug and walk over to the machine. But Knox scrambles over to me. "How do you take your coffee?" he asks, gently taking the mug from my hands. His fingers accidentally graze mine, causing me to nearly drop the mug. Knox breathes sharply, and I take comfort in knowing he's at least somewhat affected by my presence. I'm not the only one acting like a teenager, apparently.

"Almond milk, two spoons of sugar," I say, a little breathless.

"Teaspoons?"

"*Table*," I say, shamelessly.

He clears his throat as he starts my coffee and reaches for the almond milk in the mini-fridge beside the sideboard.

"You like sweet stuff." It's not a question, just a statement of fact.

"I—Yes. How did you know?"

He grins, averting his eyes. "That night after the bar. You had several fruity mocktails at dinner. Ordered two different desserts. And every time you had a bite of one of them... It was like you were experiencing it for the first time. Like this visceral thing. A small moan. A faint smile. Sometimes, your eyes would even roll to the back of your head..." He shrugs, his eyes darkening. "I noticed."

I gnaw on my lip, not knowing what to say. I've always loved sweets, but now? Sugary treats mean something different to me. I'm not trying to get pregnant anymore, and I'm not planning on letting my body control me ever again. After years and years of cutting out sugar and alcohol from my diet, enjoying a cookie or a Coke or a goddamn piece of chocolate means more to me than anyone will ever know. It means more than just having a sweet tooth. It means freedom unlocked.

And he noticed.

"You don't have to do this for me, you know," I say, a bit impatient, struggling with the feeling in the pit of my stomach. I just want my goddamn coffee and to get out of here, this office suddenly too small for the both of us. I need to get away.

And yet...

"I want to do this for you, Pretty Gi—" he cuts himself off just in time, laughing softly at my glare. "*Lottie*. I meant Lottie."

My lips quirk as I try to suppress a smile.

Damn him.

"You stole my chance at making you morning coffee last time. Just let me do it now."

Pushing my reading glasses up my nose, I tell him "Knox... You—You *have* to stop this. It was a one-time thing.

And now that we have to deal with this whole bookstore deal? It's a really bad idea."

He smiles softly despite his sad eyes. "I know. But will you at least give me this?"

After a moment's hesitation, I nod once and take my cat mug when he passes it to me. I try not to focus too much on the tattoos covering his forearms, to not think about the way I traced them with my fingertips when his arms were wrapped around my waist—a camera on his arm, a tattoo to represent each country he'd visited... The way my touch made his skin break out in goosebumps before rolling me onto my back, feeling his weight pressing me into the mattress.

"Here you go," he murmurs, his arm flexing.

I half-smile, trying to stay present as I thank him for it, just as Jenn sticks her head in the office. "Lottie, do you—Oh. Hey, Knox." A wide, wicked grin spreads slowly across her face, her eyes bouncing between us.

God.

I roll my eyes. But Knox is all smiles as he greets her with a cheerful "Morning," raising his cup in her direction.

"What's up?" I ask, half annoyed, half relieved for the interruption.

"Adriana's here to pick up her special order?"

"I guess I'll balance the safe another time, then," I mutter under my breath, closing the safe and shuffling quickly to the sideboard cover, pulling out the ten copies of the latest best-seller for her. I follow Jenn out of the office toward the front of the store with Knox close behind me.

"Yay! They came!" Adri jumps up and down in place, dark

curls bouncing while clapping her hands together. It's almost too much for me to take this early in the morning, but it is what it is.

"Yup. Good to go."

"What is this?" Knox asks, an amused look in his eyes.

"A special order for the local bookclub," I tell him. "We don't really sell a lot of mainstream books in here, so I special order them for certain people behind Walter's back. Or did." I smile, remembering how he pretended not to notice.

"And who might *you* be?" Adriana asks, suddenly noticing the gorgeous tattooed man behind me. She sticks her hand out and bats her lashes at him, turning her flirty mode on.

I roll my eyes as I ring her order up.

"Hey," Knox laughs, taking her hand. "I'm Knox. I'm one of the new partial owners of this place."

Adriana gasps and drops his hand, turning to look at me with delight. "*This* is the guy you slept with?"

Knox bursts out in laughter as I flush crimson. "Adri!"

"What?" But her faux-innocent eyes do nothing to calm my sudden ire.

"He's standing *right. There*," I hiss.

"What? He knows he slept with you, doesn't he?" She raises a brow in Knox's direction, who chokes on a laugh before nodding. "See? So it isn't a secret from him—or Ceres Cove, for that matter."

I gawk, mortified.

"This is a small town, Carlota. You went out on a date with the man. What did you expect?"

"Who told you?" I ask, eyes narrowed.

"Lizzie McCallister." She shrugs, nonchalant.

Lizzie-fucking-McCalister.

The blabbermouth.

"It wasn't a date and Lizzie McCalister can—" I stop dead in my tracks. "*Wait.* But who told you about him being the one who inherited the store with me? I haven't told anyone yet."

From the corner of my eye, I watch as Jenn shifts uncomfortably, her eyes locked on something above our heads.

I *will* kill her later.

Knox laughs in astonishment, sipping on his coffee as he watches this entire interaction unfold.

"I cannot believe that—"

"I'm Adri, by the way," my sister says to Knox, interrupting me. "Lottie's sister."

"Sister, huh?" He takes her hand, but his eyes are on me as he shakes it, smile hopeful. "I've already met your entire family, and we haven't even been on a second date. I think it's the universe's way of telling us to do it. Maybe this afternoon? After closing?"

"Oooh, you're not shy. I love a guy who knows what he wants." My sister grins, wiggling her eyebrows at me.

"You *do* know you're married, right?" I ask.

"And?"

"You don't think your husband would mind?" I raise a brow. "Plus, I would appreciate it if you didn't flirt with my business partner. It's not professional."

"He isn't *my* business partner," she says, almost snickering. "And John's not the jealous type. But we *clearly* know who is, Miss Jealousy." She laughs softly and shakes her head.

"I'm not jea—"

"Whatever." She pulls her card from her wallet. "How much do I owe you for the books, you big baby? And don't forget to give me the receipt so I can give each of the girls a copy."

I huff, muttering the total while Jenn bags the books.

"So," Adri starts again, her eyes trailing up and down Knox. "You said you've met other family members? Like who? I haven't read anything about it in our family group chat." She leans her elbow on the counter, chin resting on the palm of her hand. Wanting her to leave as soon as possible, I pry the credit card from her fingers and slide it into the reader.

Knox smiles at me before answering—that stupid, gorgeous, heartwarmingly boyish smile of his—and asks "The bartender?"

"Ah. Alejandro." She nods somberly. "And how did that go? Because Ale can be just a little overprotective of her, you know? He's seen Lottie at her worst. She basically moved in with him and his family right after the divorce, so—"

"Adriana!" I cry, mortified. Knox looks at me in concern, any trace of humor in his eyes long gone. I run my fingers through my hair, silently begging her to stop talking about my personal life, but miracles are hard to come by, aren't they? "Knox doesn't—Ugh."

"Doesn't what? Doesn't care?" She laughs once. "I doubt that because by the looks of it, he seems *very* interested in—"

"He doesn't know I'm divorced," I whisper-yell, as if he isn't two feet away. "*Didn't* know." I sigh, squeezing my eyes shut.

"Oh." Her eyes dart back and forth between us. "Well, it's not like it's some dirty thing. It happens. Sometimes you end up marrying the wrong person. Someone who turns out to be an inconsiderate piece of shit who promised to stick with you through everything but then—"

"Just take your books and leave, will you?" I beg.

"*It happens.* It's not even that big of a deal." I know she means well with that comment, but... Way to invalidate the catalyst that led to the crumbling of my entire life, sis. Like being abandoned by my husband because I couldn't give him what he wanted was standard practice and something easy to get over.

She rolls her eyes at me again. "Jeez Louise, you're such a baby. Fine; I'll go. But you better not be this big of a bitch next time, or I'll convince every single member of *Touching My Shelf*—that's our romance bookclub's name, by the way," she says, smiling and fluttering her lashes at Knox, "to start shopping for their books from *you-know-where*, instead."

We glare at an each other as I bite my tongue, using every bit of energy in my body to keep from *really* giving her a piece of my mind.

Support your indie bookstores, kids.

Jenn laughs softly before walking into the stockroom, shaking her head in disbelief.

Ungrateful little thing.

Adri takes her bag from me, but stops before heading out. "Hope to see you again soon, Knox." And with another bat of her full eyelashes and a toss of her dark hair, she exits the store leaving as much damage to my psyche as a tornado.

"God, I'm so sorry about that," I tell Knox. "She's so embarrassing."

Knox gently wraps his hands around my wrists, pulling my hands away from my face. "Hey." I look up into his eyes and, for the first time since this morning, really let myself look at him. "You okay?"

"I—I... Yes, I'm fine. I just..."

He nods in understanding. "Sorry if that was uncomfortable for you. I was only teasing, but then—"

"Yeah, the D word came up." I wince, just the memory of the past five minutes making me nauseous.

"I didn't mean that. I just meant how she..." He sighs and shakes his head. "But yeah. I didn't know you were divorced." The look in his eyes—is it pity or something else?—crushes me. It's not enough that I'm thirty-four and barren (though he certainly doesn't know that part). Add to that the fact that I'm divorced, and you've got a fully formed heap of damaged goods that could scare even the most persistent of men away. Because that's what's happening, right? That look in his eyes? He's backing away. And though a part of me has been wishing for him to do so since having him come back into my life, I didn't expect to feel so disappointed.

"Yes, I'm divorced. That's what happens when you sleep with someone older than you, Knox," I say, unable to help the curtness in my tone. "They tend to have more... history."

"Why are you so hard on yourself?" he asks, voice gentle. "Having a past isn't a bad thing."

I pull my hands from his and pretend to busy myself by shuffling papers around the register.

"How much older, by the way?"

"What?"

"How much older are you? I just want to know whether you qualify for cougar status?" he jokes and I can't help the way my lips quirk—or the way my heart swells at his distraction.

"Shoot me now." I roll my eyes.

"C'mon. You can't be that much older than me."

"I'm not, but... Well. Let's put it this way: 'Just the Way You Are' by Bruno Mars was playing on the oldies station the other day and it's the song I lost my virginity to the night of my senior prom, so..."

"I remember when that song came out," he smiles in encouragement, though I doubt he could even talk to girls back then. "I lost my virginity in the back seat of my mom's RAV-4 when I was sixteen to Sadie Lawrence. It was awkward and weird and short." He laughs in spite of himself, before stopping abruptly. "How long it lasted, I mean. Not my dick. You know what my dick looks like already, and it isn't short," he adds quickly.

I burst out into laughter for the first time since seeing him again, and I swear I feel about twenty pounds lighter. I shake my head, a smile on my lips. "Knox."

"I know. The store. We can't. Blah, blah, blah." He waves his hand dismissively, his eyes roaming over my face as if memorizing every inch of it. "But if you ever wanna break this stupid rule, let me know. Because I'm more than up for it." He smiles his trickster grin, and I can't help but laugh once more.

"C'mon. We should prep for our meeting with the business manager today."

CHAPTER EIGHT

KNOX

Two hours and a migraine later, Lottie, Jenn, and I finally finish reviewing every single piece of paperwork we could scrounge up from Walter's office with Tracey, our new business manager. That, combined with the documentation left in Leroy's care, is enough for her to tell us that we are well and truly fucked:

"You're broke," she says simply, pushing her dark braids behind her ear, eyes grave.

Jenn picks up one of the multiple sheets of paper on the desk, eyes roaming the numbers on the page. "I don't understand. How can we be broke?"

Lottie reaches out and takes the paperwork from Jenn's hands, brows pulling together. If I weren't so confused by it all, I'd focus more on how adorable the little scrunch looks, how cute she is when she's concentrating and serious.

"Makes sense," Lottie says, voice cool and collected. "It shouldn't be a surprise to us when you think about it. I mean, we work here; we can see we're not selling out of copies every week, Jenn." She reviews the page with the bottom line one last time, at once sexy and serious. I never would've imagined I'd be able to be more attracted to Lottie than I already was, but seeing her in her element like this? In full business mode? I've never wanted anyone more.

"We should've probably shut down ages ago, right, Tracey? I imagine that commercial real estate and taxes in this small town aren't high, but my god, we've barely had any customers."

"Yes." Tracey nods. "According to his files, about three years ago, Walter was on the brink of bankruptcy. But then he received a sudden influx of cash and was able to settle some debts. The store remained stable, but after a few months, he found himself in the same position. And as you can see here," she reaches out and points at one of the line items, "he found another way to pay off some bills."

"How?" I ask. "I'm not a mathematician, but he sure as hell didn't have enough money in his bank account to cover any bills. I mean, I would know. I inherited whatever was left."

"Well, it seems as though he was selling high-priced items upon request?" She points at another line item, high-lighted this time. "I would look at your sales reports, see if you recognize them... Because, honestly? It's a bit suspect."

Lottie flips through the different documents, lost in concentration.

"For example, would you happen to know what this sale for twenty-five hundred dollars could be?" Tracey asks.

Lottie adjusts her glasses and squints. "Heming Old Man Sea First Ed," she murmurs, reading aloud.

"A first edition Hemingway," I whisper, my face so close to hers. I smile briefly, eyes flicking to her lips before speaking again. "Like the ones we found upstairs."

She unconsciously licks her lips as her gaze connects with mine. Something jumps in my chest with the prowess of an Olympian, and flips again as I unwillingly lose myself in her dark brown eyes. In how much her proximity affects me.

"What books?" Jenn breaks through whatever the hell moment we were just having.

I clear my throat before addressing her. "Walter had some early editions he was restoring in his apartment. We think he was selling them. And now I'm assuming, selling them to keep the store alive?"

"Why keep it open, though? Why not just sell the store if it was drowning?" Jenn asks.

"He wouldn't do that," Lottie shakes her head, protective mode on. "He loved Adams's Bookstore—it was everything to him. And despite business not being great, the place means a lot to this town. I know it does." She continues to review the balance sheet, frustrated. "Why didn't he come to me? If he had let me help him for once I probably would have been able to save him from this. But he had to do it his way, didn't he?" There's a fondness to her voice, a smile tugging at her lips rather than the rage I would've expected had I been in her situation.

Lottie thinks his stubbornness was endearing. I, on the other hand, knew the real consequences to his pigheaded-ness and didn't find it cute for a single second. Is it possible it was me this whole time? That I was the problem? That I never got to know this great guy Lottie has mentioned and stood up for several times already?

I'm suddenly filled with jealousy, but I do my best to push it down. Useless, pointless emotion. As if there were anything I could do about it now. He's gone, after all.

"So, he basically worked twice as hard to keep a store alive that clearly wasn't working the way he wanted to, just so he didn't have to ask for help or admit to having lost?" I laugh dryly, feeling the anger build. "Typical Walter."

Lottie frowns at me. "That's not what it was."

"Hey." I place a hand on her delicate shoulder. "Don't take it personally. He was stubborn and pigheaded. From my experience, he wasn't the type of person to ask for help." She frowns at me, unhappy with my review of my father, apparently.

"Regardless, he managed to keep the lights on," Tracey says. "And anyway, it doesn't matter anymore, does it? Right now, we need to determine what *you* want to do."

"We sell it." Jenn sits up straighter in her seat, suddenly all business. Her lower lip is swollen and red from chewing on it throughout the whole meeting—she hasn't looked at ease once since it began. "Right? Maybe we won't be able to sell the bookstore itself, but the property. We sell it and we each get our cut."

"Sell it?" Lottie asks, eyes as big as saucers, panic written all over her face. "We can't just *sell* the bookstore!"

"Why not?" Jenn raises a brow. "Are you going to manage it or something? Buy us out? Because I could use the money for college, and Knox doesn't even live here, so…"

"I just—I think…" Lottie stutters. "I'm just worried about

tenants. Like, what if we sell to some awful people and they ruin the town?"

"You could vet the buyers, you know?" Tracey says.

Lottie's eyes flash darkly at our business manager for a moment, but she quickly regains control of her expression. "I... Yes, I guess so. I guess we can make sure they're the right people." But her gaze drops to her lap where she fidgets with her hands, slumped over herself.

"Perfect." Tracey claps her hands together. "You're definitely going to have to put some money into it if you want to sell it for a good price, though. Otherwise, I can just let you know now that it'll go for peanuts, because this place is a tear-down. But I'm not worried about that. Leroy mentioned that there wouldn't be too much handholding with you guys because of Lottie's experience."

"What experience?" I ask.

"I, ah, used to be Senior Vice President of Retail Operations in New York. In my past life," she mutters quickly," she says, still a little shaken. "It was kind of my job to open new stores, manage all our retail ops..." But it comes out unconvincingly for some reason. Like she barely believes it herself.

"And she was pretty good at it, I hear. She worked for a top luxury brand," Jenn says.

Lottie blushes and looks away.

"Cool." I smile at her in wonder. Because of course she was amazing at it. How could she not be? Sure, when I met her, she said her life was a mess, and of course there must be a story as to how she got from there to where she is now. But I could tell from the second I saw her that Lottie was extraordinary. *Is* still extraordinary. It just feels like she's the only one who forgot.

I can't wait to hear the rest of her story, to take advantage of this time together. All I want is to bask in her.

It's clear she doesn't realize how amazing she is, but god, I do. I don't even know her well, but I *know* her. I feel like I *know* who she is in her core. One night together was enough to find out.

And even though Walter for sure wanted to screw me over with this project, the joke is on him. Because now I get to spend all this time with the woman of my dreams, getting to know her life and the rest of who she is. Even if she won't give me the time of day in the way that I want her to.

I smile to myself, excited for the first time since getting to this town in the middle of nowhere.

"Lottie, we should use your talents and expertise to make it as good as we can before selling it so we can get the most amount of money possible. It's, like, a no brainer." Jenn rolls her eyes.

"Wait, what? No. Let's just sell it as is. At most, add a new coat of paint," Lottie says, waving her hands in front of her. "Why change it? I mean, I know it's not in the best shape ever, but it's got character."

"Why would we leave it like that?" Jenn asks. "If we can get more money—"

"It's a lot more work than you think, Jenn. I don't think I could do it all on my own. At my old job, I at least had a team."

"And what are we? Chopped liver? We all own a

percentage here. We all have a vested interest. Of course, we'd help out with whatever you need, right, Knox?"

"Yeah. Of course we'll help. It actually sounds like fun."

Lottie snorts. "Fun? It'll be hard work. And what about the money for the remodel?" "What about it?" Jenn blinks.

"Uh, maybe the fact that we don't have any?"

"That isn't exactly true, though, is it? We can just do what Walter did: sell the books we found upstairs. If they're all that valuable, we can definitely scrounge up enough to pay for part—if not all—of the renovation. Some of them looked like they were in pretty solid condition. We can reach out to past buyers, hit up some conventions." I shrug casually. "Honestly, it shouldn't be too hard to figure out. And like Tracey said, we can vet the buyers when the time comes, if that makes you feel better."

And I can't help how much I love the way I can see her mind racing, watching the way it begins to form a plan. Her expression shifts to one of excitement, a look in her eyes that tells me that maybe this "problem" is something she'd enjoy solving, despite whatever emotional attachment she may have to a store.

I love her sudden confidence—it's like she's rediscovering it, and it's nothing short of a privilege to watch it happen in real time.

"Yeah, okay." She smiles, excited this time. "Let's do it."

"Together," I emphasize, as a slow, hopeful grin spreads across my face.

Jenn exhales in relief. "Thank *god.*"

CHAPTER NINE
LOTTIE

Now covered in a kaleidoscope of Post-Its, I stand back to admire the wall of Walter's office. Taking in the rows of neatly placed sticky notes, a familiar sense of satisfaction courses through me. Of a type of peace that only comes when there's order and a plan in place.

I can see everything that still needs to be done at a bird's eye view, giving me a better sense of control, of organization. It's so well-organized and thought-out that it almost takes away the sting of parting with the bookstore. *Almost.* I put my hands on my hips and smile.

I'm ready for this. I can do this. But most of all, this is fun.

"Hey." Daniel, my older brother, breaks through my concentration. "I'm here for—Whoa. What the hell is this?"

Without taking my eyes off my masterpiece, I grin. "My battle plan."

He snorts and stands beside me, eyes roaming over it.

"You know, you could basically organize this all in a project management softwares. Or even a goddamn bullet journal, right? You don't need to wallpaper the place in office supplies."

I turn to face him and raise an eyebrow in his direction. "You're telling *me*? Of course I know that there are a ton of PM softwares available, and yes, we have one. We even have an excel sheet for it, too. But there are few bigger satisfactions in life than the feeling of ripping one of these off the wall when a task is complete."

"Is that so?" He presses his lips together to try to keep from laughing.

I glare at him and walk to the wall, searching for the orange neon sticky note with the words "Prelim. Meeting w/Daniel re: Real Estate listing" and pull it off in one quick movement.

"See?" I smile, showing him what's on it before crumpling the task in a ball, tossing it in the nearby trash. "Now let's get this over with."

He laughs softly and takes a seat, putting his briefcase on the table. "Getting down to business. I love this determined, psycho person you've turned into. It's refreshing. A nice change of pace from your other usual hot mess of a self."

I laugh a little, not taking even the slightest offense to his comment. "Psycho? I don't think so. Determined? For sure. It feels great to feel this way again. To feel like my life has a different type of purpose than just thinking of how it can go back to what it once was. I'm actually *doing* something for the first time in years."

"That's amazing, Sis. I'm happy for you."

"Thanks. But I've never been a certified hot mess, have I?"

"Nah, not really. I feel like the only way you can deserve a title like that is if you're responsible for how messy your life turns out. And you've done nothing wrong. All that bad shit from before... It all just happened to you." He smiles sadly at me, reaching out for my hand. I take it because I don't know what to say.

I wince and look away, because it didn't necessarily just *happen* to me. Everything was a consequence of choices I made. Still, I don't press the subject too much. "Yeah, well, I guess it's why I need this to work out. It's basically my get out of Ceres Cove Free card, isn't it? Take the money and run."

Daniel frowns slightly, his smile dropping just a bit, taking his hand back. "Is that your plan? To take the money from the sale and run?"

"Shouldn't it be? I mean isn't that what I've been trying to do all these years? Haven't I been here long enough?"

My brother shrugs as he takes a seat. "I don't know. What's so wrong with Ceres Cove?"

I shoot him a look as I walk around the desk and sit in Walter's chair, hearing it creak as I do. "Come on. It's not like there's anything wrong with it; it's just... You and I both know this place isn't for me. I want to go back to my old life. I hate it here. Hate this town, hate what it represents. It feels like purgatory to me and you know it."

Daniel presses his lips together and nods, pulling out some paperwork from his briefcase. "Then I guess we should get to work, shouldn't we? Wouldn't want to keep you in this purgatory longer than you can stand."

I roll my eyes. "You know this isn't about you or the people in Ceres Cove—at least not everyone, because I could definitely do without the town rumor mill. But I need more. I want more. I want to be a part of something bigger than this."

He sighs deeply, nodding as if in understanding, even though we both know he doesn't get it. At least not the way he should.

"Gotcha. So you think this money will finally help you get back on your feet?"

"Well, it's up to you. You need to find us someone who will buy the place for enough."

Daniel snorts. "No pressure, though, right?"

I laugh softly. "As if you'd ever feel it. We both know you kick ass at your job. Even in the middle of nowhere, you manage to be a star realtor." And I'm not even lying. My brother is a partner at his current commercial real estate firm. His reach is across three counties, and even in this messed up economy, he has been able to become the real estate king of middle-of-nowhere Maine.

"If you're hoping flattery will get me to drop my agent listing fee... Well, keep going, because maybe I will."

We laugh, but eventually get down to business. I manage to convince him to actually drop the agent fee, and we agree to meet up in a week or so to finalize timelines and hammer out other details. After just fifteen minutes, our business is concluded.

"So where are your co-owners? I thought all of you were

going to be in this meeting," he asks, as I pass him a freshly brewed cup of coffee.

"Jenn is finishing setting up everything for the store's going away party—are you coming tonight by the way?—and Knox is doing some research upstairs."

"Can't make it. The twins have their first ballet recital today, remember?"

"Shit," I mutter, chastising myself for forgetting about my nieces' big day. "I have a present for them at home, actually."

He laughs at my expression, the guilt I'm sure is evident in my eyes. "Lottie, they're four years old. Don't beat yourself up for missing it. If you were their parent, it would be another thing. But it's okay."

I frown, annoyed with his placation. "I know I'm not their *mom*. I'm just saying, I would've liked to have gone."

"You have work. And that's totally okay. Any other day, Best Aunt of the Year Award."

He smiles encouragingly at me and takes another sip of his coffee.

"Are we going to talk about him, though? Or are we just going to ignore the elephant in the room?"

"I don't know who you're talking about," I say, hiding behind my coffee.

"Knox?" He raises a brow. "I spoke to Adri—she told me all about him. And, like, half this town knows. Plus, I heard from—"

"If the next words out of your mouth are Lizzie McCalister, I swear to god..."

He laughs. "No, it wasn't her. Ale was the other person I

spoke to. In case you were wondering, our brother doesn't like the guy *at all*."

My skin heats in irritation, muscles braced as if ready to defend Knox. "He doesn't even know him. He barely said two words to the guy."

"I know. I'm guessing the only chance he's had to meet him was at the bar, and that was... Well. That was that night, wasn't it?" He smirks, and I want to murder him.

I throw my hands up in the air. "How is it that everyone in the entire world knows about my goddamn sex life? This is insanity."

"I wouldn't say *everyone* in the world—that's being a bit self-centered if you ask me— but—"

"And then you wonder why I want to leave this place again and never come back."

Daniel's smile drops, the entire mood in the office shifting to a more serious one. With pressed lips, he gently sets his coffee on the desk and gets up. "And on that note..."

"No, wait—"

"It's fine. I have to go anyways. Logan and I are supposed to pick the twins up together, and my husband is not a fan of tardiness."

I come around the desk, desperate to fix things. "Daniel—"

"Hey, it's okay." He kisses my cheek and puts a hand on my shoulder. "Good luck tonight, okay?"

"Well, you weren't kidding about your love for Post-Its." I lift my head up from the computer screen to find a gorgeous Knox standing in the office doorway.

"Told you it was the way to my heart." I smile and lean back in my chair, watching as his eyes pore over the sticky notes.

"Are these color-coded?" he asks, his voice tinged with awe.

"Yup. Hot pink is for all of Jenn's tasks, yours are the blue ones, mine are the orange, and then the green are just general ones."

His smile is broad as he rounds the desk to read each piece of paper. He runs his fingers over one of the notes, tracing the letters. "Your handwriting is so neat and perfect. It's very you." Knox's voice is laced with a fondness that surprises me.

I snort. "I'm far from perfect, Knox."

He laughs once. "You need to learn how to take a compliment."

"A compliment or a line?" I smirk, getting to my feet to stand beside him as he continues to take in my master plan.

"*Compliment.*" He stares me head-on, eyes serious.

I smile and nod. "Thank you, then."

"You're welcome, then." His lopsided smile makes another appearance, making my heart expand in my chest.

"So how can I help you?" I ask, wanting to get him out of the office as quickly as possible.

Despite having respected the boundaries I set after our conversation in his apartment last week, it's been impossible to keep him at much of a distance given our situation. I had hoped some of the tension would've dissipated by putting a stop to all the flirting, but I hadn't expected to be so captivated by him in general. By the sweet way he's started making me coffee every morning; the way he speaks so passionately about his work over team lunches; the adorable manner in which he *has* to carry his camera with him at all times, even if it's just around the corner or to run an errand, like a security blanket to a toddler. Knox is cute and smart and funny and spending all this time with him has been problematic since I sometimes forget that I shouldn't like him. I forget that I should probably not laugh at his stupid dad jokes, even if I find them funny. It's been a bit of an uphill battle. Which is why I need to make more of an effort to put some space between us.

"I'm just here to get you for the party. We're ready, and Jenn said people should be arriving soon."

I feel the blood drain from my face, feel myself shrink a little. We've known about the store's going away party for a while—we sent out the invites over a week ago—but it's only now hitting me how real this whole thing is.

"Wait, *what*? Already?" For some reason, my breathing speeds and I can't get it to stop.

"Yeah, I—Hey, are you okay?"

I nod absentmindedly, but he leads me back into the chair.

"Take a breath."

"No, I'm fine. Just a little in shock." But I take a deep, settling breath just the same. "It's the end of an era, you know?"

He nods, though I know he can only understand it on a surface level, not having lived it himself.

"Also, this makes it official."

"Makes what official?"

"It. *This*." I look meaningfully back at the Post-It wall. "What we're doing. Shutting down the store means the beginning of this. It's a lot." It's the end of Adams's Books.

"Yeah, it's a lot. But thank god we have you to lead the project, right?" He smiles at me, thinking my only concern is only the reno and sale project itself and not the fact that the town will be losing something that meant a lot to it. But I don't want to make things heavier, so I pretend that's the only thing on my mind.

Knox takes my hands in his, pulling me up to stand in front of him—dangerously close. I have to consciously stop myself from looping my arms around him, sinking my face into his chest and breathing him in.

"Your faith in me is—"

"Well-earned, based on all the amazing things I've heard and all the incredible things I've seen you accomplish in the short time we've known each other," he cuts me off. "Don't put yourself down. Look at this fucking list. Look at how you've already mobilized so many people and kicked off this project without a hitch. I mean, you got us a construction permit and a million others in under a week. I don't care if this is a small town, that kind of thing doesn't happen anywhere."

I smile up at him, cheeks reddening. "Ah, that was easy. All I had to do was feed Councilman Forbes's ego, tell him how great he is." I shrug.

"Still, you knew to do it. Knew how to work the system. Because you're not just book smart, you're street smart."

"Street smart?" I smirk, getting lost in the winter-blue of his eyes.

He laughs softly. "Yeah, street smart. So I know for a fact this is gonna go great."

"I know you're right, deep down. I'm just a little over-whelmed, is all."

"I get that," he says, nodding sympathetically. "Just know that not everything is riding just on your shoulders. I'm here for you. And so is Jenn. We're both part of this as well, don't forget that."

In a moment of insanity, I take a step closer and hug him. "Thank you," I murmur against his chest, inhaling his scent, never wanting to let it go.

He hesitates at first, but lets his arms come around me, warm, comforting, *safe*. He holds me tightly to him, tucking my head under his chin. "You're welcome."

We hold each other in silence for a moment. Perhaps a bit longer than what is considered normal. When I pull away, I can barely look him in the eye. I told him we needed space, and here I am initiating PDA. Still, I don't regret it. Sometimes you just need a hug, even if it is a slightly sexually charged yet friendly one.

The bell over the front door chimes, followed by a very

distinct, "Woo! Let's give this baby a kick-ass send-off!" my sister yells. I hear Jenn laugh and offer her a drink, to which Adri responds with a "Hell, yeah."

"My sister's here," I whisper, still unable to meet his eyes. "We should get out there."

"Yeah." Knox swallows once, twice, *three times*. "But, you good?"

I muster all the strength I possibly can and drag my eyes to his, finding in them exactly what I feared most: a yearning I hate to admit I'm starting to feel, too. "Yes. Thank you."

"Good. That's good. So should we…"

"Right." And without another word, we leave the whatever just happened behind in the office and walk into *Adams's Bookstore's* last hurrah.

CHAPTER TEN

KNOX

I take a sip of ice-cold beer before pulling out my camera and taking a picture of the sight before me. The bookstore is packed with people, many I have yet to meet but who all seem to know exactly who I am. Though maybe I'm just being a bit paranoid.

The space is nearly unrecognizable, its old shelves bare save for a few framed pictures of my father and the shop over the years. The middle island that contained staff picks has been turned into a buffet table filled with the most incredible finger food and snacks—all donated by Adriana, who I've discovered is a kickass cook. I've already inhaled about fifteen pounds of bacon wrapped stuffed dates with a maple glaze in the past hour. Not sure whether she added some sort of addictive quality to them or what, but that shit slaps. I'm going back for more.

"I can't believe the bookstore is just... done," I hear someone breathe beside me as I sneak another date from the island. I turn to face the voice and see that it belongs to a woman in her late seventies, long platinum hair down to her waist, and enough smile wrinkles to show that she's lived a good, happy life.

"Did you frequent it often?" I ask, curious. In the week and a half since I've been here, I haven't seen many customers. When looking at the huge turnout for the going away party, I gotta ask myself how many of these people were actual customers and how many are just here to support Jenn and Lottie. Honestly, I wouldn't be surprised if the only reason people showed up was because of the amazing food Lottie's sister brought for the party. "Knox Riddick, by the way." I stick my hand out and shake hers.

Her eyes widen knowingly, her sharp inhale a clear clue she knows *exactly* who I am. "You're Walter's boy! The one who's working with Jenny and Lottie on the remodel. The photographer." I feel the smile spread across my face as I struggle to suppress my laughter, confirming exactly what's been on my mind: I wasn't paranoid and Lottie wasn't kidding when she said everyone knows everybody's business in this town.

"Yes. That's me."

"Wow! Well, I'm Annabelle Martins. But you can call me Belle. I'm Jenny's grandmother and long-time Ceres Cove resident."

"So not a loyal customer, then?"

She snorts. "No. Don't tell my Jenny or even Lottie, but I would rather wait til the movie comes out for books. Plus, I'd say I'm more into spies and action, and Walter did not stock those types of books, anyway." I gaze down at Belle, this perfect woman in a pink floral dress and pink ballet flats, with crystal flower clips in her hair. Her makeup is light, but very intentionally put on, and everything about how she looks would've made me guess she was more into Victorian romance than murder and conspiracy theories.

"I understand. I'm not much of a reader, either. I'd rather get to know a story through photographs." I shrug unapologetically.

She tilts her head at me with a smile. "I'd gathered as much, given the camera strapped to your chest."

I look down at my Nikon with a laugh. "Yeah."

"So, you subscribe to the notion that a picture's worth a thousand words?"

"Absolutely," I say, without missing a beat. "Photographs have the ability to sometimes tell stories a human would otherwise find difficult to express or verbalize."

She purses her lips and hooks her arm around one of mine, leading me to the closest shelf. "What does this one say, then?" She points to a framed photograph of Walter standing proudly in front of the bookstore. The signage in the front looks brand new and there's a banner in the window with the words "Grand Opening" in big, bold blue letters. His hands are in his pockets, wind blowing in what little hair he had left—considerably less than the last time I saw him.

"On the surface level, he looks like a happy man, one who's proud of his accomplishment, of having achieved this feat of opening the bookstore" I start, not understanding exactly why I'm being a willing participant. "But the way his shoulders are slightly rolled inwards, the way his smile doesn't quite reach his tight eyes, and the shy way in which his fists push down into his pockets would tell me he isn't as happy as he's trying to come off.

"He's scared," I tell her. "Terrified, even. But in a way in which he would never dare confess, even to himself. Let alone someone else. That's how he was. Always proud, always stubborn."

The corners of her lips quirk up. "Is that all?"

"It's the simple answer. I could get into it, but it's a party and I don't wanna bring down the mood." I smile, but she only barely returns it. "I just thought I'd go with the first thing I notice." I shrug and we laugh softly.

"You forgot something, though."

"What's that?"

"You forgot to mention how excited he looks, too, despite the underlying feelings of terror." She chuckles. "Ready for this new stage in life he was embarking on, starting from scratch in a new town, with new people. You also forgot to mention how much you resemble each other. In looks *and* in character."

I frown, wanting to cut her off but reminding myself I should be respectful.

"Same look in your eyes, same jaw and nose. Same fear of life." She smiles and pats my arm.

"You don't know me," I try to say in my gentlest voice, a smile on my face but feeling my defenses go up.

"I'm old enough to recognize the signs." Just holds my eyes for a moment. "Your father was an amazing man. Quiet, taciturn. Seemingly indifferent to those around him. But he was the complete opposite beneath the surface. I am truly sorry for his loss. He will be—is already— missed deeply."

And with that, she walks away, leaving me alone by the photographs of my father to digest her random analysis, her condolences, and the bacon-wrapped dates.

I look around the room, at the mostly unfamiliar faces. Each one here to send off a place, when in reality maybe they're here to send off my father?

Groaning, I run my fingers through my hair. Everyone fucking loves him here. I don't get it. Who was this man so quietly adored by the citizens of this small town? And why the fuck did he never show himself to me? Why did he cut me out? Why did *I* cut him out?

I retreat into a corner with a plate of stacked with food, sulking. It's only when Lottie finds me in a corner of the party by myself leaning against the wall, two beers past tipsy, that I'm able to come out of my funk.

"Hey," she says, her voice loud enough to hear above the crowd, but soft enough to be a comfort. "You okay?"

I raise my shoulders in a sloppy shrug, causing the beer in the can to slosh a little. "S'all good."

"*Oookay*." She raises a brow. "But can I see that beer, though? Just for a second?" I hand her my can, smiling and gazing at her through sleepy eyes. She's heaven in another one of her oversized sweaters and plaid skirt look, her hair a bit more tousled since the last time I saw her.

Lottie looks tired, a little run down from all the socializing, probably, but still so perfect.

She's so fucking beautiful.

"I'm just gonna go ahead and put it here for a sec," she says, setting it far from me.

"Sad." I pout, which makes her laugh in earnest, coming

from deep within her. It lights up her tired eyes, flushes her tan skin, and makes me want to kiss her so badly I want to die. "You're amazing." And I know we agreed to let these things go and I know we agreed to just be partners, but the words burst through me, a complete inevitability.

"You're drunk. And a mess." She *tsks* and runs her fingers through my hair, combing through. I close my eyes in bliss, leaning into her touch.

"Nah. Just tipsy. Tired." *Of this achy feeling in my chest. Of thinking I'll never get to touch you again. Of rubbing myself raw every night to the memory of you beneath me...*

"Why don't you head on up to bed?"

I shoot her a lascivious smile, but she rolls her eyes with a laugh. "I meant *by yourself.*"

"You're no fun."

"Seriously. People are starting to leave anyway, so it's not a big deal. Jenn and I will clean up."

I scoff. "I'm not gonna let you guys do this all on your own." I push off the wall, but stumble a little. "Whoa."

"Okay, buddy." She steadies me with a grip around my bicep. Holds me still. "Let's get some water and coffee in you. I think you may have had a little more to drink than you think you did."

Lottie drags me through the crowd into the office, sits me down in my father's chair while she makes me a cup of coffee. My eyes never leave her as she moves, as she unknowingly turns serving a hot beverage into a beautiful performance.

"Here. Drink this." She hands me the hot cup, the one I've been using since getting here, and smile up at her in thanks.

Gaze locked on hers, I take a long, comforting drink. A warm feeling spreads through me, and I don't think it's the coffee that's responsible for it.

Lottie takes a seat across from me, watching patiently as I drink.

"Feel better?" she asks when I finish.

"Some. I guess I did have one drink too many."

She shrugs. "It's okay. It was a celebration. Did you get to meet any interesting people?"

I smile, remembering the slew of characters this town came with. "Yes, many. Though one in particular stood out."

"Oh, yeah? Who's that?" She raises a brow, looking at me with those dark brown eyes through her messy bangs.

"Jenn's grandmother? She was…"

"Intense?" A broad smile spreads across her face.

"I'd say 'uncomfortably insightful,' but intense is good." We laugh softly and I tell her about my interaction, without volunteering how unsettled I felt afterward.

"She's a character."

"What about you? Did you end up having fun at the party?"

She smiles before taking a sip of her own coffee. "Yeah. It was nice to see everyone there, supporting the store, sharing stories about it, placing bets on what will take its place. It was also nice to see how Walter became such a huge part of our community even though he was here for around nine years. That was sweet."

I frown, a twinge of jealousy I can't quite understand knotting itself in my stomach. "That's nice." I try for my best smile, struggling a bit. "Though I don't think it was *all* about him or even the bookstore. You're not giving yourself enough credit. I could tell by your interactions how adored you are here." And who could blame them? She's heaven.

Lottie looks momentarily taken aback, surprised by my assessment. "No, I think you're confused. Sure, I get along with the town, but—"

"Lottie," I start, shaking my head. Does she not realize how amazing she is? "These people admire you; they think the world of you. It's clear in every word they speak when talking about Lottie Veracruz."

"I'm sure you're exaggerating."

"I'm not," I say seriously, needing her to understand. "Your brother's wife, Bonnie, spent about half an hour telling me how you were the world's best aunt, the most loving and supportive sister, and how much everyone respects you here."

"She has to say that—she's family." Her cheeks turn a bright red, and she looks away.

"Not really, no. She didn't have to tell me about how you organized the elementary school play when the theater teacher went into early retirement. She didn't have to mention the time you helped the mailman optimize his route to decrease his delivery time during the day so he could get home earlier to spend time with his kids. I mean, who does that? And then I met one of the councilmen and *he* told me about the time you started an initiative to rebuild the rotting dock by the shore. The town didn't have the money for it, but you managed to plan a fundraising effort and exceed its donation goal."

"Jesus, they told you all of that?" she whispers, cheeks flushed.

"Yeah. They did." It was an afternoon of learning, about my father, yes, but it ended up being mostly about Lottie. It was like some of the chapters in her life she'd kept hidden from me had been revealed through the people around her, the people who loved and knew her. It was pieces of her I craved every second of every day since meeting her that I hadn't been able to get.

"I did the play thing for my nieces. And the mailman thing was a bit self-serving; Justin kept making late deliveries and it was irritating." But I know she's lying. Or if it's true, it's only a half truth. "And the dock... Well, I couldn't let the damn dock rot if I had an inkling on how to raise the money for it, could I? It was the logical thing to do."

I laugh and shake my head. "You can deny it all you want—even if it's super weird of you to—but this town loves you, Lottie. They do. And I've got a feeling you love it back."

Her face twists in something resembling pain, but I have no idea why. "Hey, are you okay?" I come around the desk and kneel in front of her. "Is it something I said?"

"No, no." She smiles at me. "I'm good. It's nice to hear I'm appreciated. There was a time in my life when I didn't really get much of that, so it kind of throws me off to think of people being... I don't know. Appreciative."

I frown, wanting desperately to pry, but all the while knowing full well that prying into her life will always lead to her raising her walls. So I give her some space, some quiet—hopefully enough to make her feel safe enough to share.

But she doesn't.

"Well, *I'm* appreciative of you, too."

"Thanks," she says with a soft smile that has me weak in the knees.

I sigh deeply, frustrated and wrecked that I'm still just outside of her, waiting to be let in—even just as friends. I glance at the office wall, the one covered in post-its, reading the notes on there to distract myself from the ache of the barrier she's put between us.

"And I do care about Ceres Cove. I just... It's just not really for me, I don't think. I really miss New York and would love to go back someday. Actually, I'm kind of banking on this whole sale to go well so I can do just that."

"You wanna leave Ceres Cove?" I ask, surprised. Seems like her entire support system is here, and while I've heard her speak about her old work, she never seems to mention any old friends, relationships, or coworkers. It makes me wonder what she's *really* wanting to go back to.

"I think I outgrew this town the day I was born," she says with a laugh. "It just isn't for me. I mean, you get it, right? You've traveled all over the world. Ceres Cove is hardly anything special."

I pull back, surprised. "Ceres Cove looks like the type of town I dreamed of growing up in as a kid," I tell her, remembering how much I would've killed to have a normal, steady, *boring* upbringing in a town like this. As opposed to the absolute clusterfuck I experienced. From my POV, Ceres Cove is awesome. From its beautiful coastal homes to its small beaches, its quaint two-street downtown and the feeling of being family with everyone even when they're not. This little town in Maine tugged at something within me I couldn't quite pinpoint. And it wasn't a negative feeling.

"And 'special' is a relative term. You'd be surprised by how many people and places have been deemed as ordinary to some, but extraordinary to others. I think you just need to change your perspective. It's what photographers have to do sometimes to catch the true beauty of the seemingly simplest things. People just need to look a little harder sometimes."

She laughs easily, throwing her head back. "I don't think you'll ever convince me that this town isn't anything more than a coastal town in the middle of nowhere with little to offer."

"That's harsh." I scoff.

"Believe me. I've been here most of my life. You're just seeing everything in rosecolored glasses. Ceres Cove isn't as great as you think it is, and you can bet your life that I'm out of here the first chance I get."

"I think it'd be this town's biggest tragedy to lose you."

CHAPTER ELEVEN

LOTTIE

Just a couple of days after the official closing, I find myself slipping into Knox's car to start the next phase of our project. The smell of whiskey and smoke and delicious leather quickly overpowers my senses as he shuts his truck door on my side. Knox has officially made his signature scent my favorite thing ever. Do they make a Bath & Body Works candle for it, by chance? Because I'd buy ten in a heartbeat. Wouldn't even wait for one of their promos.

Its effect on me is so strong, I barely notice his grin as he rounds the hood of the car, eyes never leaving mine. But I see it. And I see the way he still looks at me. And I hate the way I feel a thrill every time he does. The way I know I can't help but look at him, too.

I watch closely as he straps himself into his seat, taking in the way his muscles move beneath his white henley, the faint outline of his tattoos almost visible through the soft, worn fabric. It's the same tee he gave me to wear the night we spent together. The one I wore after the first time we had sex, while we ate shitty vending machine snacks in bed. The same one he lifted with gentle fingers, kissing up my belly, making me laugh and laugh, wishing the night could last forever.

"Ready?" He asks, unaware of how deep under my skin he's gotten, the way the ache in my chest seems to keep spreading throughout my body.

"Yes," I clear my throat and nod. "Let's go."

After a busy week of planning and calling up contractors and electricians, negotiating prices and discussing designs, work was set to begin as early as this following Monday—provided we make our initial payment by then. I was prepared to hustle somehow, or even ask one of my siblings for a loan while we figured the whole financial part out, but Knox surprised me by finding a solution before I did. It wasn't even on the to-do list I'd prepared.

He found a rare book convention that was happening all weekend about two hours away and made plans for us to take some of Walter's old books, meet with some dealers, and come back with some, if not all, of the money needed for the deposits.

I'm not going to deny that my micromanaging tendencies flared up, but I managed to hold off on getting involved, watching as he made calls and organized the meetings from his father's old desk throughout the week.

As I watched, I couldn't help but admit being surprised by his efficiency and... find it kind of hot. Maybe it's the former type-A personality in me? But watching him take charge felt better than I ever would've expected.

His proven efficiency is not enough for me to let go of full control and have him face the buyers on his own, though. It's why I was left with no choice but to go with him on the road trip—something I immediately began to question as soon as I slipped into his truck.

Can someone please tell me why I thought it would be a fantastic idea to spend the next couple of hours trapped in a metal box with him? Not just that, but I'm only now realizing that this will be the first time since that heated moment in Walter's bedroom that we'll be truly alone. No Jenn in the other room, no customer around, no guests in the front of the store. And though I thought that my crush (yes, that's what I'm calling it, because it's nothing more—I promise) would have faded by now, I've become fully aware at this point that I was terribly, ridiculously wrong. I *still* feel butterflies around him like some schoolgirl.

"You okay?" he asks, brows pulled together in an impossibly adorable way.

I nod again despite the fact that I can't—*I just can't*—look him in the eye right now. Because, my god, I'm so overwhelmed by *all* of him—his kind, yet playful voice, his warm demeanor, the way he seems to understand me despite not really knowing 100% what's wrong, and, most of all, his quiet strength, how it makes me feel safe, protected, and seen. I can barely stand it.

"You sure? Because you won't even look at me. And you kinda look like you're gonna throw up."

"I'm fine," I mumble. "Just... mentally going through our checklist for today. Everything we need to do," I lie.

"Don't worry—I got everything we need. The books are

in the back, I have the contact info for the potential buyers, the convention tickets. I've got us covered. You don't need to worry about a thing."

"Thanks." I finally look over to him and smile because I really am very thankful.

"See? You probably didn't even need to come. But I know better than to think you'd let me go alone," he says with a smirk.

I raise a brow because, even though we don't know each other very well, I feel like he knows enough of me to understand that I'm not one to let go of the reins so easily.

"I don't trust your negotiation skills and I need to make sure that we're getting the best deal, here." I hate the way the words come out, cold and detached. I'd beat myself up internally for my inability to act normal around this man, but I can't let him catch on to the fact that I love that this feels like a team, that I'm not alone. And I can't let *myself* catch on to the fact that I'm not hating this. Not even a little bit. Not even at all.

"Don't get me wrong. I'm fucking ecstatic you decided to come with me. I feel lucky I get to have hours of drive time to convince you to actually go out with me. Make my case." I glare at him, but he laughs it off, not a care in the world.

"I should've taken my own car." I roll my eyes, but a secret thrill runs through me, a part of me curious as to how he expects to break me down.

He throws his head back in laughter and shakes his head. "You're something." Knox reaches for his phone on the dashboard and passes it to me, all while keeping his eyes on the road. "Do you mind entering the address of the convention? I'm pretty sure I know how to get there, but I don't want us to get lost. My password is 4-3-2-1."

I balk at the phone in my hand, at the way he so easily handed it to me—*and gave me his password.* There are... no words. It might not seem like a lot, but trusting me with this is to me. This man, who I only just met, has given me access to his phone. I could unlock it now and go wild—read his texts, deep-dive into his search history—and he wouldn't be able to do a thing about it. He's driving, after all.

A man with nothing to hide.

My ex, on the other hand. *Phew.* He *never* let me use his phone. Never even told me what his password was. And we were *married.*

In retrospect, that should've been a major red flag. But sometimes it's easier to turn a blind eye than to admit to yourself that something's wrong.

"I know, it's a dumb password. But honestly, it's the only thing I'd ever remember."

I clear my throat, getting myself together as I unlock the damn thing. "You can't think of one significant date in your life you could use as your password? Like your birthday, perhaps?" I tease.

He shrugs nonchalantly, a soft smile on his face, and without another word, I enter the convention address into Google Maps.

For the first part of the drive, I'm quiet as I try to process everything that's happened in the past couple of weeks: Walter's death, the funeral, my night with Knox, inheriting the store, this massive project we've taken on. I'm exhausted; this whole thing has been exhausting.

But then I stare at Knox's profile, and think about how much more difficult this must be for him; about his relationship with Walter and how he'll never get to fix it.

Knox acts like everything is fine, but is that even possible? It's just a matter of time before the other shoe will drop. He'll realize he lost the only father he ever had and it'll hit him hard.

The urge to comfort him before he even seems to realize he needs it is strong. I clutch my hands together to keep from reaching out, from pulling his hand into mine to offer support.

He's not mine.

Still, he doesn't deserve my attitude, the way I've treated him since seeing him for the first time that morning at the store.

Jenn was right to pull me aside this morning, to give me shit for how I've been acting.

"*Please* be nice to him, Lottie. I don't get why you're so mean to this guy you so clearly like—"

"I'm not mean to him! I helped him when he was tipsy the other night after the party. And I definitely don't like him," I interrupted, crossing my arms in front of my chest.

"—but I would appreciate it if you could control yourself and whatever inner turmoil you're currently going through and just be professional."

I scoffed, taking a step back from her. "Are you kidding me? This coming from the twenty-year-old who asked me if

I'd ever tried edible crotchless underwear just two weeks ago at our Monday sales meeting? You're going to give me a speech on professionalism?"

Jenn placed her hands on her narrow hips and glared at me. "That was different."

"How?"

She threw her hands in the air in frustration, rolling her green eyes. "I don't know, but it just is! Just be nice, please? Because the way you've been acting recently is giving diva. We all need to work together, okay? You know this."

She was right.

"I'm sorry," I breathe. Because I am. It's not Knox's fault I'm a mess and can't handle the way he makes me feel. It's not his fault the stress of this has flared up my endometriosis to the point where I threw up from the pain last night. It's not his fault I had to reschedule my hysterectomy until after we're done with this project, frustrating to the point of pure rage because it means living with this pain, this exhaustion, for a second longer than I hoped.

It's not his fault, and I'm putting it all on him just because he's somehow made me feel more of every single emotion—good or bad—than I have in years.

"I'm sorry," I tell him again, voice stronger now.

"For what?" he asks, turning onto the highway.

For so many things. "For... for being mean to you." I fidget in my seat, tangling and untangling my fingers in my lap.

"Don't worry about it. You're not *always* mean to me. Sometimes you border on nice. I can handle whatever you throw at me." Knox laughs easily—always so light and happy—and glances over at me. "Plus, I take it as a compliment."

"A compliment?"

"Yeah. A compliment. Because I don't think you being 'mean' to me—or just a little snarky—has anything to do with you not liking me. I think it's the complete opposite, actually."

"The complete opposite, huh?" An involuntary smile tugs at my lips.

"Oh, one hundred percent. I think you're freaked out that you like me so much, so your immediate reaction is to push me away." He shrugs, unbothered. "It's basic psychology, Lottie. Come on."

I laugh dryly. "And you're positive my annoyance toward you has nothing to do with your cocky attitude?"

"Please don't confuse cockiness with confidence."

I *harumph*, crossing my arms in front of my chest and gazing out the passenger window, essentially putting this conversation to bed. He can't know that there might be *some* truth to his theory.

"Where did you find this convention, by the way? What sort of research did you do?"

"I love the subtle way you tried to change the subject." He flashes me my favorite lopsided grin. "But to answer your question, it's really amazing, actually. I tried this new thing called Google. Ever heard of it?"

I snort, biting my lip to keep from smiling back at him.

Dammit, he's good.

"You're such a smart-ass."

He laughs softly with me, thrilled by my reaction while I

almost regret the way my heart warms in my chest at the sound of his easy laughter.

"I also went through some of Walter's paperwork in his office a couple of days ago. Saw that he'd been to this particular one about a year ago. So we're good."

Impressed, I smile at Knox. "Wow."

"Can you believe it? I'm not just good at giving you multiple orgasms—I can also do research," he says sarcastically.

I glare at him, feeling a blush spread across my face.

"Come on." His laugh bursts through him. "I was just messing around. I'm just kinda frustrated that you seem so surprised I'd be able to handle something so simple."

"I haven't known you for long, so it's a little difficult for me to trust you implicitly."

He's quiet for a beat, until finally he says, "You trust me well enough to let me make you your coffee every morning." I tilt my head and raise a brow. He laughs softly and nods. "Fair enough. Ask me anything."

"Anything?" I sit up straighter in my seat, watching him with cautious eyes, tempted.

"Anything. See, while you've been doing everything in your power to keep me away, I actually *want* you to get to know me. I *want* you to like me."

"And you just assume that once I get to know you, I'll like you?"

"Yes. But not because I'm *cocky*," he says the word like it's dirty. "But because I know, even from that one night we spent together, that the connection you and I have isn't something that can be made up or faked; it's not something that disappears. I know you're pushing me away, and I'm not helping the situation by being mildly irritating—even though we both know it's a little charming; admit it. But I'm confident enough to believe that what I experienced— what *we* experienced—was real. So I'll endure the snarky comments and the eye rolls because I know it's in reaction to what you're feeling. Plus, I find them a little hot," he says with a laugh. "I'll endure them until you give me a fair shot. Only then, only when you've *actually properly* gotten to know me and can't make up any excuses, will I accept that you're not lying when you say you don't like me. So ask me. Ask me anything you want. I'm an open book—pun intended."

By the time he's done with his speech, my heart is racing in my chest, and I'm chewing at my bottom lip. With difficulty, I try not to focus too much on how his words make me feel, and focus more on the fact that he's given me the freedom to ask him about whatever I want.

Where do I even start?

The first question that bubbles up is *Why me? Why are you so into me?* Because I still don't understand how a guy in his twenties with his whole life ahead of him would want to waste his time with a woman in her mid-thirties who absolutely crashed and burned in life. Other than as a fun one-night stand, which we already had, what's the point? What would he get out of this? It's not like I'm some superhuman woman who looks ten years younger than her age. I'm someone who doesn't have the energy to follow a forty-step skincare routine twice a day, one who doesn't work out, or eat healthy. I don't have any interesting hobbies besides reading and I'm not adventurous. I'm barely surviving day by day. Who the hell wants that? Who would ever look at me and think "Yeah, that's her"? Because even when I was at my best, I wasn't wanted— easily cast aside.

Why me, then?

Instead, I choose to go the mature route and ask him an obvious question: "What's the deal with you and your dad?"

CHAPTER TWELVE

LOTTIE

The light in Knox's eyes immediately dims, the corners of his lips turning down. "Getting straight to the point, then," he says, voice tight.

"Regretting the whole open book thing now, aren't you?"

He sighs and shakes his head. "Nah. You deserve to know. Especially since we're in bed together, now. Figuratively speaking, of course. Though, I guess I should probably preface the story by telling you I didn't meet Walter until I was about ten years old."

"Wait, what?"

Knox nods, his grip tightening on the wheel with a sigh. "The whole story is kinda insane."

"Explain."

"You know how Walter used to be a Lit professor, right?" I nod. "Well, my mother used to be his TA."

I inhale sharply, my hands flying to my mouth to hide a smile. He notices my expression and laughs.

"I know what you're thinking."

I sputter a laugh. "Do you?"

"Yeah, I can see right through those beautiful big brown eyes of yours and into your dirty mind. I remember you telling me that night about your thing for romance novels." I laugh softly at the memory, at the way he teased me at first, but later asked what my favorite thing about them was.

"I'm positive I know where your mind went. But please try to remember these are *my parents* we're talking about, and I really don't wanna think about them... *You know*."

I put my hands up in defeat and laugh. "Don't worry. The 'Hot for Teacher' trope has historically never done it for me, anyway. Go on."

"Anyway, my parents started having this affair. Ma was in her senior year of college and just about to graduate when she found out she was pregnant with me." He pauses for a moment, runs his hand through his hair. "Now, according to my mother, when she told my father about me at graduation, he flat-out said he wanted nothing to do with me. Told her to get rid of the baby or count him out."

I suppress a gasp, not wanting to interrupt his story.

"To clarify, I'm all about women's right to choose. But it's a little difficult to grow up knowing that your dad wanted you to be... You know." He shrugs again, grimacing.

"Apparently ugly words were exchanged, comments about how she would only ever be a good time to him were said. Mom called him every name in the book and threatened to sue for child support. It got ugly." He shrugs.

"Of course, I know that there are two sides to every story. I understand that memories are usually tainted by emotions.

She was a vulnerable recent grad who had decided to have a kid by herself. She didn't have anyone to support her emotionally or help her financially."

Knox takes a deep breath and shifts in his seat before continuing. "Anyway, that was the last time they spoke. That is, until I was about ten when my mom got in a car accident that left her in pretty rough shape. She kinda had no other choice but to contact Walter and have him take care of me while she recovered. See, we used to move around a lot, never staying in one place long enough to build a support system, so Walter was her last resort.

"So, even though I'd never met the man, he showed up for me. Put his life on hold and rented an apartment in town. Took me to school and was there for me while Ma was in the hospital for a month." He pauses for a second while I do my best to keep quiet, realizing that this is a big moment for him, as if he's finally coming to terms with something.

"In retrospect, it was a very big thing of him to do—to drop his entire life for a couple of months just to take care of this kid he'd never met."

"For what it's worth, I can't imagine him ever *not* showing up like that."

Knox nods, frowning as he keeps his eyes on the road.

I think of ten-year-old Knox, scared and alone, not knowing who his future rested with. I think of him and how unstable he must've felt his life was. "It must've been difficult to suddenly be under the care of a man you grew up thinking didn't want you while your mother was in the hospital under critical care."

"Definitely difficult," he nods once. "But we figured it

out. Eventually. And when my mom came back from the hospital, Da—I mean, Walter—quit his job at the university and moved permanently into town to get to know me better. Or at least that's what he said." He laughs once. "He wanted to be a part of my life and my mother made it clear that we weren't moving to be a part of his. If Walter wanted to know me, he had to compromise. So he did. He stayed, which meant that *we* stayed. And I was... ecstatic. I was finally going to be in one place for a significant amount of time. I could finally have friendships that lasted longer than six months. I could... I could join a sports team or something."

I snort, and he gives me a look, a small smile. "Sorry, you just don't look like the type to be into organized sports." Though he has the body of an athlete, that's for damn sure.

He throws his head back and laughs that full, happy laugh of his. "Definitely not into organized sports. But that wasn't the point. The point was that we had help now, and my life opened up to new possibilities. For the first time ever, I felt safe."

My heart aches for the child in Knox, lost and alone, finally feeling the relief of a stable home. Did he lose that when he and Walter became estranged?

"How many times did you move? You said you moved every six months?"

"Yeah. I was born in Virginia, but my mom kept us moving north. We were living in a suburban town in New Jersey when she got into the accident, and that's where I spent the rest of my childhood."

"Wow," I say again, because it's the only thing that comes to mind.

He shakes his head and frowns. "I just want to clarify that it's not like I don't appreciate all the sacrifices and work my mom put in. She's a fucking rockstar. And it's not like everything became perfect and Walter saved us. But he helped stabilize us, you know? And I needed that as a kid."

"Of course. Your mother did everything she could with what she had, I'm sure. But it must've felt nice to have that additional support."

"Exactly," he smiles.

"Where's your mom now?"

"She works at a community college, actually. A couple of towns away from where I grew up. Not as a professor or anything—an admin. She's been doing great ever since. Loves what she does."

I smile over at him, see how his lips quirk up at the corner in admiration. From the faraway look in his eyes, it's obvious he loves his mom, admires her for everything she's done for him.

"So, how'd you end up in this fight with your dad, not speaking to each other for over a decade? I mean, it sounds like Walter showed up, in the end, right? And that's what family does. They show up."

"Ah." He bobs his head. "The official falling out story is a bit more complicated; a story for another time."

"Whoa, whoa, that's not fair." I laugh once, on the edge of my seat—figuratively and literally. "You promised."

"Ever heard of leaving them wanting more?" He smirks.

"C'mon," I plead.

He pauses, hesitating. "I... I'd rather not talk about it now, if that's okay. I'm good with talking about the genesis

of it all, but our falling out? That... I can't do that right now."
His face falls.

I watch the metaphorical shoe dangle, holding my breath as I wait for it to drop. Part of me thinks it's best for Knox to just get it out of the way as soon as possible, but the other part of me knows what it's like to grieve a life and a person. In my case, I was grieving myself, who I thought I would be. But the same principle applies, and rushing grief is never an option.

"Okay," I breathe, wanting so very badly to comfort him. I reach out and put a hand on his, right on the steering wheel.

His exhale is deep, and it clears the tension in the entire cab of the truck—not just his. He loosens his grip on the wheel and takes my hand in his, squeezing it once before placing our joined hands on the center console.

"What about you? What's your story? Jenn mentioned something about you rebuilding your life?"

I shrug and look out the window. "She just means my divorce, probably."

"Mmm," he nods thoughtfully. "It's more than that, though, isn't it?"

I sigh and, for some idiotic reason, say "Yeah." Fighting the urge to bang my head against the window, I make sure to keep my eyes on the road.

"You gonna elaborate on that?"

I swallow the hard knot in my throat and think. *Am* I going to elaborate on it? Because my marriage—more specifically *why* and *how* it ended—is my biggest failure and I *never* talk about it. But something about the way he was able to share his difficult experience with his father makes me feel like I could trust mine with him.

"I—I used to be married."

"Yes, that's generally what being divorced means."

I snort. "Yeah, well... It was to this investment banker guy in New York and..." *I don't even know where to start.*

And I guess I say it out loud because he says, "Why don't you start at the beginning?"

I nod, feeling my chest stretch due to the calm, patient look in his eyes. At least in this moment, I'm safe with him.

"For context, I should tell you that, at the time, I worked for this amazing luxury fashion brand straight out of college where I somehow worked myself up pretty quickly to VP of Retail Operations before I even hit thirty. It wasn't a common thing. I was definitely very lucky."

"I doubt it had anything to do with luck. I know how smart you are, how hardworking. I can totally see you skyrocketing like that."

My heart warms in my chest at his words, wanting to believe every single one of them.

But things have changed since then. Sure, I still have a plan to rebuild myself, to go back to having that life—at least the professional one. But even *I* can admit to myself that I had started to slow down before inheriting the store, almost giving up hope on ever getting back on track.

Just then, a chilling thought pops into my head: if Walter hadn't left me part of the store, given me new purpose and financial gain to get back to my old life, would I ever have found the opportunity to leave Ceres Cove?

I suppress a shiver.

"Well," I continue, pushing past his compliment and other intrusive thoughts. "The brand put me in charge of every single one of our retail stores in the US and abroad. Everything from how the stores were set-up, our merchandise, the way operations were run, sales... all of it, was run by me. And I was good at it. But more importantly, I loved it," I say proudly, devastated at having lost it all—willingly.

"What happened, then? Why aren't you doing that anymore? And what does it have to do with your divorce?"

"I'm getting to that." This is the hard part. This is where it gets real, and the nausea and shame start to creep in at the colossal mistake I made. If not the worst, then certainly one of the biggest. "I, uh, quit my job."

"Why? Did you decide to start your own thing or something?"

I squeeze my eyes shut and press my lips together, not wanting to get too explicit with the details. Because, yes, at the time, I did want to start my own thing: my own family. "I, ah... Yeah, sort of."

But I don't elaborate. I'm not about to embarrass myself and tell him how my manipulative husband begged me to quit my job when it seemed to be interfering with my IVF treatments. Turns out, hormone injections and my endometriosis and PCOS didn't mix well. Forget about the regular side effects of IVF—add to that an increase in already debilitating pain, nausea, and so many other fun ones that made existing downright impossible. To say the whole thing was a nightmare is an understatement.

So, Finn convinced me to leave everything I'd worked for

behind, despite the fact that I was clearly not doing well, that my health had deteriorated to an unmanageable level. He wanted me to prioritize having a kid over my health and my career.

"Who cares whether you still have a career to come back to? You know I'm going to take care of you—of us," he'd promised. *"Of course I'll support you financially. The stress from work is why you're not getting pregnant. Just quit your job, focus all your energy on this. We're going to be a* family."

And with those final six words he'd seduced me into prioritizing his wants over my need to be healthy.

We're going to be a family.

It's what I repeated to myself over and over again whenever I felt close to breaking. It was my North Star. My motivation. The ultimate goal, even though it had never been something I wanted until he told me I did. So I gave up my career, put myself through endless treatments and diets and tried absolutely everything to get pregnant—even though our doctors told us it would be close to impossible given my medical history. I was in constant pain, sick, run down... But it was all for the baby, so who cared, right? It would be worth it.

I knew motherhood was about sacrifices, and this would just be my first one.

Finn wanted me as his baby maker to continue his family line—something I didn't even see until divorce proceedings, when certain messed up clauses came up from our prenup— and I had failed.

After two years, I barely recognized myself. I told him I

couldn't do it anymore. I couldn't put my body and mind and heart through it all, only to be crushed with disappointment every time I got my period. How the combined IVF treatments and my worsening endometriosis were killing me. How I wanted a hysterectomy and he pretended to be supportive about it.

And then...

Upon seeing my discomfort, Knox's eyes flash to mine. "Hey. Are you okay? Did he hurt you or something?" There's a menacing tone in his voice, a protective one that makes me feel some kind of way.

"No, he didn't hurt me," I say softly, a small smile on my lips, because *god*, Knox is so sweet. "Not in the way you mean."

"Good," he almost growls.

"We were... having issues. I was going through some... Stuff. And... It's a long story, but I quit my job for him. Left everything I'd built for him. I... pretty much did everything he wanted me to. In the end, though, we became two pieces of a puzzle that didn't fit." I make a disgusted noise, squeezing my eyes shut. Truly, in all of this, I am my biggest disappointment.

Sure, I wanted kids. But never at the expense of myself— and that's how it all ended.

"Even so, he blindsided me."

"What do you mean?"

"I mean that one day, everything was fine, kind of,"—*or as best as it could be when your marriage's sole focus had become procreation*—"and then I was randomly served with divorce papers by his attorney while I was at home alone. I mean that I suddenly had forty-eight hours to move out because the apartment was under his name. That I was broke because he'd frozen our joint accounts and I had nowhere to go." I shrug nonchalantly, the apathy in my eyes a stark contrast to the actual agony I feel just at the memory alone.

"Whoa. Just like that? No warning?" I nod and he scoffs. "What a dick."

"Yup."

"Well, at least you didn't have kids, right? Makes divorce easier."

I don't know whether to laugh or cry at his statement, so I look away.

Thankfully, Knox doesn't push for more. I'm sure he knows there's more to the story, but he offers me the same courtesy I offered him.

There's so much I'm ashamed of, so much I'm embarrassed by. So much that broke me and made it so that I had to come back to the one place I fought to stay away from, with my tail between my legs, feeling like I failed. I failed at being a woman, a wife, a professional, and had no idea how to move forward. And even though Knox and I aren't anything to each other right now except for business partners—*maybe* friends—I still don't want him to know about all of it.

It's too much. *I'm* too much.

"Yeah. Easier."

I cringe, wracking my brain for a way to get us to talk about something else—taxes, the current state of the economy, the latest feud between the Kardashian sisters, *literally anything* other than my divorce—but there's no need:

"We're almost there." He points in the direction of a massive sign by the highway announcing the convention.

I exhale deeply, hoping that the topic will be forgotten, but knowing all too well he won't be able to let it go forever.

CHAPTER THIRTEEN

LOTTIE

With an adorable frown on his face, Knox parallel parks, the picture of concentration. For some reason, part of me finds it crazy hot that he's able to easily slide into a tight spot like that. Or maybe it's not *too* much of a mystery why I find it hot. *Ha.*

Hiding my smile behind the back of my hand, I watch as he turns off the car and gets out. He slings his messenger bag over his shoulder and pulls out the box of books we brought to sell from the back seat with ease, as if they weighed no more than a feather.

"You have everything?" I ask, eyeing the heavy-looking box under his arm.

"Yeah." He shuts the door with his hip, and I shove my hands in my trench pockets.

It's drizzling out—one of those gross March spring days where the weather can't decide whether to be cold or what. Small droplets fall all around us, and I try not to focus too much on how they look like glitter as they land on Knox's hair. The humidity in the air curls the ends at the nape of his neck in a way that tugs at my heartstrings for some reason.

He's handsome. So handsome and kind-hearted, I feel my determination to stay away from him waver.

With an ache in my chest, I sigh heavily, pulling out my phone to check the convention's website, scrolling through it to find the vendor map.

"It's in the Royal Rose Ballroom," he says, as if reading my mind.

We look up at the entrance of the rundown hotel at the same time and wince, taking in the ancient, two-star building that looks like it should be paying people to come inside instead of charging them.

"I find it a bit hard to believe this place has a *ballroom*," I tell him. "But okay."

He shrugs and we head for the front door together, his long legs matching my pace. "It doesn't look like a big place, so I don't think it'll be too hard to find the guy I've been emailing with."

We make it through the salmon-colored walls, past the front desk manned by the uninterested young woman filing her nails and find the entrance to the Royal Rose Ballroom on our own.

"Wow. This is..." My voice drifts off as we take in the image in front of us.

"Uh, yeah," Knox agrees, adjusting his grip on the box. He pulls up our tickets on his phone and shows them to the agent—a gangly, red-headed teenager with an unfortunate amount of acne—who lazily waves us in.

With its peeling salmon wallpaper and bubbling paint on

the ceiling, the ballroom looks anything *but* royal. Parts of what I think used to be a cream and gold carpet are now covered in dark beige and brown—water damage stains signaling several years' worth of improperly fixed leaks.

The hotel has definitely seen better days—and the same can be said for the attendees of the convention. As we walk around the ballroom peeking at all the different booths and vendors, it becomes painfully evident that we are by far the youngest attendees. In fact, besides the occasional hotel employee or one-off visitor, most of the convention-goers don't look a day under sixty-five.

But I don't dwell too much on the structure or the people inside it too long. It's the convention itself that captivates me. *Fascinating,* I think. My old VP of Retail brain begins to race as it absorbs the information around it, approximating the cost of a booth, transportation, and other expenses; calculating how much each vendor would have to net in order to break even; wondering what their margin per sale is; what their ROI is. It wonders whether they're all certified book conservators, how much it costs to get certified, if that's even a *thing* you need to be certified in, how—

"Okay, so keep your eyes peeled for a booth called *Lewis's Literary Lifestyle.* The owner's the one who offered to pay us three grand for this set of three, but I brought more books just in case we find more buyers." Knox cuts through my business brain ramblings, and I'm left shaken. How long has it been since it ran off with random calculations? It used to be second nature for me, something I couldn't help, considering what I did for a living. But I loved it; it always felt like a game or a puzzle to solve. It's like this whole reno and sale thing has awakened that side of me again. And to be honest? I really don't hate it.

I smile to myself once more, though for different reasons this time, and nod. "Okie dokie."

He stops in his tracks to stare at me for a second, raising a brow, processing the shift in my mood. But I just roll my eyes at him with a laugh, and lightly shove his shoulder. "C'mon. I think I see the booth from here."

Lewis turns out to be none other than a massive asshole. A tall man in his seventies with a gray comb-over and a perma-frown, he crosses his arms in front of his chest, puckering his lips when he tells us "There's a slight tear in the Ulysses. And the pages on the Kerouac are more yellowed than the photos you emailed me the other day. So I'm going to have to knock down my offer by a grand."

"*What?* That's bullshit. That's not even a tear! And the pages aren't *more yellowed* than what I sent you." Knox nearly growls.

"Young man, I've been doing this for most of my life. You think I don't know a tear when I see one? And these pages are *definitely* not in the condition you sent me. Did you alter the photos? Did you use one of those *filters* you kids use for all the pictures you take for social media?"

Knox physically rears back. "*Social med*—" He scoffs, insulted. "I am a *professional photographer*," he says, pointing to his ever-present camera bag, strapped across his chest. "I think I'd know if—"

I put a hand on his chest, whispering his name all while keeping my voice firm enough for him to focus back on me. Knox's eyes flash to mine—angry, frustrated—but he manages to catch himself. I nod, trying to convey with a look that he should probably calm down because we're *clearly* not getting anywhere here.

"Let's get out of here," I whisper in his ear, his sweet whiskey scent filling my lungs.

"No. We need the cash. I'll figure something out. I promised you I'd get the money and I just fucking lost it with him and—" he whispers back, his voice only audible to me. With a sigh, he scratches his forehead. "I'm not going to fail you. I'm not going to let you down."

My breath catches in my throat because there's so much weight behind those words; I don't think he's just talking about the sale. "You haven't let me down. This guy's just an asshole; he's not even worth negotiating with."

I turn to face Lewis once more. "I think we'll be taking our business elsewhere."

Lewis's eyes widen, his stance shifts, a snake ready to attack. "No. You kids—"

"What the hell are you doing, Lewis?" A bored, male voice from the next booth interrupts him. "Are you trying to scam more unsuspecting people?" He walks over to us and pulls our books from Lewis's table, who tries to make a grab for them.

"Erwin, go back to your booth and stay the hell out of this," Lewis growls, hands fisted on his hips.

Erwin, I assume, turns to me. "How much did he offer for all three?"

"Three grand originally. But now he's asking two."

"*Two?* Ha!" Erwin throws his head back and laughs in disbelief. "You two are little mice who walked into a snake's nest, kid." He turns to Lewis with a smile. "I'd tell you I'm disappointed in you, but I honestly didn't expect anything less. This James Joyce alone? It's worth about twenty-five hundred at first glance. Don't believe a single word out of this crook's mouth."

Slack-jawed, Knox and I look at Lewis, whose eyes are on Erwin. Through clenched teeth, he grumbles, "You know, you're getting to be really bad for business."

"You're bad for your own business," Erwin barks back. "Come with me, kids. Let's look at what you got, and I'll see if I can help you find someone to buy these from you. Unfortunately, these are out of my price range, so it won't be me." And with our books in hand, he walks off to his booth.

Knox and I turn to look at each other in confusion, until he shrugs and follows.

"Alright, so these right here will have a better shot at being sold separately, rather than in a group." He examines one of the books a little closer, inspecting it for imperfections, I suppose.

"Which one of you set up that sale, by the way? Did you even do any research?"

I shoot Knox a look, and he blushes, looking away.

"I googled," he replies, a bit defensive.

Erwin scoffs and shakes his head. "Google. *Pfft!*" After taking a few moments to carefully inspect the books, he straightens and looks at us both for a beat. "What are your names?" as if only now realizing he has no idea who we are.

My business brain wakes once more, hand shooting out to shake his with confidence. "Carlota Veracruz. Nice to meet you." He takes my hand, grip firm in a way that makes me think he had a different career before entering the world of rare book trades.

"And you are...?" he asks Knox, brows raised as he shakes his now.

"I'm Knox Riddick, sir," and for some reason the way he says it makes him look *so* young: nervous like a seventeen-year-old meeting the parents of his date for homecoming.

"Neither one of you knows anything about rare books, obviously. So how the hell did you come upon these copies?" His eyes bounce between us.

"I, uh, got these from my father. I think he was pretty involved in the community and in restoration."

Understatement of the year, by the looks of the mess he left in his apartment.

"You think?" He hums, surveying our books with ultimate care. "What's your father's name, if you don't mind me asking?"

"Walter Adams."

Erwin's head snaps up to meet Knox's face, a huge smile spreading across his face.

"You're Walter's boy? I'm so glad he finally brought you around. He talks about you *all the time*. Where is he? I haven't spoken to him in a few weeks. Started to get worried he'd finally gotten the balls to take that trip to Scotland and forgot all about us. He kept saying he hated it here, but stayed because he wanted to be close to you, so." Erwin shrugs.

As if in slow motion, Knox's chest deflates and his face falls, paling under the fluorescent lights of the hotel ballroom. All I can see is him as the shoe I was expecting to drop for the past week and a half finally does with a loud, metaphorical clunk.

"Wait. You said *was*. Is he done doing restorations, then? Because I had this one book I was hoping he could help me with and..." I barely hear Erwin's voice as he rambles on— I'm too focused on Knox. Because this is it. This is the moment he realizes his father is really gone.

He wobbles, and I'm pretty sure he hasn't taken a breath in a while.

Not able to stand it any longer, I reach for him. I run my hand down his leather-clad arm, searching for his hand, winding my fingers through his before squeezing tight.

Ice-blue eyes search for mine, panic written all over Knox's face.

I'm here, I try to tell him. *You're not alone. I'm here.*

A wave of relief crashes over me as I feel his hand squeeze mine back, his face twisted with a combination of pain and gratitude. His stance relaxes just a bit, his eyes soften infinitesimally. Still, I know without a shadow of a doubt that I need to get him out of here now.

"...reached out to him, but he hasn't gotten back to me."

Eyes still on me, I turn to Erwin. "Would you mind giving us a second? We'll be right back."

As if finally realizing something is wrong, Erwin nods, expression filled with concern.

"I'll be here."

Knox and I find a seating area in the back of the convention where we decide to park for a bit.

He leans back into his chair, eyes distant, staring off into space in complete silence.

"Hey." I scoot my chair closer, wrapping both his hands in mine. "I'm right here. You want to talk about it?"

It takes a second for him to reply. He swallows once, twice, then takes another breath. "I didn't know," he murmurs.

"Know what?" I press, voice soft.

"Didn't know he cared."

I tighten my grip around his hands, a sharp stab in my gut. "Of course he cared, Knox. He was your father. And though he made a ton of mistakes, I know deep down he wasn't a bad man."

"The things he said and did, though—"

"Were probably horrible. Horrible words and actions from a stubborn man who was worried for you and didn't know how to handle things. I'm not going to excuse his behavior, especially since I don't know the details of your falling out, but... It's clear he still cared about you. And a lot."

He can't deny it now. "He still gave a shit." His voice is full of a combination of wonder and regret.

"Of course he did. How could he not?"

He inhales sharply, pulling his hands free from mine, burying his face in them. "*God.*" I feel the pain in his voice and wish more than anything I could share it with him, take some of it off his shoulders. It breaks my heart to see him like this, because I know this is seismic, shaking him to his core.

"All this time, all these years… I thought he didn't give a shit. And it made it so much easier to hate him. But he kept tabs on me? What else don't I know?" His voice breaks, muffled by his hands, and I can't take it anymore.

I kneel in front of him, pulling his hands away from his face only to stare into his red, teary eyes. "Don't. I'm so embarrassed." He sniffs, looking away.

"For what?"

"For breaking down like this. *Jesus*." He wipes his eyes with the back of his hand, still unable to meet my gaze, but there's no way I'm leaving him.

Slowly, I reach up to cup his face, expecting him to push me away. He looks back at me, face contorted, but leans into my touch.

"Hey," I whisper, relief flooding me as he holds my hand to his cheek. "You don't have to be embarrassed. Honestly, I was starting to doubt whether you were even human at this point."

His lips twitch. "Because of my otherworldly good looks?" he jokes, sniffling.

I smirk and drop my hand, but he takes it back into both of his. "Glad to see you feel *a little better*," I tell him. "But no, it was because you seemed to act like your father's death didn't bother you one bit. Like you didn't care at all."

"I care," he whispers, unshed tears shining over his ice-blue eyes.

"Of course you do, Knox. And that's more than okay."

"I don't know if I can go back there, Lottie." He exhales, looking over his shoulder at the rows of vendors while running his fingers through his hair.

"I know it'll be hard. But it *could* give you the opportunity to find out more about your dad. Plus, I'm going to need help with negotiations."

Knox looks back at me with a raised brow. "You know you don't need my help for shit."

Laughing, I get to my feet, extending my hand to pull him up. "Oh, I know that. But at least you'll be something nice to look at."

With a smirk, he takes my hand and gets to his feet. I start to walk away, but he uses his grip on my hand to pull me back. Gone is any trace of humor—only Serious Knox remains. And, *god,* can Serious Knox give good smolder. "Thank you, Lottie," he whispers, his free hand pushing my curtain bangs from my hair. "Really."

My chest tightens as it adjusts to the ten sizes my heart grew in the last five minutes. He stares down at me with those blue eyes of his—the ones that remind me of a winter chill. But I'm warm all over.

"No problem," I murmur, unable to look away.

He kisses the back of my hand and my stomach drops, because it's right then that I realize how fantastically screwed I am.

CHAPTER FOURTEEN
KNOX

I wanted this trip to help prove that I could be responsible and am just as much an adult as she is, no matter the age difference. I wanted to prove to Lottie that I'm not some infatuated kid and that she could trust me with important shit. But no. I had to go and have a meltdown over my father.

My dad.

In all honesty, I thought I had everything together, but hearing Erwin say Walter had *talked* about me, that he'd mentioned me more than once...

The whole thing was too much to handle.

It takes some time, but after a few minutes of breathing and easy small talk with Lottie, I manage to pull myself together. Even if I'm mortified and gutted that I may have ruined this thing with her (though after our conversation on the way here, I'm beginning to think my age or maturity level is not necessarily why she keeps pushing me away). Eventually, we make it back to Erwin's booth as cool as two cucumbers—*business* cucumbers, that is.

"You're back," Erwin greets us with a hesitant smile. "Thought you'd run off."

"Not just yet." I force a smile. "Sorry about that, by the way. I... I needed a second."

"He's gone, isn't he? Walter, I mean. And not to Scotland." Erwin frowns, brows pulled together.

"Yes, he's gone," Lottie whispers. "About two weeks ago."

Erwin looks down at the floor and nods. "I am truly sorry to hear that. In all honesty, he hadn't been looking great the last few times I'd seen him."

After a brief pause, he lifts his head up and forces a smile. "Well, then. How about I introduce you to your father's world? Get to know him a little better."

And without another word, we follow Erwin, weaving through the crowd. We let him guide us for the rest of the afternoon, during which I can feel Lottie's eyes on me. She watches as I'm introduced to my father's old friends, how they greet me with the same kindness and pleasant surprise Erwin did. She watches how I break the news of my father's passing to them and, every time, I see her brace herself, ready to provide me with any kind of support I might need. And whenever I feel my composure begin to slip, she squeezes my hand, reminding me that she's right here. She's not going anywhere.

"We're meeting up for some drinks in a bit. Would you like to come?" Erwin asks. "It'll be a group of your father's friends. We can toast to his memory, answer any questions you may have?"

I wince, my control slipping just a bit. Today has been a lot. Enough that I'm not sure whether I could spend a whole night listening about more parts of Walter's personality that I never got to meet.

"I don't know…" I start, looking to Lottie for support. She shoots me an encouraging smile, threading her fingers through my own once more.

"It might be nice to get to know this side of Walter. I didn't know it either."

My eyes lock on hers, trying to read what's in them: support, affection, strength. She's there, this woman I've known less than a couple of weeks. There for *me*. And though she's pushing her heart away, just out of reach, she's still been more emotionally supportive and available to me in the past couple of hours than anyone has in my whole life. Throughout this entire day, she's never left my side, never been without a word of encouragement. Throughout this entire day, Lottie has been my rock.

"Okay. Yeah. I guess it would be cool to know more about him."

Half an hour later, we meet Erwin and a few people from the convention at a nearby bar, some we'd met already earlier in the day.

"He talked about you a lot, you know?" Allison, one of the traders, whispers to me. She bought two books from us for much more than we expected and pointed us in the direction of three other buyers. Thanks to her and Erwin, we sold the first editions in less than an hour, making more than six times the money we were hoping to come back with. We're officially going home with enough to cover the demo, electrical work, and some of the renovation. Not enough to cover the full cost of the remodel, but now that we have an in with the rare book trade crowd, those last copies in Walter's apartment will definitely help us get there.

I look back at Allison, her silver-threaded raven hair shining under the bar lights, in surprise. "He—He did?"

"Oh, yeah," Broderick—another man from Walter's gang —pipes in. "He always bragged about his son, the photographer. Even told us about that award you won? The—the—" He snaps his fingers a few times. "The World Photography Awards for travel photojournalism, right? Wouldn't let us forget how talented you are." He smiles kindly at me, patting the back of my hand.

My jaw slackens, eyes dropping to the table.

That award was my proudest achievement. I had the privilege of spending five weeks at the Yutajé camp in the Venezuelan Amazon, photographing everything from the beautiful foliage to the most dangerous animals, and epic waterfalls and river banks. It was more than I could've ever dreamed of, and to be recognized by such a prestigious award was life-changing. It validated all of my hard work over the past couple of years. All of the bullshit assignments.

And Walter celebrated my win with me from afar.

"He bragged about it? And how did he even find out? It was a couple of years ago—we weren't even speaking when I won the award."

Lottie's hands reach for mine under the table and I look gratefully back at her with a sheepish smile.

"Dad always said photography was stupid. That I was making a mistake by pursuing it as a career," I tell her. Her eyes widen, maybe because it's the first time I've used the D-word out loud since this whole thing happened. It feels monumental and pivotal to my relationship with Walter, even if it is posthumously.

She squeezes my hand again, speaking in a low voice. "I'm sure most parents of children who choose to pursue the arts live in constant fear of their child's success or lack thereof. And I think everyone at this table would agree with you in saying that Walter was not one for being sensitive to others' feelings. He loved in his own unique way." She treads carefully, as if trying to avoid detonating any minefields she might find.

And I officially hate myself for breaking down. Is this how it's going to be from now on? Am I some fragile kid to her?

I suppress a frustrated sigh as Walter's friends continue to tell us stories of their time together, ordering another round of drinks and pub food.

By the end of the night, Lottie decides to drive my car back home. Partly because I drove us to the convention and she thinks it's only fair she take on the other half of the long drive home; partly because I had a couple of beers and she didn't. Mostly, though, I think it's because I just had an intense day, and she probably thinks I need time to process it.

The drive is quiet, for the most part. I don't feel like talking, and Lottie doesn't pressure me into small talk. It's like she can read me, can tell what I need most right now. She waits patiently as *I* open up to *her*.

After we've been on the road for over an hour, I finally

break the silence: "That's why we got in a fight," I say quietly, apropos to nothing. "The photography thing. Kind of, anyway."

She turns to look at me for a second, headlights from the other cars illuminating her solemn face in the dark car. She doesn't speak, giving me time and space to continue should I choose to.

And I do. I wasn't lying when I said I wanted her to know me.

So I keep going.

"God, it seems so stupid now, but it's how the whole fight started. Me telling him I wanted to go to an art institute and study photography; him disagreeing with me, telling me how stupid he thought it was. And he did not hold back, let me tell you." I shift uncomfortably in my seat, remembering every cruel word exchanged, every ounce of resentment revealed.

"I know I shouldn't have cared, should've just done whatever I wanted and ignored him. But I needed him to be a cosigner on my loan for art school—Mom didn't qualify— and he wouldn't do it. Not for his own financial reasons, but because he said it was a dead-end profession. Of course, me being a teenager, I escalated it quickly. Told him he didn't have a leg to stand on. He had an English degree—that he was a failed college professor who had conned his TA into falling for him. Then I leaned into the savagery and pulled the abandonment card. Told him he didn't have much of a say considering our history and he owed me. I told him how disappointed I was in him that he was never there, that he was a failure of a father and, subsequently, a man." I put my face in my hands, chest tightening. In a second, the possibility of breathing becomes nearly impossible. "He didn't take that well. Said some vicious things. So I said some more back. And then... Well, I said maybe it would've been best if my mother had lied and told him I didn't exist after all."

"Jesus," she mutters.

"And you wanna know what he said, Lottie?"

"No, because I have a feeling it will affect the impression I have of Walter," she whispers. "It's no secret he wasn't an easygoing man, but I loved and respected him despite it. You should tell me anyway, though."

"He said he wished she'd never told him either. He wished he never knew I existed."

The memory of that moment slices through my chest, the pain so visceral I have to look away. The look on his face, the sound of his voice, his stance... It's the same reel that runs over and over in my head every time I think of him. And it cuts deep.

I hear Lottie's sharp inhale, followed by a soft whisper, barely audible to my ears. "*What the hell were you thinking, Walter?*"

Out of the corner of my eye, I watch her bite her lip, holding something back.

I groan. "Shit. I shouldn't have said anything. Now you're going to feel all sorry for me and this isn't exactly making me look too good, is it?" I feel my cheeks heat, for the *second time* today feeling like a child, embarassed out of my mind.

"No, no. I—I... Well, I feel utterly devastated. For you. For Walter, too. Especially since I *know* Walter wasn't a bad man. Was he the bad guy in your story? Yeah. I guess so. But I know that deep down, he was a man who cared. If he didn't, he wouldn't have offered me a job, wouldn't have offered all those words of wisdom and advice. He was cynical and jaded, snarky and sarcastic—yes, at times unrelenting when he disagreed with someone—but never *bad*." She pauses. "No, *never* bad."

She blows a puff of air through her lips, mussing her bangs up in the process—but she doesn't seem to notice. "He made a mistake, which hurt you both deeply, and he didn't know how to fix it. I don't know why he said the things he said, or acted the way he did, Knox. But from what we saw today, it's clear he regretted it. It's clear he wanted to be a part of your life, and continued to do so from afar. He kept tabs on you, told his closest friends about you." She glances back at me, but I look away again, not wanting to meet her gaze. "That doesn't sound like someone who is disappointed in their son. He was proud of you. He *loved* you. He just didn't know how to."

It takes a moment before I can reply, my voice thick with emotion. "Thank you."

"For what?"

"For being here. For holding my hand through it. Literally and metaphorically speaking."

She reaches over the center console for my hand like she did earlier today, and takes it in hers, holding it for the rest of the ride home.

"This is me," she says, pulling over close to the curb and putting the car in park. She turns the engine off, unbuckles her seatbelt to look at me, and waits for me to open my door and make a move to take over the driver's seat.

Instead, I look up at the house and smile, taking in the two-story white Victorian with wide eyes and admiration. "It's really nice."

She snorts. "It isn't mine. I live in the loft above the garage," she mutters, cheeks reddening.

"Oh. Sorry, I didn't—"

"It's fine. I rent it from Alejandro. He owns it."

"Right," I bob my head, uncharacteristically mono-syllabic.

"So..." she drags the word out. "I guess I'll see you tomorrow?"

"Yeah." I unbuckle my seatbelt, sliding out of the car. Lottie does the same, rounding the hood, meeting me on the sidewalk. I stare down at my feet for a moment before looking up into her eyes—whiskey brown, so beautiful I could get drunk off them. The tightness in my chest, the one that's been growing silently all day, suddenly expands to every inch of my body. And I can't just let things end like this today. I don't *want* to.

"Okay, then," she mutters right before she walks away.

But before she makes it far, my hand wraps around her wrist, gently pulling her to a stop.

"You okay?" she asks when she turns to look at me.

The answer is clearly written all over my face, my body. The way my other hand shakes as I wrap it around her free wrist.

No, I am most definitely not okay. For so many different reasons.

"Can I come up?"

"Yes," she says without a hint of hesitation. She loosens my grip on her wrists, threads her fingers through mine, and pulls me to her apartment. Together, we climb the stairs slowly, stopping only to search for her key at the bottom of her purse.

CHAPTER FIFTEEN

LOTTIE

With a shaky hand, I push my front door open, painfully aware that *I just invited Knox to come into my apartment*. Alone. *Alone together*. But there is no way I'm going to leave him by himself tonight—at least not before knowing he's okay.

"Jesus," I hear him whisper behind me, looking into my apartment over my shoulder. "Your place is *almost* like Walter's apartment, except everything is bright and insanely organized."

I smile, hanging my coat and toeing off my white Converse, leaving them on a small rack by the door. "You mean because of the books?" I toss my keys on my kitchen table next to my ereader while Knox unlaces his boots, setting them beside mine. I feel a pang in my chest at the image, something about the domesticity of it all reaching a part of me that craves it—with him, specifically.

"They're *everywhere*," he says, his voice filled with awe, taking in my collection. The built-in shelves wrap around almost every wall of the loft—one of the best features of the place. Organized by color rather than author, the books stand out in a wild rainbow from the rest of my apartment—white bookshelves and furniture, cream blankets and linens, off-white flowers tucked between books or resting in glass vases on every surface of my place. I know some people consider it sacrilege to organize books that way, but the aesthetically pleasing look brings a small, yet significant, joy in my life.

"I love it," he breathes. "It's so... bright. A far cry from the brown- and black-spined books from the store."

I smile, an odd sense of pride filling my chest. It took a lot to make this place into something I could see myself being happy in. But I did it.

Knox looks around the apartment, absentmindedly running his hands over the back of my loveseat, a soft smile tugging at his lips.

I snort. "I know. Ale gave me free reign to renovate it however I wanted when I moved in. It was originally being used for storage and kinda dark and musty. I wanted the complete opposite of that. And I know Walter would've killed me if he saw how I organize my bookshelves here, but I just wanted the place to look beautiful."

"That isn't a bad thing. To want to make things look beautiful. Though I should tell you, as a photographer, there's beauty in everything." He grins his lopsided smile.

"As you've mentioned before."

He laughs once and nods. "Right. But as far as conventional beauty, you succeeded. This place looks amazing."

I smile ruefully. "Once in fashion, always in fashion. I

can't help but merchandise my own place, I guess. Plus..." I hesitate, considering confessing the truth. "I—I wanted it to feel happy. I desperately needed that after my divorce. A happy place that would help me want to get out of bed in the morning." As soon as the words are out of my mouth, I wish I could reach out and pull them back in. I groan internally, cursing myself for bringing it up.

"It's great," he says with genuine admiration. "I totally get what you mean by it."

"It's total 'coastal mom vibes,'" I say self-deprecatingly with a shrug. "But, yeah."

"It's bright and cozy. And I can just see you curled up under a blanket on that little loveseat, reading one of your many books." He smiles softly, almost as if lost in a daydream. "Or maybe binging a show on your laptop— something from the nineties or early two-thousands— with a mug of tea."

"Accurate," I grin. "Though don't most people do something along those lines, too?"

"I guess so. But something about you being the one doing it makes it special." I inhale sharply, my eyes widening as I zero in on Knox.

Shit, I think I've caught feelings.

His eyes—so goddamn beautiful—land on mine almost sheepishly. His words, the way he's looking at me, his scent... It's throwing me for a loop and I desperately need to get a handle on things.

I shake my head slowly, readying myself to have an uncomfortable conversation.

"Knox—"

"Tell me what you'd do on a regular night," he says, his voice almost commanding, rough.

For some reason, I blush. "What? No. That's boring. And weird."

"I want to know." He walks over to me and cups my jaw, glacier eyes serious.

It takes me a minute to be able to answer, and when I do, my voice comes out high, shaky: "Well, I... I guess I'd change into something more comfortable. Probably leggings and an oversized tee."

"Hot," he smirks, and I laugh a little. "Keep going." He takes a step closer.

"I would binge-watch something, probably. Either *Buffy the Vampire Slayer* or *Gossip Girl*—the original one, *not* the new one." It's an important distinction to make, because the revival is crap and nothing will ever beat the original. *Long live Queen B.*

"Of course," he grins, his hand sliding down my neck, my skin heating and bursting into goosebumps at the same time.

"And then I'd probably read a book before bed. Maybe on my e-reader," I go on, breathing growing shallow.

His eyes widen at my words. "An e-reader? My god. You work at a bookstore. How *could* you?" he asks in mock-honor, pulling his hand away.

Biting my lip as I stare up at him for a second, I consider telling him the truth. After a short pause, I do what I always seem to do with him: share more of myself than I planned to: "Well, when you read as much as I do and you don't have a library close by, you need a cheaper alternative to physical books. Plus, there are some novels—*romance* novels—that I enjoy reading but wouldn't necessarily love to have on display when my nieces and nephews come over, if you know what I mean."

His eyes spark with a combination of intrigue and amusement. Suddenly, he stands up straighter and his trademark trickster grin is back. "Oh, yeah? What kind of books are those, then?"

"Just... Some books whose content I wouldn't want just anyone knowing I enjoy. But you know this about me."

He raises a brow. "You said you liked to read romance novels. You didn't specify what kind."

"I like *all* romance novels. From the sweetest to the... Well." I look up at him through my lashes, simultaneously turned on and freaking out. On the one hand, something about this conversation is making me want to throw myself at him. On the other, I want to die for having it in the first place. Are we seriously talking about this?

"Oh, yeah, Pretty Girl? You got some kinks I don't know about?" We both laugh softly, but I stop as soon as his hands come to my waist, his eyes darkening.

Shit, what is happening?

My heart beats a deafening drum, so loud I wonder whether he can hear it. I can barely catch my breath as I look up at the hungry expression in his eyes—one I'm positive I'm matching, despite my best efforts.

"Maybe I do," I whisper. Knox's grip tightens on me as his jaw clenches.

"I don't remember any specific kinks from that one night we shared, and we had all that time to explore. Shame. I would've been up to do whatever you wanted to do." For the millionth time in the in the past couple of weeks, my brain flashes back to that amazing night. To all the things we did together, the dirty words he whispered in my ear.

It was so good, I didn't *need* anything other than him.

The hunger I've been trying to control resurfaces with a vengeance. Restraint slipping, the need for him, for us, for *this,* is too strong to hide anymore. Not that I was any great at it to begin with. All other thoughts have flown the coop, and all that's left is Knox. My skin buzzes as I think of all the ways I wish he'd kiss me, touch me, *fuck* me, and I just can't take it anymore.

"I can help you with those, you know? Acting out your kinks, I mean." His voice is gravelly when he speaks. He slinks an arm around my waist, pulling me into him with one rough movement. Knox digs the fingers of his other hand into my hair at the base of my neck, keeping me from looking anywhere but at him.

A small gasp escapes my lips as I feel every line of his body on mine. Every curve, every plane. My body recognizes his as if it were yesterday. It knows his, knows what he likes.

Keeping a firm grip in my hair, he uses his other hand to hold both my wrists behind my back, causing my body to arch into his, breasts pressing into his chest.

My breathing is ragged when I'm finally able to speak up: "I don't think you'd be able to keep up."

He smiles lasciviously before ducking, skimming the delicate skin of my neck with his nose from the base to the line of my jaw and back down again to my exposed collarbone. He inhales deeply before speaking. "You'd love to think that, wouldn't you? You'd love to think there's no way I can give you what you want, what you fucking *need*. You'd love to think I can't give you any of those things because then you'd have nothing left to hide behind."

I stop breathing because he has it the other way around. For a moment, I panic and almost push him away. *I'm* the one who will never be able to give him what he wants. *I'm* the one who will never be able to give *anyone* what they want. *I'm* the one who is only part of a person—will never be whole.

I will never be enough for anyone, and he thinks I think the opposite.

I start to pull away, but he doesn't notice, too caught up in the moment. "Knox—"

"You're so beautiful." The words burst through his lips, like he couldn't help them. With his hands still in my hair, he angles my head back a bit, giving me a clear view of his eyes, pupils blown now.

"Fuck, can I kiss you again?" he asks, before biting lightly at my neck. His tongue licks softly over the same spot, sending shivers down my spine.

I whimper at the sensation, of feeling him all around me, feeling him take control of everything. And more than anything, I want to hand it over, so tired of being in charge of so many different things.

But then a small, yet significant part of my brain reminds me of *why* I let him come up and of everything he went through today. Walter, the convention, his father's friends...

"Lottie? Can I?"

"What about today? What about earlier? Shouldn't we talk about it?"

He shakes his head, eyes locked on mine. "I'm okay. I mean, I'm not *okay*. But I'm fine.

You were so amazing today, there's no way I would've been able to survive it all without you."

"I just wanted to be there for you." I pour everything in me into those words, wanting him to really understand.

"I know." He smiles, kissing the tip of my nose. "You were. You were everything. You *are* everything."

Knox pulls me back in for another kiss, slower this time, deeper. My hand comes over his heart where I feel it beat against my palm, fingers curling into his chest. He's hard against my stomach and all I can think of is ripping his clothes off and touching him again, wanting to feel his skin on mine, to be closer in more ways than one.

I fist his leather jacket, desperately trying to hold on. This kiss—this kiss that feels like falling—is making me weak-kneed and I don't know how much longer I can stay upright. He's all around me and I can't think, can't breathe, and I'm losing myself in him, in *us*, and I'm shaking. Literally shaking from struggling to stay on my feet, from fear because this feels so good and I don't know what to think, because any inch of my body he's not touching feels too cold, too bare, and I need him there. I'm overwhelmed by sensation and emotion and am slipping—*literally*—clutching at him because my mind and heart are on overload.

I never want to let go.

As if sensing my current predicament, Knox's hands— big, warm—move down my body, stopping to squeeze my ass once before sliding down to the back of my thighs. In one swift movement, he picks me up, my legs wrapping easily around his waist as if it were synchronized. I break the kiss with a moan as I twist my hips experimentally and a burst of pleasure shoots through me. The sound ignites something in him, something brighter and hotter than what was already burning before. His grip tightens, fingers digging into my skin in a way that's more pleasure than pain. "I can't wait to be inside you again," he growls through his labored breathing.

"Not just to feel you but to—"

I press my lips to his again because I know exactly what he means, exactly how he feels. He's talking about more than just sex. He's talking about this invisible gate that's opened between the two of us. The one I let him walk through the night we spent together but have kept him locked out of ever since. And deep down, I've wanted so desperately to let him come back in, but it's been impossible in more ways than one. But with his lips on me, his teeth bared on my skin, words like *"I've missed this so much"* and *"You feel so good"* breathed against my ear, all the reasons to keep him out have disintegrated in my mind and heart and I'm ready. At least for this.

Almost shaking in anticipation, Knox moves to walk us to my bed, stopping right by my bedside table. I barely notice as I try to process the taste of his lips, the dizzying scent of him, the delicious way in which he touches me.

"Take your top off," he commands. With my legs still wrapped around him, I pull away just enough to tug my sweater over my head—

—and accidentally knock the vase of flowers on my bedside table to the floor.

Glass shatters at Knox's socked feet, water splashing everywhere. It takes me a minute to wade through the fog and process what happened: my clumsy, sex-crazed ass knocked everything over, totally ruining the moment.

"Shit, I'm sorry. I—"

"Ignore it," he says before pressing his lips back to mine. "We'll clean it up later."

But I take it as a sign to stop, pushing at his chest. "Careful! There's glass everywhere and you're not wearing any shoes." The glazed look in his eyes is gone now. Disappointment spreads across his face in its stead. I pretend not to notice as I maneuver myself out of his grip, falling gracefully atop my bed, managing to completely avoid the glass-covered floor.

"Don't move," I tell him, trying to ignore how hot he looks—panting, running both his hands through his hair, massive tent pitched he doesn't even bother hiding.

"Come back," he whines. "We can clean it up la—*Shit!*" He looks down at his foot and winces. "I think I stepped on some glass."

I roll my eyes and put some shoes on. "I *told* you not to move." Sensing my seriousness, he proceeds to *finally* stand still.

"I'm so sorry for being so careless," I apologize once I'm done picking up the glass and mopping up the water. "I guess I was really into it and didn't—"

"Whoa, never apologize for being *too* into it." His

lopsided smile makes an appearance, and my lightheaded ass can barely take it. "And it's not that big a deal."

"Let me get the first aid kit."

"I don't need the first aid kit. It's just a—"

"I insist."

With a resigned, amused look in his eyes, he nods.

In the bathroom, he takes the kit from my hand and sits on the lip of the tub. "I'm a big boy. I can do it." He kisses my forehead when I sit next to him, my heart doing backflips in my chest. Knox presses another kiss to my cheek, the sudden tenderness making me ache in that all-too-familiar way it does whenever he's around.

With a smug look on his face, he removes his sock—stained bright red from the blood— and tends to his cut. I wince when I see the small gash, marveling at how something so small could cause so much damage. "You sure you wanna be here for this? You look like—"

I shake my head. "It's not that I'm squeamish, I promise. I have lots of experience with needles and blood and stuff."

He snorts. "What? Were you a nurse or something, too?"

I sit up because once again I've said too much. I've invited more questions through stupid slips of my tongue.

"No, I—I just had to go through some medical treatments a long time ago, and it required me to give myself regular shots. So I kind of grew numb to the whole thing."

His slacked jaw is everything I need to realize that I'm an idiot and should've probably just lied.

God, when am I ever going to learn that we're hostages to the things we say, and free from the things we don't?

"Were you sick? Are you okay now?" I watch as the panic

settles in, my heart twisting at his concern. "Seriously, Lottie. I'm going to need you to answer me now."

I pull one of his hands and hold it between both of mine. "Hey, stop. Everything's fine."

It takes me a few seconds to understand where the extra concern is coming from. But then I realize: he just unexpectedly lost his *father*. The thought of losing someone else right now—even if I'm just his business partner he's hooked up with—must not be easy to process. "I'm good now."

But he doesn't let it go. "What happened? Tell me," he pleads, while I try to search for the words that will please him enough to stop asking questions.

There's no way I'm telling him the truth. There's no way I'm going to sit here and tell him how I underwent years of every type of therapy available in order to get pregnant. How I had to learn to stomach giving myself shots, ignore the bruises it left behind—both the physical and emotional kind.

"There's nothing to tell," I shrug. "There was just a time in my life where I needed to give myself regular shots. I have this health thing and... But I don't have it anymore. I mean, I don't have to get the shots anymore. And I never will." *Never, ever again.*

He stares back, wide-eyed. "Lottie, c'mon. You gotta give me more than that. Are you serious? You're going to shut down on me *now*? After the day we've had, what we just did, and everything we talked about?"

I rear back. "Shut down? Just because I don't want to tell you about something *private*? About my *medical history*? Do you realize how unreasonable you're being right now?" I say, anger coursing through me. "See? This is why I didn't want to do this. I knew you were going to ask for things I could never give you. This is why I didn't want to say yes to any of it."

Knox gets to his feet, cut still untreated, bloody sock in one hand. "Fine. You don't want to tell me about your medical history, okay. But give me *something*. I need *something* from you. I need you to trust me."

"You don't *need* anything from me. And I can't just give you my trust. That's something you *earn*."

He scoffs and shakes his head. "I'm starting to think that no amount of showing or proving myself to you will ever earn me that luxury. I can't even convince you to go out for goddamn dinner with me, for fuck's sake. A romp in your loft? Sure. But talking about your feelings? Getting personal? Not something I'll get to experience."

My jaw drops and I can't think of a single word to say, a different kind of fire coursing through my veins than the one from ten minutes ago.

"I'm gonna get outta your hair, now."

As I watch him walk out of my bathroom and into the loft, I will myself to call out his name. But nothing comes out. I have nothing left to say.

CHAPTER SIXTEEN

LOTTIE

When I worked in fashion, I was fantastic in crises. Thrived in them, even. I was the goddamn problem-solving queen of luxury. Even now, through this whole bookstore renovation, I've felt myself slowly awaken from the state of numbness I've been in. Problem-solving has always made me feel professionally empowered and knowledgable. I love it. But when it comes to my personal life? Experience has taught me I have no idea what the hell I'm doing. I need help.

Are you there, Goddess? It's me, Carlota, your favorite hot mess. I'm in my mid-thirties and my life is a goddamn joke. Any tips?

Though, if I'm honest, I don't think appealing to any sort of deity will do me any good here.

Because I'm a coward, I avoid the store and daydreaming about our amazing make-out session all of yesterday. Daydreaming about how close we got to getting together again, and mortified because of how abruptly it ended.

We definitely need to have a conversation—that's clear. The other night proved to me exactly why we wouldn't be good together: he's asking too much of me—or at least more than I can give. And though I know all of this and I've had time to think about it, when I walk into the store Monday morning, even thirty-six hours after the incident, I still have no idea what to say.

How exactly would it even go?

Hey, Knox. Just wanted to say sorry for making out with you and then shutting you out emotionally. Truth is, I've liked you since the second I met you—a fact that terrifies me to the bone— and don't know how to handle it. I want to jump your bones and stay in bed all morning the next day, cuddling and laughing and just being with you, but I'm fucked up and you're too young, and we'll never be able to be anything at all. I'm a failure at life and love and work and I really don't want to get attached to you because it'll kill me when you go.

Yeah, no. I don't think honesty is the right plan here. He'd run for the hills, screaming the entire way there, regretting the second he got into bed with this crazy-pants.

Still, I know I owe him *some* kind of explanation. And even though I had mentally prepared myself to have a diffi- cult conversation, my stomach still drops when I walk into the office and find him making himself a cup of coffee. I was already struggling through paininduced nausea (the stress of everything was causing me to have an endometriosis flare- up, which was *super* fun), but seeing him standing there, watching his muscles move beneath his tshirt as he poured himself a cup, made everything I'd eaten since yesterday rise up in my throat with even more intensity.

I fist my hands at my sides and swallow hard. "Hey," I squeak.

He tenses, his body frozen for a few seconds before turning to face me.

"Hey." I can barely hold his glacier-blue eyes. The hurt from my rejection is still clear on his face, and it kills me. Because I know this isn't because I turned him down for sex; it's because I shut him out emotionally. Knox is an open book and I'm just... not.

"I was hoping we could talk?"

"Really?" He nods and looks down at his coffee, stirring it occasionally with a frown on his face. "About what? The weather? What kind of sports you're into? Or is that too personal a conversation for you to have?"

Ouch.

I nod. "I deserve that, I guess. But you need to realize it's not that easy for me to open up. I've been through... some things. And being so honest and transparent about everything isn't in my nature."

"We all have our shit, Lottie. But we gotta work through it."

"I *know*." I sigh, adjusting my oversized sweater over my stomach, praying it hides how bloated I look today. "But it's not like I didn't share anything. I told you about my divorce." He raises a brow. "Yeah, but I didn't get the whole story there, did I?"

"No." The word comes out whispered, followed by his scoff.

I blow a puff of air through my lips. "Anyway, I'm sorry that I closed myself off and I'm sorry that I keep pushing you away, but it was never my intention to hurt you. I'm just not someone who opens up easily.

"I think you're an amazing person, Knox. Truly. I really like you, but I'd like it more if we were able to work well together—I think it's the right thing to do here. So I was wondering if it were possible for you not to hate me." I pause for a minute to let him absorb my words.

He nods once, still not meeting my eyes.

"Thank you."

But I'm not done: "I appreciate you understanding, but I do need to let you know, however, that I *am* entitled to privacy. To decide what I share and when and with whom. So while I get where you're coming from, I hope you get where I'm coming from, too."

His uncharacteristically hard eyes turn soft, pleading. "I like you. *So much.* So please don't blame me for wanting to get to know you better."

A deep blush creeps up my neck at his words as I marvel at how easily he's able to express every emotion without fear when I'm barely able to admit I feel the same way about him to myself.

With a look of resignation, he says, "But you're right about wanting privacy. You're entitled to share whatever you want with me and I promise to adhere to your boundaries."

"Wow. Okay. Thanks." That was... surprisingly mature of him. I expected a little more back-and-forth, to be honest.

"You like me, though?" He asks, light in his eyes.

Ah. There it is.

"Of course *that's* what you focus on." I roll my eyes, though I'm happy to have left the uncomfortable tension behind. "And I do. Obviously. But I don't think that we should pursue this. I *do* promise to stop being as snarky, though." I smile, trying to add levity to the situation. "I'm just... disappointed you wouldn't want to share things with me." I grimace because I wish more than anything that I could.

"What about a friendship? Is that a type of relationship you'd be willing to have with me?"

I bite my lower lip in hesitation. "Yes?"

He frowns, lips pressed together.

"I mean, sure. Yeah. *Yes.* Friends."

"Great." He smiles, back to his regular unbothered behavior. Knox, I've come to learn, bounces back faster than a dodgeball, most times. Even after his break down at the convention, he was able to get back to business after only a few minutes.

"Can I say something before we move on, though?"

I stifle a smile. "Sure."

"You look really pretty today." His eyes shine bright, but he isn't joking, and I know he isn't saying it as a line. Knox just wants me to know what he's thinking, and I hate how I can't help the way his words make me smile.

"Thanks. But I'm not even wearing any makeup. I look like a mess," I almost whisper, flushing. I look down at my comfort-over-fashion outfit, reconsidering my leggings and old sweater combo. Maybe I should've squeezed into something else? But this morning was awful as I struggled to find something that fit me and made me feel comfortable at the same time. I woke up more bloated than I have in months, unable to fit into anything that required buttons or a zipper. Stupid endometriosis.

"Nah. You look great."

"Are you ready for today?" I ask, because we're veering back into non-friend territory despite the conversation we just had.

"For the demo? Sure. Why wouldn't I be?"

I shrug, turning back to face him. "I don't know. Personally, I find it kind of sad. Although, I guess it's different for me, you know? I worked here. Walter gave me this job when I had nothing. The bookstore means—*meant*—a lot to me. I guess it's all kind of hitting me now, you know? Some random retail store is going to take over this spot and it'll all be gone."

"Yeah," he says, nodding thoughtfully. "To me, it's just something Walter left me in his will." And something about the way he sounds feels like a stab to the chest.

Knox puffs out a breath. "Sorry, I didn't mean to sound glib or indifferent or—I... I just realized last night that part of me might be a little jealous of you."

"Of *me*?"

He scratches the back of his head. "Yeah, you—You got to know him well. I only knew him as a temporary father figure, you know? He wasn't even in my life for a full ten years and it's not like I got to *know* him the way you did. I was a kid. But I know he was a huge influence and support for you and Jenn. And I guess I can't help but feel a little jealous." He shrugs, bashful. "I guess sometimes I'm not as okay with this whole thing as I expected myself to be, and Saturday proved that."

"Grief comes in so many different shapes and sizes," I say, recalling my own experience—with Mom and Dad *and* with the life I lost back in New York. "Speaking from someone who knows of loss, I can tell you that much is true. I remember the days and months after my parents' death... The countless emotions I went through. It'll come in waves, and sometimes you won't recognize it for what it is. Grief is fickle like that."

"I didn't know about your parents," he says, his voice quiet.

I nod. "Yeah. It happened a while ago," I shrug. "They both died in a car crash—drunk driver."

"Jesus." Knox winces, running his hand through his hair. "I'm so sorry. That's terrible."

I take a beat, feeling the familiar sting behind my eyes whenever I think too hard about my parents' death. "It's fine. I mean, it's not." I shake my head. "I want to say that you keep going, that you'll find your groove again. But it's not true. You'll eventually have to find an entirely new one and *that's* okay. It has to be. But you'll never get over it. Grief will forever be a part of your life."

"I'm not grieving him exactly—"

"You might not be grieving *him*. But I think you can't deny that a part of you is grieving the life that you could have had. The life he could've offered you. Like, if he had been a present father, involved in your life. I mean, from what we found out Saturday, it's not that he didn't care, but I think it's more he didn't know how to that was the problem. And...

it's okay to be sad and therefore grieve something you never even knew you wanted or could have had."

"I…" He swallows once, eyes wide, gaze locked on mine. And it's in that moment that I know I've hit the nail on the head.

I feel my heart fill in my chest, aching to comfort him. It's almost as painful as it was on Saturday.

"Don't," he pleads with an awkward laugh. "I know that look, and you're feeling sorry for me again." He looks down and fidgets with his mug, avoiding my gaze.

"I don't feel sorry for *you*, I feel sorry for *him*. Because he never got to truly know you.

At least as an adult. And I think you're pretty great."

His smile is tender when he finally looks up at me, heart-break still in his eyes. "You think I'm great?"

"Come on, Knox. You know I do. I just told you so not two minutes ago."

He shoots me a rueful smile, and nods. "I think you're pretty great, too. And I can do the friend thing, I think."

I laugh softly. "You think?"

He shrugs with a lopsided smile. "I'll make an honest effort. I don't want to push you away. Plus, it's not like you're wrong; we do need to still work together. Can you imagine finally giving in to this sexual chemistry we have? We'd never get anything done."

I snort and laugh in earnest. "I love your confidence."

"What? It's true!"

Shaking my head, I put a hand on his chest and push him away from the coffee maker.

"Now, get out of here. I need to make myself some coffee."

It's hard to pay attention to Luke, our contractor, as he walks Knox and I through the final demo strategy and budget. All I can think of as he talks about knocking a wall down is what the place meant to me, how it took this moment right now to realize that this store might've been responsible for saving me when I came back to town.

I wince as Luke talks about breaking down built-in bookshelves, I stop myself from objecting when he discusses getting rid of the current register for something more generic, and I do my best to keep a straight face when we agree to remove any signage pertaining to *Adams's Bookstore* today. But when we discuss gutting Walter's office, I nearly lose it.

I look away and blink back tears, blocking out whatever it is the two men are discussing while I try to gather myself.

What is *wrong* with me? I mean, it's just a stupid office. I know—

Luke snaps his fingers in front of me, bringing my attention back to him. "Hey," he does it again, and Knox's hand comes flying in front of my face, slapping Luke's fingers away.

"Hey, don't ever fucking disrespect her like that again.

She's a fucking person, not a dog, asshole." His voice is vicious in a way I could've never imagined it could be.

"Whoa, whoa. Let's calm down, okay?" I slide in between the two of them, suddenly on high alert.

Luke glares at Knox, moving to stand squarely in front of him, clipboard in one hand, a fist in the other. Fear skitters down my spine in a cool chill. Luke is as dumb as a rock, but he's also built like one. A giant boulder of a man, he stands a couple of inches taller than Knox, and more than a few inches wider. With his buzzed hair, tattoos covering almost every inch of his body, and ripped muscles, he is exactly what you'd see if you googled "smoking hot construction worker." He could definitely take Knox if he wanted to.

"Hey guys, hold on." I put my palm on both their chests, trying to ignore the way Knox leans just a little bit into it. *It's fine. We're fine.* "Luke isn't going to do anything like that again, right Luke?" I look to him, who's still glaring at Knox. He grits his teeth and nods once.

"Sorry, babe," he replies, enjoying the way Knox rolls his eyes at the pet name.

I press on, ignoring them both. "And Knox, you're going to apologize to Luke, right?"

Knox's head snaps to look at me. "*What*? Are you joking? He was an ass to you!"

"He was. And Luke knows that, as I've reminded him nearly every day I've seen him since we broke up in high school."

"You dated this clown?" He throws a thumb in his direction.

Shit. That was definitely the wrong thing to say. I also

happened to sleep with him when I first came back to town. I was at my lowest of lows. But I don't mention it since there's no point in stirring the pot. Instead, I sigh and say, "Ages ago. But he's also the best contractor around." *The only one, really.* I feel rather than see Luke's smug grin spread across his face. "So we need him even if he is as big a tool as the sledgehammer currently hanging from his belt."

Luke grunts in anger, but Knox smirks, light slowly coming back into his eyes.

"Okay. So we're good?" I ask Luke.

He rolls his eyes once, but nods.

"Cool, let's forget this silly testosterone competition and start the demo, shall we? But we're leaving the office as is. It's still our mission base. Now let's get to work." I clap my hands once and Luke walks away over to his crew, muttering something under his breath about "crazy exes." Unfortunately, Knox hears this and takes a step toward him. But I stop him with a strong grip around his bicep.

"Don't."

"He's a jerk. If he's gonna act like that then I don't want him working anywhere near you."

I snort and shake my head.

"What? I don't like him. He doesn't treat you right."

"Newsflash, buddy. He's the only game in town. And don't worry about him. I know how to handle Luke."

"I don't know." He sighs, looking over at Luke as he goes over the blueprints with his crew. He runs both hands through his hair looking torn. "I don't like the way he looks at you."

I shrug and gently place a hand on his cheek, pulling him back to face me. "Don't worry about him."

We both freeze, suddenly realizing at the same time that I'm touching him—something I haven't allowed myself to initiate since Saturday night in my loft. I should drop my hand now, but as if it had a mind of its own, it slides to curve around Knox's jaw, prickly with stubble, down his smooth neck, and stopping at his hard chest. A little rattled by my brazenness, I try to take a step back and move away. But Knox is faster than me, quickly pressing his own hand over mine, taking another step forward.

Both of our breaths come out a little faster, skin heating like wildfire. I feel it spread from my cheeks, down my neck and chest.

"I love your blush." His voice is so low, it's as if he's saying it just to himself. "You look beautiful today."

"You already said that," I whisper.

"Did I? I can't stop staring at you."

My gaze remains glued to our hands because I cannot—*I just cannot*—look up into his eyes. I know the second I do I'll crumble and break my rule.

Instead, I push out an awkward laugh and say, "I noticed." I wince, wanting to head-slap myself because this is flirting, and *we. Aren't. Supposed. To. Flirt.*

I feel the rumble in his chest as he chuckles, moving his hand to thread his fingers through mine.

"Sorry. I shouldn't have said that. That wasn't very friendly of me, was it?" I sigh.

"Hey," he gently tilts my chin up to meet his eyes. That mischievous spark is back—the one that makes my insides twist, the heat build low in my stomach. "It was very, very friendly."

I laugh, and pull my hand free, slapping him gently against his chest. I take a step back and move around the front desk, needing to put distance and an actual piece of furniture between us because, my god, I am two seconds away from throwing myself at this man. "Stop. I don't want to send you any mixed messages."

"Sure. We wouldn't want that, would we?" He sighs and shakes his head knowingly like he can read every single dirty thought running through my head. "Lottie," he breathes on a sigh, his eyes a mix of humor and longing.

"Stop. Don't." I raise a finger at him. "I don't want to hear it."

He rolls his eyes, laughing. "C'mon, we like each other!" He throws his hands in the air. "Go out on a date with me, please."

"We did already."

He laughs once. "Let me take you on another one, then. Show you I'm actually a good guy."

"I *know* you're a good guy." That's the problem. "Still, it's a no."

He purses his lips to keep from laughing and nods. "Okay, but I'm not giving up."

"What happened to our talk this morning? What happened to you accepting this wasn't ever going to be a thing?"

"Nah, I'm not doing that anymore. I'm gonna make you like me so hard you won't be able to deny me any longer."

You really don't have to try that much.

He pauses. "And I mean that in a non-stalker, non-creepy, and I-won't-pressure-you way."

I laugh a little lighter now. "You know what would make me like you?"

"What's that? Tell me, because I'd pretty much do anything right now."

"I'd like it if you helped Luke with the demo and leave me alone so I can finish reviewing the info my brother sent us. He'll be here in a couple of hours to walk us through the whole sale process. So it would be *uh*-mazing if you would make yourself useful somewhere else."

He snorts, but doesn't look offended. "Okay, Pretty Girl." I roll my eyes at the nickname. "You want me to help with the demo? I'll help with the demo." A dimpled grin pops on his face while he walks backward toward the crew, wiggling his eyebrows.

Laughing once, I pick up my things from the counter in one swoop before heading for the back office.

I lose myself in paperwork for the rest of the morning until Salt-N-Pepa's *Push It* blares suddenly from my phone, breaking my concentration. My hand flies to pick up, the personalized ringtone already alerting me to who the caller is.

"Hey, bro. I was just—"

"*Where the hell are you?*" Daniel snaps at me from the other end of the line, whisper-yelling.

Taken aback, I sit up in the desk chair. "In the back, going through some numbers before we—"

"Well, I'm here in the bookstore and you need to get the hell to the front. Because— *Jesus*, Carlota." Daniel stops and exhales to catch his breath. My stomach drops as my mind begins to race. He only calls me by my full name when something is really wrong.

"What is it?" I say, getting up so quickly, I trip on my way out.

I run to the front of the store where I see my brother standing by the counter, mouth slightly open, phone in hand, but no longer pressed to his cheek. "What? What is it?" I ask anxiously.

Daniel raises his hand slowly, pointing in the direction of some very, very loud banging.

And that's when I see him.

Knox.

Sweaty and shirtless.

Sledgehammering away at the old bookshelves.

"Oh my god," I groan. "How much more is one girl expected to take?"

CHAPTER SEVENTEEN

KNOX

"So, I'll make sure to send you guys the final paperwork once you get a chance to review these." Daniel hands Lottie, Jenn, and me a packet containing several documents. I feel the weight of it, dreading having to read them all. I know Lottie is more than capable of studying them closely and making sure that things are in order, but I wanna prove that I'm just as much an adult as she is.

"Sweet," Jenn says, flipping through the paperwork with a furrowed brow. "And once we e-sign we'll list the property?"

"I would suggest waiting until the reno is completed, but if you want to try to sell it during, we can try. It will just add to the cost."

"No, no," Lottie interrupts. "We want to get a good price, here. The higher the better, obviously. I know you're anxious to make your first deposit for school, Jenn, but I'm pretty confident we'll be able to sell it in time for the deadline. Right, Daniel?" "Hmm. When's your deadline?"

"August first." Jenn bites her lower lip, shifting in her seat.

"And work is projected to be done when?"

"Mid-May to early June. Project's supposed to be done by May sixteenth, but I'm hedging two weeks extra because I don't fully trust Luke." Lottie grimaces. "Plus, he's short-handed, he said. It's why Knox had to help today."

I frown, my previous irritation over that douche canoe coming back. "What? If you don't trust him, then why the hell did we hire him for the job?" I ask Lottie.

"You know why. He's the only contractor in town. Unless we want to pay extra to get someone from somewhere else in here, I suggest you take a chill pill." I grit my teeth and look away, trying to suppress my irrational jealousy.

"Is that enough time to sell the place?" Jenn asks, steering us back on topic.

Daniel nods thoughtfully. "I think so. Especially with summer approaching, since this town is about to get an influx of tourists."

"Perfect."

We go over final details and expectations, wrapping things up with a final cup of coffee before Jenn heads back home. Reaching for his second cup, Daniel looks up at the post-it wall, the completed tasks from this week already gone, leaving open patches.

He turns back to look at Lottie with a fond smile on his face.

"What?" she asks, almost exasperated.

With a shrug, Daniel smiles. "It's nice. To see you like this, I mean." "Like what?" She narrows her eyes at him.

"To see you this excited over something. I don't think I've ever seen you like this. Plus, you're good at it. At the project management and the business decisions and keeping everyone in check. Like, really good at it. Don't you think so, Knox?"

I smile proudly at her. "Definitely. I've told her about a thousand times."

She snorts. "Of course I'm good at this." But I can tell despite her confidence that she wasn't expecting the compliment.

He rolls his eyes at her. "I just think you're making a mistake."

"A mistake? What are you talking about?" She crosses her arms in front of her chest, leaning forward in her chair, pinning Daniel with a glare.

I sit back in my seat watching the interaction quietly, realizing that there's something beneath this conversation that I don't quite understand.

"You know exactly what I'm talking about, sis. I'll obviously help you list the place if that's what you want, but is going back to New York really something you want to do? You wanna go back to living like that? To be surrounded by the same people who turned their backs on you when things got difficult for you?"

"So what are you saying? That I should just take over the store and stay here for the rest of my life, stuck?" Her voice is sharp, cold—but Daniel looks unbothered by it.

"Stuck?" He laughs once, humorlessly. "You keep thinking it's this town's fault that you're stuck."

"*Daniel.*" There's a clear warning in her voice.

"I don't get it. Why are you holding on to a life that never seemed to want you to begin with?"

She looks away, but I catch her red-rimmed eyes glazing over with unshed tears.

What the hell?

A shot of adrenaline courses through me, so I reach out to her. But she pulls her hand away. Always pulling away. "Lottie—"

"Can we not talk about this anymore?" she whispers.

"I've spoken to Brandon about this and... We want to offer you the money. As a loan. To buy out Knox and Jenn."

"What?" Her head snaps up to him.

"I believe in you, Lottie. We all do. So, if you want to take the money, it's there for you. Buy them out and do your own thing. You just need to believe in yourself again. And when you finally do, just know your family will be here to help you through it."

They enter into a stare-off, glaring at each other with the fire of a thousand suns. We're all quiet for a beat, the tension palpable. Finally, she breaks the silence: "Knox, would you mind leaving us for a sec?" Her eyes never leave Daniel's.

"Of course. Yes. I still need to shower after the demo, so..." I push out of my chair, simultaneously wanting to get the hell out of there as fast as I can and wanting to be a fly on the wall for this conversation. Ultimately, though, I know the latter isn't a possibility, so I hustle back upstairs to shower as quickly as possible.

Once I've washed all the dust and sweat from my day demoing, I bounce down the stairs hoping to catch Lottie before she heads home. But as I reach the office door, I hear voices— Lottie and Daniel's—uttering my name.

"Now that we're done discussing that, would you mind telling me what's up with you and

Knox?" Daniel asks her.

I inhale sharply, freezing where I stand, hoping they didn't hear me come down the stairs. I know it's wrong, but I *need* to hear this conversation. I press myself against the hallway wall and do my best to listen. Am I finally going to get the unfiltered opinion of what Lottie thinks of me? For a moment, I hesitate. We all know what they say about eavesdropping: you're bound to hear things that aren't nice about yourself. But when I hear Lottie sigh, gearing up to deny everything, I decide I don't give a shit.

"I have no idea what you're talking about," she says, her voice sounding almost innocent.

I almost snort at the sound of her voice, at the fact that she thinks Daniel is going to let her get out of this one unscathed.

He scoffs once. "Please. You know exactly what I'm talking about. I'm talking about how obvious it is that you like this guy. How obvious it is that you want to jump his bones."

"Shh! Are you insane?" she hisses, shifting in her seat. "He'll hear us! And you've only seen us together once just in this meeting where all we did was talk about Real Estate for an hour with you and Jenn. I didn't even flirt with him once. So how would you know that I like him?"

Daniel laughs softly. "So you admit you like him, then?"

My heart races in my chest as it fills to the brim with happiness. I knew she liked me—and not just for sex. But having her admit it out loud—even if it was an accident—feels great to know. It gives me hope, it tells me there's something I can work with here, and it tells me we're not a lost cause.

Lottie is incredibly special, and if there's even the slightest chance that she'll let me be a part of her life that way, then I sure as hell am gonna try.

"I'm ignoring you now." I hear her sift through some paperwork, imagining how she would avoid meeting her brothers gaze. It hasn't been eons, but I've known Lottie long enough to know she's not one for admitting anything that might put her in a vulnerable position.

"When you told me about this guy on the phone, you neglected to mention how hot he was."

"I told you he was attractive," she mutters.

I grin stupidly, suddenly wondering why the hell everyone makes such a big deal about eavesdropping and karma. All I'm hearing is good shit.

"And I was sure Adri must've said something too. There's no way she's been sitting on that information and didn't tell you about it." I can practically hear her roll her eyes.

"Yeah, but you know she can be *a little bit* dramatic. I took all of it with a grain of salt. And when you and I spoke... I mean, *Jesus*, Carlota. Tell me why you aren't all over him?"

Yes, Carlota. Do tell.

This is what I've been waiting for. The moment of truth —the *real* one. Not some fictitious, pathetic excuse.

"He's my business partner. Plus, it would be dumb of me to start something given that he doesn't even live here."

Okay, the business partner part isn't new, but me not living here is definitely is.

My stomach twists because there's no immediate solution to that problem. But I stand up straighter, determined to find it. If this is what's keeping us apart, then—

"He won't always be your business partner. And honestly? The whole not living here thing should be a bullet point in you *pro* column. He could just be a temporary good time." I frown, not liking the turn this conversation is taking. "Especially since you vowed to never be in another relationship again, right? I don't get what the big deal is." *Wait...*

...never be in another relationship again?

"Stop," she groans.

"Seriously. I don't know how you've held off this long. He's really attractive—that much is obvious. Even after he put his shirt on for the meeting, it took everything in me to focus on the numbers and not think about those tattoos and ripped body. Why do you think I caved so quickly on the realtor's fee?"

"Because you're my brother," she deadpans.

"No way." He scoffs. "Damn, I almost feel like I cheated on Brandon or something because of how much I struggled not to *look* at the guy that way. But it was mostly his charisma.

He's so *charming*, you know? And sweet."

"Yeah, of course I know. It's not even about the way he looks, which is so infuriating. I keep trying not to like him, but... It's like we can't help flirting with each other. And he's adorable and it's so goddamn frustrating because it's not like he does it to manipulate me or try to get me in bed. I mean, I'm sure part of him is. But what I mean is that he does all the same nice things he does for me for everyone around him and it's just…" She sighs, frustrated. "He's the best."

I smile, the knot in my stomach releasing, replaced by a sense of warmth and comfort.

Lottie.

Daniel snorts. "Yeah, he actually seems like an amazing guy. Not to mention the amount of sexual tension between you two was way more than I was comfortable with. You *are* my sister, after all."

"That's gross. Don't ever say the words 'sexual tension' to me ever again, please."

"You're so stupid." He snorts. "But seriously, I think you should just go on a damn date with the guy. Put him out of his misery. Maybe sleep with him, a little," he snickers.

Yes. Date me. Date me, Lottie.

"I've already slept with him, remember?"

"You know what I mean."

God, I knew Daniel was a cool guy. I should buy him a coffee or a cookie or something as a thank you. Though of course I wouldn't be able to tell him why I'm thanking him, could I? "I don't know." She sighs. "It feels like playing with fire. I… I'm kind of terrified, Daniel."

"If this is about Finn… I only spent about thirty minutes with Knox, but even in that limited time you can tell he's not—"

Finn? The ex?

"No, it's not that. I know he isn't anything like Finn.

There doesn't seem to be a bad bone in his body. It's just..." A groan from Lottie.

He gasps. "Oh, shit. You *actually* like him. It's not just some crush. That's why you won't date the guy."

I hold my breath, waiting for her answer.

"We'll hook up and then, once everything is over with the sale, he'll either go back home or... or want more. And you and I both know I can't give him more. Not now, not ever. That's what's stopping me. Either way, I end up with a broken heart. So what's the damn point of it all?"

So this is about her? Not me?

I want to bust through the office door, to start demanding some answers nearly overwhelms me. But I stop myself just in time because I know I'll never come back from that if I do.

"I get what you're saying, Lottie. But I also think you're getting ahead of yourself. To be honest, you don't know whether he'd want more. And despite his young age," they laugh softly, "he's a big boy who can make his own decisions. It looks like he's willing to enter into something despite not living here. So I think you're getting ahead of yourself, sis."

"I don't know..."

"Just have fun. Enjoy life while you have a gorgeous twenty-something year old man who looks more like a tatted-up Greek God than anything else who's interested in you."

She laughs once, followed by a sniffle. "What?"

"It's just nice. Seeing you like this over a guy again. Especially over one who looks like he would worship at your feet." She snorts, but I'm pretty sure I'm close to doing so, if we're being honest. "Seriously. I just hope you don't ruin this by letting your baggage get in the way."

"My baggage won't get in the way, because there's nothing to get in the way *of*. I told you. The plan is simple: renovate this store, sell it, and get the hell out of Dodge."

He sighs deeply, and I can hear the chair creak as he sits back in it, exasperated.

"Let's change the subject," she says. "I don't want to talk about him anymore."

Shit. Is that it? I'm not getting anything else? What am I supposed to do with that information? Besides the part about her thinking she's the problem, I didn't overhear anything I didn't already know.

Frustrated, I decide this is my cue to make myself known. I quietly back up down the hallway before turning back toward the office, stomping loud enough for them to hear me. "Shh! I think he's coming," she whispers to him.

"Hey, you guys are still here," I say innocently enough as I step into the office.

"Yeah, we were just wrapping up. How was your shower?" she asks. Lottie winces. "Shit, that was really weird of me to ask. Sorry."

I laugh softly, because I've never seen anything more adorable than a mortified Lottie.

"It's fine. And good. It may have been the best I have ever taken in my life."

"That's probably due to the fact that you must've washed away a thick layer of wood chips, dust, and sweat." A wide smile spreads across her face, the sight of it bringing one to my own.

"Ew, Lottie. No." Daniel gives her a look.

"No, she's right." I laugh. "Maybe that's what made it amazing." I wink at her, and she immediately stops laughing. Lottie clears her throat, cheeks flushing, and looks to her brother, quietly asking for help.

"Er, so, Knox. You have any plans tonight?"

"No," I say, looking between Daniel and Lottie. "What about you guys?"

"Well, I have a date with my husband and my two girls at the movie theater a couple of towns over." He gets up from his seat and gathers up all the documents, slipping them into his briefcase. "I am in for a wild night of Paw Patrol."

"Exciting." I grin at him. "What about you, Lottie?"

I wait anxiously for her reply, the three seconds it takes for her to do so feeling more like hours. Is this my in? Is this how I get her to say yes to me? If I ask her to go on a date with me tonight, right now, will she say yes?

"I-I'm actually having dinner with the girls," she says a bit nervously.

Daniel's face falls. "Oh, right. I forgot tonight was your—"

"My girls' night out," she cuts him off, an urgent look in her eyes. She shoots her brother a glare before gazing back at me. "It's just a regular girls night out with my sister, Jenn, and a couple more people. Nothing super special." She fidgets in her seat.

"Right..." I stop myself from pushing, from asking what she's hiding, because I know it will only make things worse. "Well, I think it's great you're getting out. You've been working really hard. Hope you enjoy yourself tonight." But the disappointment is clear my voice, no matter how hard I try to sound happy for her. For some reason I thought today would be the day I'd convince her to take a chance on me. For some reason, after hearing her conversation with her brother, I thought she'd want to try.

I have to remind myself that I have a history of people not really wanting to be invested in me, so I shouldn't be surprised.

CHAPTER EIGHTEEN

LOTTIE

I absentmindedly listen to Adri and Bonnie drone on about who-knows-what while I nurse my cosmopolitan. Normally, I'd probably go for a martini like I did the first night I met Knox, but it's my uterus's going away party, and only pink drinks are allowed tonight—as per Jenn's rules. I don't mind it though. The drink is sweet and cold and perfect and it takes the edge off of listening to my sisters passionately discuss something I couldn't care less about. Maybe some issue concerning their kids' Little League team? Honestly, not to sound like a horrible person, but shouldn't the topic of children be banned tonight? Isn't it a little off-brand for the occasion?

Suppressing a sigh, I try to keep myself entertained with the paper cocktail napkin, doing my best to shape it into a butterfly despite the material not being optimal for origami. It was a habit I picked up to help with my anxiety when I first started trying for kids, but as the years went by and Finn and I were still childless, keeping my hands busy worked for shit at managing my anxiety and depression. When the IVF isn't working for you or a surrogate and the door to adoption has been slammed shut in your face due to your husband's youthful indiscretion of cocaine possession during his time in college, there is little that can help in that regard. No amount of paper butterfly-making could keep my mental health in check. At a certain point, it became less of a therapeutic tool and more of a constant, glaring reminder of my body's failure—*my* failure. Hundreds of paper butterflies all over my home and office, each one reminding me of a missed shot, of my inability to reproduce, of how things were *my* fault.

Yeah, origami didn't help much.

That's the thing about coping mechanisms: they're helpful in the beginning, but if the problem in question goes untreated, they're nothing more than a Band-Aid for a stab wound.

Just as I mull this over and make my final fold, Adri's hand comes over my work of art. "What the hell, Adri?" I whine, watching her crumple my butterfly in her fist.

"Where the hell are you, Lottie? We're all here *for you*, we organized this party *for you*, and your head is anywhere but here. Can you please involve yourself in conversation, at least?"

I glare, doing my best to keep from going off on her. There are so many things I wish I could say right now. Like, for example, whether she thinks I would truly be interested in talking about her kids' baseball league mommy drama, because literally no one else cares—especially on one of the few nights out we get. I want to tell her that, even though

I've come to terms with my infertility and my hysterectomy, I don't really think talking solely about your kids during my uterus's goodbye party is really appropriate.

But I stop myself, knowing that anything like that will have her questioning my decision to have the surgery again, begging me to cancel it or live to regret it. And I just don't have that fight in me right now. Not tonight. I'm too tired from all the work we've been putting into the store, too tired from the flare-ups. Too tired from the emotional roller-coaster I've been on this past month.

So I force a smile and say, "You're right. We had to drive forty minutes to get to the nearest nice-ish bar just to have a girls' night. So we may as well enjoy it. I was just thinking about the bookstore."

"Girl, please do not bring work up while I'm on my night out," Jenn groans, taking one of the three shots in front of her.

I wince as I watch her do it, dying for the days where I could still wake up fresh as a daisy after a night of drinking. Not because I'd kill for a night of shots and dancing, but because I miss the body I had in my twenties. My endometriosis and PCOS weren't horrible back then—things were bearable. Also, certain body parts hadn't yet been affected by gravity, if you know what I mean.

"I know, sorry. I was spacing out. Sorry. Just wondering what kind of place is going to replace the bookstore, you know? I feel like it's been there forever."

"God, maybe they should put in one of these places so we don't have to make this damn trip every time we want to have a girls' night out. I feel like coming here every time involves vacation-level planning and coordination."

Adri snorts. "Right?"

"I doubt we'll ever get something like this in Ceres Cove, even if it would help with tourism. We're not cool enough for it."

Preach. Finally, someone on my side.

"What was that space before Walter came to town?" Jenn asks. "I don't remember." The rest of us chuckle at her.

"I forgot how young you are," Bonnie says, gently patting Jenn's hand.

She pulls it away with a glare in my sister-in-law's direction. "Well?"

"It was still a bookstore; it just belonged to someone else. It wasn't really super successful at the time, but that was more so because we had much less tourism then. I'm not sure whether it'd do so poorly nowadays, if I'm honest. It wasn't like Walter's shop; the old owner actually stocked popular books and some bookish merch."

Jenn nods thoughtfully.

"How's the reno going, by the way?" Adri asks.

"Great. We're making a ton of progress, actually. The demo went off without a hitch."

Despite the emotional toll watching my safe space getting torn down to its bare bones had on me. *Or* the near-heart attack Knox gave me. Seeing him shirtless and sweaty, sledgehammering away, reached my most basic instincts in the most cliched way, I know. I was a flustered mess the entire time. I am 100% sure he submitted himself to working for my ex during the process *just* to get me to pay attention to him.

He knew what he was doing, though. But it isn't his body that's been keeping me up at night, no matter how amazing it is. It is how he has been my constant throughout this. At first glance, Knox looks like a tatted-up young man with a free spirit, no real responsibilities, who could never be able to help in running a business, much less take on a significant role like he has.

But he's left me standing corrected at every corner. Yes, he's young and lives the life of a young man with no ties to anything, but at no point has he ever made me feel like I'm alone in this project, that I have to carry this renovation and sale solely on my shoulders. He's been an incredible partner and new friend, who's always there for me. A man who notices if I haven't eaten, who asks what I did the night before and actually cares about the answer. A man who pays attention to the small and simple things about my life which feel... big. I am fully aware it's because he has a crush on me, but it still feels nice. Especially since I have a crush on him, too.

And I know this all sounds so ridiculous. I know that if a friend came to me with this situation, I'd go off on her and tell her to just seize the day, to at least date him while he's here— the whole "It's better to have loved and lost than to have never loved" of it all. But that's exactly what I'm scared of. It's taken me *years* to recover from the fallout that was the explosion of my old life. I barely feel recovered now. So of course I've turned into this total cliché, terrified of getting hurt again, wanting to put up boundaries between us that would rival the Great Wall of China.

Sigh.

I just wish I didn't care about him. It would make this whole thing so much easier.

"What comes next?" Bonnie asks, before taking a sip from her own drink (a Shirley Temple, because she's DD).

"The actual remodeling. Making the whole space a little more generic to appeal to different type of businesses. Then paint and stuff. After that, we list it and pray to the gods we find a buyer quickly." I feel an unexpected pang in my stomach at my own words, the idea of someone else taking over that space suddenly unsavory. That's *the bookstore.* It has always been the town's bookstore.

But I shake off the feeling because why the hell should I care? My main goal is to get the hell out of Ceres Cove ASAP. When I'm back in New York, I won't even notice it will be gone.

"Whoa. Can you guys afford all that work?" Bonnie asks before taking a sip of her own drink.

"No," Jenn and I both reply at the same time with a laugh.

"We'll be doing the painting ourselves, so that should save us some money. Plus, Knox is going to take the pictures of the place for the actual listing, so we won't have to pay a photographer there."

"That's great to hear," she says, in earnest. "Sad that I'll need to either start ordering books online or drive an hour and a half to the closest bookstore, though."

"I can still order your book club's books for now. Plus, every cent that comes in helps."

Adri's face falls as she slouches a little in her seat. "Oh, you don't have to worry about that." She waves her hand in the air as if dismissing me. "We're not doing book club anymore."

All three of us whip to face my sister, practically slack-jawed. "Excuse me?" Bonnie breaks the silence.

"We're done with it," Adri shrugs, her gaze on her drink, steadily avoiding eye-contact.

"How—? What—? *When*—?" Jenn stutters. For all her apathy, even *she* knows how important the bookclub is to the town. Though it's saucy name is new, it's been around for *decades*. Touching My Shelf is the town's most exclusive (and only) club.

"What? What happened to the book club? Isn't Touching My Shelf like, I don't know, harder to get into than Studio 54 in the seventies?"

"Studio *what*?" Jenn asks, making me shiver.

"Seriously, Jenn?"

"Nice reference, Bonnie. Are you secretly sixty-five?" Adri rolls her eyes.

But my sister-in-law ignores her, pressing for more answers. "Seriously, what happened? That book club was so important to the town, and not to mention what it did for you when—"

I kick her under the table, trying not to bring up how that it basically helped save my sister's life through the darkest point of her depression. It's what got her out of bed during a very low low.

"I—" Bonnie coughs. "I mean, I thought you were really into it."

But the book club shutting down isn't upsetting just because of what it could mean for my sister. It's also huge for our small community. You wouldn't believe it, but it has become the lifeline for so many of the women in this town over the years. For some, Touching My Shelf is the only place they feel safe enough to blow off some steam and get some space from the people they see every day—a necessity in Ceres Cove.

"Of course I was into it," Adri sighs. "But you know Melanie? Melanie Miller? Well, she met this rando online on some Discord channel for train model collector's and fell in love. Now she's moving down to Florida, which means we can't keep the club going. Out of all of us, she was the only one who could host the meetings. So we have to shut down since we have nowhere else to go."

"What?" I scoff. "How is that possible? *None of you* can host?"

"Well, there's no way *I* can host," she snorts. "We live in a two-bedroom with three boys and a husband who watches sports on loud from the very *second* he gets home, in case you've forgotten. There would be absolutely no peace and quiet. And honestly, one way or another, it's kind of the same situation for all of us. Touching My Shelf isn't just about reading books and discussing them. It's—*was*—our girl bonding time. And now it feels like we lost the safe place to do so."

"Are you telling me Melanie was the only reason this club could keep going?" Jenn asks.

"Kind of. She's divorced and has no kids. The only other one that could work is Casey's house, but she has three cats and two of the girls are super allergic to them."

"I find it really difficult to believe that eight women can't find a safe space to talk about *books* and blow off some steam. Like, can't you ask your husband to take the kids for like three hours or something? Or find anywhere else to do it that isn't one of your homes?" Bonnie asks.

"Where? Tell me if you can think of anything, because we're stumped," she says, looking defeated.

"What about our place?" Bonnie asks.

Adriana grimaces. "No offense, girl. But your house, though bigger, is busier than mine. Don't your girls always have friends over from their soccer team or any one of their other extracurriculars and stuff?" I open my mouth to volunteer my loft but—"And before *you* offer up your place, do you really think you could comfortably fit eight women in your tiny living area?"

I puff, wanting so very badly to find a solution. "What about a restaurant? The bar?"

"No, no." She shakes her head in frustration. "The restaurant is too family-friendly and we don't particularly like to filter ourselves. And the bar is too seedy. Like, I don't think it would be all that great to talk about the hot guys we read about with the gross ones from town or even passersby hitting on us, the smell of stale beer drenching our clothes. No. No, thank you."

"What if you admit a new member? Someone who'd be down to give you guys the space to participate?"

"Lottie, sweetie. We tried. A lot of people don't think Touching My Shelf is cool anymore." Adri frowns.

"It *did* originate during the Fabio days," Bonnie says.

"*Who?*" Jenn looks around at us like we're speaking Klingon.

"Oh, honey," Bonnie whispers, patting the back of her hand.

But I ignore them, looking back at my sister. "I just think—"

"Can we stop talking about this, please?" Adri says, putting her foot down, final.

We sit on this news for a beat, quiet as I'm sure we all process the information.

"Well, I'm sorry to hear that. Truly. I feel like our town is just…" I sigh. *Shit*, is what I want to say. But there's something keeping me from saying it, holding me back. Because while I realize I may not like it here, so many people still do. And based on my brother's reaction from earlier, I should probably start keeping some of those opinions to myself.

Plus, Jenn already stated the fact. No need to bum everyone out by expanding on it, right?

"Yeah, it's definitely lacking a few necessities. We should at least have a cool hangout, for one. It's kind of ridiculous that we had to drive over forty minutes to get here just so we could have a night out at a decent place."

Adriana takes a sip of her drink and shrugs. "It is what it is."

"I know what you mean," Bonnie sighs. "Adriana's right. I love my girls and I'm so happy they're happy with their friends and their goddamn soccer team. But I just want to take some time to myself. Have a place where I can relax." She downs her drink. "God, I'm a terrible mother."

"*No*," I tell her. "You're a human with perfectly normal needs."

Bonnie nods, but looks away guiltily.

Always with the perfect timing, Jenn swoops in to steer the conversation elsewhere: "I think we should get back to a more cheerful topic. To the reason why we're all here tonight. I'd like to raise a toast to the uterus we hate the most!"

"*This* is more cheerful?" my sister mutters, rolling her eyes. She hasn't kept her opinion on my hysterectomy a secret.

Jenn ignores her comment and raises a shot glass in the air, laughing. Bonnie and I follow suit, but Adriana is slow to join.

My favorite redhead reaches out to clasp my hands in hers. "I know you've postponed the surgery while we finish this project, but I want to congratulate you for taking charge of your body, for being brave. I'm so happy you'll finally find some relief."

My eyes water at Jenn, my little Gen Z firecracker. I'm going to miss her so much when I'm gone. When we're *both* gone.

"Thanks, Jenn. Seriously. And though I thought this whole thing was weird as hell, at first, I'm so glad you planned this for me." A bit teary-eyed, I raise my glass a little higher in the air. "Thanks for the memories, uterus of mine. I can't wait to get rid of you."

And with that, we all take a sip of our drinks. Except for Jenn, of course, who knocks back another shot.

I chuckle at her puckered face after she downs her lemon drop, shaking her shoulders.

She's so young.

"How are you even drinking, by the way? You're nineteen."

"I gave the hot bartender my fake ID," she shrugs. At my mock-disappointed face, she rolls her eyes. "Chill, *Mom*."

Adriana sucks in a breath. *"You can't call her that*, Jenn," she practically hisses.

"Especially not tonight."

I roll my eyes at my sister and sigh. "Thanks for coming to my 'defense'," I air-quote, "but it's unnecessary. I can take a joke."

"It's just *sad*. And this whole night is fucking sad and stupid. No offense, Jenn. I know you organized this thing thinking it would be cool and fun and a way to make things easier on Lottie. But I just think this whole night is depressing and never should've happened."

"Adriana," Bonnie warns.

"Seriously. How is this even okay? I don't want to celebrate the fact that you're sterilizing yourself. I don't want to celebrate the fact that you're giving up. And I sure as hell don't want to celebrate you securing yourself a lifetime of loneliness and solitude just from a little pain, some silly, little cramps."

Rage strikes my body like lightning, coursing through my veins, lighting my skin on fire.

"*A little pain*? Silly, little cramps? *Are you fucking kidding me?*" I struggle to keep my voice down, to keep from losing my ever-loving shit on her. Still, a few people in neighboring tables turn to shoot me a wary look. "Did you know that the pain from endometriosis has been compared to *labor pains*? Do you even realize what that means? And it's not like it happens just when I'm on my period. It's almost *all the time* now. Almost every goddamn day. Debilitating, exhausting pain. And the bloating, the sick joke of looking six months pregnant when several doctors have told me that while it isn't impossible for most women with endometriosis to have children it is for *me*. It's sick and fucked and I. Am. *Tired*. I am... I'm done. That, combined with the PCOS? I'm over it. I can barely stand it anymore. The surgery won't cure the endo, but maybe it will help."

Bonnie and Jenn pretend to look anywhere but at us, successfully predicting where I'm about to go with this.

"I just—I just think if you hold on, if you just hold on for the right man or do some more fertility treatments, if you just *wait*, then—"

"I held on for as long as I could. I did all the fertility treatments. I've done *three* endo surgeries to remove the tissue and every time it comes back. I put my body and myself through hell. And I am so fucking tired of it controlling my life. Moreover, I no longer feel like my world is going to end because I can't have kids. I look at it as having an entirely new window of opportunity open for me."

"But you won't get to have a family, and what if you meet a man who—"

"I don't need a man in life. I want to focus on my health

getting better, on getting my career back on track after everything I've been through."

She shakes her head vigorously, tears running down her cheeks. And it makes me *angry*.

I should be the one crying. *I* should be the one throwing a bitch fit right now.

But I've done my time. I've cried my tears. I've been through all the stages of grief several times. I don't need this.

"Who's going to take care of you when you're older, huh? You're going to die alone."

"Having kids shouldn't be about *breeding* a future caregiver," I hiss.

"You know what I mean." She grimaces. "I think you're making a mistake by quitting like this—"

"I'm not quitting!" I throw my hands in the air, frustrated. "I am doing the opposite of quitting, Adriana. *I am taking back control.* Of my life, of my body. Of my goddamn future. For way too long I focused on *one* thing, on *one* image of what my life was supposed to look like. But I can't keep holding on to that because it is just not in the cards for me. Having kids is not in the cards. And you know what? That's *okay*. Me having this hysterectomy? It doesn't feel like giving up. It feels empowering. It feels like taking lemons and making lemonade. I have choices now. I can focus on myself. I can stop having to think about another's person's wants other than my own."

Her lower lip trembles, and I can tell she's just bursting with more words I can't stomach right now. It's taken a lot for me to be "okay" with my situation. But I am. And I will not let myself be dragged down again by whatever conventional ideals my sister has for me.

"I feel so sorry for you that you think this is okay."

"*Adriana*," Bonnie bumps her shoulder, shooting her a look. "Stop."

"No, don't try and shut her up. I know exactly how she feels about this whole thing—it isn't a secret. I was devastated when I finally realized I couldn't have kids. And trying wrecked me for years—we all know this. But I love being an aunt. I love not having to deal with the kids after we're done playing. But instead of supporting my decision, of trying to understand it, you keep pushing these ideas when I've already come to peace with my decision."

"How can you come to peace with the fact that you're going to spend the rest of your life alone? You just told us you won't date another man because of what happened with Finn, because they'll want something you can't give them. You won't even try to date a guy who tells you he doesn't want kids because you're scared he'll take it back."

Because that's what Finn did. He didn't want kids, and then he took it back.

"You're going to be *alone for the rest of your life.*"

I chew on my lower lip, shaking in anger, wishing I could suddenly develop magical powers to get out of here with the blink of an eye. "I'm not going to die alone. And it's not like I'm done with men forever. I can still have flings."

She scoffs. "Honey, you won't even go out for coffee with Knox, a man who seems like a prime candidate for a fling. You really expect me to believe you can handle that? You're too scared. And don't you dare deny it because I can see it in your eyes. You're not strong enough."

It's like a record scratch cutting through all the noise in the lounge, like an atomic bomb in the shape of a single sentence. It cuts through the room like a samurai sword, leaving everyone speechless.

"*Dude,*" Jenn whispers, dropping her face in her hands.

"*I'm not strong enough?*"

We've garnered the attention of everyone in the room by now, the patrons of the place having overheard the most intimate details of my life thanks to my sister's stupid outburst. And I am done. So fucking done.

Her lips tremble, eyes teary as she shakes her head.

"I think you lack resilience."

I scoff, and if I wasn't seething with rage, I am now. "I keep resilience in fucking business, Adriana. If there's someone at this table who truly knows what that is, it's me."

I fist my hands at my sides, a million more rebuttals running through my head. I want to tell her where she can go, I want to tell her to mind her own business. I want to tell her all about the judgments I can also make about her life but choose to keep quiet everyday because it's her life, not mine.

Instead, I choose to do the right thing: I pick up my bag, my coat, and walk away, my head held up high.

I'll show you just how strong and resilient I can be.

CHAPTER NINETEEN

KNOX

I click through this week's images—the before and after of the demo, the crew working, some shots around town, Jenn helping pack up some more rare books to sell, and Lottie. Dozens and dozens of pictures of Lottie.

I can't help it—she's my... muse? I gag. I've always hated that word, associating it more to artists suffering from obsession and a self-centered someone loving the attention. But what I feel for Lottie isn't that. It's based on real experience and knowledge of her as a person. And if there's someone who's less of a Pick Me Girl, it's Lottie. She'd hate it if I ever called her my muse. But as I scroll through, she's in almost every frame of my memory card, making it a little difficult to pinpoint exactly who she is to me if not that.

Sure, she's my business partner—friend, even. But fuck me if looking at pictures of her doesn't make my chest tighten in a way that tells me that's not at all what she is to me. I pore over each and every single frame: Lottie focused at her desk, brows scrunched in that way I find nothing short of adorable; Lottie alone in the office, gazing at her Post-It mural with admiration; Lottie laughing with her sister and Jenn at the store closing party, her face shining with a lightness that wasn't there the night I met her all these weeks ago; and so many more I wish I could print and wallpaper this entire apartment with (in a super, non-creepy way, I promise.).

Lottie Veracruz might not be my *muse* per se, but she's become the center of my universe, that's for damn sure. There's no other reason why I should be thinking about her at one in the morning while I'm home alone in bed on a Friday night. There's no other reason why my mind should be filled with her laugh and her voice and her strength 24/7.

I need it to stop. I need it to stop, because we agreed that nothing would happen and what I feel for her has only gotten stronger and I can't keep going like this.

I groan, running my fingers through my hair as I put my computer away, too wound up now to go to bed. "I need a cold shower," I mutter to myself, throwing the covers off myself in frustration. But as soon as my feet hit the cold floor, there's a knock on my door.

I freeze, thinking maybe I've lost my mind and am imagining Walter's ghost has come back to haunt me. Or maybe it's some local trying to murder me.

Or maybe you've been watching too many true crime documentaries on Netflix, you dumbass.

Another knock, a little harder this time, has me jogging quickly to the door, peeking through the peephole.

"*Lottie?*" I pull the door open, fully ready to ask her what she's doing here so late when I see her full outfit.

And I want to die.

Because standing right in front of me, Lottie looks hotter than I've ever seen her before. In a flared red dress with a low neckline where the skirt hits a couple of inches over the knee, she stands before me looking like every straight man's dream. And those heels... I can't help but immediately wonder what they'd look like with her legs wrapped around my neck.

I groan and pinch the bridge of my nose, squeezing my eyes shut. "Jesus, Lottie. You can't just show up to my apartment late at night looking like this. I'm already dying every day when I see you. But now I'm gonna have this image burned in my brain forever."

I want to photograph her for hours from every angle. Then I want to strip her, fuck her, and photograph her naked body even more. I need even more photographic evidence that a woman of this caliber even exists. That *she* fucking exists.

I squeeze my eyes shut to concentrate, remove the temptation of wanting to wrap my arm around her waist and kiss her crazy. "This is gonna sound horrible, but please tell me no other guy saw you dressed like that. It'll fucking kill me." She chuckles half-heartedly. "Seriously, though. I know it sounds possessive and uncool, and it's not like we're together, but I do not give a shit."

She snorts. "If I look so good, then why won't you look at me."

"I can't," I swallow and shake my head. "I'm trying hard to respect your boundaries, and I'm pretty sure I won't be able to keep myself from gawking at you right now. That, and I don't know if I'd be able to concentrate enough to understand what you're saying."

An exasperated sigh, a shuffle of feet. "Knox. Please. It's important."

The serious tone of her voice puts me on high alert, pulling me out of my fog. Is she here because she's in trouble? Is that why she's here this late at night?

"Everything okay?"

"*Yes*. Can you please open your eyes and let me in before I lose my nerve, you weirdo?"

I steel myself and open one eye with caution, which makes her laugh. "C'mon, silly." She shoves me lightly and pushes through into my apartment, leaving me awestruck at the door. Was that... flirty? Or did I imagine it?

I close the door behind me, pulse racing, as she takes the apartment in.

"It looks so different now," she breathes, brown eyes scanning the apartment. "Total day-to-night transformation. In the best possible way."

"Yeah?" I smile, eating up her compliment.

"Absolutely," she nods, grinning back at me. "Gone are the rebinding supplies and the stacks of books. Gone is the dust and the clutter. Walter's apartment went from near-unlivable conditions to being neat and almost, dare I say, *homey*." She gasps, her eyes falling on the corner of the loft where my bed is. "You even have an accent rug and blanket!" she points out, pleasantly surprised.

I bark out a laugh. "I found them hidden in the back of a closet, where I moved the rest of the books to. Then I threw some other random shit in boxes and stuffed them into the front closet. It's all squished in there, ready to blow, but I made it work."

"So you went through all his stuff?"

"Not yet. Haven't had the time," I lie. For some reason, I haven't been able to bring myself to sift through Walter's things. Every time I sit down to try, I get this horrible pit in my stomach, filling me with the need to walk away. Eventually, I decided to pack his things up and hide them in the front closet. Outta sight, outta mind.

"I can help you. If you want." The corners of her lips quirk up.

"Yeah?" It *would* be nice to have someone there to help me go through it.

"Yeah. Definitely." Lottie nods. "It must be hard. To deal with this part all on your own. I'd like to help, if I can."

"You cold?" I ask when I watch her rub her arms gently.

"Shoot, I must've left my coat in the cab."

I run over to the hook by the door before she has a chance to respond and gently place my leather jacket over her shoulders, ignoring the way seeing her wearing it makes me feel (i.e. like a caveman. *Mine*, I think).

She burrows deeper into my jacket. I think I catch her putting her nose to it, inhaling its scent, but it's probably just wishful thinking.

"Thank you. For the jacket." Her smile is soft, and I can tell there's quite a bit of hesitation.

I almost beg her to keep it, wanting to see her wear it every day for the rest of my life. "No worries."

An awkward silence falls over us as we just stare at each other. I try to ignore the fact that those high heels have brought her lips at least three inches closer to mine, but it's a little difficult to do when she's standing *right there*, looking so good, smelling of caramel. *Mouthwatering.*

"So, not that I mind—because I really, really don't—but what exactly is so urgent that it brought you to my place at one A.M? I know my talent for décor wasn't it."

She laughs softly before worrying her lower lip with her teeth. I watch her cheeks blush as she looks down at her feet, wrapping my jacket tighter around herself. "I wanted to talk to you."

"Yeah, I figured you weren't here to play a couple of rounds of backgammon."

"Backgammon." She smiles.

I shrug. "First thing that popped into my head."

She takes a deep breath before meeting my eyes again. "God, you're going to hate me," she whispers. My stomach rolls, every possible scenario—from the best to the worst—running through my mind.

"Not possible. Ever. Just... tell me."

She sighs. "I know... I know we talked about this multiple times. About us being friends and being professionals..." She pauses, wanting to torture me, apparently.

"Yeah?" My heart beats so fast it could sign up to race in Formula 1. But I try like hell to play it cool because if there's even the slightest chance that this is headed where I think it's heading...

"Well, so I was thinking..." She exhales and takes a step closer. The palm of her right hand comes over my chest to rest just above my heart. I'm sure by now she can feel how hard it beats against my ribs, the way her mere presence affects me—especially when she's looking like this. It's warm and comforting and makes me want to melt against her. Her touch, inviting as it is, seems more like a surrender, an admission, rather than an intentionally seductive act.

She swallows once, her eyes on her hand, my chest. "I was thinking," she continues, "while I was out... I was thinking that I really like you." Her fingers curl, lightly fisting my shirt in her hands. "And I guess I just thought you should know. Just thought I would be honest and stop trying to hide it. I want to—" She pauses. "I was thinking maybe we could give this a shot. *Us.* Go slow. Keep it casual. But... But give it a shot."

There's a ringing in my ears as I process everything she says, half of me not trusting it. Am I still dreaming? Is this all a sick dream my subconscious decided to throw at me? A car alarm blaring outside and the cold gust of air coming from my open window, raising goosebumps on my skin alerts me to the fact that I'm not.

This isn't a dream; I'm awake. And she's here, looking better than I ever imagined she could. But this all seems too good to be true.

"Are you drunk?" I blurt out. I knew from our earlier conversation today that she had plans to go out tonight. And by the looks of her outfit, it definitely wasn't anywhere in town.

Where did they go? Did they meet up with some guys? Was she with anyone earlier?

God, the thought alone makes me nauseous.

"What?" Her eyes widen as she physically recoils.

"I'm sorry, but I have to ask. You went out with your friends at a girls' night to a nightclub—"

"Lounge. And I'd barely call it that," she corrects me.

"Whatever. You were just out with your friends, drinking, and now you show up at my doorstep in the middle of the night looking like pure sin and telling me you want to stop denying that you like me? Are you gonna regret this tomorrow? Because I don't wanna go through the same thing I did the first night we met. Unlike you, I can very openly admit that I like you and want something to happen here." I point back and forth between us. "I don't wanna end up feeling like I was a mistake all over again." I do my best to not let the pain her abandonment caused bleed into my voice, but I'm not sure I do such a great job.

Dammit.

"I made you feel like you were a *mistake*?" she whispers, frowning, eyes filled with regret. She shakes her head, as if disappointed in herself. "I have *never* felt that way about you. Did I feel like it was..." She winces, struggling to find the right words. "*Inconvenient* given the situation? Yes. But *you*—you were never a mistake to me."

"I don't know that '*inconvenient*' sounds any better, here," I grumble.

She closes her eyes and blows a puff of air through her lips. "I just mean that it sucked that we were thrown into this situation because I hated walking away from you that first night. And when you first walked into the store, I was both terrified and ecstatic to see you again. But then when we found out we were inheriting the business together, that we had to work side by side... I knew it was wrong to pursue anything. So the whole thing was, yeah, *inconvenient*."

I nod, hands on my hips. "So, if all the same facts remain as before, what's changed that I don't know about? Why are you here at one A.M. in my apartment telling me you want to give it a shot?" I have to ask, because I can't take her flip-flopping us one more time.

She shrugs. "I feel like I deserve to go after what I want. And I feel like, if we set boundaries—"

"*More* boundaries?"

She smiles. "*Different* boundaries. If we set different types of boundaries, maybe we can enjoy each other's company in a different way."

I narrow my eyes at her. "What kind of way?"

"C'mon, Knox." She looks away, blushing. Still, she takes a step closer toward me, both hands on my chest, now. "You know what I mean."

I fist my hands at my sides, fighting the urge to put them on her hips, her waist, every inch of her smooth and soft body. Because I am not touching her until I know *exactly* what she means.

"Lottie. You need to tell me what you want." My breathing is ragged—embarrassing. I'm a horse gearing up for a race, the tension building as a gate holds me back from the finish line: *her*.

"I want *you*, Knox. I want you."

CHAPTER TWENTY

KNOX

I swallow and shake my head, certain I'm dreaming now. "What?" I've been waiting so long to hear those words come from her mouth.

"But—" *Ah, here comes the catch.* "But I can't handle anything serious with you. I care about you, and I want us to —to hang out, see each other. But you're leaving after we sell the bookstore, going back to your old life, and I sure as hell am gone as soon as the check clears. And... There are just things that I'll never be able to—" She stops and takes a deep breath, her expression switching to a more serious one. "I just think we really like each other and are both adults and should be able to have a casual relationship while you're still here."

"And by *casual* relationship you mean...?"

"A sexual one, yes." She clears her throat while I choke on my own spit. "And dates, I guess."

"You guess?"

She takes a deep breath. "I like you, Knox."

I grin down at her, placing a hand on her hip and pulling her in a little closer. "I mean, if we're being honest, you've done a shit job at hiding it, Lottie, so I'm glad you're done with that. I think what you mean is that you're done denying it."

She looks up at me with warm chocolate eyes but doesn't say anything. I cup her face in my hands, all humor gone. "But are you serious? Is this what you want? Because I'm done with the back-and-forth. I don't want you flip-flopping. Honestly, at this point, I'm so into you I don't think I could take it." My voice comes out a little too pained for comfort, but I rally. She just asked for *casual*, and that definitely didn't sound like it. "If we're going to do this... If we're gonna do this, I need your word that you're not gonna wake up tomorrow and disappear on me. That you aren't gonna just up and change your mind. Even if this whole thing is *casual*."

"Knox... I can promise you that it is highly unlikely that I will wake up tomorrow and change my mind about this. Short of finding out you're a serial killer, I think we're good for now. But no one can guarantee the future. I can't make any major promises. I won't. So for now, given our circumstances, how about we decide to just live in the moment? Relationships are messy. Let's just... *be*. Hang out together. Enjoy each other's company until we each go our own way."

"Jesus," I drop my hands from her face, shove them into my hair. "I'm not asking you to move in with me, marry me, have my kids." She winces, her eyes dropping to my chest. "Hey, look at me," I say softly. "I'm just asking you not to disappear in the middle of the goddamn night again. Can you promise me that?"

Her hands slide up my chest, lace behind my neck as she presses up against me. And I can't help the way my lids drop halfway at the feel of her—her warmth, her softness.

"How about this? How about I commit to us for now, and promise to say goodbye before I leave again? And you do the same."

The thought of never seeing her again, of her disappearing from my life leaves an unsavory taste in my mouth I can't wait to get rid of. And why are we talking about endings before we've really even begun? I get she's coming into this after her divorce, but she reads enough romance novels for me to say with certainty that she can't really be *that* jaded. She can't be. Someone who doesn't believe in love wouldn't be able to read about two people (or sometimes more, according to her e-reader) overcoming all obstacles to find love. She's hurt—at the very least a little bruised still— and just needs me to be patient.

I can be patient.

I can show her that I'm not going to purposefully hurt her. That I'm not here to get in her way or use her. Until then, I'll take whatever I can get.

"Okay. Let's agree to enjoy whatever time we have together. I'd like that."

I try to give her my best smile, ignoring the nagging feeling that, despite her fears, *I'm* the one who's more likely to get hurt here—not her.

"So... Are we good?" There's a slight tremble in her voice

—it warms my chest, makes me grin so wide I feel it in my cheeks.

I want to say yes. I'm fucking *dying* to say yes. But this woman has been the center of everything for me—all I've been able to think of for the past few weeks. And if I say yes to this, to her, I'll be agreeing to expiration dating her. To letting myself fall deeper and deeper, all the while knowing that I can't keep her forever.

For a split second, I almost consider saying no. But then she looks up at me through those long lashes of hers and I know that I'm done.

"Knox. Are we good?" she asks again. "Because I've been dreaming of kissing you again for ages."

"The feeling is mutual." And without another word, I band an arm around her waist, pulling her even closer still, tilting her chin up to me with my other hand to press my lips to hers.

I'll take whatever you give me.

The kiss doesn't start off slow—not even for a second. As soon as our lips touch it's like a flame to tinder, a fire erupting through us. There's no doubt, no small hesitation. We melt into each other, our bodies molded perfectly in the same, familiar way they did all the other times we kissed before.

You were made for me, I think. *And I was definitely made for you.*

She whimpers in my mouth when I tug on her lower lip with my teeth and I almost lose it, my already hard dick now like stone. As her tongue teases my lips, parting them with a moan, I realize that this isn't lust I'm feeling. The way she cups my face, angling it to better kiss me, the way my hand spans her lower back, holding her tightly to me... It's so much more.

As I spin us both to press her against the wall by the door, my lips traveling down her neck, I can't help but breathe everything I'm feeling against her sweet skin. *Beautiful* and *feel so damn lucky* and *can't believe this is finally happening* and *I never want this to end* all while a fist tightens around my heart.

I'm so goddamn terrified by how much I want this.

I gently nip at her neck as I push my jacket off her shoulders. With satisfaction, I watch Lottie's skin cover in goosebumps at the loss, making me want to run my tongue over them.

"Cold?" I tease, laughing into her neck.

She pants, fisting the back of my shirt. "The opposite, actually."

"Oh, yeah? Then maybe we should stop. Let you cool down?"

She glares at me. "On second thought, I'm cold. Freezing, really. Need some warmth. Body heat."

"Ah, well, I can definitely help with *that*." I grin, covering Lottie with my body once more.

My fingers play with the zipper of her dress, lightly tugging, wordlessly asking for permission. She grabs my face in her hands and nods before pulling my lips back to hers. I work it quickly, the *zrrp* of the zipper combining with the sounds of her moans and whimpers making it the most erotic soundtrack I've ever heard in my life.

Desperately, we work together to push her dress down her body, letting it fall at her feet before she kicks it away.

"Jesus Christ." I pant, eyes roaming every inch of her body.

Lottie's face and chest flush in embarrassment for some reason.

"You're beautiful." The words burst through me, just like they did before. "So goddamn beautiful." My hands travel on their own accord up and down her sides while my eyes soak in the view in front of me: gorgeous, soft Lottie in a forest green lace lingerie set, hair wild, eyes low-lidded, perfect lips kiss-bruised.

She is my fantasy come to life.

I run the tip of one finger over the line of her bra raising a new set of goosebumps over her skin. I want to pull it down over her breasts, run my tongue over her hard nipples. But, *slow*. I want to take things *slow*. Savor her and this moment.

"You look like a dream. Did you wear this for me tonight? Or for someone else?" My fingertips dig possessively into her skin, grip tightening. And I hate how the thought of another man popped into my head, almost ruining this moment. And I certainly don't wanna come off as the possessive asshole who—

She smiles, bites her lip. She... likes the possessiveness?

"No," she shakes her head.

Intrigued, I test out my new theory.

"You sure?" My voice is gravelly, a bit harsh as my grip around her tightens just enough. "Because you're *mine*, now."

Her eyes widen with excitement, but she controls her

features, shifting them into one of innocence. "I know I am. But I didn't wear this for anyone else. I wore it for myself."

"Fuck, that's even hotter. I love your confidence." I groan, running my finger between her tits, down her abdomen, to the edge of her thong. "You weren't wearing anything like this the night we met. Not that I'm complaining. It's just... *Fuck*." I lean in to give her a drugging kiss, but it's my knees that grow weak as my lips travel down her neck, in between her chest. "You look incredible in lingerie and heels. Good enough to eat." As if to prove my point, I nip at her collarbone, licking the sting away before moving below. I flick her nipple with my tongue over her bra, wetting it, biting it through the thin delicate fabric.

"Noted," she gasps, her arms looping themselves around my neck as if she's lost all ability to support herself.

"Don't worry. I've got you, baby," I growl in her ear. My hands slide down her waist, under her panties, cupping her round ass, pulling her closer to me so she can feel my dick pressed against her.

"Knox—"

"I know. But not yet."

My mouth moves over to her other breast before hooking a finger into each bra cup, pulling them down and over, exposing and pushing her tits up.

"*Jesus*," I groan, before ducking to pull one of her nipples between my teeth, twisting and pulling the other with my fingers.

She moans my name, gasping when I pull harder, twist tighter, making me harder than I've ever been in my entire life. "Hold on tight to me," I order, because I need one hand on her tit while I send the other on a *very* important mission.

"No," she whines. "I need your hands on me."

I laugh gently against her breasts. "Oh, don't worry. They'll be on you. I just need to check something."

My right hand travels south, dipping into her underwear and— "You're *soaked*." I groan, nearly coming in my pants.

She gasps in my ear. "*God,* yes."

I part her folds with my middle finger, tapping her clit in a way that makes her entire body shiver. And her *moans*... The way she says my name as I enter her, first with one finger, then with two... I nearly lose it in my pants. I move in and out of her, mimicking the movements I plan to do with my dick later, all while pressing my heel to her clit. Her little moans nearly bring me to the edge, so I punish her with a sharp tug of my teeth on her nipple and a calculated stroke and then—

She's coming, moaning my name as her channel clenches around my fingers, her hands gripping my shoulders, pulling on my hair as she convulses in my arms nearly bringing me to my knees.

"Did you just—"

Flushed, she begs, "Take me to bed. Take me to bed *now*."

"I will, but you need to understand that *I'm* in charge now," I growl. Without another word, I throw her over my shoulder, fireman style, and walk a whole ten steps over to the bed, tossing her on the mattress in a way that makes her whimper.

"I'm going to make you scream."

CHAPTER TWENTY-ONE

LOTTIE

"Ohmygodyesplease." I moan, barely coherent now.

I sit up, working the straps of my shoes, only to have him stop me with a hand around each wrist. "Leave them on."

I smirk at him. "You have a shoe fetish I don't know about? Because it's fine if you do."

"No. Just a *Lottie-naked-in-these-heels* fetish." He laughs, pulling his white t-shirt over his head in one fluid movement. My mouth waters, taking in every muscle, every ripple and valley of this man's chest, eyes tracing the ink so carefully drawn over his taut, tan skin. "How often do you work out. My god."

"Never." And I believe him.

"Ah, to have a twenty-seven-year old's metabolism."

Knox rolls his eyes at me with a smile before ducking to kiss me. He pulls away and cups my face in his hands. "You're beautiful."

For a moment, we don't speak. We just stare into each other's eyes, his glacier blue, yet warm at the same time.

The way his gaze roams over me, a combination of heat and hunger and something else, has my pulse racing even quicker, my breathing coming in even shallower. I want him, yes, but more than anything I crave his closeness, the feel of him. It's not the orgasm I find myself chasing, but the chance at connecting with him once again.

Suddenly overwhelmed by this unnamed emotion, I pull him down and over me, his body covering mine. Quickly, we move to pull down his pajama bottoms and underwear all at once, watching with awe as he springs free. Almost immediately, though, he pulls away, sitting at the edge of the bed despite my protests.

"Shit."

"What? What's wrong? Come back." I don't care if I sound like I'm begging. The way I feel right now, I'd happily do so.

"I—*shit*—I don't have anything."

"You don't have anything of what?"

"I don't *have* anything."

"Okay, that still doesn't say—"

He looks at me like I'm dense, and maybe I am, but there's very little my brain can process when he's naked like that.

"I don't have a condom. I used everything I had that night we spent together. Haven't purchased any since."

"You've been flirting with me shamelessly for weeks, but never thought to purchase a box of condoms just in case?"

"Didn't want to jinx it," he says bashfully. "For the

record, I'm clean, haven't slept with anyone since you or anyone for a long time before that. But..." He drops his face into his hands, groaning in frustration.

"Oh, I—" I swallow, considering my options. "I haven't had sex without a condom since my ex and I separated, and I'm good. I went to the doctor recently and..." I cough a little, suddenly feeling a little embarrassed. But we're adults, goddamnit. "And, well, birth control wise..." How do you tell a man you're about to sleep with that you can't have children? Situationally, it's good news. But in reality, it's a freaking bummer, right? I don't want to ruin this night by bringing it up. This thing between us, it's not meant to be permanent at all. Which means he doesn't need to know that I can't do the one thing women are supposed to do. That I'm broken. "You don't need to worry about the birth control part. We're good." It's the best I can do without getting into it.

He turns to look at me, eyes wide. "Yeah?"

"Yeah."

"You sure?" I can tell how hard Knox works to maintain his self-control, but the mask drops as he licks his bottom lip, his eyes dropping to my chest, my legs. He reaches out and runs a hand over my calf, travels up over my knee toward my inner thigh. His light touch sparks the heat inside me once more, the possessive squeeze he gives my legs just inside my thighs running an electric current through me. "Because we could also just do *other things*." The look in his eyes, starved, predatory, has me melting atop his bed as he hooks his fingers into my lace thong and gently, so slowly, pulls it down.

"How about we do those *other things* and more?" I sit up and pull his face to mine, kissing him, running my tongue over his lower lip.

"Yeah," he whispers against me. "Yeah, that sounds good." "Good." I grin, looking up at him.

His eyes darken and his hands come to my shoulders in one quick movement. "Now be a good girl and lie back while I taste you." I gasp as he pushes me back, my body shivering with the sound of his commanding voice.

"I love it when you take control," I can't help but say. I blush in embarrassment at the confession, covering my face with my hands.

"I know you do," he says against my skin, kissing what feels like every inch me, stopping to unhook my bra.

"You do?" I look down at him, watching him watch me as he travels down my body.

"I do. Because you spend the entire day in control of everything else, working, managing people, making sure things are going well. And by the end of the day, I know you must be tired. I *see* you, Lottie Veracruz. I see you and how you are every day. And I know losing control from time to time is exactly what you need."

He sees *me.*

I gasp. "I... I think you're right."

He grins that lopsided smile of his, his eyes full of the mischief I love. "I know I am. And now you're gonna just sit back and enjoy this."

Knox wraps his hands around my thighs and pulls me further down the mattress in one movement. And without any further preamble, he dips his face in between my legs and presses his lips there, kissing my pussy as if it were my mouth.

"*Jesus,*" I moan, my back arching off the mattress.

He groans into me, the vibrations from the noises coming from deep within his chest making the whole thing ten times better. Just as I'm recovering from the initial pleasure of his lips on me, of his hot breath on my wet folds, I feel the slow drag of his tongue over my clit and—

I feel incredibly empty, my body *aching* to be filled. God, it feels so good, but—

As if he could read my mind, Knox slides two fingers in me, making me almost cry in relief. He murmurs words of approval into me, but I can barely make them out, too caught up in a fog of pleasure and pure, unhinged happiness. Eyes closed, hands knotted in his hair, I come hard as he hooks his fingers in me, hitting me in just the right spot. My mind blanks, clenching around him during this life-altering moment.

He waits until I come down from my orgasm, but then he's on me, in me, and I am so deliciously full. He's big and it's a tight fit, but I'm pliant and wet from my come. His warm body over mine, pressing me into the mattress while he's inside me feels like the best thing I've ever felt.

"You feel better than I remember," he pants into my neck. "God, so good. It's so fucking good."

I want to scream *yes* and *it's better than good* and *I want this all the time*, but I can barely catch my breath as he moves in a near-punishing rhythm. Without warning, he sits up on his knees, pulling my legs to rest on his left shoulder. He wraps an arm around them while his right hand grips my hip and I fist the sheets below me.

"Your tits are incredible." He watches as they move with every one of his thrusts, absentmindedly kissing my ankles. His body is perfect and already glistening with a sheen of sweat when I run my hands over his chest, his abs. He's hard and soft all over, skin smooth and covered in tattoos and a smattering of hair.

I want to get to know every tattoo, every story behind them. I don't want to leave a single one out.

I watch as something in Knox's expression shifts, letting me know how close he really is.

"*Fuck*," he groans, pulling my legs at his side once more before falling over me. His right hand comes between us, his thumb circling my clit in quick, decisive movements and—

I'm so close. I'm so close.

"Good. That's good." He's breathless, growling like an animal, both of us sweaty from the exertion. Right before I feel the orgasm come over me, I tighten my legs around his waist and dig my nails into his back, unable to hold back the scream that rips through my chest.

I come in waves, over and over again. It feels never-ending in the best possible way. And when I'm finally done, I can tell he's on the edge, so close it's painful.

"Can I come inside you?" he barely manages to push out.

"*Yes*," I say, gripping him to me as it's his turn to lose control now.

CHAPTER TWENTY-TWO

LOTTIE

The softest of pressures against my forehead wakes me from my sleep, an arm tightening around my waist.

"Sorry," his voice is low and gravelly in my ear, its sound flooding me with memories from last night. "Didn't mean to wake you."

"Mmm. What... time is it?" I ask, mid-yawn, not even hiding that I don't want to move an inch from where I lay. I groan when I stretch, feeling the soreness in my joints and between my legs. The former, I'll wear with a badge of honor. I was bent in the most delicious ways last night. The latter serves merely as a reminder of the inconveniences of endometriosis: sex hurts sometimes. And not in a good way.

Don't let it ruin this moment, Lottie.

Knox wraps his other arm around my waist and tackles me when I try to sit up, rolling effortlessly on top of my body. Caging me between his arms, Knox starts kissing a line down my neck and chest. With a laugh, I put my palm to his forehead and push him away.

"Knox," I plead.

He sighs like I've just taken his favorite toy away from him, and rolls onto his side, resting his head on his elbow as he looks at me with a broad smile, dimples popping. "Still early. Around seven." He takes my hand in his and brings it to his lips, kissing each finger softly. I suck in a breath, trying not to get distracted by the tenderness of the moment, by the dangerous look in his eye. Not because it's the same predatory one he used before taking me, but because of the depth of the emotion I can see in them.

Knox's boyish grin makes another appearance before kissing the palm of my hand this time, pulling me away from the intense feeling building in my chest. "I had a lot of fun last night."

Throwing caution and restraint out the window, I roll into him, wrap an arm around his shoulders, and burrow into his chest. "Me too," I whisper.

"I wish we could stay in bed all day."

"Same," I breathe.

All too soon, he pulls away, reaching for something on his nightstand. I groan, pulling at him. "Come back."

He laughs softly at my whining. "Hold on, I want a picture of this."

"What?" I shriek, pulling the comforter up to cover myself.

Knox rolls his eyes at me, camera at the ready. "I'm not talking about photographing you naked. Although I'd be totally into that if you're interested. I just meant this moment right here." He aims the camara at me, although not quite directly at my face. Adjusts the zoom a few times, and snaps away.

"What moment? There is no moment."

"How can you say that?" He looks over at me, a smile in his eyes though he's completely serious. "This, right here. This is a moment. I wanna remember it always. I want there to be a record of this. You and me, waking up together for the first time." He makes it sound like we'll have a thousand more mornings like this, and I want them all.

My heart tightens in my chest, and suddenly I find myself at a loss for words. Panic creeps up my throat, tightening my airways. Does this behavior fall in line with "casual"?

But then he buries his face in my neck, inhaling the scent of my hair while holding the camera above us and I can barely think.

"And if *I* don't want to remember?" It's meant as a joke, but my voice comes out colder than expected.

He flinches for a second, pulling away. But his eyes are gentle when he says, "You're just gonna have to fight me on it, I guess." Knox launches himself at me after that, covering me with his entire body. With a squeal, I struggle to get away, laughing, but he holds me down, straddling my hips. With one hand, he takes hold of both my wrists and pins them above my head; with the other, he snaps another picture. "I'll keep you tied here all day if you don't cooperate." He laughs softly, hiding behind the camera.

"Stop, I give up!" I laugh, and he releases me, lying back down to flip through his photos with a gentle smile on his face.

"Can I at least see them?"

He smirks, glancing between me and the camera. "I don't think you're ready for what the camera has to say yet."

"Oh, yeah?" I sputter a laugh.

"Yeah."

"What, exactly, can a camera say, then?"

"Sorry, have you never heard of the expression a picture is worth a thousand words? It can say a whole lot."

Laughing, I roll to sit on the edge of his bed and stretch. I feel the heat of his chest against my back, his lips on my bare shoulder, inching up towards my neck. Strong arms wrap around my waist in a vice-like grip just as I turn my head just in time to meet him with a kiss.

"Don't go," he whispers gruffly against my lips. "Stay all day in bed with me."

I moan, pressing another kiss to his lips. "I can't. Have to open the store in a couple of hours. I need to go home and change before I meet with Luke again." I hear the slight rumble in his chest at my ex's name and suppress a smile.

"Easy, cowboy. We have to start building the new shelves and stuff, so there's a lot to review. I have responsibilities, you know. Grown-up stuff."

He releases me from his possessive grip, and I almost beg him to pull me to him once more. "And I'm not a grown-up? I seem to remember doing very grown-up things to you last night." His hands travel down my sides and to my front to cup my breasts.

I smirk, playfully slapping his hands away and getting to my feet, quickly pulling the tee he wore last night where it lay on the floor over my head. I sneak a deep inhale of it, snorting the scent coming off the softly worn fabric like an addict. "You know what I mean."

"Whoa, why are you covering yourself up?"

"Did you just miss the conversation we just had? I need to go."

"I already forgot. I was a bit distracted."

"Seriously, Knox. I need to get home, get dressed, and come back to work." I scuttle around his apartment, picking up my purse, dress, and underwear, searching for my bra under the bed. "Have you seen my bra? I can't find it."

He stretches out onto his back on the bed, feet crossed at the ankle, arms behind his head, body like a tatted up Greek god. "Nah. Tossed it sometime between orgasms the first time around."

I snort, checking under the bed again. "I can't believe you —" I stop dead in my tracks, my eyes catching on the midnight blue object on his nightstand. "What is that?" I ask, my voice trembling.

"Oh." He laughs, sitting up in bed. "Your e-reader. I may have taken it from your place when I was there."

"*What*? I've been looking all over the place for this," I shriek, taking it in my hands. I feel myself blush beet red in mortification. The amount of books I have on there that are just for spank bank material... "What the hell are you doing with it?"

"Research." He shrugs with a laugh, staring up at me with adoration.

"Re—*What*? Oh my god."

"You know, I was a little surprised to see just how many different romance sub-genres there are, but I gotta say, they're all really hot. Even the alien-human ones had me going there for a second. I can totally see why you'd be into them after reading parts of one."

My jaw drops, mortification freezing me in my place. "I cannot believe you went through my reader. That's like—that's like reading someone's journal."

"After everything I read, I think it's more like going through someone's browser history." He shrugs nonchalantly. "I don't know why you're so upset about this." He smiles up at me, pulling me towards him on the bed.

I press my hands on his chest, pushing him away.

"C'mon, Lottie," he says with a laugh. "You can't actually be mad. Sure, I stole it from your place. But I think it's hot. And no one said we couldn't recreate a few of the scenes in there. I'm actually looking forward to it. I can't take you to another planet or anything, and I wouldn't be down to have sex in the snow—shrinkage and all that—but I'm not opposed to a little body paint if you really want to recreate those alien books."

"Oh my god," I groan, skin heating, every inch of it covered in a deep crimson blush.

"That one book about the former child actress who does the dance competition has that incredibly hot sex scene in the park that I think we could totally recreate and—"

"Whoa! Spoiler alert! I haven't read that one yet. And how did you get through so many books in such a short amount of time?" I never pegged him as a fast reader.

He shrugs. "I've only read five of them, and just skipped to the good parts. All scenes we'll recreate in due time."

I snort, unable to resist his cheeky smile, the brightness

in his eyes as he talks about future plans between us. But I can't focus on that now, instead moving my thoughts to more pressing matters. "I am a sexual person—"

"I *definitely* know that."

"—and I will not be shamed for reading the books I read." "You shouldn't be. Read what you like." He shrugs.

"And I read other stuff besides smutty romances. I read contemporary romance, too. And thrillers and personal development books. I read business strategy, books, too. Did you not see those on there, too?"

"Duh, but I wasn't going to read those. I was more interested in other stuff. For research purposes. And you'll find no judgment from me. I'm not the type of guy to shit on someone's tastes. In fact, I think I might encourage this particular one. It gives me hope."

"What do you mean—?" But my alarm cuts me off, taking me back to more pressing matters. "We can talk about this later. Can I borrow a pair of sweats or something? I don't want to risk running into anyone dressed in last night's dress when I walk back home."

"You'd rather they see you in men's clothes?"

"It's just sweats—no one will know. In all honesty, I'd rather they think I'm a slob than a trollop."

He bursts out laughing. "A *trollop*? For sleeping over at the guy you're seeing's apartment? Really?"

My stomach lurches. For a split second, I start to wonder whether maybe he misunderstood last night. We agreed this was just casual, right? I begin to nervously run the conversation through my head, staring down at my feet.

"Hey." He moves, pulling on a pair of boxers before

walking over to me and taking my hands in his. "Stop freaking out. We're good, remember? We talked it all through last night."

"Right. Yes. And we're on the same page. About all of it? About us taking things easy?"

"Yeah, absolutely."

"Okay, good."

He leans down and presses a kiss to my lips, then another, before pulling away with a groan. "I hate that you have to leave." He drops my hands and walks over to one of two dressers below the window and pulls out a pair of grey sweatpants. "Here you go. Be careful of them slipping off or something. They might be too big."

I scoff. "That's cute of you to say, but we both know I have humongous hips." I take the sweats from him, placing my clothes atop a chair while I change.

"Jesus, why are you so mean to yourself?"

His words almost make me fall as I balance on one foot while I pull my sweats on the other. "What?"

"You're always making mean comments about your body. Why? So you're not influencer thin. Who gives a shit? You're fucking gorgeous."

"I—"

As if to prove a point, he walks over to me and runs his hands up and down my sides, cupping my bare ass as I officially drop the sweats and give up on my task. "I love your body." His eyes darken with need as his lips come down hard on me, demanding, punishing, telling me off for not appreciating myself and owning up to the curves he's shown me over and over again he so loves.

My hands lock in Knox's hair, body pressed up against his. It only takes a second for our bodies to kick into action. I feel his heart beat as quickly and as hard as mine, his breathing coming in just as ragged and choppy. And when one of his hands drags down my body, curving down my ass and squeezing it before moving down my thigh and hooking my leg over his hip, I feel his hardness against my stomach.

The heat builds between my legs, wanting more than just his kiss and touch, but Knox pulls away all too soon. "You're beautiful, and if I could, I'd fuck you every second of every minute of every hour of every goddamn day." I exhale unsteadily, trying to settle my breathing as his gaze locks on mine. The fire in his eyes dims slightly, cupping my face in his hands in that tender, loving way of his. "You're beautiful and smart and funny." A quick kiss. "And I can't thank the universe enough for ever leading me to you—especially given the circumstances. You are perfect, Carlota Veracruz. I just wish you'd believe it too."

I'm barely able to push out a, "Thank you," grasping his biceps, trying hard not to collapse.

"Plus," he continues, his expression losing some of its intensity, the corners of his lips quirking up. "Men love wider hips."

"Do they?" I smirk.

"Oh, one hundred percent. It's a whole biological thing. Ingrained in our nature, you know?"

"What are you talking about?" I laugh, shaking my head, recovering from the way his lopsided smile and words almost brought me to my knees.

"Wide hips are better for child bearing. Easier deliveries,

you know. That's why straight men like big butts and hips stuff. It comes from some primal instinct to reproduce."

Suddenly, all the air is sucked out of my lungs, my body paralyzed. I know it was a joke, but...

I can't hear Knox as he talks, laughing about something while he pulls a shirt over his bare chest. I turn around, my back to him while I try to regulate my breathing. In a sort of trance, I pull the sweatpants over my legs, pick my clothes, shoes, e-reader, and purse from the chair where I left them, and say,

"Okay, well, I guess I'll see you later."

From the look on his face, he was in the middle of a thought, my sudden change in demeanor disorienting. "You don't even want me to drive you?"

"Oh. I... I can walk."

Knox's face falls. "Are you serious? You'd rather walk in heels and sweatpants all the way home than be in a truck with me right now? Is this because of the kids comment?"

"I—"

"*Jesus*, I thought we went over this. I get it, we're taking it easy. No one's talking about a long-term commitment right now." It's the *right now* that's making it really difficult not to run for the hills. "I promise I'm not getting down on one knee after a night with you, okay? I really like you, Lottie, but gotta give me a little credit. I'm not an idiot." He huffs and walks over to his dresser, pulling out a pair of jeans and a sweater.

After he dresses, he drives me back home, the entire car ride enveloped in silence. When he parks outside my house, I don't immediately get out of the car, choosing instead to measure my words before I speak them aloud:

"I'm sorry. I don't know what got into me," I lie. "I guess I'm still getting used to this thing. You and I haven't really been a slow progression, you know? We went from meeting one night, jumping into bed together, to not seeing each other, to having you pursue me, only for me to fold after just a couple of weeks." I turn to look at him, but his eyes are straight ahead, lips pressed together. "Though we agreed that this was going to be a chill, easy... *thing*, it's the first time since my divorce that I've wanted to be exclusive with someone. That I've had the guts to do it. This isn't easy for me. And I know it sounds like an excuse, but it isn't."

I want to tell him the whole truth—I truly do—but the thought of him knowing every bit of it makes me feel too vulnerable to handle. I don't want him to look at me the way people do when they find out I can't have kids. It would kill me to see the pity in his eyes. Or worse, to have him look at me like less of a woman, or something broken to be repaired just like Finn did.

I spent too many years beating myself up about something I couldn't control, blaming my body and hating it every time I looked at myself in the mirror.

I don't want that anymore. I don't want him to start asking questions. I don't want him to say stupid shit like "Have you considered adoption? What about IVF?" Because that's what people do when they find out. They ask you to elaborate on the most personal thing ever, thinking they're going to end up helping you solve the issue that is your fertility as if you haven't explored every single option out there for you.

"I like you," I sigh, looking down at my hands. "I like you a lot. More than I ever expected I would. But you and I? This thing? It scares me a lot. And if we're going to do this, just know that I'm trying my best. But I'm gonna have freak outs, okay? And if that's too much for you to handle, I totally get it. I come with a lot of baggage." *More than you know.* "So it will be no hard feelings if you decide not to do this with me anymore."

Knox's hands tighten on the wheel, pressing himself back into the seat with a deep sigh. "I can be more understanding. I'm sorry if I haven't been. I'm just impatient, I guess. I like you a lot, too. Obviously. But I hate it when you shut me out." He takes a deep breath, unbuckles his seatbelt, and turns to look me straight in the eye. He reaches out to cup my face in his hands and kisses my forehead like he did this morning. "I'll do my best to calm down, to stop being so needy."

I smile, grabbing his hand by the wrist, and turning my face to kiss the palm of his hand.

"And I'll do my best to be as open and honest with you as possible."

"Okay, then." His crooked smile makes an appearance before ducking to kiss me again, this time on the lips. "Now, you better go upstairs and get dressed quickly. I'll wait here until you're ready and will give you a ride back to work."

"What? No. I need to shower, too. It'll take me at least twenty minutes if I hurry. If you're going to stay, just come upstairs."

"Nope. Can't do that, sorry. Gonna stay in the car."

"What? Why?"

"Because if I go up those stairs with you into your apartment, we won't make it out of there until dinner. Seeing you in my clothes, sex-haired..." He shakes his head. "I can't. So, get a move on, will you?"

With a smile, I kiss Knox on the cheek and open the door.

"Wait! Can you leave your e-reader with me? There's this chapter I want to finish..."

Laughing, I toss it in his lap and run upstairs.

CHAPTER TWENTY-THREE

KNOX

I grin stupidly as I bring the cream and blue mug to my lips, relishing the taste of the bitter roast.

Though the coffee I sip on is scalding, it's not the only thing that's got me hot. It's Lottie's determined face, her furrowed brow and stern expression as she speaks to our contractor. The authority and respect she commands has me dying to take her into the office, bend her over the desk, and fuck her crazy while the entire crew hears us from the site.

I smirk at my fantasy and pull the camera hanging from around my neck, quickly snapping a couple of pictures of her, focusing on her chocolate eyes, fierce and fiery.

"We can't do it by the end of the month, Lottie. It just isn't possible." I watch as Luke, a six-five beast of a man, wider than a linebacker, cowers under the glare of the beautiful brunette before him.

"I think you're lying, Luke. Or not trying hard enough. Either way, it's not my problem. It's yours. We already agreed on when the project was to be completed—check the contract—and you're going to stick to it. *Or else.*"

He grinds his teeth before speaking. "I understand, but that was before you asked us to redo the shelves *and* knock down the bay in the middle of the—"

"Luke," Lottie sighs and closes her eyes, placing a hand on his shoulder. For a second, I feel the slightest bit territorial—that is, until I realize she's patronizing him. I stifle a laugh, and shake my head, because no one can stand up to this powerhouse of a woman. If only she were able to see that herself sometimes.

I snort as he recoils, causing him to look in my direction for the first time since my arrival. Luke sizes me up before asking, "Can I help you? We're in the middle of a meeting, here."

"Luke." Lottie sighs, and squeezing her eyes shut, pinching the bridge of her nose in exasperation. "Can we not have a rehash of last time, please? You guys were working so well together up until now."

"*Barely,*" he growls back at her. "Your guy caused more trouble than help during the demo."

I scoff and take a sip of my coffee.

"We both know you'd be even more delayed if it hadn't been for my help."

"Especially seeing as you were two men short, and he saved your ass by stepping in during the demolition," she adds.

Trying to intimidate me, Luke shoots me a killer glare. I laugh at his attempt, which only seems to piss him off and make me happier. He can try and come at me, but it's agility and finesse that wins fights, not always strength.

"Luke, Luke, Luke. Can we get back to the topic at hand? You keep telling me no and it's not possible, but we both know you could finish by the previously agreed-upon date if you wanted to, right?" She looks up at him, squeezing her grip on his shoulder. Unconsciously, I take a step forward. "Don't lie to me and tell me you can't just because you want to take extra long breaks—" Luke opens his mouth to interrupt her, but she holds a hand to stop him. "Ah-ah! Don't try to deny it. I saw it when you did my loft, and I've seen your boys in action this week."

He's been to her loft? He's seen her bedroom? Suddenly, I look the man over once more, no longer appraising him as the contractor to our business endeavor with the problem with authority, but as a potential opponent in the battle that is obtaining Lottie's affection. I know she says they dated a long time ago, but I don't like the way he stares at her sometimes. Like the last time they were together wasn't over a decade ago.

She's mine, asshole.

And I have the scratches on my back and she has the love marks on her chest to prove it.

"So, are you going to deliver what we talked about by the date we agreed upon?" She asks, voice sweet but laced with lethal venom. He pauses before licking his lips and surrendering with a nod. "Good. Remember, as per our contract, we get a ten percent discount every week you delay the project further."

He sighs in defeat and removes his backwards hat to run

his fingers through his blonde hair. Luke clutches his Red Sox cap to his chest and says, "Fine. Walk me through what you want for the build again, then."

Lottie shoots a victorious grin over her shoulder at me with a wink, making it impossible not to smile back. My chest tightens when I think how amazing she is, how commanding and intelligent. She knows exactly what she's doing and has no idea how sexy she looks doing it.

I'm an absolute goner for this woman.

After an hour of torturing Luke, she finally makes her way back to the front of the store, where Jenn and I have been going over our remaining inventory.

"I've spoken to a few bookstores in nearby towns, and many have agreed to buy *some* of our books at cost, but not all. Unfortunately, since Walter didn't like to purchase best sellers for the store, it's not a lot." Jenn frowns, looking down at her printed inventory sheets.

"What percentage of our inventory is it, though?" Lottie's brow, pull together, she crosses her arms in front of her chest —all business.

"Roughly forty percent?" Jenn winces, but Lottie nods in encouragement.

"That's not bad, Jenn. I'm actually surprised you managed to sell so much of it, considering." Jenn's grin is wide and splitting, her chest filling with pride. "As for the balance, we can donate to local libraries, which *could* give us a tax break—we'll have to double-check with an accountant or something—or include it as part of the sale of the store itself."

Jenn nods seriously, reviewing the charts again. "Sweet.

I'm gonna go back into the office and keep calling stores, though. Just in case. If I can't sell more inventory by the end of the day, then I'm gonna call it."

"Great. Knox, you should go over the balance of rare books that Walter has upstairs. We still need to pay off the rest of Luke's fees eventually, plus the electrician. Once you're done with your coffee, of course." She shoots me one of her smiles, the ones she saves just for me. "I have some paperwork to go through today, so I'll see you guys around." She walks away, leaving me a nice view of her ass on the way out.

"Oh, man, you are *so* far gone it's hilarious." Jenn shuffles her paperwork, gathering it up in her arms before starting for the office. She chuckles and starts to head for the office, but I follow.

"What are you talking about?"

"I'm talking about you being a total smitten kitten. A love bug. A complete—"

"Alright already. I get it. You think I'm into Lottie. And I am. It's not like it's a secret or anything. We all know I've been dying to go out with her again. And we've been... kinda seeing each other. *Casually*," I add nervously. "It's... It's *casual*."

"Oh no, my friend." She laughs, dropping the stack of papers onto the desk and taking a seat. "You are way past being 'into' her and 'casual'," she air-quotes. "I'm not sure that I'd use the L-word yet, but I think you're for sure on your way there."

I could try to deny it, tell her she's insane. But something inside me repels the idea of saying so. So instead of trying to deny her claims, I laugh, a bit bashful. "In all honesty, what's not to like? She's incredible."

Jenn grins smugly, eyes shining. After a few seconds, though, her expression shifts. "Just be careful with Lottie. Because she may act all tough, but she's been hurt a lot, and I *will* mess you up if you hurt her."

I frown, disappointed in Jenn for even thinking for one second I'd ever do that to the only woman who's ever had this hold on me. Though of course, she doesn't know that, does she?

"I have no intentions of hurting Lottie. I really, *really* like her."

"No one starts a relationship off intending to hurt the other person—unless you're like a villain, or something. But it happens. People end up hurt by love more often than not. Happily Ever Afters aren't as common as we'd love to believe. And, despite her addiction to reading romance novels, unfortunately Lottie has been at the forefront of the deepest of heartbreaks."

"I'm not divorced or anything, but we've all had our hearts broken. I'm not naive enough to think—"

"I can assure you, you haven't been hurt in the same way she has." She presses her lips together, eyes narrowed at me in warning.

I pause and watch Jenn turn the computer on, typing away as I stand there like an idiot just staring at her.

I know Lottie is amazing and beloved, but the protective instincts she seems to inspire in everyone around her gnaw at me, making the hunger and curiosity to find out more even stronger. She said her ex-husband didn't hurt her *that way*—meaning he didn't get violent with her—but I'm sure there's so much more to the story. I want to pry, to ask what *really* happened because I feel like I'm just getting small pieces from everyone around us. Lottie's told me what happened in her divorce, but I've always known there was more she was hiding the night she barely opened up. But after our argument that night, I haven't wanted to push. And though some might make the assumption that I could probably ask her now seeing as the nature of our relationship has changed, I'd gather it's the exact opposite. I'd stake my life that if I were to press her now on her past relationship, she'd end things with me in an instant.

By closing time, Jenn, Lottie, and I have discussed next steps for the upcoming weeks.

Between shipping out sold inventory, helping out the construction crew, restoring and reselling Walter's books, and then repainting the store, we definitely have our work cut out for us. But I'm not worried about it—Lottie's at the helm of this boat. She knows what she's doing and this whole project seems to have breathed a new life in her.

The entire day, I've watched her in awe. Eyes bright, shoulders back, commanding respect and attention from everyone around without even having to say a word. It's inspiring, and admirable. Most of all, it's sexy as fuck.

"You going home already?" I ask as she shuts down the office computer.

She smirks, shoving some folders into her purse. "It *is* closing time, after all."

"Yeah, but as that song goes, we don't have to go home; we just can't stay here." She throws her head back and laughs, giving me a look.

"Aren't you a little young to know what that song is?"

I repress the urge to wince. "C'mon. What're your plans for tonight?"

"You want the truth?"

"Always."

She grimaces a little. "I was going to go home and read something spicy on my e-reader, but I guess that plan is shot to hell now, isn't it? *Thief.*" She smiles.

"You want it back? I'll give it back to you right now if you want." A small part of me falls, regretting the offer. I kind of liked looking into her collection, a little piece of her soul, always giving me hope for something more.

She considers my offer for a second and shakes her head. "You can keep it a little longer, so long as you're actually using it."

"Oh, I plan to use it alright." I smirk smugly, not wanting to tell her just how much I've been able to get through. I'm not a fast reader by any means, but I suddenly found myself getting sucked into these stories, and I'd be lying if I said I didn't want to read a couple more.

"So what are you up to, then, now that some evil person has taken away your e-reader?"

"I guess I'm just going to have to find someone to do all those things in real life. Keep me occupied." She smiles and walks out the front door, leaving me slack-jawed.

I don't hesitate to follow her.

CHAPTER TWENTY-FOUR

LOTTIE

Knox drives to my place in loaded silence, the tension in the car palpable. Over the past couple of days, things have been easy between us. I've felt giddy and light, giggling like a schoolgirl whenever he catches me looking at him or vice versa. My mind has been in a half-daze, getting lost in flashbacks of happy moments with him—a never-ending dose of serotonin boost. He's taken to finding any excuse to subtly touch me, to graze his fingers over my heated skin with the lightest of touches, driving me mad. Always subtle enough that no one notices (I hope), but electrifying enough that, by the end of day, the need for him has been built to impossible proportions, necessitating immediate relief and therefore requiring us to stay at his place.

But tonight is different, and it's only when we hit my street that reality sets in, and I begin to actually panic: he's coming home with me tonight. Like, *to sleep over*. And I know that we've been doing more than that for the last couple of days, but it's always been at his loft—never at mine. And though I've dated in the years since my divorce, I've never brought a man back home—and this would be the *second* time I'd be doing so with Knox. Except the assumption is that, unlike the time after the convention, he'd actually be sleeping over tonight.

Until recently, I'd been strict about the boundaries I put in place in my dating life (i.e. don't have one), but he was able to knock them down fairly easily. Looking back on it, I feel like I never stood a chance against his charms. I try to tell myself that it's okay to indulge and succumb to the sort of connection and chemistry that we share because it won't be permanent. But I feel the danger that comes with it; its bitter taste coats my tongue. Knox is such an incredible guy, engaging in this kind of casual relationship feels like tempting Fate.

My stomach turns as I contemplate ending this now, just as I'm beginning to grow attached. But then I turn to look at him, a soft smile permanently plastered on his handsome face, and I can't help the way my chest tightens, my heart aches. Even in the dim light of the car, he's still the most handsome man I've ever seen in my entire life. And the sweetest I've ever met.

He parks at the curb in front of the house, pulling me away from my overthinking and back to this moment. Knox turns the engine off, but doesn't make a move to get out of the car. Instead, he keeps his eyes straight ahead. "If you've changed your mind," he starts, voice low and soft. "That's okay, too. I was happy to drive you. Any time we spend together..." He shrugs bashfully, finally turning to gaze at me with those perfect blue eyes of his, navy in the darkness.

"I..." But I let the sentence die.

"I don't want you to feel pressured. Even though the past week has been incredible, I want you to know that I don't... I don't *expect* anything. I hope you know you can always say no. Would it be nice to go upstairs right now and have mind-blowing sex again? Yes. Have I fantasized about fucking you on every available surface of your apartment since being there? Absolutely." We both laugh a little. "But, in all serious-ness, if all I get tonight is a kiss on the cheek and a smile from you, I'd still feel like the luckiest guy in this town."

I can't help the stupid grin that spreads across my face or the way my heart races and jumps and does a whole track and field event in my chest at his words.

He says all *the right things. He does* all *the right things.* And maybe that's wrong.

"I—I *am* really tired..." And sore. So damn sore. I had forgotten how sex can hurt with endo. For the most part, I'd been able to power through our adventurous nights—it had been that good. But as I squirm in my seat, I can't deny that while half of my body is craving another night with him, the other is begging for a break. Because Knox is *big.* "I have this weird health thing... And I'm *fine,* but I still... And I just don't think that..." I stop myself before getting into it.

I see him wanting to ask more personal questions, to push. But past experience has taught him not to—especially not when it comes to my health. Not after the last time he was at my apartment.

His hand comes over mine on my lap, squeezing it

encouragingly. "Hey." He brings it to his lips and kisses the back of it lightly. And just that gesture of reassurance, the fact that he can read that I need him, even though I'm scared of losing him, tells me so much about Knox. About *us*.

I swallow once and squeeze his hand back. "Don't worry about it. I'll see you tomorrow at work?" He kisses my hand once more before letting it drop softly on my thigh.

Suppressing a sigh, I regret the loss of contact instantly. Because I *don't* want to be without him tonight—not really. And I *don't care* if he sleeps over. I just want to be with him, sex or no sex. And isn't it the whole point of this arrangement? We're together until we're not?

So I shove my fears and insecurities down my shadow self's throat and ask, "Dinner?"

"Sure." The way his face lights up once the question is out of my mouth has the panic creeping up once more. Again, though, I push it back down. "When?"

"Now," I say, before losing any ounce of courage I can dream of having.

"Now? I thought—" He cuts himself off and shakes his head. "You know what? I'm not gonna question it. I'm just gonna get out of the car before you change your mind."

I laugh halfheartedly and watch as he pulls his camera bag from the back seat. He gets out of the truck and slings it over his shoulder. A wide grin on his face, he opens my door and helps me down, shutting it behind me. With gentle pressure, he places a kiss on my forehead— one that paralyzes my lungs, makes it so difficult to breathe. I lean into him just a bit as my entire body shivers in pleasure.

When he notices, he whispers against my temple, lips grazing my suddenly heated skin.

"You're cold."

I open my mouth to tell him it's the opposite, that I'm blazing hot because just his proximity has me on overdrive, when he takes his jacket off and slips it over my shoulders. And I melt, because the feeling of being wrapped in his leather jacket is second only to the feeling of being wrapped in his arms. I don't ever want to give it back.

"Thank god you didn't send me away, Pretty Girl. It would've broken my heart." He smiles, wrapping his arms around my waist.

Are people in casual relationships supposed to be talking about broken hearts like this? Isn't the whole point to keep things separate? But as I run my hands over his chest, I know that, at least in this exact moment, I don't care.

I slide both hands over Knox, feeling him beneath my palms, recognizing every ridge and valley there—every single inch. Just like he's discovered mine. Over the past couple of days, we've become a topographical experts of each other; masters of each other's bodies in a way I didn't know could be possible.

But it isn't just that. This thing between us isn't just sex. It's everything. It's the way he takes care of me in ways I didn't even know I needed or wanted. It's the way I love to be teased by him in public and the way I feel I can let myself go in private. He knows me, we *know* each other—and there isn't a thing I would change about him. Though I'm sure he wouldn't say the same about me, if he knew *all* of it.

Though it shouldn't matter, should it? Not if it's *casual*.

God, I'm starting to really hate that word.

I inhale deeply, letting his signature scent fill me up and weaken my knees. He pulls me tighter into him, holding me up against his body. He cups my face with his right hand, tilting it back so I can meet his eyes. "You're incredible, you know that?" Knox whispers, eyes never leaving mine.

I open my mouth to reply, to ask him how I'm ever supposed to say goodbye to him, to tell him we should probably stop, call this whole thing off before it's too late and—Alejandro's front door slams loudly, pulling us immediately off each other. Knox and I turn to find my brother standing on his front porch, Cindy, my baby niece on his hip.

"What're you doing outside, lurking like that?" he barks.

"Lurking?" I push away from Knox, placing my hands on my hips.

"Lurking."

"I'm not *lurking*. I'm just standing here, having a conversation. You're the one lurking in the shadows like a creep, you lurker."

"This is my house." He points at his chest, reminding me once again that my place isn't really *my* place, is it? I live above my brother's garage. *God.* "I came outside to check out the couple of weirdos who were standing outside in the dark in front of it."

I sigh, trying to ignore how adorable my little niece looks struggling against my brother's hold as she reaches out to me. Not able to help the massive—and smug—grin on my face, I walk over to the front porch and take her from him. "We were just talking. But don't worry—I'm done bothering you and will hopefully soon be off your property."

I'll be in New York again, soon. I'll be out of this stupid town, and back where I belong.

Alejandro's face immediately softens, guilty eyes on my hurt ones. "Come on. You know that's not what I meant."

"I know," I smile, kissing Cindy on the cheek before returning her to him. "But still. We're headed up to the loft now anyway."

The front door opens again, and my sister-in-law pops her head out. "What's up? I thought we were—*Oh.*" A slow smirk spreads across Bonnie's face, her eyes bouncing between me and Knox.

"Hey there, Knox," she sing-songs, wiggling her eyebrows at me.

I suppress a groan, realizing now that the last time I saw Bonnie was the night of my stupid uterus's goodbye party, which ended with a blowout and a discussion on my emotional capacity to fuck Knox with no strings attached. Kind of.

"I haven't seen you since the bookstore party."

"Yeah. Bonnie, right? Good to see you again. And you, too," he says with a smile, nodding to my brother. "Alejandro?"

Ale grunts but manages to at least nod once.

"I didn't know you were coming to *jueves familiar.*" She says it with a strong American accent, but at least she tries.

"What is *jueves familiar?*" Knox asks, though his comes out perfect. I think we all take a step back, surprised by it. "I mean, I know it means Family Thursday, but, like, what do you mean by it?"

"You speak Spanish?" I ask, jaw still a little slack-jawed.

"You didn't know he spoke Spanish?" Alejandro bites back, raising a brow. As if this delegitimized my knowledge of who Knox is as a person. And, well, maybe he's right. There's still a lot to learn.

Knox laughs softly. "Yeah, I picked some of it up while traveling through South America."

"Well, *jueves familiar* is I guess a Veracruz tradition? It used to be *domingo familiar* when Lottie and Alejandro's parents were still alive. I guess in Barranquilla their parents always had family barbecues or lunches on Sundays without fail. It was a way to get everyone to clear their busy schedules and make time for family at least once a week. But after they passed, and everyone started having kids—" Bonnie glances furtively at me. "Well, almost everyone— Sundays became about homework and rest, and we decided to move it to Thursdays." Bonnie shrugs, smiling down at Knox. "It's part of their heritage and it's a nice way to make sure we never lose touch with each other."

"That sounds kind of great." He grins. "I never had anything like that growing up."

And how could he have, with a single mother and no extended family until his estranged father showed up out of nowhere only to disappear again a few years later? *Jeez*, sometimes I forget how lucky I am in that respect. I have my family. I had parents who loved me and were there for me until the day they died. And not everyone gets that.

I stare at the side of his face, a pang in my chest, as I think of how lonely it must've been for him growing up. Because for all my complaining about my siblings I wouldn't trade them for anything in the world.

"Meh. I could live without it. Most of the time they're just fishing for gossip," I joke, shooting my older brother a look to lighten the mood.

"So, wait, if you don't know about tonight's dinner, does that mean she didn't bring you here tonight for it? Were you guys just... going over to Lottie's place?" A wide grin spreads across Bonnie's face as realization dawns. I roll my eyes behind Knox's back because I know

I'm going to have to answer some questions now. What did I do to deserve such a nosy family? Having a faulty reproductive system wasn't enough?

Shit.

"Uh, no. I've been so distracted with work—" i.e. sex with Knox "—that I kind of forgot about tonight, to be honest."

Bonnie takes Cindy from my brother's arms and smirks at me before looking back at

Knox. "Well, now that you're here you *have* to stay and have dinner with us."

I panic. "Oh, no, I don't think—"

"I'd love to. Thank you!"

"Bonnie," Ale whispers. "Do you really—"

"Oh, stop. It'll be fun!"

"Absolutely. I'm looking forward to it. I think I still have a couple of members of Lottie's family to meet yet." Knox smiles, genuinely excited at the opportunity.

I balk "I... But..." I shake my head, trying to come up with excuses to keep him from intertwining more with my life. It will only be so much harder to untangle him from it when the time comes.

"We have peach cobbler. Homemade," Bonnie pipes in.

"Peach cobbler? I *love* peach cobbler," he says, his lopsided grin weakening my ire. *Dammit.* "And I haven't had a home cooked meal in... I don't know. The last time I visited my mother? Like a year ago?"

Bonnie *tsks* and shakes her head, taking Knox by the hand to pull him to the main house. "Unacceptable. Both the fact that you haven't visited your mother in over a year and haven't had a homecooked meal since."

"Do sandwiches count? Because I can make a mean turkey sandwich."

I open my mouth to object one final time, but it's too late. They've already crossed through the threshold, leaving me and Ale out alone on the porch.

"Jesus," he mutters. "Come on, let's get in. It's cold out." But I'm at a perfect temperature, protected by Knox's jacket.

"Your wife is..." I sigh, shaking my head, walking past him into his house.

"*Involved?*"

"Meddlesome."

"Preach."

CHAPTER TWENTY-FIVE
KNOX

It doesn't take long before Lottie's brother's house turns into full pandemonium. Just a few minutes after our arrival, the rest of her siblings and nieces and nephews descend upon Alejandro's house like horsemen of the apocalypse. They bring with them chaos and destruction, but in a fun way. I love it.

As soon as Adri sees me, she wraps her arms around my shoulders in a way that shows more familiarity than my own mother has often showed me. I relax into her hold, loving how almost every member I've met of this family always makes me feel like part of their own.

"Knox! So happy to see you here for family dinner." She smiles, mouthing *Finally* at Lottie over my shoulder. If I wasn't supposed to see it, then Adri is definitely the least discreet person in the world.

For some reason, Lottie gives her the cold shoulder. The animosity toward Adri is obvious, but I have no idea why it's there. Lottie hasn't said anything...

My stomach twists as I'm reminded once again that though I have her now, I don't really *have* Lottie. The walls she built between us are still up, only I have a limited pass to get over it, only allowed through at her discretion.

Before I spiral, Adri brings me back. "This is my husband Jim and my son Stephen. I have two more running around the house somewhere," she moves and waves in the direction of a tall, bald man with a heavy build and an infectious smile on his face.

"Ah, you're Knox?" he asks, struggling to speak from the chokehold his son has him in.

"Fucking family group chat won't stop babbling about you."

"Daddy. That's a bad word!" His kid calls him out and Lottie snorts beside me.

"You're right, buddy, sorry. Daddy is just finding it a little difficult to concentrate when you're keeping him from having a steady flow of oxygen to his brain." He claws at his son's hold and carefully manages to set him on his feet, releasing him like a hellhound to join his cousins and brothers.

"Sorry about that, man."

"It's all good. Nice to meet you," I laugh, greeting him with a slap on the back. "So, you've heard a lot about me?" I wiggle my brows at Lottie while she watches this comfortable exchange happen in shock.

"Is that Knox I hear?" I hear Daniel's familiar voice as he walks through the front door, open once again. "Adri told us you'd be here."

"*How?*" Lottie screeches. "This wasn't planned, and we only *just* got here."

He shrugs before calling out over his shoulder to his husband. "Brandon, he's here!"

"Oooh, let me look at him." A horror-stricken Lottie and I watch them jog up the porch steps through the open door, their twin girls on each hand.

Meanwhile, she groans, putting her face in her hands. "I can't believe this is happening. Someone shoot me."

I laugh and wrap an arm around her waist, pulling her into my side before placing a soft kiss on her temple in an effort to calm her down. "Why are you freaking out? I'm just meeting the rest of your family—it's not like they're murderers or something, is it?"

She glares at me and shakes her head. "No."

"So?" I give her a soft kiss on the lips and whisper, "Everything is going to be okay."

"Oh my fuc—*freaking*. I meant *freaking* god. How *cute* are you two?"

Lottie sighs, cheeks heating.

God, she's adorable when she's nervous.

"Fight or flight? Fight or flight? Fight or flight?" she whispers to herself, eyes on her feet.

"What the hell are you mumbling about?" Daniel asks her.

"I'm wondering which I should choose. I'm leaning heavily towards flight, but I swear to god I'm not opposed to fight if someone else comments on how cute we are."

"Daniel, she's blushing," Brandon whispers to his husband.

"I *told* you."

"I hate you all," she groans. My grip around her waist tightens, wanting to reassure her once more.

"Ignore her; she loves the dramatics. Can I get you a drink?" Daniel asks.

"How kind of you to offer someone a drink in *my* house," Alejandro snaps from behind us.

Daniel rolls his eyes and pushes past him. "Yeah, yeah. You own the damn house. We get it. C'mon, Knox. Let's make Lottie even more uncomfortable." He pulls me into the kitchen, leaving Lottie to deal with the aftermath of the tornado that was her family.

Which I loved.

After a few minutes of introductions—more aimed at Lottie than at me—I feel myself relax and grow even more comfortable with everyone. With the exception of Alejandro, who seems to be more hesitant about my presence, each and every one of them has gone out of their way to make me feel welcome—and make Lottie feel uncomfortable. It's a hoot.

"They're just getting started. The inside jokes? The embarrassing stories from my childhood? That's just the beginning," she whispers nervously while downing a glass of wine before dinner.

"I understand why you're nervous, but I gotta say I'm loving it, Pretty Girl," I whisper back. "Also, I would've killed for this. To have a family, a support system like the kind you had and currently have. I... didn't. Not really. Ma tried her best and things got better for a while when Walter first came into the picture, but you know how that ended. And after art school... It became impossible to keep in touch with people. Especially given what I do, traveling the world and all. All of this. It's everything I wanted and never had."

Years of solitude flash through my head, watching kids in school out with their families, making plans for the holidays. Meanwhile, I spent most of my childhood with my mother. And while I love her to death, I would've been thrilled to have had a sibling to share my childhood with.

Lottie's face softens, smiling up at me in understanding. "I guess I'm just being a baby. In all honesty... I think I kind of like you here."

"Good." I grin, wanting to get lost in the chocolate swirl of her eyes, flecks of gold and green sprinkled near her pupils.

She cups my face and brings it down to meet hers, kissing me in earnest.

"*Ew*! Tattie is kissing her friend!" Alejandro's oldest, Elena, cries out. "Blegh."

The adults in the room laugh softly as the kids—with the exception of the baby—all pretend to go through various levels of physical trauma in disgust (i.e. mock throwing up, passing out, fake crying).

"Where did the nickname Tattie come from?" I ask as we take our seats at the dinner table.

"When the kids first started talking, none of them could say Auntie Lottie. What kept coming out was a combination of the two—Tattie. I think it was the first moment I truly, *truly* felt like an aunt. Don't tell anyone," she whispers conspiratorially. "I think in terms of nicknames, I more than lucked out." Lottie smiles proudly. It's clear she loves being an aunt and loves her nieces her nephews to death. And though I agreed to this *casual* thing, I can't help but wonder what she'd be like as a mother. Before I go too deep down that road, I stop myself.

Casual. Expiration dating. Nothing more.

My heart twists. I suddenly want to hold her tight to me, never want to break my hold. I reach out for her hand under the table, needing the contact. Trying my best not to show how rattled I feel, I kiss her forehead. "Beautiful." I grin, focusing on her as if we were in our own little world at the dinner table.

"Sorry if seating is a little tight." Bonnie's voice calls our attention, breaking the connection between us. "We're not used to so many people, but we're so happy you're here with us."

"It's a little tight, but I don't mind." I grin down at Lottie, shooting her my flirtiest smile. I'm actually *loving* being forced into being this close to her. Rarely do I ever get to touch her in public, so this is more than nice.

"Problem, Knox? Not enough room for you there, buddy?" Alejandro's voice is cold, he's daring me to complain.

"Not at all. But if I'm making things too uncomfortable for everyone, I'm happy to sit at the kids' table." In unison, we all look over to the kids just in time to see Adri's middle boy throw some Mac n' cheese at his little brother. With a sigh, Jim gets quickly to his feet to stop a war while Bonnie slaps her husband's shoulder.

"Oh, don't worry. You're not the one making us feel

uncomfortable," Daniel tells me before glaring at his brother.

"Daniel, please." Brandon places a hand on his husband's shoulder.

"Alejandro doesn't mean anything by it. Do you, Ale? We're all so happy you're here," Bonnie tells me with a smile.

Alejandro forces out a "yeah." One thing is clear: he looks anything *but* happy.

"So, Knox. Where are you from, originally?" Jim asks, volunteering as tribute to change the topic.

"All over the place, actually. Growing up, my mom and I moved around a lot. Eventually, we settled in a little town in New Jersey. After that, I went to art school, and haven't really lived anywhere for more than a month or two since."

"Wait, really?" Jim asks. "How did you manage that?"

"Well, I'm a freelance photographer—photojournalist— for a lot of travel magazines and websites. So I basically travel the world most of the time and take pictures wherever they send me. I'm never home, so I thought it would be pretty much a waste of money to rent my own place. I guess, technically I live with my mother?" I grimace. "But that's just for legal reasons— a place to send my mail, keep some of my photo equipment, park my car when I have a trip overseas. That kind of stuff. But when I'm in town, I just stay at an AirBnB or something." I don't want her to think I'm a twenty-seven-year-old weirdo who lives with his mom.

Lottie smirks up at me, tightening her hold on my hand. "Don't worry. I don't think less of you for it. I *am* a thirty-four-year-old divorcée living in her brother's garage, after all." She means it as a joke, but I know her well-enough to recognize when her self-deprecation is a coverup for how she truly feels about herself.

"So you're a nomad," Alejandro says.

"Ah... Yes. I guess so, yeah."

"Not one for staying in one place." It's not a question.

"Uh... By trade. Not so much by choice."

"What does that mean?" Lottie's brother barks, raising a questioning brow.

Brandon groans.

"Ah, fuck, man. Come on, drop the protective brother shit and leave him alone," Daniel begs.

"*Alejandro*," Lottie bites back. She looks at me apologetically. "Sorry my brother is such a loser," she whispers, low enough only I can hear.

I mouth, "*I got this.*"

I turn back to Alejandro. "It just means that, right now, my job requires me to travel. It's what I do."

"So that means you just come and go as you please, then? Like a sailor." Alejandro looks pointedly at me, and suddenly I get it: he thinks I have a woman in every port.

"Whoa. No. Not like a—"

"Okay, that's enough," Bonnie cuts in. "We've heard enough about Knox's boring job. Let's talk about something else."

"Right. Because traveling to exotic locations and taking pictures on someone else's dime is boring?" Lottie mutters in my defense, but no one seems to hear her.

"Baby, she's just saying that to change the topic," I whisper, squeezing her hand in mine, letting her know I'm fine. An uncomfortable dinner with a dickish relative is nowhere near my limit of things I would do just to spend time with Lottie.

She nods once in understanding, a hint of a smile on her face.

Daniel clears his throat. "Tell us about the store reno. How's it going? When can I start sending potential clients your way to check the place out?"

"Not for a couple of weeks. But things are good." Lottie sits up a little in her seat, genuine smile spreading across her face this time. "Really good, actually. I somehow managed to get Luke to stay ahead of schedule—"

"Through fear, no doubt," Brandon snorts, but proudly gazes at his sister-in-law.

"Absolutely," I pipe in. "The other day she threatened to—"

"*Excuse me,*" she cuts me off. "There are *children* present." She nods towards the kids' table. The table bursts out into laughter, Alejandro included. "But yes. I did tell him I would cut off and feed him certain body parts if he so much as stepped a toe outside my schedule. And it felt good."

"I bet."

"Nice! I like to hear my sister's kicking butt," Daniel beams at her—just like everyone else at this table. Her siblings and in-laws all look in her direction as if they're seeing her for the first time again in years.

As we say our goodbyes to everyone at the end of the night, I slip my leather jacket over her shoulders. Leaning in, I take advantage of the situation to breathe in her scent, feel the heat of her body on my fingertips.

"What are you doing?" she asks softly.

"It's cold out," I shrug.

She gives me a smile and blushes. "It's a thirty second commute back to my place, Knox."

I open my mouth to tell her I don't care, that it's more about her wearing it for my sake than hers, when I feel a tap on my shoulder. "Can I talk to you?" Alejandro asks when I turn to face him.

Lottie looks nervously at me, but I plead with my eyes for her not to say anything. If this is an opportunity to talk to him and convince him that I'm not some guy who's going to screw over his sister, I want to take it. I nod and follow him back into the now-empty dining room, but not before placing a comforting kiss on the corner of her lips.

Alejandro grimaces, standing quietly with his arms crossed in front of his chest. "I wanted to apologize for my behavior tonight."

"It's cool, I—"

"No, it wasn't. I was a jerk, and there's no excuse. I'm just very protective of my little sister, and it looks like she likes you. A lot." I try to control the sudden thrill coursing down my spine at his assessment. "I know you don't have siblings, but even as adults, you never lose the sense of protectiveness over each other. And I've seen her go through hell and back and, frankly, I'm a little terrified you're going to make her go through it again."

"What? *No.* I would *never*—"

He raises a hand to cut me off. "Listen, you look like a good kid." Alejandro sighs deeply as I try to suppress my annoyance at the word *kid*. "I don't know you, but you don't look like the type of asshole that will hurt her or have complete disregard for her feelings like her ex did. But Lottie is older than you. And she's lived through a lot. And you're still young. I don't think you'll want to hurt her, but I do believe that you will eventually—regardless of whether it was intentional or not—for the simple fact that she will never be able to give you the things that you want. And that reason alone will destroy her the closer she gets to you."

I scramble for the right words. On the one hand, I respect the fact that he wants to protect his sister, to make sure she's okay. Lottie is amazing, and I wouldn't want anyone else hurting her either. On the other, I don't appreciate the whole intimidation tactic thing going on here—if that is what he's doing.

I would love nothing more than to tell him to fuck off, to tell him I would never hurt her and that he shouldn't make assumptions. But I only *just* got Lottie to agree to see each other, and I don't want to shit the bed with her. Who knows how she'll react if I tell him what I really think?

Instead, I say, "I hear you, man. I promise you I have no intentions of hurting her."

He stares down at me with a frown on his face, silver threaded dark hair a little disheveled. "That's not the problem," he sighs. "But it's useless to try to explain. It isn't my place."

"Knox?" I hear her call out my name from the foyer. "Where'd you go?"

"Over here, I call back," leaving Alejandro standing pensively in the dining room all alone.

"Let's go." Her dark eyes widen suggestively, and I struggle to smile, still irritated with her brother.

We say our final goodbyes and walk hand in hand to the loft. It's only when we get to her front door that something Alejandro says sticks out.

She will never be able to give you the things that you want. And that reason alone will destroy her the closer she gets to you.

LOTTIE

"You good?" I ask, slipping his leather jacket off and hanging it on the hook by my front door.

"Yeah," he mutters unconvincingly as we both take off our shoes. I watch him struggle to grin before kissing me on the forehead, lips stiff.

"You know it's impossible for you to hide anything, right? We haven't known each other for long, but it's been enough that I can tell when you're not feeling your joyful, optimistic self."

This time, his smile comes more naturally. "You think you know me by now, huh?" He reaches out to grip my hips. "I kind of like that." I don't tell him it kind of terrifies me.

He leans down to kiss the tip of my nose, the top of my head, before wrapping his arms around my waist and bringing me into a tight hug. Not able to help myself, I melt against him as my hands glide up his back, the feel of his muscles beneath my fingertips sending shivers down my spine. "I'm sorry about tonight. My family is... a lot."

He quickly pulls away enough to cup my face and look me straight in the eye. "Hey, *no*. Your family is amazing. I loved getting to know them tonight. Seriously. And getting to see you with them was a blessing. You are so loved, Lottie."

I smile softly up at him, remembering how excited everyone was to meet him, how easily and quickly they accepted him and brought him into the fold. The way even the kids seemed to love playing with him. "Yeah, they seem to have really liked you too. It was kind of cute."

"It was fun. Although Alejandro didn't seem to be particularly fond of me."

Ah. There we are.

"So that's what's bothering you?"

Knox hesitates, pulling his brows together. "Not exactly. He's just—He said some things before we left that—"

"What did he say when he pulled you aside?" I pull away from Knox's arms and angrily search for my phone ready to unleash a fiery storm of rage on my brother.

He takes my hands, stopping me from my frantic search. "Hey, stop. It's fine."

"It's not fine. Did he threaten you or something? He had no right to do that and—"

"He didn't threaten me, for Christ's sake. He apologized for being an ass at dinner."

"He... *Apologized?* Alejandro Veracruz? I have literally never heard my brother apologize to anyone other than his wife. *Maybe* my parents, but he was the favorite, so he could get away with anything."

Knox shrugs, and pulls me back into him, pushing my

bangs away from my face. "Can we not talk about your brother? Or about anything else for that matter."

I nod, quickly falling prey to his blue eyes as they lock on mine. I had my own awkward family interaction tonight by way of my sister apologizing for her behavior last week. Or should I say her *half*-apology.

"I'm allowed to have an opinion," she'd said as soon as she was able to get me alone at Alejandro's. "But I know I'm not entitled to give it unrequested—especially when it comes to this topic. And I'm sorry for bringing it up again despite you having asked us several times to stay out of it."

"So you're sorry you said it, but you're never changing your mind about it?" I asked.

With a sigh, she pinched the bridge of her nose. "I'm being honest, here, Lottie. I'm sorry I upset you. But I'm not going to change my mind. I *will* however shut up from here on out."

"At least there's that," I muttered.

"I see our talk did have positive consequences, though." The corners of her lips quirked as she nodded toward Knox, her voice dropping to a whisper. "You're welcome."

It's the closest I've ever been to committing murder in my entire life.

Knox's hands travel to cup my jaw, he runs his thumb softly over my lower lip, and I leave everything that is us tucked away in a drawer inside my brain. I can't remember the last time anyone looked at me like that—like their world begins and ends with me. The look in his eyes is everything I want and don't want to see, so I shut mine to control the swell of emotions building inside. How did we get here so fast?

As if not able to control himself any longer, Knox presses his lips to mine. He groans in relief, like he's been waiting years to kiss me even though it hasn't even been an hour.

"I've been fucking dreaming of being alone with you again all day. It's been killing me. And I finally have you, and I really don't want to waste time on things that don't matter, like— no offense—your brother's opinion on me or our relationship."

I nod in a daze, barely even processing his words as every atom in my body aches for him to kiss me again and never stop. Thankfully, Knox reads me perfectly as I fist my hand in his soft Henley and he bends down once more to take my lips in his. This time, it's more forceful, the air charged with the knowledge that we're finally alone, locked away in my loft, the whole night ahead of us.

With a whimper, I let him tease my lips with his tongue before opening my mouth, succumbing to the onslaught of emotions brought on by the taste of him. I slide onto my tiptoes, needing to get closer to him as fast and as much as possible. With a hungry growl, Knox nips at my lower lip, sliding a leg in between my thighs. I pull away in a gasp, needing to catch my breath as the heat growing low in my belly starts to spread, the hunger becoming too difficult to deal with.

"God, you have the most incredible lips, Lottie. Kissing you feels like..." He shudders out a breath, eyes still on my mouth.

"Like?" I smile against his mouth.

"Everything."

The scent of whiskey and leather overwhelm me when Knox's hands fists into my hair, tilting my head the way he wants to in order to reach my neck. I mourn the loss of his lips on mine until I feel his hand on my lower back, moving me back and forth over his thigh. The way I'm panting is almost embarrassing, the noises coming out of both of us intense. We haven't even had sex and I'm already so close to orgasming it's ridiculous.

But I'm sore, and it's equal parts pain and pleasure. Still, I power through because I just don't want to make it uncomfortable. However, on a particularly hard downward stroke, I wince, and he notices.

"Just a little sore."

"I haven't been giving you enough breaks it seems." I don't mean to burst his bubble—or reveal intimate information about my health—so I let him think it's all the fucking that has me in pain, and not the endo. "Come here. Let me kiss it and make it better." He gives me a deep, dizzying kiss, swirling his tongue inside my mouth, showing me what he plans on doing in just a few moments' time on a different part of my body.

Nearing total combustion, Knox walks me backwards to the edge of my bed, biting my neck, following it with a sweet kiss before tossing me onto the mattress. He pulls his shirt over his head in one swift movement before barking, "Take your clothes off. Now." But I'm hypnotized by his body, his tattoos; by the way he moves, every muscle flexing effortlessly and beautifully as he unbuttons his jeans and pushes them down along with his underwear. Once he's naked and fully erect standing before me, I'm wet and my mouth is watering.

"Lottie. Take. Your. Clothes. *Off.*" I shiver at his commanding tone, but don't hesitate another moment.

"Good girl," he says, eying my naked body with admiration once I've stripped.

"You have the most amazing tits," he says, his voice more like a growl than anything else.

You should've seen them ten years ago, I almost say. But I don't want to remind him of our age gap or think of how much better I looked when I was younger. So I crawl towards him instead, needing him inside me. Wanting to forget everything that isn't us, now.

"*No*. On your knees, hands on the headboard." His voice is almost a growl. I inhale sharply, staring wide-eyed. "Now."

I scramble to get into position as I feel the bed dip behind me. Not long after, I feel the heat of his body as he scoots below me between my legs, his arms wrapping around my thighs, holding me by the hips as he lines his mouth just below my core. I claw at the headboard, feeling his tongue tease me, swirling patterns on my inner thigh.

Whimpering, hips moving, aching to feel his tongue on me, *in* me, anything to relieve this need.

"Please," I beg. "*Please.*" Legs shaking, I can barely breathe as I wait for him to do something, *anything*.

He chuckles against me, hot breath on my wet folds, and I can't help the moan that bursts through my lips when he finally, finally presses his lips to them. His kisses me deeply there as if it were my mouth. Like fucking. Kissing that feels like fucking.

And I'm a mess, rocking on his face, wanting more, needing more, crying out when he presses his tongue flat against my clit. I'm hot and cold and my world shatters around me but makes sense at the same time as he laps at me, tastes me. I call out his name once, which makes him growl and tighten his grip on one thigh, before I feel him release my other.

I barely notice the way the bed begins to shake, off-beat from my own rocking. In a fog, I look over my shoulder to see his left hand move furiously up and down, wrapped around his cock as he tongues me. Suddenly, the need to have him in my mouth and pussy at the same time overpowers me. I make to move, to reposition myself, which he isn't happy about. "What are you—?" Until he realizes what I'm doing, that is. "Fuck, yeah," he groans, helping me turn over his face, growling into my pussy as I fold over his body.

It's clumsy at first as I try to balance myself over him while working him with my mouth. It's nearly impossible not to lose my focus when he hooks a finger inside me when he sucks on my clit. I don't know how I manage, but I do. On shaking arms and legs, I feel the intense satisfaction of what it means to please and be pleased at the same time. To understand what it's like to drive someone crazy as you're being driven to your wit's end. It's like a vicious cycle of giving and taking and it takes over my entire mind and every other sense in my body beside touch and sound have taken a back seat. All I can think of are his hands and tongue on me, the noises he makes from between my thighs, and I can barely stand it any longer. It's building, I'm building, and then I'm falling in his arms, between his legs, as he pumps his hips up into me and falls at the same time.

The soft click of a camera wakes me the next morning. I open one eye to catch his lens aimed at me, a sly grin on his face. Groaning, I roll onto my other side and bury my face in my pillow. It smells like sex and sweat and Knox.

"You're being a total creep," I say, my voice muffled by the pillow.

He laughs softly as I hear him place the camera back on the nightstand, dipping into bed and pulling my back to his bare chest. "*I* don't think it's creepy."

"It's totally creepy." But I smile into the pillow. "I'm sorry I fell asleep last night while watching the movie."

"It's okay," he says with a shrug, placing a kiss on my bare shoulder. "The book was better than the movie, anyway."

"The books are always better than the movies." I yawn, relishing in the soreness I feel in almost every muscle in my body.

"Speaking of books," he says between open-mouthed kisses on my skin, "would you like your e-reader back now?"

I struggle to keep my breathing level, to not let him distract me as his tongue begins to travel between my breasts, circling first my right nipple, then my left.

"I told you," I swallow once, trying not to let him see how

affected I am by his ministrations. "Keep it for now. You can learn a thing or two from fictional men." Although, I currently have zero complaints.

He pinches my side and I jump, laughing.

Thankfully, he stops what he's doing—at least temporarily—so I can finish a coherent thought. "I don't *need* to read books with sex, Knox. I just enjoy them. And if I happen to crave reading one, Henry Cavill and I can just use the app on my phone." I shrug. He raises a perfect eyebrow before asking, "The guy from *The Witcher*?"

Jesus Christ.

"He's not doing the show anymore, but yes. And he was also *Superman*. Not to mention Charles on *The Tudors*, but you might be too young to remember that show."

He grimaces, but otherwise ignores my comment about his age. "What does he have to do with your dirty books?"

"Don't call them *dirty*," I say defensively. "Calling them that implies that sex is wrong or something, and it's not. It's completely natural and can be part of a healthy relationship or just for fun. As we both know, it's not just for procreation purposes." It took me a while to get back to thinking of sex in that way; as something that wasn't just about making a baby, but something enjoyable too. Not that I've had very much of it since my divorce (at least before Knox came around). But it felt good to reclaim that part of myself. Of my body. Sex is more than just about having kids.

"Well, I know *that*." He smirks. "But I get what you're saying. The word association isn't deserved. What should I call the book genre, then?"

"Spicy?"

"Gotcha." He laughs once before dipping his head to kiss and bite my clavicle once. "But you still haven't answered my question. What does Henry Cavill have to do with your *spicy* books?"

I blush and laugh, burying my face in his chest. I run my hands up and down his biceps, over his tattoos, each one telling a story I'm dying to hear but for some reason can't bring myself to ask about. Like I'm too scared to know him even more. Like I feel the need to leave at least *one* part of him uncovered.

"It's what I named my vibrator," I finally tell him, my hands traveling all over his chest.

His eyes widen for a split second before he bursts out into laughter. "Are you saying you *named* your vibrator? Is that something women do?"

"I don't know, but this woman does."

He pushes my hair away from my face, cupping it gently between his strong hands. "I only care about the woman right here in my arms."

Heart flipping in my chest, my smile falls. Already I feel myself getting too attached to him, my mind racing with images of what my life will look like after he leaves this town —leaves *me*. Everything will go back to normal; nothing will have changed. Not really. So why the hell does the thought cause a yawning void in my chest that almost leaves me breathless?

"Does it bother you or something? That I have a vibrator?"

"Hell no." A wicked grin spreads quickly across his face. "I think it's hot. Actually, I think we should incorporate

Henry. Invite him to participate from time to time. Have a little ménage-a-vibe."

I laugh at him, but he ignores me and reaches for his camera on my nightstand.

Immediately, I become the subject of his photographs once again.

"I look like a mess."

"You don't look like a mess." He kisses my neck, breathing me in as if his life depended on it. "Also, it's my job to find and photograph beauty in everything. If I can find it in the most difficult of places, what makes you think I can't find it in the most amazing woman on the planet? *Especially* when she looks so incredible in the mornings."

My heart. It aches and I can't breathe, I can't move. All I can think of is how much I want to stay in his arms. All I can think of is how badly I want to run away.

"We've never really talked about your work," I say, needing to change the subject while doing my best to keep my voice level and breathing steady. My heart, I realize, is a lost cause as it beats wildly against my ribs.

"What about it? I take pictures for a living." He says it matter-of-factly, as if he were no more than a passport photo photographer, and not the award-winning photojournalist I know him to be.

I snort. "Yeah, but I only know the basics. I want to know why you got into it, for example. What made you want to pursue it enough to fight Walter on it? How did you get started?"

"Ah, well. Walter gave me my first camera—*his* camera— when I met him and came to town to take care of me. A

Nikon with actual film—very old school." I laugh softly, marveling at how "old school" film sounds to him. I'm sure he barely even remembers what "one hour photo" really means. "I found it in one of his boxes when he was moving into his place when he first came to town. I started playing around with it and he just gave it to me."

"Did he teach you how to use it?"

He nods before taking a deep breath. "Yeah. It's kinda how we bonded at first. And then he'd take me hiking around the area and we'd take pictures. It was... kinda our thing. Then he got me my first professional camera when I turned sixteen—used. But it was perfect. It changed everything for me. Started participating in competitions and stuff and..." He shrugs. "Yeah, I was good at it."

"Why did you choose to travel? To do photojournalism?"

He raises an eyebrow at me like it's the dumbest question. "I get to travel to remote places on another person's dime doing something I love. What's not to love?"

But I don't buy it. "There's something else; that's not why you did it," I accuse him, narrowing my eyes at him.

He's quiet for a moment, chewing the inside of his cheek, carefully considering his words. He scratches the back of his head and grimaces before saying, "I... I guess, in the end, I knew I didn't have a home to go back to after art school. Mom was living somewhere new, Walter and I weren't on speaking terms, and nowhere felt like home. So I made everywhere my home." His voice is muted and soft as he speaks, a tinge of regret in his words.

"You never wanted to stop and be in one place?"

He shrugs. "Sure. Maybe. Just not used to it, you know.

Never had that. Except for those few years with Walter. In the end, it seemed easier to just travel. I'd done it before." He scowls and looks away, jaw tense.

I sit up, covering my chest with the sheet as my hair falls over one shoulder. "Show me."

He looks up at me with a questioning brow. "Your photos, I mean."

His smile is lopsided, fingers playing with the ends of my dark hair. "Not yet. You're not ready."

"Ready for what?" I narrow my eyes at him.

"Ready for the pictures to speak to you."

"You're kidding, right?" I deadpan.

"Nope."

"Not even your old ones?"

"Nuh-uh."

"You know I can just Google them, right?" I raise a brow, making another reach for the camera and failing.

"You could. But you wouldn't be able to appreciate them." He shrugs, unperturbed. Like he knows that I'm not about to hop on my phone and give him a quick Google.

Dammit.

"At least let me see the ones you took of me. I'm entitled to that."

"Are you insane? Absolutely not. Those are the ones you're *least* prepared to see. You won't be able to handle it." He shakes his head vehemently.

"Knox... Come *on*," I plead. "Aren't the ones on your camera just pictures of the town? The remodel? What's the big deal? It's not like it's some hidden gem ready for me to discover. Nothing I haven't seen before; nothing special."

His smile is blinding as he sits up and wraps his arms around my waist, pulling me back down to the mattress with him. "*That right there.* That's my point. You're not ready. My job is to show you the beauty in what can be misconstrued as mundane. But only if you're open to it. When you're ready, I'll show you."

I huff, almost call him out on being hokey, but he manages to distract me with a kiss on the neck, followed by a soft nip of his teeth in the same place.

"*Fine*," I capitulate. "But I think you're being ridiculous."

"You often do." He kisses me on the neck once, twice. A third time that's slower and has my skin heating.

But I'm sore and tired, just a few days before I get my period, bloated and feeling incredibly unsexy right now. Sleeping with a younger guy as hot and energetic as Knox has its advantages—a mile-long list, if you ask me. However, it definitely comes with its *dis*advantages. He's insatiable, which I should be flattered by, but my inability to constantly be at the ready— whether it's from pain or exhaustion or spotting—even when I do want it, is getting to me. I feel like shit when I softly push him off me, rolling away with a forced smile on my face that I know would never ever even be considered for an Oscar—more like a Razzie Award.

For a second, I reconsider. There's an amazing twenty-seven-year-old man who looks like a tatted up male model naked in my bed staring at me with a heated look in his eyes. On the other, my gaze drops down to my swollen belly while I try to ignore the sudden onset of cramps.

It makes me wince, make me immediately feel the need to pull some clothes on.

"Breakfast?" I ask, pretending like everything is fine. "I have pancake mix."

Knox quietly stares at me from the bed, his hair sticking out in every direction. His eyes are soft and something about the look in them tells me that he understands there's something I'm not ready to talk about with him. Something about the way his eyes are on me tells me that he's not only *looking* at me but *seeing* me.

I just hope he doesn't see too much before he goes.

CHAPTER TWENTY-SEVEN
LOTTIE

I trail my fingers over the rows of rope, feeling the difference in textures beneath my fingertips.

From the goofy smile on my face, you would think I find them fascinating or something.

Beautiful, even. Or that I'd equate trips like this to the hardware store to going to Disney World. But you'd never know all that's running through my head right now is Knox. And the way he tied me to his bed last night. You'd never guess I'm trying to find a way to sneakily buy the blue rope in my hand without Jenn noticing or raising suspicion from Frank, the cashier.

I could come back later. I could come back when I'm alone and pretend like I need it for the reno and—

"Girl, what are you doing here?" Jenn's voice, so close to my ear, makes me jump.

"We're supposed to be in the paint section picking out a color."

"I—I was just... I got distracted. Sorry."

Jenn follows looks at the items before us and raises a brow. "By rope?"

"I...Yes? I thought the color was pretty," I say, trying to come up with a semblance of a believable lie. "For the walls. Of the store."

Shit.

"I thought we were going for a neutral tone. Picking a color like that would make it harder for buyers to imagine themselves in the space, right?"

"Right. No, you're right. Let's—" I clear my throat once, leading her out of this aisle and toward the paint one. "Let's go. We need to start painting soon. No more dilly-dallying."

For the next fifteen minutes I watch Jenn review each paint sample available, comparing pricing and quality. And I watch her in fascination, loving how this teensy bit of responsibility has caused her to blossom into this... *adult.* Or maybe she's always been this way. And I just haven't been able to see it.

"Okay, so, like, I feel like we should go for more of a cream, you know?" she says, her brows creased in concentration. "This white is giving asylum, and no thanks, no one's gonna want to buy one and dove grey is boring AF."

I snort and take the paint samples from her, comparing them side by side. "Absolutely. I agree with you."

"Where's Knox? Shouldn't he be here to approve this?"

"Why are you asking me?"

Jenn scoffs. "Puh-*lease.* You two have been attached at the hip."

I don't because I know it's all over my face. Instead, I own it. Laugh about it. Because I love it.

"Knox is—"

"Right here! I'm right here. Sorry I'm late." He plants a quick kiss on my cheek as if on instinct leaving me stunned. A huge grin spreads across Jenn's smug face while Knox catches his breath. "What're we looking at?"

"Uh, the reason why we're supposed to be meeting here in the first place?" Jenn rolls her eyes.

He laughs. "Right. Paint. Sorry. Is this what you guys got it down to?"

"Yes." She takes the samples from my hands and passes them to him. "We were between these three. You're a dude, so I don't expect you to know the difference, but—"

"The cream, right? The white is too clinical. Wouldn't work for the sale. And the grey is just... *Meh*."

Jenn's jaw slackens but I smile, unsurprised. Knox is all about attention to detail—in work and in his relationships.

"Am I right or what?"

Jenn smiles. "Right. Good job, Riddick! Making me proud."

"Thanks?" he laughs.

"Okay, so let's get a couple of gallons—you carry them. I'm gonna go check out doorknobs and stuff. We still need to replace essential hardware. And that way you guys can have some alone time and Lottie can go back to that gross happy expression she had on her face when she was fantasizing about you five minutes ago."

"I—"

But she holds a hand up to stop me. "Ah-ah! Don't try to deny it, babe. See you at the cash register."

Knox winds his arms around my waist as soon as Jenn walks away, placing an openmouthed kiss on my neck.

"I missed you," he murmurs in my hair.

My chest tightens, and I want more than anything to admit that I missed him too. But *casual*. Need to keep it *casual*.

I place a soft kiss on his lips and dig my fingers into his hair, pulling back just enough to look him in the eye. "What took you so long?"

He laughs. "So long? I was only like five minutes late, Pretty Girl." I raise a brow in reproach, but it only makes him smile wider. "Was at the park, getting to know the rest of the town. Ceres Cove is kinda idyllic."

I make a face, ready to tell him all the ways in which he's wrong but decide against it. No need to bring this vibe down.

"It *is*. I took some pretty sick pictures of it. One day, I'll show them to you."

I snort and pull away from him. "Okay, Helmut Newton."

He inhales sharply, hand to his chest. "You did not just call me by his name. I don't think I've wanted to fuck you more," he says with a growl.

I laugh when he pulls me closer to him, nipping at my neck and whispering all the things he wants to do to me as soon as we get a second alone.

There's no denying I want him just as bad, heat building between my legs. And just as I come up with the perfect excuse to feed to Jenn so Knox and I can take the day off, a voice breaks through my fantasies.

"Carlota?"

And as I open my eyes and slowly push away from Knox, it's like a record scratch to my heart, my body—everything.

"Jason." His name comes out on a whisper, mouth dry. I try once to swallow while I take in his appearance: tall, runner's build, blond hair with light brown eyes—kind ones. He was always so kind. Standing before me, he looks just the same as the night I got up suddenly from our last date, cutting our dinner short.

Except this time around, he has a baby strapped to his chest.

His smile is warm and welcoming, like he's genuinely happy to run into me even after the way I treated him. "It's so good to see you."

"I..." *I can't say the same.* "It's so good to see you too." Like an idiot, I go in for a hug, stopping short when I realize *he has a fucking baby strapped to his chest.* "Oops, sorry." I laugh awkwardly. "And who's this little guy?"

"Girl." Jason looks down, beaming at the baby who beams right on back at him. "This is Katie." He makes a face at her, and she giggles. "Say hi, Katie." He grabs her little hand and waves it before kissing it.

"Hey, I'm Knox." I jump at his voice as he stretches out his hand to Jason, who happily takes it.

Jason grins at him. "You're Walter's son! It's so good to meet you. I've heard a lot about you."

"I'm not surprised," Knox says with a laugh. "Seems like this town is good about keeping everyone up to date."

Jason laughs easily and nods.

"I thought you moved away," I say, voice detached. And I

wish I could take the words back as soon as they leave my mouth because *what the hell.*

The vibe shifts, the air grows a bit tense. Jason's face falls when he turns to me. "Yeah, I did. But Saskia, my wife, and I are here visiting my parents. Katie and I are here buying a couple of things to help my dad with a project at his house."

"Got it." I nod, forcing a smile.

After a painfully awkward silence, he nods once with a tight smile. "Well, it was good seeing you again, Carlota. And it was good meeting you, Knox."

"Good to meet you, man."

Knox has the decency to wait until Jason is out of earshot before prying: "So how long did you date for?" I can tell from the sound of his voice that he's trying so hard not to sound jealous. Or eager for information. Or both.

I take a deep breath and look him straight in the eye, trying my best not to look devastated. Not because I'm not with Jason anymore. Not because he's moved on. But because of what he represents. And there's no way I can be that honest with Knox, is there?

"Not long. About three dates."

His brow furrow, and I'm certain it's due to the short length of our non-relationship. "He end it?"

"No. I did."

He sighs, frustrated. "You gotta give me more than that, Lottie. Not to sound like a jealous boyfriend or whatever, but you looked like you saw a ghost. You're fucking white as a sheet. I'm trying really hard to respect your boundaries, but..."

"I just... We didn't fit." I close my eyes, remembering that last dinner. Feeling the hope at the beginning of our date, realizing I was really starting to like him, that I was ready to move on and start another relationship. Only to have it all come crashing down after one little conversation.

"I really like you," he'd told me, my hand in his. The candlelight hit him in a way that turned his light brown eyes into a warm gold hue. "And I want to be clear about what I want. From us. *For* us."

I remember the way my stomach dropped, knowing exactly what was coming.

"I can see this long-term, Carlota. House, kids—the whole nine yards. What about you?"

"I—" I remember trying to speak, trying to say something. He wanted it all. "Kids?"

"Three," he had said with a warm smile.

I had stared at my hands in my lap, wondering what to say or do. All I could think of was how much I needed to get out of there. So I did. I got to my feet and without another glance in his direction, I walked away, vowing never to seriously date another man again. What was the point?

He wanted it all and I had nothing to give.

Jason, being the good guy that he is, called and messaged, asking whether I was okay—but I left every attempt at communication unanswered. It wasn't until I Venmoed him for my part of dinner that he got his answer: I was through with him. And I was through with everyone else, too.

Until Knox.

"It wasn't going to work. Ever. So I'm really happy he got his family. I promise you my expression had nothing to do with any sort of remaining feelings for him—of which, to be clear, there are none—and more about my shock of running into him."

I watch Knox grind his teeth, biting back questions he deserves answers to he knows he'd never get.

"Okay," he says after a bit with a single nod.

"Okay?"

"I mean, *not* okay. You know you've left me with more questions than answers. But okay. I'm going to respect your privacy. Trust you."

"Okay," I whisper before pressing a soft kiss on his cheek. "Thank you."

He sighs heavily and brings a shaking hand to mine. "Let's get the stupid paint and go."

Guilt weighs on me as I follow Knox to the check-out counter, fully aware the tension in his shoulders isn't from carrying the heavy cans. But it's *casual*, I remind myself. And *I can't have kids* is not a casual conversation to be had. Or relevant to our relationship. Because, again: CASUAL.

"Lottie-pie!"

I look up to find my parents' old neighbor, manning the cash register. "Mr. Pierce. How are you?"

His smile lines deepen as he reaches over the counter to pat my cheek. "Good now that you're here. Haven't seen you in a while, my girl."

Knox smiles, so I don't even bother pulling away. Let him be distracted.

"I know Mr. Pierce, I'm sorry I haven't visited more often." And I mean it. He and his wife used to babysit us whenever our parents needed help and were there for us when they passed.

"You know, Molly and I were talking about setting you up with our daughter's brother-in-law. But then I heard you were with this guy now!" Mr. Pierce throws a thumb in Knox's direction.

I choke, but Knox bursts out laughing.

"Mr. Pierce, have you even met Knox yet?" I ask, embarrassed for the man. He's pushing eighty, but still.

"No," he says with an easy shrug, looking Knox over. "But I don't need to in this town. I'm pretty sure I know all about him, now."

"I'm honored to be such a widespread topic of discussion, sir," Knox says with his lopsided grin. "But how about I introduce myself just the same?"

Mr. Pierce looks down at his hand, then at me, then back at his hand before shaking it.

"He's a nice man, Lottie. Good lookin', too."

"Oh my god," I whisper, putting my face in my hands.

"I'll tell Molly we should put off introducing you to other men for the time being, okay?"

"I would greatly appreciate that, sir," Knox says. "I'm not one to share."

CHAPTER TWENTY-EIGHT

KNOX

"Okay, let's do this thing." I pull out the final box from the back of Walter's closet, handing it to Lottie to place next to the others.

"Are you sure you want to do this now?" she asks, biting her lip.

I shrug as casually as I can. "I have to deal with his things at some point, don't I? I can't just leave these things forever. And who knows? Maybe there are more valuable books in here that will help us out with the renovation."

"Do you want to go through them all at once? Or go slow?" Her voice is soft, cautious. Measured so as not to pressure or scare me. Unconsciously, she pulls her sweater over her stomach, which looks especially bloated today. Not that I care. She's beautiful either way. But it does make me wonder if that's what her health problems are about. Is it some digestive thing?

Like Crohn's or something? She mentioned needles. Do Crohn's patients require treatments with needles?

I wish she'd tell me. I wish she'd let me be there for her like she's here for me now.

"Knox?"

I smile, heart tightening in my chest like it does every time I look at her. "I'm good. We can do whatever." She doesn't know that having her close is enough for me to keep it together.

"I only ask because I need to go home soon and don't want you to go through them alone.

So if you want to do them all at once, we should probably set some time aside for tomorrow. Otherwise, we can do one tonight and then open the rest over the next couple of days." She puts her hands on her hips, biting on her lower lip as she gazes down at all the boxes. Sexy Project Manager Lottie is back, but she isn't all business. Behind her serious voice, I can tell she's concerned.

I take her hand and kiss the back of it. "I'm good," I murmur against her skin. "We can do one tonight. The rest another time. That okay?"

She nods seriously, eyes wide. "Whatever you need. I can take the day off tomorrow. I'll just text Jenn quickly letting her know..."

While she does that, I pull the box closest to me and open it, heart racing. Two hours ago, I was wrapping up some last-minute to-do's, completely unconcerned by what I had planned for us tonight. But now, faced with having to go through my father's remains, I can't think of anything I'd want to do less.

Notebooks. Dozens of notebooks.

I'm frozen to the spot, a memory unlocked in my brain:

Walter journaling first thing in the morning, last thing before going to bed. In black leather-bound journals that looked exactly like these.

Sensing my sudden distress, Lottie comes to my side, places a comforting hand on my shoulder. "What is it?" But when her eyes land on the box in front of me, I'm pretty sure she knows exactly what I'm looking at.

"Oh. You... You don't have to read them right now. Or ever."

But the temptation is too big, to find out what Walter *really* thought about me all these years. Mixed signals, and all that.

"Are you sure you want to do this now?" She rubs my back in circular motions, and I want to lean into it. But I can't make myself move. Or talk.

I potentially hold in front of me the answers to so many questions I was left with. And so many more I haven't dared to even dream of.

"*Fuck*," I groan, rubbing my eyes, squeezing them shut. "No. I can't deal with the journals now."

"Do you want to stop?"

I shake my head, because even though I can't handle Walter's deepest thoughts at this exact moment, part of me needs *something* now. Something to feed my curiosity.

She rummages around another box, double-checking it, I guess, before revealing its contents to me. Making sure it's safe. Taking care of me when all I want is to take care of her.

"Let's try this one; it's full of photos and knick-knacks. Might be fun to see pictures of a young Walter. We can do the rest tomorrow."

I brace myself, take a deep breath, and turn towards her. With careful eyes, she pushes the heavy box toward me, and I dig into part of what's left of my father.

The next day, I pace anxiously around the office, sipping coffee, not really tasting it. Lottie's an hour late and hasn't replied to a single one of my texts. We were supposed to meet to go through the rest of Walter's boxes today. Did she forget? Does she not know how torturous it was to sleep in the same room as those goddamn journals all night? It's why I've been mainlining caffeine—I could barely sleep. That, and the fact that I didn't have Lottie in my bed last night, something I've grown used to way too soon.

I glance at the clock above the sideboard once more, my anxiety building. The nauseating feeling in the pit of my stomach grows as I let my mind wander through catastrophic scenarios— any and all my mind can come up with. Did she get in an accident? Is she okay? The light drizzle from earlier this morning could have caused a speeding car to slip on the road, crash into her.

My stomach rolls again, coffee rising. Before I accidentally drop my mug, I set it on my dad's desk.

Walter.

Walter's desk.

With a frustrated groan, I pull my phone from my back pocket, scrolling through my last text exchange with her. A simple "Made it home safe. Goodnight. xo." she sent over last night. My thumbs hover over the screen, wracking my brain for what to text, or even whether I should be texting at all. I don't want to come off as too needy, but... the fact remains that I *do* need her.

Now, especially. A terrifying thought, given that I'm leaving as soon as this thing with the bookstore is over.

Except that the idea of going back to my old life doesn't seem as appealing as it used to, lately. And the idea of having to go through my father's things is even less so. You could say I'm putting off the inevitable, avoiding what needs to be done. You can say whatever you want, and I won't deny it. I *don't* want to deal with that shit. I *don't* want to learn more about the life my father chose to live without me.

To kill some time, I scroll through my emails, my tired eyes stopping briefly on one from my agent—a request for a freelance project that I'm sure will pay me peanuts, just like the last one did. With a sigh, I scroll past it, my mind not able to process the request, deciding to deal with it later.

With newfound determination, I search for Lottie's contact and consider calling her—just to check in, just to make sure she's okay and on her way. I could pretend like I have a question about the construction, pretend that there's an issue. But would she see right through that?

This is ridiculous. I'm being ridiculous. I should be able to just call her. Why am I so nervous?

After a few more seconds of hesitation, I lock my phone and put it back in my pocket, only to pull it back out a few seconds later.

"*Goddammit!*" I say under my breath, glaring at the

stupid smartphone, begging it to catch on fire. At least that way I'll know I'm not getting her messages because my phone isn't working, and not because she's choosing to ignore me.

"Are you okay?" Jenn's voice startles me, causing me to almost drop my phone and *actually* break it.

"Yeah, I'm good. Just... Drinking my coffee."

"Uh-huh. You sure you're okay?"

"Absolutely." I nod, a little too eager.

"Okay. Well. Luke's here to talk to us about the progress he's been making. Do you want to join? I know Lottie isn't coming since she texted me yesterday."

Yeah, because she was supposed to be with me *upstairs.*

"Ah. Luke. Yeah, not a fan, really."

She laughs and nods. "It's cool. I'll send you my notes. You can ask Lottie—I take great ones."

I snort. "Have you spoken to her today?"

"No. But she takes a lot of sick days, so when she texted me last night, I just assumed it was—" Jenn realizes her mistake at my sharp inhale. Her eyes widen, her face the perfect picture of the phrase *I made a mistake.*

"So she gets sick often?" My voice is too high to play it cool, but I don't care. Because I *knew* something was up. And I need to go find her. Help her.

"I—I don't—" Jenn sighs once. "Please don't put me in this position. It's her business."

I groan in frustration, but nod. "*Fine.* But I'm going to find her."

The drive from the bookstore to Lottie's house takes ten minutes. I make it in six, running every red light, heart beating so intensely against my chest, I'm almost scared it will fracture my ribs.

I barely remember to turn off my engine when I park the car, running to the garage, taking the stairs to her loft two at a time.

Please be okay. Please be okay. Please, god, please be okay.

CHAPTER TWENTY-NINE
LOTTIE

There's a loud banging coming from somewhere, interrupting the much-needed sleep my body is craving. Ignoring the disruption, I squeeze my eyes shut and burrow myself deeper into my pillow, willing the noise to go away. Only it gets louder.

"Lottie! Lottie, open the door!"

"What do you want?" I yell back, brain foggy, not moving an inch from my safe, comfy haven. The cramps aren't as bad my last period, but the pain is bad enough that it's spread all the way down to my legs, the stabbing feeling in my abdomen leaving me in a crippled state in bed, making it nearly impossible to move.

"I came to see whether you're okay. Please let me in," he says through the door.

I groan, throwing myself back on the bed, burying my face in my favorite pillow. "Go away," I moan, not wanting my super-hot, young... friend-with-benefits? Situationship?

Casual boyfriend? God, who even knows at this point—to see me like this.

"Not a chance. Open the door."

I take a deep breath through my nose, exhaling through my mouth. "Even if I wanted to, I wouldn't be able to." I haven't been able to move from this spot for the past two hours. The nausea combined with the pain have made it so bad I'm scared to get up. A problem, seeing as I stupidly left my pain medication on the counter of my bathroom.

Though I know inviting him in probably isn't the best idea, the temptation of my prescription grade medication far outweighs my mortification. "The key is under the mat," I call out, rolling onto my back, cradling my swollen abdomen with both hands.

Back in the days when I was still trying to get pregnant, I'd get through the worst of my period pains by doing exactly this. Imagining that I was growing a child inside me, that I didn't get pregnant that month because it would be the following one when it happened. I told myself it was the universe's way of getting us to want this even more, so when the child would inevitably come, it would be loved more than any kid ever had.

I looked at every possible silver lining I could think of so as not to feel the absolute crush of failure at not being able to conceive, and resentment toward my body. But none of it mattered, in the end.

Positive vibes and "manifesting" aren't what get you pregnant. It's fucking biology.

I hear the slide of the key into the lock, the *click* as he turns it, and the soft way he enters my loft before gazing up into his concern-stricken eyes.

"Hey," he says softly, his brows pulled together as his blue eyes trail all over my body, curled up under my favorite fuzzy blanket in a fetal position. "You okay?"

All the shits I swore I didn't give suddenly make an appearance. Mortified by how I must look—matted hair, no make-up, puffy red face from crying, and, *god*, so bloated he must think aliens impregnated me between now and the last time he saw me.

"Super. I'm super." I adjust the heating pad under my blanket and over my stomach, hoping it helps hide the big bump.

Knox removes his shoes, tossing them by the rack at the door before walking over with purpose, a man on a mission, to my bed. He kneels beside it before speaking. "I got worried when you didn't show up this morning."

"Oh my god, I completely forgot! I'm so sorry. I should've texted you."

"Shh, it's okay." The back of his hand comes gently to my forehead, a look of deep concentration on his face as it does. His scent and touch and mere presence are soothing, like a balm. It's not enough to make the pain disappear, but enough to give me a small boost of energy.

Enough to want to stay awake for a moment longer before I very kindly ask him to fuck off.

"I'm not—I'm not feeling well."

He nods and rounds the front of my bed, pulling the blanket up, slipping in beside me.

"What are you doing?" I ask, horrified.

"Uh, settling in?"

"You cannot *settle in*." My voice rises an octave, the panic creeping in.

"Are you contagious?"

In spite of myself, I laugh. "No, but you shouldn't be here. We... This isn't part of the deal."

"The *deal*?"

"Yeah, I mean..." I scratch my forehead, trying to form the words, but the exhaustion is getting to me. "Like, you don't *have* to do this."

"I know I don't *have* to. I *want* to. Plus, I have the universal cure right here for you." He wiggles his eyebrows, that lopsided grin on his face.

Irritation courses through me. "*God,* why is it that all men think their sperm is this universal cure? The last thing I want is—"

"Whoa, Lottie, hey." Any hint of humor disappears from his face, his hand coming up to cup my jaw, fingers digging into my hair. "I was just joking. I'm not here to offer my *magical cure.* I'm here because I was worried about you. You didn't show up and— I just wanted to make sure you were okay. Maybe take care of you if you needed it. Make you some soup, get you some cough syrup. Though..." He looks down at the long cable poking from under my blanket, the Dove Dark Chocolate wrappers everywhere, and the empty cans of ginger ale lined up on my nightstand like fallen soldiers against period pain-induced nausea. "Though I think your thing isn't a cold, am I right?"

After a moment's hesitation—because aren't all guys scared of periods?—I say, "You're right. So you can leave now. As you can see, it's shark week and I'm closed for business."

He looks affronted by this, almost recoiling at my words. "Periods don't gross me out. And I'm not gonna stop talking to you just because you're on it. I'm not that kind of guy. Plus, the relationship we have goes beyond that."

I shrug, considering his words. He's not wrong; we are business partners, after all. Friends, even. I feel like nowadays he's my *only* friend. My best friend who has sex with me and stays over and wakes me with soft kisses in my neck, pulling me into him every morning like he's scared of letting me go. Totally normal, friendly relationship.

"I guess you're right," I tell him, and for some reason my answer makes him beam.

Though I'm sure I'm imagining it.

He kisses the tip of my nose and smiles. "Good. Now, tell me what you need."

"I don't need anything," I grit out, my hands fisting the sheets below me, trying to hold back a groan as another wave of pain runs through me.

"You're such a bad liar." He laughs softly. "Do you need help getting to the bathroom? Need me to get you some painkillers?"

My entire body lights up at the suggestion. *God,* pain killers and a shower—better yet, a bath—sound unbelievable right now.

Knox watches my expression shift with a satisfied smirk. "Shower? Pain meds?"

"*Bath* and pain meds." I groan, trying really hard to stay in the moment and not think about how nice it is to have someone around. This situationship with Knox is a one-time thing; him taking care of me is a one-time thing. In just a few weeks' time, he'll be off to god-knowswhere and I will have used the money from the sale to move back to New York and rebuild the old life that came crashing down years ago.

"Let me help you to your feet," he offers. But I throw the covers off, toss the heating pad onto the ground, and make to get out of bed. He stops me in time, scooping me up and into his arms. I squeal in fear and mortification—I am *not* a dainty girl. I have real curves and can gain up to ten pounds while on my period. Yet Knox scoops me into his arms as if I were as light as a stuffed animal. "What are you doing?" I ask, mildly terrified as he carries me to the bathroom.

Ignoring my question, he takes me to the bathroom and sets me gently on my feet. "Sit," he commands softly after putting down the lid of the toilet seat. I do what he says partly because I don't have it in me to argue, and partly because it's been years since I let someone take care of me and... it feels nice.

"I'm going to run you a bath and get some water for you to take your meds." I watch him in awe as he kneels by the tub and adjusts the knobs on the wall until he gets the temperature just right. Once he plugs the tub, he gets to his feet and disappears out of the bathroom, only to come back with a glass of water. "Pain meds? Ibuprofen?"

"Naproxen," I point to the orange container.

"One pill?"

"Two." He hands me the pills and the glass, which I take with a happy sigh. Partial relief is coming. I pop them in my mouth and down the hatch, keeping my wide eyes on him as I let the cool water lower my heated skin.

"Do you need help getting undressed?" he asks as I hand him the empty glass.

His question is genuine—not a hint of a suggestive tone in his voice—but the tenderness of the moment, the way it's rocked the foundation of whatever the hell it is we've been building, shakes me. "Of course you'd say that," I snap back. "No, I don't need any more of your help. You can go now." The words are like ice and venom and a sharp blade all at once, and I regret them as soon as they leave my lips. But I don't take them back. I can't let myself accidentally hope for something more—not with Knox, and definitely not when I'm wanting to leave this place, too.

He stares back at me for a beat, both of us quiet without saying a word, before he nods in understanding. "Gotcha. I'm gonna head out, then, if you don't need help in the tub."

"I don't," I say, my voice cracking, my eyes stinging with the tears I know I'm going to start shedding the moment he walks out that door, maybe to never come back again. Knox leans down to press his lips to my forehead, and nods once before leaving the bathroom. I wait until I hear footsteps walk toward the front door, open it, and close behind him.

A wave of grief washes over me, of despair and disappointment at myself for being so cruel to a man who only wanted to take care of me. God, I'm such an idiot. I wipe my nose with the back of my hand and undress myself, easing into the hot water with a heavy heart, wishing with every bone in my body that I could just let myself be happy for one second.

CHAPTER THIRTY

KNOX

I use the same key from under the mat to unlock the front door once more, knocking a few times, as I do just in case she's naked in there or something. But as I slowly push the door open, all I hear is a surprised "Knox? Is that you?"

"Yeah," I say, moving into the loft, my eyes searching for Lottie. I find her laid out on the bed, right where I first found her just an hour ago. This time she looks better, though. There's more color in her face, more light, and while I can tell she's still in some pain, she doesn't look consumed by it anymore.

Phew.

I exhale the breath I seemed to be holding the entire time I was out shopping.

"You look cozy." She's perfect and beautiful, wrapped in her comforter like a cocoon.

"I am. But. I mean, what are you doing back?" She sits up

in bed, gnawing at her lower lip. Guilt. Guilt is all over her face. "Not that I'm not happy you're back, it's just—" "I just left to get more supplies for you." "S-Supplies?" Her lower lip trembles.

"Yeah. I didn't know whether you use pads or tampons, or which brand, because I didn't get the chance to ask you. So I got a bunch of different ones. I got a sales lady to help me out with that, though. So don't worry." Her jaw drops slightly. "You... what?"

"She got a kick out of it, too." I laugh but stop abruptly when I see her start to cry. "Hey, no. What's wrong?" I run to the side of her bed, showing her the contents of the bag. "Don't cry—I brought some snacks, too!" But that only makes her start crying harder.

"You're so sweet and I was h-horrible to you before. I'm s-so s-sorry." She wraps her arms around my neck, pulls me into a tight hug. "Thank you for coming back."

I smile into her neck, my chest constricted. "Of course. Of course I came back. I was always gonna come back, Pretty Girl." She sniffles once and nods, but I just tighten my grip around her, relishing in the feel of her body against mine.

When I can still feel her crying, I try to lighten the mood. "By the sheer amount of wrappers all over the apartment, I figured you were a Dove Dark Chocolate Squares girl, so I got you some more of those." It works, because she pulls away and looks at me with a wet smile, cheeks flushed.

"Yeah?"

"Yeah. I also got you some cookies, chips, and my personal favorite: Cinnamon Toast Crunch." I pull the box from the bag and hold it up like a trophy. "Plus, two types of milk for the cookies and cereal—almond and regular—so that I don't have to drink that nut water you love so much."

She stares back at me, eyes red-rimmed, lips trembling. "You did all this for me? Why?"

"Isn't it obvious?" *Because I'm falling in love with you,* I almost say, surprising myself. If I'm being honest—truly, one hundred percent honest with myself—I've been falling for this girl since the second I laid my eyes on her that night at the bar. She's a goddess and I want to worship at her feet every day for the rest of my life. I'm not going to deny it's how I feel any longer. At least to myself.

To Lottie, however... I can't tell the most skittish woman in the world that she's it for me, even if it feels that way. Not when she's been so adamant about keeping boundaries between the two of us. Not when she continues to put up a new wall, as soon as I knock one down. So instead of telling her how I feel, instead of telling her I'm here to support her because I care for her in ways that would terrify her, I say, "We have a kind of odd relationship, right? But even with that, we *are* friends. And you're not feeling well. So we're gonna hang out, and I'm gonna help take care of you, okay? Just like friends do."

I want to bang my head against the wall for how many times I brought up the F-word, wishing I were brave enough —that we were *both* brave enough—to delete it from our vocabulary once and for all.

"Thank you, but I don't need your help, really. You don't have to do this." But she doesn't say it in the tone she normally would, like she's trying to push me away in earnest.

"Lottie," I say, setting down the rest of my loot on her small kitchen table. I walk back and take a seat on the edge of the bed, taking her hands in mine. "You're not okay right now. And I wanna help. So I'm gonna hang out for a while. You can sleep and I can chill on the couch— read a little, maybe. Or we can watch a movie together. Whatever. Let me help you. Please?"

Her eyes travel over my face for a second, searching, before she smiles softly and whispers a hesitant, "Okay."

My stomach flips at the opportunity to be able to do this for her, to show her I care, to help her while she isn't feeling well. "Okay, then. Let me prepare us some food and snacks while you set up your favorite comfort movie or show for us."

She grimaces and shakes her head. "I—I don't have a comfort movie."

I laugh once. "Lies." I make my way to her stove, searching for the box of Mac 'N Cheese so I can get it started. Turning to give her a look, I say "We all have a comfort movie. Bonus points if it's embarrassing."

I grin when I watch her sink lower into the bed, cheeks flushing. "Promise not to laugh?"

"Absolutely not."

Lottie rolls her eyes. "That's not fair. You need to promise."

I laugh. "Come on," I whine, but she stands firm. "Okay, I promise not to laugh at your guilty pleasure comfort movie."

"It's, ah, Twilight. My comfort movie is Twilight."

I press my lips together to suppress a laugh, but I'm

honestly not surprised. I'm too young to remember the book frenzy, but I know a lot of women my age are obsessed with the movie franchise—though I have no idea why. The idea of a sparkly vampire and werewolf romance doesn't particularly appeal to me. But for her, I'll watch it.

Still, I laugh. "You don't strike me as a Twilight fan, if I'm being honest." Though by now I know her hard exterior is a consequence of being hurt bad by life and love, not because she doesn't have the capacity for it. To be filled to the brim by it, to be able to give it to the right person.

Hopefully me, someday.

She huffs, sitting up in bed. "I'm not exactly a Twihard," she starts. "But you could say I was a—ahem—fan of the books. I confess I did have an *Alice Cullen Fan Club* t-shirt at one point."

This time, I can't help the laughter as it rolls out of me. "Ooh, I can just see you waiting in line at midnight outside of the bookstore for the last book in the series."

She shoots me a look, cheeks tinged in an adorable pink.

"So, which one are we watching? I haven't seen any of them, but I'm sure I'll catch up quickly."

She eyes me suspiciously for a moment. "You're staying?"

"Of course I am. I'm making you food, aren't I?"

She crosses her arms in front of her chest, her hard exterior making a reappearance.

"Okay, but I'm doing a marathon. Watching all five of them," she threatens. "It's the only way to do it."

"*Jesus,* there's five of them?"

"Four books, five movies."

Five movies is around ten hours of uninterrupted Lottie

time. "It's fine. We can watch them all," I shrug, like I don't care. Because honestly, I don't. My heart is already racing in anticipation at getting to spend this time with her, one-on-one, just being together. It's all I want right now—more than sex.

We make it two minutes into the movie before I laugh in her hair. "You're so cute right now. You're so into the movie. But don't worry; I'm not judging."

"The books were better," she grumbles, cheeks reddening. "Though we've already had this discussion about book adaptations in general, haven't we?"

"Yes." I press a kiss to the top of her head, obsessed with everything about this moment. I'm in her space, holding her. She's letting me take care of her while feeling safe enough to be vulnerable and share her guilty pleasure. Tonight feels like we aren't expiration dating, don't have this deadline or dagger being held over our heads. Tonight feels like it would if this were real. I'm on cloud nine and she has no idea.

"So are you Team Edward or Team Jacob?" I ask, midway through New Moon, her least favorite movie ("God, I hate and love them so much," she's repeated three times now.).

"Because this Jacob guy is coming on *real* strong. But isn't Edward supposed to be the love of her human and eternal life or some shit? And why is Jacob *always* shirtless? When does Edward come back?"

"Whoa, okay." She snorts, shifting in my arms. She pauses the movie and looks me straight in the eye. "Okay, you need to listen to me *very* closely. You will need to make up your own mind about which team you're on. And not to put any pressure on you or anything, but this thing between us will immediately be over if you get it wrong. Because, despite what people say, there *is* a right and wrong answer."

"Is there, now?" I smirk, fighting the urge to kiss her.

"Yes."

I run my fingertips softly up and down her thighs. "Oh yeah?" Her cheeks flush, breathing speeds. "And you're not gonna give me a hint on where you stand?" My eyes roam hungrily over her body, and even in her current state of loungewear—leggings, fuzzy socks, New York University oversized sweatshirt, messy bun, and glasses—I've never seen her look sexier.

Because she's *her*. She's Lottie. She's letting me see her naked, even if she's covered in layers.

"Stop that," she whispers, her eyes closed.

"Sorry." I pull my hand away immediately, slightly ashamed of myself. "I didn't mean to make you feel uncomfortable—especially since you're in pain. I... I forgot." I shrug, wincing at my lame excuse, even though it's the truth.

"It's not that. I'm not in as much pain anymore, thanks to you." Her smile is soft, but it lances through my heart every goddamn time. And I'm sure I'll never forget it, not if I live a thousand years. "I'm just... you know. And what you were doing..." She reaches out now, her fingers moving softly from the palm of my hand all the way to my inked forearms, tracing the lines of my tattoos. "It just felt really good."

I smirk. "You know, in all my googling, it said orgasms were good for period cramps."

She laughs awkwardly and looks away. "That's nice, but I'm not into that."

"Orgasms? Weird of you to say, since you look like you do whenever I give them to you."

She rolls her eyes, her pink cheeks turning crimson. "I meant *period sex*," she says in a low voice, terror in her tone.

I sputter a laugh. "Why are you making it sound like it's something dirty or something? It's completely normal."

"Periods or period sex?"

"Both!"

She looks at me like I've lost my mind. Like I've just told her I love to eat my own boogers for breakfast or something gross like that.

"Maybe it's a generational thing." I shrug. "*My* people don't care about shit like that."

Lottie snorts and smiles fondly down at me before returning to her rightful place in my arms. I pull her closer into me as she makes herself comfortable on my chest. "Regardless, this old lady isn't into it."

"Okay, Lottie. Though orgasms aren't limited to sex. There are other ways to get you off."

She glares at me, shooting me down with a look. I chuckle and kiss the top of her head, inhaling her scent. "Let's keep watching, then." I squeeze her tightly and she hits play.

Lottie lasts only a few minutes into the third movie before she falls asleep. Gently, I remove her glasses and place them on her nightstand, turning off the light. I could leave now, but I don't move an inch, letting her doze on my chest while I watch her. Soaking in every moment I get with her, memorizing the feel of her body against mine. I run my fingers through her hair as the tightness in my heart grows, the thought that I'll have to leave soon, that as soon as we finish renovations and sell the store she'll drop me like a hot potato, whether she stays or really does move back to New York. And me? I'll go back to my lonely life as a nomad, taking pictures of other people's lives, not living my own. Except...

Except it doesn't have to be that way, does it?

CHAPTER THIRTY-ONE

KNOX

"Are you ready?" Lottie whispers in my ear, running her fingers through my hair.

I swallow hard—twice. Clear my throat—once. "I don't know."

Sitting on the floor of my loft, we're surrounded by the remaining boxes of Walter's things. The ones I haven't been able to go through alone. The ones we were supposed to get through together last week.

"You don't have to do this. We can just throw these out. Or put them in storage. You don't have to read every single word written by your father. It—"

"There's no way I would ever throw these out. And I'm definitely not going to read them all. But maybe I do need to read *some*. Because coming here has left me with more questions than answers." My chest tightens, my breathing stutters. This is... much harder than I ever thought it would be.

"When I first got here... I didn't really *know* him. Or rather, I only knew this one side of him. And then, of course, our last exchange being what it was… And then he died. And he left me the store and this stupid loft with no explanation but—" I stop, and she waits patiently as I gather myself so I can keep talking. "I just… Since being here, I feel like I've gotten to know him better through other people. And I'm both happy and disappointed, you know? Happy because I can accept he wasn't the awful man I thought he was. Disappointed because I didn't get to see most of it."

"I get that." She takes my left hand in both of hers and squeezes it.

"I've come a long way since first arriving to Ceres Cove. And I'm scared of what I'm gonna find here, you know? Like… What if it turns out he really is a dick? Or what if he regretted his entire life and how he left things with us? I don't know what to do. Don't know which would be worse."

"You're allowed to *not* read them, Knox." Her voice is soft, enticing.

"Tempting. But I have to. For me. At least some of it."

I take a deep breath, steel myself, and pick up a random journal from the box. And because Fate is a dick, it's the one with the year of my birth foiled into the cover.

I burst out laughing. "You've gotta be kidding me."

She peeks over, comprehension dawning on her. "Whoa, okay. Maybe let's start with something easier? Save the year of your birth and… maybe the year you fought for last?" "Or for never?" But I know deep down there's nothing that will keep me from the temptation of reading the words I'm so scared of reading. I *need* to know what he was thinking.

I set the journal aside for a later time and, with a shaking hand, pull one from the bottom of the box this time. One from seventeen years ago. From when I first met him.

"*Shit.* None of this is going to be easy, is it?"

"No. But I'm here with you. We can do this. Together."

I cup her face, choking back a sob. And... it's fucking embarrassing. I feel like crying. Because I've lost my father. Because I never really knew him—not the way I wanted to. And because I've fallen in love with the most amazing woman. One who wants to walk by my side while I figure this out.

I love you, I'm dying to tell her. To ask her to stay with me forever. But I don't want the first time we have this discussion to be when the moment isn't about anything but *us*.

So instead, I lean over and kiss her. Just once. Just enough to get my fill, some strength, before I tackle the first journal. I flip through the pages, anxiously searching for entries around the time of my mother's accident. Finally, in neat, near-perfect cursive handwriting, my name pops out at me from a page.

September 16th

She called today. After ten years of not knowing where she'd gone or why she'd left so suddenly, Melissa called. After breaking my heart and leaving me to die, to rot in academia, she called me.

From a damned hospital bed, no less.

The tear-filled way in which her voice broke when she'd first greeted me... My heart dropped when she told me she had been in a terrible car crash.

"Tell me where you are and I'll come get you. I'll take care of you," I'd said. It's all I'd ever wanted. I didn't care that she'd abandoned me all those years before. I loved her. I would always love her.

"I don't need you, Walter." Still, the same words over and over again from the day she left. "But our son does."

Our son.

She had told me there would be no son. She had told me she was going to get rid of it. She had told me she didn't want to be the student who had gotten knocked up by her professor during some torrid affair.

Her words, not mine.

I wanted her. I wanted us. I couldn't wait until she graduated for us to be free to be together. Was even willing to quit my job for her. Anything. And then she'd said she was pregnant and it was bliss. For a few seconds, life had been bliss. Until...

"I'm getting rid of it," she'd said. "And

I'm leaving and never coming back." She'd destroyed me. Left me bleeding. And now...

And now she was calling me to her, like some spaceship back to their home planet.

I leave tonight.

By tomorrow, I will have met Lennox.

My son.

I exhale, but it comes out choppy and I don't know why. My face is wet—*is the roof leaking or something?*

"Shh, it's okay." Lottie is rocking me back and forth, arms wrapped tightly around my waist, face in my neck. "I'm here. I've got you."

The pages of the journal are shaking and it takes me a moment to realize that it's because

I am. I'm shaking and crying and it's—I'm in too much pain to even care.

I think it, but the words aren't easy to push out. I think it, but it takes me a minute for me to be able to process it properly. I think it, but it isn't until I focus on Lottie's comforting caramel scent that I can finally speak the words: "He always wanted me. He never wanted me gone."

She nods, lets me sit with it. Because she told me so. She told me she found it hard to believe he never wanted me. But why didn't he make me believe it when he was alive? Why was I fed this random story?

"Where are you going?" she asks when I get to my feet, searching through my things for my cellphone.

"I'm calling my mother. Need to straighten this shit out *now*."

"*What?* Knox, no." Lottie comes up behind me, reaching around to pull my phone from

my hands. "Absolutely not. You are way too upset right now. And you're only *one* entry into the journal. We don't know anything. Obviously, you're going to have to talk to your mother after this, but... I mean, does she even know you have these?"

"No. She knows why I'm here in Ceres Cove, obviously. She's been... nervous about the whole thing. But we've never spoken about my dad directly before since being here."

Her eyes widen at me. "You... You called him your dad."

I shrug and look away, wiping my nose with the back of my hand.

"Can you leave? Please? I—I need space." I can't look at her right now. Don't want her to look at *me*. It's... too hard to put up a front. She's the queen of boundaries, so I know she'll respect them if I—

"*No.*"

I can definitely look at her now. "What? Are you kidding me?"

"I'm not leaving you alone like this. And I am *certainly* not leaving you alone so you can call your mother. Not two seconds after reading this entry. Not until you've had time to process it."

"I cannot believe you, of all people, think you have the balls to—"

"Yeah, yeah. Call me a hypocrite—I don't care. I'm not going anywhere. And I'm not giving you your phone back. You're gonna have to pry it from my cold, dead hands. In fact, I might enter the wrong password enough times to have it be blocked for an hour so you can't use it even then." My lips twitch at that. "You're not doing this."

I just stare at her. Can't keep my gaze off those vicious, chocolate brown eyes of hers.

She's fierce, my love. A protector. I want to be hers, too.

"Okay. I'll let you stay." I pull her into my arms because I *need* her right now, and I don't care who knows it.

She scoffs. "*Let* me stay? More like, can't stop me from staying." She burrows into my chest, inhaling my scent in that cute way she thinks is subtle, but absolutely is not.

We hold each other just like this. I never want to move.

"Are you up to reading more of them?" Her voice is cautious, quiet. Like I'm a baby deer she's approaching in the middle of the forest.

I've never felt more ashamed of myself. Never felt so weak.

"Because, like I said, you don't have to if you don't want to."

"I do want to." *I just don't want to break down in front of you.* But then again, I'm not sure I could make it through another one of these without her by my side.

"Same journal?"

"Yes. I want to see what he thought of me that first day."

"Okay. But let's move to the bed, shall we? Get more comfortable. Maybe it will... make things better."

I smile. "The bed will make things better?"

"You're underestimating the power being wrapped in a comforter cocoon has over the human psyche."

I laugh softly with a pathetic sniffle. Together, we make ourselves more comfortable, slipping into bed, wrapping ourselves up in the comforter as per Lottie's instructions, before moving on to the next page.

September 17th

Today was one of the worst days of my life.
I met my son and—

I take another break. "The day he met me was the worst day of his life?"

"Stop. Keep reading. We don't know everything else." She takes the journal from my hands, and decides to read aloud.

September 17th

Today was one of the worst days of my life.
I met my son and I have never been so crushed.

I will never forgive Melissa for what she's done to me. For denying me the opportunity to be part of this boy's life. I will never forgive her for not letting me get to be the father I could've been for the past ten years.

I feel like I have missed everything.

He's... incredible. Lennox. Knox.

Knox is amazing. Smart. Creative. So brilliantly creative. And no one has noticed,

because his mother has been to busy working, trying to support them. From what he's told me, they've moved too much for anyone at his schools to realize it.

But I'm not going anywhere. Not now, not ever. From now on, I will be here for Knox.

Melissa thinks I'm just going to help her through her recovery, but that's not how things will go at all. I haven't told her I resigned or that I've already put in an offer on an apartment in town. I have enough savings to hold me off while I figure things out.

I'm here for good.

And Melissa... Well, I can't even look at her. I thought there would never be any pain like that of losing her. But this? Finding out I have a son she never wanted me to know feels like death. It feels like finding out someone died and realizing they're never coming back. Those first ten years of his life I lived without knowing him. Those first ten years of his life I could've experienced with him. I missed so many mile-stones. So many big moments. And she took that from me. She's taken a piece of my life I'll never get back.

But I'm here now. And I'll be his father. And after only one day of knowing him, I know he's already made me proud enough to call my son for the rest of my life.

"Jesus. I can't. Stop, please." I'm crying again. Because I failed him. He thought he'd be proud of me for the rest of his life, but then… "I disappointed him. He told me so. I let him down. That last time we talked—" I choke on a sob.

"Hey. That's not true, remember? We found out it was never true. He *constantly* told his friends about you. That he was proud. Talked about you non-stop. What he said that day you fought, it must've been in the heat of the moment. Or a misunderstanding."

"No." I shake my head, heels in my eyes. "No, I let him down. I let him down. I wasn't the kid he thought I was. I was a terrible son. And I disappeared."

"Knox, hey. Hey, you need to breathe. Please."

I can't make myself stop hyperventilating. It's like my lungs forget how to work. "I—I—"

"Knox, *please*." And now she's crying, too. Pulling me into her arms, wrapping me tightly against her chest. "Feel the rhythm of my breathing. Try to match it. Please. Focus on me."

So I do. My true north. I close my eyes and listen to her breathing, trying to match my own to it. I focus on the way her fingertips trace my skin softly, the way she runs them over the lines of my tattoos. Her scent floods my lungs, and I welcome it with open arms, letting it soothe me like a balm.

"Lottie."

"I've got you." She wraps her arms tighter around me. "Just like you had me, I've got you. It's my turn now."

CHAPTER THIRTY-TWO
KNOX

I watch with wide eyes as Lottie shoves another thick sweater into a very large suitcase. My god. "How much are you packing, exactly?" I chuckle when she shoots me a look bent over the gigantic blue roller.

Her once pristine and organized loft decorated in a white, cream, and birch palette, is now littered with clothes, shoes, and makeup on what looks like every available surface.

"I have to be prepared for every occasion."

"*Every* occasion? We're going to a book trade convention. For three days." Except she doesn't know the surprise I have waiting for her.

I pull out a sparkly silver dress I'd kill to see her in from the heap of clothes on the floor.

"Yes, but you never know." She shrugs, my little over-packer.

"Well, I can assure you we have no plans for anything that fancy. But I can certainly make something happen just so I can see you in this dress." I watch as she tries to suppress a smile, as she struggles to keep up her annoyed act. But I know her better by now. She's just fighting off the excitement she feels at the prospect of us having three days to ourselves. Even if it is just a business trip.

Because, even though these past couple of weeks together have been epic, we've also had to contend with a lot. The first being, of course, what happened while going through my father's journals. After my breakdown, I couldn't get past another entry. Not then. And I think certainly not now.

"With time, you will," Lottie had said.

I knew she was right. With time and especially with her by my side, I could do it. But for right now, I wasn't ready to keep reading his innermost thoughts. The things that are in those journals will have to be unpacked carefully, too delicate to just go through haphazardly while finalizing everything with the renovation and sale.

The second thing we've had to deal with lately is the constant watchful eyes of the members of Ceres Cove. Though I love how supportive people close to us have been about this... situationship, sometimes it feels like the entire town is watching. Like we're their favorite reality show, unveiling right before their eyes.

Normally, I wouldn't mind, because even though it's incredibly weird, I've never been happier. But since I know Lottie, I'm always scared I'm one busy-bodied comment away from losing it all.

Last Sunday, for example, we decided to spend the morning at the local park. I wanted to explore more of the town since arriving anyway, so I took my camera and a well-packed basket. I was excited to spend the day just lazing out in the sun, kissing her, and maybe getting to act out a particular scene from one of her many romance novels.

Unfortunately for us, we were ambushed by what Lottie calls The Mommy Mafia—a group of young mothers around her age that power walk around town with their strollers during weekend mornings as they gossip and plot the demise of whoever goes against them in town (her words, not mine). As soon as we heard their saccharine voices, I could tell something was off. Lottie tensed, her spine straightened, and the blood drained from her face. In a split second, I saw my beautiful, strong, confident Lottie turn into a submissive, self-effacing version of herself.

Lottie had stuttered through a greeting, trying to control her features as one of the Mommy Mafia announced a pregnancy. She only answered in short, precise sentences when asked about how the store reno was going. And things got even worse when they looked over at me and one of them asked, "Well, aren't you going to introduce us? Who's your friend?" Even though every person in this nosy town already knew who I was.

Sensing her reluctance, I chose to answer for her, shooting the women a smile. "Hey. I'm Knox Riddick, part owner of the *Adams's Bookstore*."

We engaged in polite conversation surrounding how saddened they were to hear about the death of my father, how excited they were to see what new business would come to town, and how happy they were to have met me. Lottie was mute throughout its entirety, her eyes glazed over as if lost in thought.

I couldn't wait until the women left us and went back to whatever the hell it was they were doing before they ruined my day. I wanted my girl back, and they had completely fucked the rest of my afternoon, even though I had no idea why.

Again, I asked Lottie what was wrong, asked her why she called them a *mafia* when they looked perfectly nice and non-murderous. And again, all I got from her was a vague non-answer. Slightly irritated by feeling her pull back from me once more, I decided it was time to do something about it.

I couldn't change the way this town reacted to us dating —I still don't understand the fascination behind it. But after an uncomfortably quiet rest of the afternoon together, I went back to my apartment after dropping her off before dinner and devised a plan to get us some alone time.

I hoped the time away from this town, these people who so lovingly keep a watchful eye over our relationship and the woman I'm beginning to care so deeply about, would give Lottie the space to focus on us. I wanted the space for *both* of us to focus on each other. I want her to see that we can exist outside of this damn town, outside of the store reno. Because the project's days are numbered and, whether I like it or not, so is our relationship.

This time with Lottie has meant so much to me, there's not a chance in hell I won't fight for it to continue after. I need to make her want to fight just as hard for it, too.

I'm not quite sure what will come for me after this reno and sale is all over—I've lived a transient existence for most of my life, so staying in one place isn't exactly my forte. But for her, I'd more than try to make it work. We could do long-distance while I travel for photo assignments, or she could even come with me to the non-dangerous locations. I wouldn't care either way.

I want her to be my home base.

Trying not to dwell on what the future might bring, I tell her, "Well, I can tell you we will absolutely not be going anywhere where you'll need this, Pretty Girl. But I wouldn't mind you wearing it for me in the privacy of our own room." I shoot her a lascivious grin and she bites her lower lip, trying not act like she isn't thrilled about this getaway.

"I packed matching shoes," she whispers, pulling a pair of silver stiletto sandals from her suitcase and showing them to me.

"*Fuck*," I whisper, kneeling by her to take her face in my hands. "I want to see what they look like on my shoulders while I fuck you."

"Should I try them on now?" she jokes.

I ignore her, kissing her so deeply and intensely I feel the need for her build almost instantly. When her hand brushes over my hardness, I groan in her mouth, the hunger nearly overpowering me. The taste of her lips on mine is like alchemy, and it's not long before we're naked and I'm over and in her on her living room floor.

"Are we there yet?" She whines, leaning her head on my shoulder.

Keeping my eyes on the winding roads, I tilt my head to press my lips to the top of her head. "Soon."

I shift gears and feel her hand come above mine on the stick shift, squeezing it lightly before moving it over her thigh and lacing our fingers together.

I pull our joined hands to my lips and kiss the back of hers before setting them back on her leg. We drive the last twenty minutes in comfortable silence as the excitement at spending the next three days alone together builds in my stomach.

It's only as near the B&B that a growing sense of unease begins to build within me. All I can think about is how much I like this woman, how much I care about her. In just a matter of weeks, she has become the brightest spot in my life in the darkest and murkiest time. The way I feel about her now is exciting and new and intense—but terrifying. We're more than casual now, right? You don't go away for the weekend with someone you're just seeing *casually*. This means more to me. This *has* to mean more to her, too.

Right?

The sudden terror that we're not on the same page grips my heart, rooting me in place. This long weekend was supposed to bring us closer together. It wasn't just about business or even spending time alone, away from everything. But what if being a *we* is not what she wants? Not long-term, at least.

My heart races, thoughts of being on unequal ground

causing a wave of anxiety to wash over me. But as always, she's able to pull me back to the present.

"Thank you," she breathes. "I think we really needed this." I look down at her wide eyes, warmth spreading through me. *We.*

We.

We. We.

The word drums in my chest with every one of my heart-beats. *We* implies there's an *us*. It must.

It *must.*

"It's a business trip."

"Yeah, but I'm sure you picked one far enough for us to be alone, didn't you?" She smirks, seeing right through me.

I don't reply because she already knows the answer to that. Instead, she leans over and kisses me on the cheek.

There's no way we're still doing the casual thing.

No way at all.

CHAPTER THIRTY-THREE

LOTTIE

"This place looks…" I exhale, looking up at the gorgeous luxury B&B as Knox searches for parking in the lot.

"Perfect?" A wide grin spreads across his face, pride in his eyes.

"*Expensive.*" I frown. "A little too expensive to justify for a business trip."

He laughs softly as he slips into a spot and shuts the engine off. "I know. Which is why *I* paid for it."

I stare blankly at him as he gets out of the car, jogging over to open my door for me.

"You… What? That's insane. I mean, it's beautiful, Knox. Don't get me wrong. But it's a waste. We're going to be at the trade show all weekend."

As soon as I'm out, he pulls me into his arms, kissing the tip of my nose once, my forehead, and my nose again. He shoots me that trickster grin of his and says, "The trade show only lasts a day. Tomorrow. We're here for three."

336

I freeze, gazing up at him in shock before looking back at the beautiful log cabin waiting for us. "You... You planned this for us?" I breathe.

"Yeah," he whispers, kissing my neck.

"Where'd you find this place, anyway? Your precious Google?"

"No, actually. I found an old pamphlet for this place in one of my dad's boxes."

I miss a breath, hoping he doesn't notice. He said the word *dad* again. My heart expands in my chest. Watching this man learn to love his father after his passing has been a privilege— and an emotional roller coaster. I don't point out his slip, though. Don't want to make him feel self-conscious.

"I wanted to give us time away from that town," he continues. "Time away together. It was... getting intense being there. With those women in the park and people finding out we're sleeping together." I freeze, bracing myself for whatever it is he's hesitating to say.

"We're having a great time—or at least *I* have been—but we've also had to contend with small town life and... other things." He shrugs. "It is what it is. And though I love the support and enthusiasm we've received from people who know about us, they seem heavily invested in it. Which is... charming but also kinda annoying at the same time?" He winces.

I grimace and nod, knowing exactly how he feels. "Yeah the other day..." I shake my head. "I'm sorry about that. With the Mommy Mafia."

"It's not like it's your fault." He scoffs and shakes his

head. "But it was so hard to control myself from saying something. I saw how they made you feel. And I hated it."

My eyes widen in disbelief because I thought I had managed that situation so well. Mortified, I ask, "Really? I-I mean, yeah, I don't really like them that much." A part of me can acknowledge, however, that it may also be that I will never even qualify to be part of their group.

Maybe that's what's truly irritating about them.

"I figured. Regardless, I felt like we needed space. Which is why I booked us for the two extra days away."

I exhale deeply and lean into his chest, pressing my ear to his heart. "Thank you." I feel myself relax in his arms, breathing in his scent.

Knox's lips press to the top of my head before he whispers, "Anything. Anything for you. Always. I don't think you realize the lengths I would go to make you happy."

His words linger in my head, my heart, as he checks us in, holding my hand throughout the entire process. I watch him talk through scheduled spa treatments and dinner reservations with the B&B manager, in awe with everything he organized. I'm in a trance, so distracted by the realization that I'm falling deeper for this guy I'll never be able to permanently keep that I barely notice someone calling my name.

"Lottie?" My blood runs cold because I recognize that voice. "Lottie Veracruz."

I wonder whether I can still make a run for it, or whether I am well and truly fucked. Because standing just a few feet away from me, looking more glamorous than I remember, is none other than my former assistant.

"Madison Shelton."

Once small and mousy, my favorite former employee stands strong and confident before me, not just looking like she's ready to take on the world, but like she already has.

"Oh my god. It *is* you." She runs up, pulling me into her arms.

"I... Hey." I quickly assess myself, feeling 100% confident in that I look like utter shit. I'm bloated, just got here after a three-hour road trip, and have probably gained around twenty pounds since the last time I saw her over four years ago. "Wow, you look—I mean, I haven't seen you in—" "A while," is the best I can say.

"Right." Her smile is broad and eager, her hazel eyes bright as she takes me in, and I know right then that she's managed to stay true to who she is—a nearly impossible feat in the fashion world. "I'm so happy to see you. I've missed you!"

And damn, did I miss her, too. Something I didn't even realize until this very second.

Madison was a breath of fresh, naive air, filled with enthusiasm and dreams of a simpler industry; someone unharmed yet by the dangers of not knowing how to "play the game." It's for that reason and that reason alone that I let her pull me into another hug. And this time, I return it.

"It's so good to see you."

"What are you doing here? Romantic getaway with Finn?" She smiles.

"Uh, no actually. Finn and I... We're not—I mean, we..." I scratch my forehead and sigh.

"We're not together anymore."

"Oh, I—I'm sorry to hear that."

I snort. "Don't be. Seriously."

She smiles back. "Good. He always gave me bad vibes, anyway."

"Right."

"I'm here with my new guy, who's over there." She points proudly at a man in the front room of the B&B. The definition of the phrase tall, dark, and handsome, he looks up briefly from his phone screen and shoots us a little wave.

"*Madison*." I say with a laugh.

"I know. The man looks like a hotter version of Michael B. Jordan. Didn't think that was possible. And such a sweetheart." We giggle like two schoolgirls at recess. "What about you? You here with anyone?"

"Uh... No. I'm—I'm here on business."

Ever the man with perfect timing, Knox walks over to me, placing a possessive hand on my lower back. It's an unconscious move, I know, and I probably wouldn't even have noticed it usually. But suddenly running into my assistant from years ago makes me wildly self-conscious of everything around me. What I say and do, what I look like.

Who I'm with.

Madison's eyes flit briefly to his hand, her expression curious, so I pull away just out of

Knox's grasp.

"And who is this?" she asks.

Knox shoots her one of his charming, lopsided smiles. "Hi, I'm—"

"This is my business partner." The words come out before I even get a chance to process them. Before I even know what the hell I'm saying. And I can feel his eyes on me, burning with questions.

"Business partner?" Madison's gaze bounces between us.

"Yes," I say, standing up straighter. "Knox and I own a bookstore together, which we're flipping."

A little disoriented, he sticks his hand out to shake Madison's. "Uh, yeah. Hi. Knox Riddick, nice to meet you."

"Mr. Riddick? Your room is ready," the concierge calls from the desk. "I'll have our staff take your things up for you and your partner."

Every muscle in my body tenses and, for some odd reason, an unbidden wave of embarrassment washes over me.

Madison gives me a knowing smirk, but it isn't a judgmental one. More... like she's proud?

"Right. Well. How long are you here for? I'm leaving tomorrow afternoon. But would love to see you before then. Are you available for coffee or something? To catch up?" she asks hopefully. "I miss you."

"I... No, actually," I say, half genuinely disappointed I won't be able to see her, half relieved I have an excuse to avoid the inevitable download on what happened to my life. "We have meetings all day tomorrow."

"I can handle the one morning meeting we have tomorrow on my own, if you guys would like to get breakfast together." Knox shoots me an encouraging smile.

"Oh, that would be amazing!" Madison claps in place, her usual enthusiasm just as contagious as it was when she was first starting out. "Should we meet down here at around eight, then? I can't wait to hear more about what you've been up to! And I have news for you, too." She grins before kissing me on the cheek.

"Babe, we gotta go," Madison's boyfriend calls.

"One sec!" She rolls her eyes and shakes her head. "Men."

We agree to a time and place before parting ways, double-checking we still have our old contact info.

When we make it to our room, Knox doesn't hesitate to broach the subject. "What the hell was that?" he asks, dropping his camera bag gently on the nightstand.

"The hell was what?" I pull my makeup bag from my duffel and power walk into the bathroom. It's cowardly, I know, but I don't think I can manage to look him in the eyes.

"Business partner? Really?" I hear the hurt masked by anger and frustration in his voice.

Knox stares at me, hands gripping the frame of the bathroom doorway on either side.

"I—I didn't know what to say. She's an ex-employee of mine—my former assistant—and I guess my professionalism kicked in from before." I struggle to find the words, but we both know it's just excuses.

"C'mon, Lottie. Cut the shit."

I fidget with the contents of my bag, keeping my eyes locked on them. It isn't until I feel his hands on my hips that I look up to meet his gaze in the reflection of the mirror.

"I'm ashamed."

"Of *us*?"

"No. *No*." I turn to cradle his face in my hands. Sighing, I search for the right words. Because even though I'm not ashamed of *us*—not really, anyway—I do feel painfully self-conscious about our age difference sometimes. "When I saw her... It was like a knife to the gut. A reminder that I had a kickass career—it was solid, I was respected—and now it's gone. A reminder of all the things I'd lost from before."

Knox hesitates, pulling my hands away from his face but keeping them in his. "Like your ex?"

"Yes, but not in the way you think. I wouldn't ever go back to Finn. Like, ever. Even if he wanted me back, I would never be able to be with a man who so easily cast me aside." Even if I really was, well... easily cast-asideable. "But it's a part of my life that failed, just like work. And that isn't something easy to face, you know? I've spent the better part of the last few years recovering from it, figuring out what my next move should be. And just when I think I'm getting my shit together... It's there. She's there. The sweetest person I ever worked with, but a reminder that, despite how hard we've been working these past couple of months, I already failed once before. And I just wanted to give myself clout. Wanted to emphasize that I was here on business and not just on a romantic weekend getaway with some guy I've been sleeping with."

Scoffing, he drops my hands and walks away, shaking his head. I hear him mutter something that sounds like "...*some guy I'm sleeping with...*"

"I... That's not what I meant. You know that I—"

"You what?" He turns the full force of his blue eyes, fiery ice, on mine. "Know that I'm just *some guy* you're sleeping with?"

"You're not *some guy*. But even you just said not ten minutes ago that we're sleeping together."

"Yeah. That they could tell we're sleeping together, yes, for sure. But not that I'm just *some guy*—"

"Would you please stop saying it like that?"

"Jesus, Lottie. What the hell are we even doing here?"

Horrified, I stare at him with widened eyes. "I... I..."

"I *care* about you. I want to *be* with you. I've shared things with you that I would *never*— " He drags a hand over his face. "But am I just *some guy* you're fucking? Is that what this is for you?"

I can't breathe. It's like all the oxygen in the room has suddenly been sucked out of the room, the B&B, the entire goddamn planet. My heart beats a fast rhythm in my chest, the sound so loud it's almost deafening.

I squeeze my eyes shut, digging my hands in my hair as I try to calm myself, steady my breathing. Because *of course* I care about him, but we had an arrangement. And I didn't want to fall for him. I never meant to fall for him.

Goddammit. I fell for him.

"We agreed. We agreed to keep it—"

"I swear, if I have to hear you say the word *casual* one more time, I'm gonna lose it."

"Knox..."

He takes a deep breath. "Sorry. That wasn't fair of me. It's —It's what I agreed to in the beginning. What *we* agreed to. But... Lottie. Things have *changed*. Haven't they? Because they have for me."

My lips tremble, a sob caught in my throat. "Yes, they've changed." It's all I can manage right now.

"Do you care about me?" he asks, brows furrowed.

"Of course I do. What are you even talking about? How could you ever believe otherwise?"

"Because if we're sleeping together and you say you care about me, then what's left to discuss?"

There's... so much left to discuss. So much I haven't said. So much I need to say.

"But—the age difference."

He looks at me like I'm crazy, because at this point, I'm just grasping at straws. In the two months we've been together, I can't remember the age thing ever really being a problem. Not really.

"Are you seriously using that as an excuse?"

I take a deep, sharp breath.

"No," I whisper, because it *is* a pathetic excuse, I realize now. Especially after all this time.

"So? Are we together or not?" he asks, panting, every muscle in his body tense as if he were bracing himself for a huge blow.

"I—*Yes*, but—"

"No. No buts. Yes or no, Lottie. Because I'm here. I'm in this. I *want* to be here. I don't want to be with anyone else but you. I don't want to kiss or fuck or hold anyone but you. I want to share my days with *you*. I don't want to expiration date anymore. I don't want this to be a *for now*. I want us to figure things out together. To make this long-term."

But there's so much I can't give you. There's so much we need to discuss. There's so much that doesn't fit.

I can't have kids. And you'll want them some day.

But I can't make the words come out of my mouth. The best I manage is "There's so much we don't know about each other, still." I feel a tear stream down my cheek, which he catches with his thumb just in time.

"We have time to get to know each other. We'll learn. We'll grow. And we'll do it together." He wraps his arms around my waist, which I'm incredibly thankful for because I feel myself losing my footing.

Ever the coward, I swallow hard once and ask "What about your job? You travel for a living. You don't even have a permanent residence—not really. The only reason you probably haven't left is because we've been working on the damn store."

He shrugs nonchalantly, unbothered by the concept of having an income or stability. "Not a big deal. It's because I don't have a set home base that this will make things easier. I can even take shorter projects so I can spend more time with you." He swallows hard once, his Adam's apple bobbing. "Wherever you are will be my home base. If you'll have me. Even when you move to New York. I don't care about where I set my roots, so long as they're where you are."

I press my hands to his chest as my breath catches, feeling his heart beat a steady rhythm beneath my palms. I keep my gaze on my fingertips, doing everything to avoid the smoldering look in his eyes I know he's giving me.

"So we're just going to do this?" I ask, a little dazed, a lot in awe.

He laughs softly. "Be in a relationship?" he asks, pressing his lips just below my ear. His hot breath tickles as he speaks, making me weak-kneed. His arms tighten around my waist, pulling me closer to his chest, and suddenly, I really don't mind.

"A real one."

"Yeah, I think that's the next logical step here." I can practically feel his smile against my delicate skin.

"I..." I can't breathe. And I know I need to tell him. I know I need to say the important part. But the truth is, I've never been this happy. Not really. And the thought of having to ruin this with reality—with the entire truth—is a little heartbreaking. Being with Knox hasn't just been a breath of fresh air, it's made me feel seen. Understood. I'm not ready to give up the happiness of being with someone who cares about me, who I care so deeply about, by telling the truth. And I know it's selfish, and I know I'm just delaying the inevitable. But as I stand there in his arms, his lips pressed to my ear as he whispers how much he cares about me, how often he thinks of me, how he never wants to let this go, I decide I don't care anymore.

I'll cross that bridge when we get to it.

CHAPTER THIRTY-FOUR
LOTTIE

The smell of warm syrup, baked goods, and bacon as I walk into the dining room of the B&B is glorious. That and the three rounds of sex over the past twelve hours lift my spirits up this morning.

I'm trash for a good breakfast. Give me some crispy waffles, smothered in butter under a tsunami of maple syrup (legit Vermont maple syrup, at that!) and a side of sausage and I turn into a big grin emoji for the rest of the day. So the second I see the self-serve all-you-can-eat buffet and I am living for it, already mentally mapping out my first plate—because I will definitely be going back for seconds.

That is, until I spot Madison waving eagerly at me to come over to her table and remember what I'm doing here in the first place. I cringe, but the mouthwatering scent gives me hope that no matter how painfully awkward this meeting could end up going, at least the food will be good.

"You're here! Yay!" She gets to her feet, perfect locks

bouncing, and comes around the table, wrapping her arms around my waist.

Taken aback by her enthusiasm, I whisper "Hey. Yeah."

She pulls away and takes a seat, motioning for me to do the same. "I have to tell you, Lottie. Part of me really thought you'd bail."

A wave of guilt falls over me because I battled with coming up with an excuse to avoid this meeting up until five minutes ago. But I brush the feeling off, and slap on a smile. "Why would you say that?"

"Well," she says, her smile dropping, gaze locked on her fingers as she fidgets with them on the table. "You disappeared from New York. Just into thin air. When I woke up this morning, part of me thought I'd made you up. If it hadn't been for my boyfriend who saw you, too, I could've sworn it was a dream."

"That's a little..." *Melodramatic.* "Unfair. I quit my job, yes. But, I—I never *disappeared.*" Anger flares inside me, but my head's too much of a mess to make sense of everything I felt at that time of my life. Frustration that my body didn't work right, devastation that I had given up on a career I had worked so hard on, hope that it would be for the better only to have it be crushed a couple of years after that. "I was just... going through a lot at the time. I may have... disconnected for a bit, but not disappeared."

Or did I? Was I the one who pulled away from my life in the city and not the other way around?

"Right," she whispers, shrugging under my heated gaze. "It's just... Well. I called. A bunch of times. And... I missed you. You never answered. At one point, I thought something had happened to you. I was kind of devastated because you know, you were my *mentor*. I respected you—still very much do—and felt a little lost when you were gone. It wasn't until I overheard some girls in the marketing department talking about how they saw you at a restaurant the night before that I knew you were still alive."

I laugh dryly, but she glares at me.

"I'm being completely serious, Lottie."

I exhale. "I know. I'm sorry I left and just dropped off the face of the planet. I was going through some shit and... Well."

"Was it because of Finn? Was it because you were getting divorced?" She asks softly.

"No. No, Finn and I weren't there yet. That came a couple of years later. I quit because..." I sigh, already exhausted from this conversation when it's only barely begun. "I quit because I was trying to start a family with him. And it didn't work out."

She raises a questioning brow before looking down at the table again. "I'm not going to ask for any details if you don't want to give them to me. I feel like anything related to family planning is extremely personal and so many people don't realize it. So... if you want to share details, I'm here. If not, it's cool, too. No pressure."

I smile, my heart growing about two sizes as I stare at her compassionate face, remembering how much I loved having her work for me. Madison was smart, hardworking, clever, and, more importantly, had an incredible ability managing people. She was only an assistant, but there wasn't a person in the office she had to work with that she couldn't handle.

The second I interviewed her, I knew she was going far. By the looks of her radiating confidence and the way she carries herself, she has.

"Thanks," I say with a genuine smile, glad I made myself show up this morning. "I really appreciate that. And yeah, people don't really know when to not ask those types of questions."

I don't volunteer more information, so there's a brief pause while she stares at me, wideeyed, and I watch her gears turn, wondering what to say next.

Madison clears her throat after another beat before speaking. "So, how are things, then?

What have you been up to since leaving the company?"

"Well, we covered the family planning and the divorce." I laugh softly and shake my head, wishing I had at least a stack of chocolate chip pancakes to dig into at the same time as I dig into my life. I keep my gaze on the wall just over Madison's shoulder, unable to look her in the eye as I tell her what I've *really* been doing these last couple of years. Something about the familiarity of Madison makes me open up.

"...After everything that happened with the divorce, I went back home for a bit and just... Took a break. Started working at a bookstore. Read a lot and did not much of anything else," I say, a little bashful. "My plan had been to take a beat for a year to recover—financially, physically, and emotionally—and eventually come back to New York and get a new job, but it's taken much longer than I expected."

She sits up in her seat, a small smile tugging at her lips. "So you're back in the city?"

"What? No, I—I'm not back *yet*. The project I'm currently

working on is in my hometown. I hope it will be what helps get me back on track."

"The same bookstore you mentioned?"

I nod. "I'm renovating and revamping the retail space and intend to use the cash from the sale to move back to the city, give myself a big enough runway of time to find a good job. I know I probably won't find anything at the VP level since I've been out of work for so long, but—"

"Wait, stop!" Madison waves her hands in front of me, a huge smile spread across her face, eyes as bright and excited as a child when they receive the perfect birthday present. "You want to come back to the city? To work in fashion again?"

"Uh... Yeah. I mean, yes. That's the plan. I was thinking I'd—"

"No. You were thinking nothing! And you don't need to think of anything! Because... well," she bites her lower lip. "I'm starting my own company and I want you to be part of it."

"You ready to go?" Knox asks, leaning down to give me a quick peck on the nose, holding both our weekend bags.

Breakfast with Madison was yesterday, but I still haven't been able to digest everything—and I'm not talking about the pounds of food I anxiously ate as she discussed her job offer. I mean the weight of her offer. How it could change my entire life. I waded through the crowds of people in the trade show afterwards, letting Knox handle the negotiations and sales all while I ruminated and relived my conversation with her. She handed me everything I was looking for and then some on a silver platter. It was more than I could've dreamed of, more than I had planned for myself, and I still don't know how I feel about it.

"A COO role," she had said before taking a sip of her coffee—though her excitement had her bouncing so much in her seat, I considered suggesting she lay off the caffeine for a bit. "Right now, it's just me and one other person—Beka, an associate designer from where I'm currently at, who is just wasted talent at her level. She's amazing and is going to be big one day, and I want to be the one to help make it happen. I'm currently wrapping up getting investors as start-up money, but it's pretty much a done deal at this point. We're both putting in our two weeks' notice on Monday. Beka'd be Creative Director, of course, and I'm CEO, but we've been looking for a good COO, and..." She sighed happily. "It's just fate, because I know you're it."

I know you're it.

The words floated in my head all weekend, pulling my attention away from everything around me—including the amazing romantic weekend activities Knox had planned for the two of us.

She wants me. She wants me to run the operational side of her new company. Someone is trusting me enough to do what I've been dreaming of doing since I began my career and... And I'm even excited about it.

My first thought was *I need to tell Knox; he's going to be so happy for me.* But I couldn't, for some reason. Sure, we had talked about him following me wherever I decided to move to just the night before. But something about this whole thing made me rethink that. How could I have let him agree to that without him knowing the truth about me? It was something I would have to tell him *before* we began making plans to move.

The truth of the matter is that after this weekend, we'd made enough money to make final payments to our contractor, the electrician, and even hire professional painters to spare us that job. According to Daniel, there was already one company sniffing around the place, asking questions about when and if it would be up for sale. Which meant that I was at the end of the line. It was time to come clean.

But what would happen once I did?

"Lottie? You ready to go or...?" Knox breaks through my panic.

I nod before locking my hands behind his neck to pull him back down to give him a deep kiss. My tongue parts his lips and Knox groans in the back of his throat, dropping the bags to wrap his arms tightly around my waist.

I'm hungry for him. Starved for Knox since Madison offered me a dream job and a ticket out of Ceres Cove. Like I can't and will never get enough of this perfect man. Need builds in the pit of my stomach, between my legs, and my mind is empty of anything and everything that isn't him. Heat spreads all over my body, putting me seconds away from ripping his clothes off in the B&B lobby.

"Pretty Girl," he whispers against my lips, gently pulling away. "You're torturing me. I already checked out of the room—it's not like we can go back before hitting the road." He laughs softly as he pulls my hands from where they hold him to me at the back of his neck. Pressing gentle kisses on my knuckles to soften the blow, he gazes at me with *that* look in his eye.

The one that tells me how much he wants it, too.

But not nearly as much as I do. Because I haven't told Knox about Madison's offer, and the whole thing fills me with dread. Every second that's gone by since he asked me how breakfast went and I replied with a simple "Fine," I've felt the weight of our inevitable end. Sure, he'd said not twenty-four hours before meeting with my former assistant that home was wherever I was, so I know he would move to New York if I asked. But the more and more I process this new potential avenue, the more I think that it might be kinder to Knox to just let him go.

But then his glacier eyes bore into mine, holding me still, and I can't think of anything else but the absolute bliss, the joy, of a life shared with this man. At having him by my side always.

My stomach turns as I struggle to suppress a sob, because I don't want us to end.

He frowns and cups my face. "Baby, what's wrong?"

I want to groan in frustration, because though I love how easily he can read me, it's also one of the things I hate the most about our relationship.

"Nothing, I..." And because I know it will be impossible to pretend like everything is dandy, I say, "I just don't want to leave. It was... such an incredible weekend."

He smiles and pulls me into him, kissing me once more.

"I know. Though I could tell you had a lot on your mind." I press my face into his chest, inhaling his scent, making sure I remember this feeling, this very moment, exactly as it is so I can carry it with me always. His strong arms around me, the way they embrace me protectively, his heart beating loudly against his ribs.

"I understand how upsetting it must've been to run into your old assistant and see her thriving in her current role. In all honesty, I thought it would've been a fantastic opportunity for her to help you get a new job. I didn't know it was gonna end up this way."

I raise my head to look at him. "You what?"

"Yeah. I was a little disappointed when you told me that it was just breakfast and catching up. If she idolized you so much back then, why can't she help you out now? Help you find something? You did tell her you were looking to move back to the city, right? That you were looking to start over?"

"I—Yes, I... think I did. Pretty sure." An understatement if there ever was one, as Madison and I went so far as to discuss potential starting salaries, equity, and benefits. She even offered up her spare bedroom in New York (which, Jesus Christ, she can afford a two-bedroom apartment in Manhattan on her own? Who is she, a Rockefeller?).

"And she still didn't offer up any help?" He frowns, holding my hands in his.

"I... Just help on my resume. She also said she could help put me in touch with some people, maybe," I lie, kicking myself. Why is it so hard? Why am I holding back? He would be happy for me—no, he would be *ecstatic*.

"Still, she should've—"

I clear my throat and peck him on the lips once. "It's okay. She gave me her number, so maybe I can call her next week," I tell him, trying to appease him. "Let's head home. This weekend was amazing, but we still have a lot left to do."

CHAPTER THIRTY-FIVE
LOTTIE

From: Madison Bakay <bakay.m.e@mail.com>

To: Carlota Veracruz <carlota-vera15@mail.com>

Date: Wednesday, May 18th - 3:07 P.M. EST Subject: Re: L&M Designs - COO Role

Hey Lottie,

It was great seeing you last weekend!

I was so happy to see your email this morning asking for more info on the role. I've attached the deck we've been passing around to potential investors. Take a closer look and tell me how you feel about it.

I've spoken to Beka and we both agree that based on your background and just who you are, you'd be a great fit.

When you and I worked together, I used to dream about being part of something big like this with you, because I knew we'd both be able to go far. I can't believe it's actually happening!

Let me know your thoughts and we can talk salary. And like I said, you're more than welcome to stay in my second bedroom while you find your own place in the city. Best,

Mads

I slip the phone back in Knox's coat pocket, snuggling into it, letting its weight and warmth soothe me. The email is burned into my brain, but I keep pulling it up in my phone over and over again, rereading it in disbelief at the twins' birthday party. Knox is busy playing with the kids in the backyard, getting tackled by a dozen mini-NFL players. Meanwhile I watch him, sulking in a corner at my brother's house.

I take a sip of some organic healthy juice pouch thing (whatever happened to *real* Capri Suns, anyway?) and wince. Because I am pathetic. It's here. My ticket out. More than just the means to move out of Ceres Cove, I have an actual *position* waiting for me. A job. I finally have exactly what I've been working so hard to get since the second I came back to this town. And I haven't told a single soul about it. Not my brothers. Not Jenn. Not my sister. And certainly not Knox.

Why, you ask? I have no idea.

But I have to tell someone. *Soon.* Or I swear I'm going to explode. Except that I don't know what to say. *Hey, I got everything I wanted and more but I don't know why I'm not more excited about it?*

I squeeze my eyes shut and lean on the porch rail. "God, what am I even *doing*?"

"What's with the emo vibe, dude? There's free cake and hot dogs. It's perfection." My eyes fly open in surprise.

"Ale."

"You gonna tell me why you're acting all depressed at the twins' birthday party? You're gonna scare the kids if you don't get it together."

I laugh once and slap my older brother softly on the arm. "Just stressed. Adulthood, and all that."

"That's showbiz." He nods and lifts his juice pouch in solidarity. "Now do you want to cut the shit and tell me what's really wrong?"

"*Language*, Alejandro. Your kids might hear you." I shoot him a smile, but he's not having it.

"They've heard worse. Now be serious. Is it Captain Dipshit over there?" He nods in Knox's direction, who's being chased by the entirety of the kids at the party. My heart squeezes in my chest when I catch his eyes and he grins at me. Distracted, he trips over his own feet and rolls on the grass, only to be tackled once more by the little monsters.

"Don't call him that."

Alejandro rolls his eyes. "Fine. Knox. Is it about Knox."

"I... In a way."

"Okay. And what way is that?"

"I, ah... I'm going to tell you something. Something I haven't told anyone. I don't want anyone to know yet because I don't know how to feel about it for some reason." I play with my juice pouch's straw, unable to meet his gaze. "I just... I may need some *solicited* brotherly advice on this one."

I look up to see Ale's brows raised in surprise. "*Solicited*? As in, actively seeking *my* advice?"

"Stop. Don't be a drama queen. Can you help or not?"

"I don't know. Why don't you tell me what this is all about."

I pause and take a deep breath. "Okay. Okay, well. It turns out, this past weekend, I ran into an old coworker from my old job..."

I tell Alejandro everything. How we ran into Madison as soon as we arrived to the B&B and her job offer. I even tell him about Knox and I making the decision to stay together, how he promised he'd follow me anywhere. "And even though we agreed on all that. And even though I was offered a dream job. I still feel weird about it."

He nods thoughtfully. "Do you think maybe it's because you're not as into Knox as you think?"

I pause and look for him in the party, watch how he kneels in front of one of the twins and hands her a lollipop as she cries. Watch the way the rest of my siblings stare at him with googoo eyes. Knox gives my niece a lopsided grin which she can't help but return, wrapping her arms around his neck. He returns her hug, catching my eye from afar, smiling widely at me in victory. My breath catches, my chest filling with light and something more and I can't breathe. He's everything that is good in my life. He's my cheerleader and my support. And I love being those things for him, too. I love him, I think. Not having him in my life just seems unacceptable.

"It's not that," I tell Alejandro. "It's definitely not that. I... I might be falling in love with him." I *know* I am.

Beside me, my brother goes still. He slowly lifts his own drink to his lips and drinks before responding. "Are you sure, Lottie?"

"I..." I feel the stinging behind my eyes build, my lower lip trembling. So I turn around with my back facing the rest of the party to avoid anyone else from seeing me like this. "Yes. Pretty sure."

Grinding his teeth, Alejandro takes a beat to process this info.

"I know you don't like him, but—"

"It's not that. It's not that at all. He's... He's actually really fucking cool. I don't have a problem with him. Maybe when I thought he was just some fuck boy trying to get laid, someone who was going to dump you in a heartbeat. But the way this kid acts... He's more gone for you than you are for him. Anyone can see that. If it wasn't already obvious, then today made it so. He's spent the entire afternoon playing with your nieces and nephews. That doesn't scream casual booty call to me."

"No," I murmur.

"And, this is gonna sound gross, but I can tell he's kind of... devoted to you. The way he looks at you... It's like you're his center of gravity or something."

I feel a tear run down my cheek, but I catch it quickly with my hand.

"But it worries me, this intensity of emotions. Because of what happened last time with Finn. Because of his age. And because I have a feeling you haven't been exactly forthcoming with him about your... health stuff, have you?"

I shake my head.

"I'm scared for you. I was there when you came back, your spirit broken. We all had to watch this ghost for the first year after the divorce float around town in a kind of trance-like state. Seeing you like that..." He shakes his head and looks away. "It was tough, Lottie. So tough. I've never seen anyone so heartbroken before."

"It wasn't about Finn, though. You know that, right? It

was about everything else. The kid thing, the job, having to come back, having no money. Finn was... a dick. But losing him was the least of my concerns. It was more about... about not being enough for anything or anyone."

"I know. But it worries me that you're going to end up in the same situation. Or a version of it at least."

"What do you mean? I can't imagine Knox ever being as cold-hearted as Finn."

"He's young."

I raise a brow, waiting for my brother to finish, but he doesn't reply. "Duh."

"He's *young*, Lottie. So his priorities and what he wants in life might shift a couple of years down the road. And then where will that leave you? Unless you've changed your mind about kids."

My stomach rolls, heart racing. *Kids.*

"No, I haven't." My voice is small, and shaky. "And I don't think I ever will."

"Have you asked him what he wants?" I shake my head, unable to speak.

"I see."

I'm going to throw up. I swear I'm going to throw up any second now.

"Can I make an assessment, then?"

I nod.

"I think you haven't told him or anyone else about New York because you know you have to tell him about the kid thing first. And you're scared because it not only destroyed your last relationship, but the life you had built. But you know it would be unfair to the *both* of you for you to tell him, move your things to the city, only to wait until he's ready for kids to let him know you have no intentions of ever having them. Because I have *never* seen you this happy, Lottie. Not with anyone. That's the truth. And I guess that's why I feel extra overprotective with this guy. Because the higher you are, the harder the fall."

CHAPTER THIRTY-SIX

LOTTIE

"... **I** also spoke to Daniel. Told him that the painters had finished a couple of days ago and that I'd be taking pictures of the space tomorrow for the listing. I have some lighting equipment I brought with me. Not my best stuff, but it'll work. So we should be able to do that," Knox says, his hands on my hips. I slip the key in the lock, still shaken from my earlier conversation with my brother. But Knox doesn't seem to notice my distress, too distracted by our to-do list—and honestly, still probably on a sugar high from all the cake and treats from the birthday party.

When I push the door to my loft open, breaking free from his grasp, I immediately toe my shoes off and hang his leather jacket on one of the hooks. I'm three seconds away from making a run to the bathroom so I can cry in the privacy of my own shower.

"Knox—"

"And then I guess with Walter's apartment, we're almost there. The wall between the store and the stairs has been shut, and the street entrance is done. So we're good there. I need to finish clearing everything out before putting it on the market, but we should have time to do that before we move, right? Or do you have a specific timeline? Because that's cool, too. I just need to let my agent know, because she found me this job—it's just a two-week assignment—but I do need to let her know soon. She also offered a three-month one, but I told her I won't be taking those anymore. Of course those bring in more money, but I don't need much to survive, so—"

"*Knox.*"

He hears the urgency in my voice and immediately stops.

"I'm—I'm tired. Can we talk about this tomorrow?"

"Oh. Okay." He kisses the tip of my nose and slips off his shoes, setting them beside mine. And what once made my heart flutters, what once made me crave this domesticity, now rips at my chest. Because I know what's coming. I know what needs to be done.

"I'm just a little wired, you know? Excited about what's coming." He wraps his arms around my waist, grinning down at me like I'm some coveted prize he's just fought for and won.

Like I'm everything.

And I can't handle keeping him in the dark anymore, because Ale is right. It's time to come clean. Tomorrow, though. Tonight, I just want to enjoy the time we have. I want to—

"I love you."

The metaphorical glass shatters, sharp pieces everywhere.

Air. I need air. I can't breathe. "W-What did you just say?"

His eyes travel all over my face, ice-blue, but warm all over. "I love you, Lottie. I can't wait for us to take this next step together."

"You... You love me?" I don't know why I sound surprised, because I shouldn't be. He agreed to move with me to New York. You don't just do that for anyone. You don't agree to uproot your life all willy nilly.

He huffs out a laugh, tightening his grip around me. "Of course I do." "I—I..." I have nothing to say.

No. That's not true. I have so much I *should* say, but nothing I want to.

Seconds that feel like hours drag on, his expectant gaze on me. Suddenly, his arms feel more like a net ensnaring me rather than a comforting hold. I push out of his grip and turn away, needing the space.

"You... You don't feel the same way." His voice is low, resigned. *Heartbroken.* I have to swallow back a sob.

"That's not it," I whisper. "It's just... I... Before I say it back, before we move forward with our relationship, I need to tell you something."

"You're making me nervous."

I laugh once and turn back to look at him. I'm the one shaking, here. "Yeah."

"Okay. So... spit it out, then. I feel like I'm losing my mind. Because there's very little you could say that would ever make me think twice about being with you. I know you joked about serial killers before, but honestly, the way I feel about you, I'm pretty sure I could live with that too because—"

"I can't have kids." There's a pause while he waits for me to elaborate. "Those health problems I told you about? Well, I'm fine and everything, but... But it means I can't have kids. I have this thing—well, a couple of things, actually. I have endometriosis and PCOS—that's polycystic ovarian syndrome. And it comes with a bunch of issues, like severe pain and bloating and other stuff, but also includes fertility issues. And it's not like you can't have kids when you have either of them, but I have both and from what my doctors have said, it's pretty much impossible in my case because they're both pretty severe. So... I can't have kids. I'll never have kids."

He freezes. Stares back for a second. Scratches the side of his nose. "That's... That's it?"

I recoil. "'*That's it*'? How can you act like it's nothing?"

"I mean, it sucks that you're in pain and it explains a lot and I'm happy you finally told me, since I think this is what you've been hiding this entire time. But you prefaced it like it was going to be this huge thing. This relationship-ending thing. I mean, I'm sure it must be difficult for you, but that doesn't matter to me."

Shock. Pure shock. It's the only way I can describe how his reaction makes me feel. Because this flippant response? It proves that he doesn't get it at all. If he knew what it really meant... Either he doesn't see a future with us—not really— or he's truly clueless.

"Do you not understand what I'm saying here?"

"Of course I do. You... You can't have kids. And that sucks.

I'm sure it must be incredibly difficult for you and I hope you're able to open up more about why that is, since it's obviously a huge deal. But I truly don't **see** how that's an issue for *us*."

"So... So you're okay with it. With not having kids. *Ever*."

He shrugs. "I was secretly kinda hoping one day I'd get a daughter who looked just like you—maybe with my eyes—but it's okay. I think there's very little we can't handle don't you think?"

I smile, that tight fist wrapped around my chest squeezing once more, but in a good way.

But I can't let myself get off track.

"Are you sure? Because I've spent years—*years*—retraining my head and heart to *not* want this anymore. To be happy with this. Finn and I... It's part of the reason why we ended things. I'm sure if we had been a better match, we could've survived it, but... It's all our marriage became about. Having a damn baby. Treatments and forms and diets and negative pregnancy tests and not meeting enough criteria and money. So much money. Sex stopped being about us and instead it became this... this *tool* to make a baby. And it's all I could think about. All my life revolved around. It wasn't healthy. *I* wasn't healthy." I take a deep breath, try to calm my suddenly defeating heartbeat. "It took me years to not only accept this decision, but to embrace it. To be happy with it. To look on the bright side and look *forward* to a life without having kids. And I'm just scared that if we keep doing this, if we keep going where we're going, you're going to want it. And you're going to try to convince me to want it, too. And I can't go through that again. I can't do that to myself or to us. I want to give you everything because I love you, Knox. So much. But I need to love myself more."

"I told you. No one's asking you to have kids. I can live without having my own kids." There's a hint of panic in his voice when he takes a step closer to me, reaching out to take my hand in his. "Did I assume that I would have kids at one point? Yes. Do I like them? Yes. But we don't have to have them to be happy, to be together. I can accept this. I can live with this. We can be together and not have to do the whole 2.5 kids thing. I don't have to want it."

It kills me to say it, and for a second I don't know that I can. But he deserves better than me. "But you'll want them. You will, Knox. And you deserve it because you're an amazing person. And you shouldn't have to sacrifice something so huge—so massive—just to be with me. I love you enough to not take that away from you. You should find happiness with the right person who can give you the things that you need. And if we keep doing this, you're going to change your mind. And I can't put myself in a position again where I'm with a man I love who will leave me because I won't give him what he needs."

"But I don't need that. I need *you*." His eyes are red-rimmed, moisture building. My heart shatters.

For a second, I believe him. I begin to think that maybe this won't be a problem; that he gets it. Because this is happening. Because we *can* get through this together. I underestimated him. I underestimated *us*. And I'm so happy I could fling myself into his arms and—

"I mean, I know you said you tried everything, so I get if you don't want to try the natural way anymore. And it doesn't have to be now or even any time soon. But maybe we can try adoption, you know. A few years down the road. Maybe we can—"

And there it is.

"*No.*" That's when it all comes to an end. Because I won't even accept the *suggestion* of it anymore.

"That's it? We're not... We're not even going to discuss this?"

"You started this off by telling me you were okay with not having kids. Thirty seconds into the conversation, though, you start talking about adoption, about exploring the option together. That's evidence enough that you *can* change your mind. I told you, I'm not doing it. And it isn't because I love you less than Finn—because I *know* I love you more than I ever even hoped to love him. It's because I know what it did to me and what it did to our relationship. And I've seen it through my perspective, and it sucked. And even when everything goes right, like how it went with my brother and his husband, it's a lot. I am forever burnt out by it. I don't want it. I don't want to ever have it. I want to learn to be happy with my career. I want to make something of myself and—my god—I know some people might think I'm a horrible person, but I *know* I can have a happy life without kids. It's not worth the effort for me."

"Fine. We won't have kids. I'd rather have you, anyway. Please don't do this." He grips my biceps, his blue eyes wide, pleading—filled with hurt.

I did that. It's all my fault. I let this go on far too long.

I shake my head, something wet and salty on my lips. "I don't believe you. I think you believe that that's true, but... I thought we could, but then... Today, seeing you playing at the birthday party with my nieces and their friends... You love children."

"I... I do. But just because I'm good with kids, doesn't mean I have to have them. It doesn't mean I wouldn't be happy just being an uncle or something. Didn't you tell me you loved being an aunt? I can love being an uncle. We'll— We'll spoil them. We can just be the favorite aunt and uncle."

"No, Knox. You're always going to have this small ember of hope that I'll change my mind. And it's not happening."

"There's no fucking ember! There's nothing else! All there's ever been since the second I laid eyes on you is *you*. Please, Lottie. Don't do this."

"You're still young. This is what you think you want, but you'll change your mind."

"Don't tell me what I want."

"I won't go through the same thing again, Knox. I just won't. This needs to end. Tonight. Now. We can't keep going on like there's a future here."

"So that's it?" His voice breaks. "You're not even going to give me a chance to prove to you that I can love you through this? That we don't need kids or a 'conventional' life to be happy? For fuck's sake, Lottie, you aren't being fair."

"I'm being the most fair. I'm giving you a chance at a happy life. And myself. I'm undoing my mistake. *This* was a mistake. I'm sorry. We're over."

He holds my face in his hands and presses his forehead to mine. "I won't be happy without you." His eyes water, as his thumbs caress my cheeks, wiping tears off my face. "Please don't do this to me. Don't do this to *us*."

"You'll thank me in five years," I say through my tears, sniffling. "When you're traveling the world, unattached. Or even in your backyard watching your kids chase each other around next to a wife who's closer to your age. Who could give you all the things I couldn't—wouldn't. You'll think of me fondly, as the woman who once loved you enough to let you go and allow you to have the future you didn't think you wanted but now can't live without."

"But I love you. So much."

"I know."

I hold onto his wrists and pull his hands away from my face. He doesn't fight me anymore—he knows I've won. There's no way I'm backing down. I kiss him for the last time, on the cheek, feeling his tears beneath my lips.

"Please go."

CHAPTER THIRTY-SEVEN

KNOX

I adjust the tripod height and the light umbrella, making sure the shot catches the best angle of the light coming into the bookstore. Or rather, empty space. We've staged the place with a few knick-knacks on the new shelves, put a fake plant in a corner, and a vase of flowers by the register. But other than that, the space looks depressing and bare in comparison to the organized brown chaos it used to be.

I sigh, checking the time on my phone once again.

She's late.

She should've been here for the photoshoot over an hour ago, and she's nowhere to be found. The last time she was late she was bedridden—couldn't even get up from the pain. What if it's the same thing now? What if she needs me to come get her? I could take care of her. Show her that I can be there for her, no matter what. Show her that last night was dumb and we should just *be* together. I don't care about the kid thing because all I care about is *her*. She makes me happy.

And we *can* be happy, just us two. We can get a dog or something. I'll even agree to a cat, if that's what she wants.

I consider dropping the shoot and heading straight home to her, but I stop myself. Because I know better than to push her. Even if I'm running on exactly zero hours of sleep. Even if it feels like every muscle in my body is sore. Even if it feels like my heart has been ripped from my chest and kicked across the floor.

I know better.

Plus, we do need to get this done—it's one of two remaining sticky notes still hanging from Walter's office— and I'm not going to let a bump in our relationship stop me from finishing this. Because it *is* a bump. It's *gotta* be. Lottie and I cannot be over. Last night... Last night was just a glitch in the matrix or something. We're still together. We'll get through it. She just needs time.

The bells above the store doors jingle making my heart somersault in my chest. I exhale in relief.

"*Finally*. I've been waiting all day for—"

"Hey, man. I just came to see how the photoshoot was going." Daniel walks in, briefcase in hand, sad smile on his face.

He knows.

"Hey. Yeah, it's going good. I'm pretty much done." There's no use in hiding the disappointment or misery in my voice. Literally could not possibly care less right now. There's only one person I wanna see today and she still hasn't shown up. "Sorry. Thought you were Lottie."

"Lottie?" Daniel furrows his brows. "I... No. Why would you even think that? Of course not."

I freeze, something in the look in his eyes sending a shiver down my spine. "What—" I clear my throat. "What do you mean *of course not?*"

"Well... I—Because she left."

No. Because... because *no.* Absolutely not.

"She *left?*"

His face falls, drags a hand across his mouth. "Are you saying she didn't even bother to—" He exhales, shaking his head. "She didn't tell you?"

"Daniel. You're going to need to explain yourself. Because if what you're saying is true. If—If—" I will lose it. I will officially lose it.

Daniel looks like he'd rather be anywhere but here—doing his taxes, scrubbing his toilet bowl, having to sit through three hours of C-Span—literally anywhere but in front of me right now. So when he tells me the words I've most dreaded hearing, I know he made it to the bookstore out of the kindness of his heart to check up on me.

"She's gone, man. I—I thought that's why you broke up? Because she left."

"Where the—" I take a breath, try to slow down my heart as it beats a deafening drum against my ribs. *She's gone.* "Where did she go?"

"I think you know."

New York.

"Right." The need to scream is almost overpowering, but I can't make myself speak over a whisper.

"That friend of hers. The old coworker? Lottie took the job she offered."

What job? Madison offered her a job? She never told me

about a goddamn job. Never told me Madison had come through with anything. "Right." I nod as if I knew. As if she'd told me. As if she cared enough to keep me in the goddamn loop about her plans. As if we really had been partners like I thought we had evolved to and not just the fuck buddies we started off as.

"I'm sorry, man. I really am. I thought she would've... I did think it was all very sudden. She hadn't said anything all day yesterday at the birthday party and then this morning I got a call from her and..." He shrugs, looking a little helpless.

"Yeah. No."

He says something else, but I'm not listening anymore, the past two and a half months flashing in my head like some kind of torturous reel.

I didn't even merit a fucking goodbye?

I can't be here anymore. I really can't. I need to figure out what my next steps are. Figure out what I'm supposed to do for the rest of my life now that...

"Daniel," I interrupt whatever the hell he was saying. I don't care. "I think I'm done here. In more ways than one."

He opens his mouth to speak, but immediately closes it. I can see in his eyes how apologetic he is, how much he wants to help. But no one can help now. Finally: "I understand."

I grab my camera and pop the SD Card, slapping it on the counter. "Here are the photos for the listing. Obviously unedited and maybe not enough of them, but you can hire someone else to do that for you. I'm done." I don't want them in my life—all those photographs of this town, of her, of us—of this fucking relationship we were building even when we thought we weren't... I don't want the reminders.

The temptation to revisit them when she's made it very clear it will never be a reality. They are merely photos of a moment in time—nothing more.

"If she's gone, then... Then I'm gone. I can't be here anymore."

"Wait. *What?* No. What about the rest of the tasks we need to complete? And the sale?"

I start breaking everything down, packing up my equipment. "Jenn can handle whatever's left. It's not much, and she's honestly more than capable. And you have my email for everything else. And with regards to Walter's apartment... There's still some stuff there—I haven't cleared everything out. But I'll just hire some guys to put it all into storage. I'll pay you to clean it up and stage it."

I'm done. I'm gone.

It doesn't take long for me to pack up my things; I just need the basics. Like I told Daniel, I schedule some movers to get the rest of my stuff—Walter's stuff—for the following week. They'll shove it into some storage somewhere out of sight, out of mind. All I decide to take with me are my camera gear and some clothes. But as I'm wrapping up the last of my packing, I don't reach for my leather jacket. The sight of it tears at my heart, shreds it, the mix of her scent with mine too difficult to bear. I think of how sexy she looked wearing it, each time she did waking my caveman instincts. *Mine* was all I could think of, despite never realizing she was far from that. Always keeping me at arm's length, even after thinking that I'd brought all her walls down.

Never mine.

I toss it on the bed, leaving it behind. Don't even want to look at it anymore.

It takes me a moment to get to a place where I feel comfortable driving. I have a nine hour trip ahead of me to my mother's place and it's not a good idea to drive this distracted, is it? With your heart torn to pieces and your mind a jumbled mess?

Because it isn't just the reason why I'm leaving that's got me rattled. It's my destination. After all of this, after reading all those snippets of Walter's innermost thoughts, there is no other option but to confront my mother. And even if I didn't, even if I choose to avoid the topic altogether, the fact that most of my professional gear is stored at her house means that I won't be able to avoid her regardless. And I know myself. I know that after everything that's happened, everything I've learned, there's no way I'm not going to question her.

I realize I'm the one who's throwing myself out of the pan and into the fire, but I can't keep avoiding my father forever. Or our sudden similarities—both suffering from unrequited love, both betrayed by the women they worshipped.

Finally, I get it together at least enough to walk, only to trip on one of the boxes I left by the front door. Walter's journals—so many of them still unread. With Lottie's help, I'd gotten through some, never able to face his words by myself. But now I'm alone. And it's something I'm going to have to accept, whether I like it or not.

I swing my camera bag strap over my chest on my left

shoulder, my duffel bag on my right, and carry one of the boxes of journals all the way to my truck.

Before I start the engine, I shoot off an email to my agent accepting the three-month job—fuck it, who's gonna miss me anyway?—and slam my hands on the steering wheel hard and loud enough to draw some looks from multiple passersby.

It's fine. The outsider is leaving. They can add that to the list of shit they'll say about me.

And without another thought, without any other ounce of hesitation, I leave just like she did.

I wake up the next day in my mother's guest room just at the break of dawn—just a few hours after having arrived to the house. Last night, I didn't stop once for food or bathroom breaks, laser-focused on one thing and one thing only: the truth. Because it seems to me that I haven't been getting much of it over the course of my life. Not from my mother, my father, or the person I thought was the love of my life. Using the key under the mat, I let myself in, snuck into the spare bedroom, and tried to fall asleep despite knowing the tough conversation that awaited me this morning.

The sound of dishes clattering together, cabinets being opened and closed, alert me to my mother being awake, despite the early hour. And just from that, I know it's an admission of guilt.

Because Melissa Riddick is far from a morning person.

Heaving a sigh, I throw the covers off and pad out of the bedroom and into the kitchen. I stop in the doorway, arms crossed in front of my chest, as I stare at her. In her messy top-knot and pajamas, sitting at the worn kitchen table, my mother looks more vulnerable and frail than the hero I've always regarded her as.

"Ma. You're up early."

With obvious effort, she meets my gaze with wide, blue eyes. Same as mine. Lips trembling, tears building, she knows exactly why I'm here.

"I heard your truck when you came in last night. Been up since."

"Sorry I woke you." But even I can tell from my flat voice that I couldn't care less. Not now. Not after everything. Not before I get some answers.

"It's fine." She sniffles and looks down. Waiting.

"I think it's time we talked. Don't you?"

She nods once, taking a sip from her coffee. "I knew it would come to this the second you told me about the inheritance. When you told me you were going see it, stay and help sell it. It was only a matter of time."

I sit at the kitchen table, the same one that traveled around with us each time we moved to a new town. Scratches and crayon stains from when I would sit here and do my homework or play while Ma cooked us dinner. Years of just her and me, thinking we were a team, when all this time it was just her choosing what was best for Melissa. Not us.

"If you truly believed that, don't you think it would've been best if you'd just told me from the get-go? Or, better yet, when I was a kid?"

"I don't know. I was so young when I got pregnant. So scared. And everything with Walter was so intense. High highs, lowest of lows. I didn't think I could handle that for the rest of my life. Because that's what having a kid with someone means—even if you never marry the person. They will forever be in your life."

I grind my teeth, white-knuckling the table. "Yeah, but it could've meant something better for *me*. I would've had a father growing up and not just those few years after you came clean. Maybe if Walter and I had had a stronger relationship, we would've survived our stupid fight before I went off to college. Maybe he wouldn't have passed away while we were still estranged. Maybe I would've been able to forgive my father and said goodbye to him. Did you ever think about that?" I don't mean to raise my voice at my mom, but it's hard to keep my emotions in check when I'm suddenly letting myself feel them so viscerally for the first time.

She wipes her nose with the back of her hand. "Obviously."

"Because I get pulling your kid away from his parent if you think they're a bad guy. But from what I've learned over the last almost three months, Walter wasn't the man you made him out to be. He showed up for *everyone*. And Ma, he was..." I push out a breath of air. "He was so fucking devoted to you. You should see the shit he wrote about you. About your relationship—"

"*What*? You've been reading his journals? Is that how you found out about everything? Knox, that is a complete invasion of my privacy."

"*Your* privacy? Are you kidding me? If anything, it's an invasion of *his*. And he left everything to me, so as far as I know, he *wanted* me to read them. I think he knew you gave him the wrong end of the stick and he just had to deal. From what I've read, he never wanted to come clean about every-thing and cast a divide between the relationship you and I had. But it didn't mean he was okay with it, either. He was hurt. And he wanted to be my father just as much as I wanted him to be."

She looks away, swiping at a stray tear. "I... I don't even know what to say other than

I'm sorry. Other than to tell you that I was young and so... so *terrified* of how much I loved him, Knox. But for how much we cared about each other... He was fourteen years older. And I was just graduating and everything was so intense. And of course, there were so many times before the accident when we were struggling that I wanted to call him. But I didn't, because I knew I wanted him back in our lives one day. I just didn't want that day to be because we needed him. I wanted to make him proud. But we struggled so much and part of me was scared he'd take you away. And then the car crash happened, and we didn't really have a choice..." She shakes her head at the memory, my eyes going straight to her neck, to the only visible scars from the accident from where the glass shattered and cut her up. "I regretted keeping him out of your life the second I held you in my arms and thought how awful I was for not letting him be here and share this moment with me. With us."

"Then why not just call him, Ma? From the hospital, the second I was born. He showed up for us almost ten years later. He would've done the same." My chest aches from the loss, so different than the one I feel from that of Lottie. Grief, like she said, comes in so many shapes and sizes and for different reasons.

My mother sobs, putting her face in her hands as she cries. "I-I know you're looking for a good reason, but there isn't one. There just isn't one, Knox. Other than the fact that I was a coward or scared that he was going to take you away from me... There was no other reason."

"Ma." My voice breaks. "You let me believe he never wanted me in the first place. You let me believe he asked you for an *abortion*."

"I know. I'm so sorry. I'm s-so s-sorry." She can't get any more words out, choking in between sobs. Not able to stand it anymore, I kneel beside her and take her into my arms, rocking her gently from side to side.

"Shh. Ma."

She claws at my shirt, burying her wet face in my neck as she finishes crying. After a few minutes, when she seems to have calmed down some, I pull back, and say, "I don't know how to forgive you for this."

"I know."

"But I think you talking about him, about your relationship, about *you* might help. I can't be kept in the dark anymore. I'm... I'm full of regret and—" My voice breaks. It takes me a minute to gather myself again. "I need to know."

"Okay. Anything you need. Anything. I promise."

"I also think you need to read his journals with me."

She pulls back in a panic. "What? No. No, I don't think I'm strong enough to do that. To see what he really thought of me. It's selfish, I know, but I can't have all my worst fears confirmed because... I wouldn't be able to bear it, Knox. I-I-I..."

"Ma." I put my hands on her shoulders. "He loved you.

He said so over and over again. You broke his heart, but he always loved you. So please. I need someone to help me go through harder passages. You owe it to me to stand by and answer any questions I may have. You owe me."

She swallows hard once before nodding. "Yes. I'll—I'll sit with you. We'll go through them together."

"Okay. Because there's one entry I've been wanting to read but haven't been able to bring myself to. It's the one after the last time we spoke." It's the one Lottie was helping me gear up for. The one she promised we'd face as a team. And I know I could do it alone now, but I want my mother beside me. I want her there as we explore things together. I want her to answer questions about him that Lottie would never have been able to provide.

Without an ounce of hesitation, I bring in the boxes of journals from the truck, setting them in the living room. My mother walks in with the mugs of coffee and sets them down on the table while I find what I'm looking for: the journal from the last year I spoke to my father.

Mom and I settle into the couch, sitting side by side. I flip through the pages, and, while I don't remember the exact date I told my father I never wanted to see him again, I guess the month. From there, we flip through each day, skimming its contents before going back to them at another time, before arriving to the date we want.

Thursday, June 7th

CHAPTER THIRTY-EIGHT
KNOX

Thursday, June 7th

Knox and I argued this afternoon. He's been trying to convince me for the past couple of months that his destiny is to go to art school. While of course, I think of the arts as being important, I want more for him. I see the life he has now—the life Melissa and I can provide for him—and it isn't enough. Yes, as a university professor I made enough money to keep me quite comfortable after my tenure, but in this economy, it isn't enough for me to give the two of them the life they deserve. Especially not after having paid Melissa's medical bills. Or most of them.

I'm scared for Knox. And can't help but wonder what the hell he's thinking about wanting to take this path after the way he and his mother struggled financially for so long.

Becoming a successful artist... One who can support themselves, let alone a family, is so rare. A one in a million shot. And he's just going to jump into it head first?

I admire his confidence and I am proud that photography—something that was our thing, something I taught him—is his passion. But can't he pick something more stable?

I tried to reason with him, but it was impossible. And once he started raising his voice, calling me all these names, insulting me... I realized the resentment he still felt for me after all these years. It runs deep.

I don't blame him for it. I know that it's Melissa who fed him the lies. But like I've said many times, he already has a broken relationship with one parent—I'm not breaking the only one he still has.

I'm a disappointment to him. Someone who could never come through. I'm someone who doesn't support him.

It crushed me, to see him like this. To hear what he really thinks of me.

Which is why I said what I said. Those horrible words I wish I could take back.

"I wish your mother had never told me about you."

But it wasn't about him. God, never about him. Knox is brilliant and so talented. All I meant is that maybe, if I had never known about him, he could've maintained this nebulous, vague idea of who I was. Without having evidence to how awful of a father I am.

I hate that I've been this monumental let down. I hate that he will forever think of me as this awful man who abandoned his mother in her time of need, who never wanted him, who is disappointed in him and unsupportive.

I wish I could tell him how much I love him, how happy I am he exists, how proud of him

I am. But he'll never believe me.

Maybe once he cools down—once we both do—we can get through this.

I am just utterly terrified that I've ruined everything. That he hates me more now that he knows me. That maybe he'd liked me better if I had stayed away.

. . .

After I finish reading the passage aloud, neither my mother nor I speak a word for a good moment. There's... so much information to process, my head is spinning with it. His relationship with my mother, for one. The fact that he never expected our argument to last ten years. How proud of me he truly was. His concern for my future. But more importantly, what the last words I ever heard him speak truly meant.

I don't know what to say to my mother, so I go with the first thing that pops into my head: "He helped pay for your medical bills?"

She sniffles, and it's only then that I realize she's crying. "Yeah. He... He didn't want me to have any debt hanging over our heads."

I nod, my eyes still on the pages, running my index finger over his handwriting, feeling the indentations in the paper. "Did you love him?"

She clears her throat. "Yes... And no. Not the same way he loved me."

So we're both winners in that regard. Walter spent his whole life loving a woman who wouldn't love him back—the same destiny that waits for me now. What other similarities do we share other than heartbreak?

"I wish I had. But I realized that maybe I was looking for something different in our relationship. A protector. I was never really sure whether I loved him as much as he loved me. I didn't trust my feelings."

"Right."

"I... You can't help how you feel, Knox. Or how you *don't*."

I laugh once, humorlessly. "You'd get along so well with someone I know."

I flip through the journal, words jumping out at me, calling to be read. But I need a minute before I move on.

"Thank you." My mother kisses my cheek. "For making me listen to this. It's... incredibly difficult because I did really care for your father. But I appreciate it. I needed to hear this."

I swallow once, shrugging. "Yeah."

"How about I make us some breakfast so we can keep reading together? I'll take the day off from work."

We spend the time flipping through journals, picking out random years and months, going as far back as the day he met my mother.

It's wild to me, how he was able to record his entire life in these journals without missing a single day, the oldest one dating back to his first year of teaching. By the end of the day, we still have years and years to go through, but I feel like I've gotten one step closer to getting to know him.

"What do you know about his life in Scotland? About growing up there and his family?"

"Not much," my mother admits between sniffles. "I know the name of his hometown and a bit about his childhood, but I never met any family members of his. Never knew him to be too open about them. I did know he missed Scotland quite often. He'd visit at least once a year, but I never went with him, obviously. He invited me several times, but... I never agreed for some reason. It didn't feel right."

"Do you know when he moved to the US?"

"Right after he finished his doctorate in Cambridge. He

chose to pursue teaching in an American university. Said it was his way of doing charity work for illiterate populations." She smirks, as if getting caught in a memory.

I laugh softly. "What an ass."

"Yeah." Mom sighs deeply, wistful. "But I think he always planned on going back."

I nod. "He had told his friends the same. Except that he didn't want to leave me behind.

We weren't even talking, and he stayed here, just in case I chose to forgive him."

Guilt doesn't even begin to describe the depth of my emotions now. The regret. The *despair.*

"Ma. You certainly were the origin of this... this misunderstanding. But all three of us are at fault, here. He could've cleared things up and asked to come see me—especially when he found out he was sick. He should've talked to me and told me the truth. And I could've grown the fuck up and tried to talk to him, too. I could've sat down and let him explain everything to me. Forgive him. And now he died the way he did, alone."

She gasps. "He was alone?"

"Not literally. Not the moment it happened. Lottie. She... She was one of his employees. She was there." Just saying her name makes me wince—another slice, another ache. "But what I mean is, he got sick and went through all that alone. He didn't tell anyone. He knew he was dying and chose to keep it quiet."

"Oh."

"All I'm saying is, you're not the only one who should feel guilt. There's enough blame to go around."

"Still, I'm sorry for the role I played in this. You deserved better."

I exhale, pushing my fingers through my hair. I lean back against the couch and stare up at the ceiling. "God. How did everything get so messed up?"

"Well, what you just said. With—"

I shake my head and put my face in my hands. "Not just us. With... other people, too."

"You mean with that girl you've been seeing? Is it the one you just mentioned?"

"How did you... How did you know I was seeing someone?"

"You haven't stayed in one place for more than a couple of weeks since art school. In the past, you would've been there to help, but there's no way you would've been able to stay there for longer than a month without taking an impromptu trip to some desolate place or something."

"I went to a B&B in Vermont for a weekend away. Does that count?"

She snorts. "No. It sounds more like a romantic getaway, not a Knox getaway."

I snort. "You're not wrong."

"So, what's up with this girl? Is she still in that town?"

"No. She's gone." I can't bear to look at my mother, to see the look in her face. So I keep my eyes on my feet.

"And you two...?"

"Are done. She broke up with me."

"Then she's an idiot."

I laugh and shoot her a look.

"What?"

"It's just, I keep comparing my situation with Lottie to that of yours and Walter's. The whole unrequited love of it all. So, in a way, you just called yourself an idiot."

She laughs too. "I feel like we already established that, though. I agreed."

"True."

"So what's next for you?"

"I was planning on taking this assignment. It's in Kenya—an amazing opportunity to be with the Masai for three months. But." I sigh.

"But?"

"But I want to learn more about Dad. I want to... I think I want to head over to Scotland. Find his family. Learn more about him. I think I owe it to him and to myself. And it sucks, because I will never get to have a relationship with him, but... This way I can finish getting to know him. I think I need this."

"I think you need this, too. I think it's a fantastic idea, hon'."

"Yeah. It'll piss off my agent, though. I literally just agreed to this other assignment yesterday." But I honestly couldn't care less. It's time I got to know this mysterious man who'd only revealed himself to me in death. It's time I dug deeper. For him and for myself.

"Your mental health is more important than any of that, Knox." And I know she's right.

"How long would you be gone for?"

"I don't know, Ma. As long as it takes to get to know him better? To find answers to questions I didn't even know I had?"

She nods, serious. "I have some money saved up, if you need it. You can—"

"I don't need anything. I have enough money saved up until the cash from the store and apartment sales come through."

"But if you—"

I take her hands in mine. "Thank you. I know you're just trying to make it right—do your part. But this is the part I do need to do by myself."

CHAPTER THIRTY-NINE
LOTTIE

It's never been more obvious to me—or probably anyone, for that matter—that I'm a transplant. What's a transplant, you ask? Someone *not* from New York City who currently *lives* in New York City. Which is hilarious, because in the 14 or so years I lived here I never once felt like one. Not even during my freshman year at NYU. I would sit on a bench in Washington Square Park surrounded by other students and New Yorkers and never once feel out of place— or look it. So as I do the same right now, as I sit at the very same bench with my good friend—and now business partner—at my side, I wonder when I started feeling this disconnect.

I used to feel like I was *born* for this city. Like maybe someone made a mistake and the universe somehow dumped me in a small coastal town in Maine on accident. It was the stork's fault—they were disoriented. Then the devastation I felt when I had to leave the city only seemed to reinforce this idea in my mind that I belonged there. That I craved those special New York moments—you know the ones. That I needed the hustle and bustle of all five boroughs (yes, even Staten Island), each one, special in its own way.

And they are. They are all amazing. But I'm starting to wonder whether I've changed too much. Whether I no longer feel the same passion for the industry I used to work in. Whether I'm just... over it. Or if it's something more. Is it what I've left behind that's making me feel unsettled? Is it Knox? My family? Or is it both?

"So where are we with factories, then?" Madison stabs a big helping of her salad and shoves it in her mouth.

God, I had forgotten all about the damn massive salads for lunch. I hate them.

"I spoke to the one in Florence. I think we should steer clear of Spain, since they basically shut down all of August. I mean, Italians take the summer off too, but I feel like they're better at keeping business going."

"Amazing. *God,* this is going to be so great. I can't wait."

Madison is two seconds away from detonating from excitement. Meanwhile, I keep waiting for the rush of satisfaction to course through me. For that intense shot of adrenaline I get whenever things seem to fall in place the way I felt during the reno, or even before in my last job.

But nothing. I get nothing. It's been a month, and still nothing.

I don't understand. I'm doing something bigger than I ever did—a dream job. I'm living *rent-free* in New York City— unheard of. And I have fantastic business partners in Madison and in Lucy, who turned out to be exactly as described: sweet and incredibly talented. And yet I feel unfulfilled and so fucking lonely. I miss my family so much, it's almost embarrassing. And Knox? Sometimes I can't *breathe* when I think about him or the way we left things.

The most surprising bit of it all? I miss Ceres Cove, too. I miss the stupid small town gossip. The way everyone knows everyone. And the bookstore. I miss working there and all the fun I had renovating it.

Deep down, I'm devastated by the sale. It happened quickly, the money having come through just last week. But it isn't just the fact that it's gone, that my final connection to Knox has been severed. It's also the fact that I won't be there to see who is replacing Walter's spot. I didn't know the buyer, so the thought of giving up this piece of my town to a complete stranger who could be taking away its charm...

God, what if they put in a national chain or something?

I shiver.

"You okay?" Madison breaks through my doomsday musings, shooting me a look.

No, I want to say. No, I'm not okay. Because I'm currently going through one of the worst endo flare-ups I've ever had, missing home and my family and Knox so much I can hardly breathe. I'm not okay because I have everything I asked for and more, and yet I'm still not happy. If possible, I'm even more miserable than I was six months ago. Because I found something that made me happy and *someone* who made me happy. And I traded them both in for this idea I had in my head of what success and true fulfillment were.

I'm kind of miserable.

I try to keep a handle on my emotions. I really do. When I open my mouth to reply, it's just to feed her an excuse. But...

Before I know it, the words are out of my mouth: "Mads, this isn't for me anymore."

"What isn't for you anymore?"

"This life. New York. This job. I... I am *so* sorry. I'll help you find and train someone else, if you'd like. And I am so thankful you let me stay with you all this time. But... I can't, Mads. I am so unhappy."

"Lottie... Are you serious?"

"I need to go home."

If you've spent some time in New York City, I'm sure you've probably seen some crazy things. So two women hugging on a park bench while one of them sobs into the other's neck?

Not really something that would alarm anyone in the vicinity. That's the thing about New York. You can be having a major emotional breakdown in public, but feel so isolated from everyone, you may as well be alone in your room.

To her credit, Madison never once gets upset with me. She holds me through my entire verbal diarrhea as I tell her all about Knox and the town, my family and the bookstore. She asks questions about why I loved working there so much. She makes comments when my face lights up and holds me tightly when I cry harder.

"...And it's just ridiculous, because all this time I've been working towards getting back to exactly where I am now. But now that I'm here... God, I've never felt more lost."

"What made you want to leave Ceres Cove to begin with?"

"Initially, it just felt like there was nothing there for me. But maybe I just wasn't looking hard enough. Because my family is there and... I don't know. I guess, in all honesty, I only started feeling at home when I started working on the bookstore renovations and sale. It gave me purpose. And it felt good to be making something *better*. In a way, I knew I was giving back to the town as well as riding the high of being good at my job."

"Hmm. Honestly, Lottie, I don't know how you haven't realized what you need to do by now."

"What do you mean?"

"I mean, you're obviously not happy here. And it sounds like what actually made you happy wasn't just your boyfriend. It sounds like it was being part of something bigger that brought joy to your life. And while this job, starting this company, is about being involved in something bigger... It certainly isn't the same. I think with the bookstore you got to give back to your community. The work brought you back to life, but it was the people and the bookstore itself that made you connect to your town and to yourself."

I bite my lower lip and look around Washington Square Park, processing Madison's words. I love this New York. I really do. But it's not a part of my present anymore. It's a chapter in my life that belongs in the past.

"You know, while doing the reno, I kept wondering what kind of business would take its place. And I'd be filled with so many ideas. So many ways I could make the town better, bring more things to it to make it feel more complete and independent from the outside world. And... it kind of kills me to not be part of that, you know?"

"So why not go and be a part of it, then?"

"*How?*"

"I can't answer that question for you, Lottie. To quote the great Taylor Swift, 'You're on your own, kid.'"

I snort and wipe my nose with the back of my hand.

"I have an idea. But it's buck wild and... and I'm gonna need people's help."

"It's more than okay to ask for people's help. That's how you learn. That's how you taught me everything I know."

I laugh, and it comes out a little wet, a little sniffly. "I could make a lot of people really happy. I could make them feel safe, too."

"What about you, though? Will it make *you* feel happy and safe? Because that's what matters."

I take a deep breath and pause, running through the different ideas I'd been flirting with for months, now. As if by some exterior force, they begin to piece themselves together, materializing into something greater in my head. *A concrete plan.*

"Yeah. Yeah, I think it will. I just need to make a call."

CHAPTER FORTY

KNOX

As I drive down Main Street on my way to the cemetery, I try not to let my mind—or my gaze—wander too much. I'm here for one reason and one reason only: to visit my father's grave and to say goodbye.

In the months I lived in Ceres Cove, I never once did this. I never once gathered up the strength or courage to visit it. I missed his funeral by an hour, so that opportunity was lost, and I kept making excuses to myself about why I couldn't go after.

Truth is, I was scared. I didn't know how to feel about Walter back then—certainly not in those first days. Now, though, after months of reading his journals and traveling all around Scotland, after reaching out to extended family and friends, I feel like I have a grasp on the kind of man Walter—my *dad*—was.

He was a quiet Scot, from a minuscule town, who was looking for adventure after his doctorate. It's why he made the crazy decision to go straight into teaching in America. He was a secret romantic who fell for my mother the second she walked through his classroom door. They fought it for a long time, but eventually let themselves fall in love. From what I'd heard from his brother (I have an uncle!), Dad knew immediately Ma was *it* for him. The trouble was that, even though my mother had strong feelings, I don't think she knew how to follow through on them. He was devastated when she left, spent many years wondering about her as he continued to teach, hoping one day she'd come back. Was both enraged and overjoyed when she did, pissed for hiding me but thankful I existed. He loved me through all our fights and arguments, through the decade we weren't speaking. Kept tabs on his son like the devoted father he truly was. Took care of my mother, even when she didn't ask for help. And in his final days, after he'd been diagnosed, he wanted to leave me with something he thought would bring me eternal happiness.

And no, it wasn't the bookstore.

I turn onto the gravel driveway, following the directions in my email while I wind through the cemetery. It's my first time in one, so I can't help but feel a pang of sadness as I think about all the people who lost loved ones. I drive by a couple laying flowers on a headstone, leaning into each other with solemn faces. And then the guilt hits me, because I don't think anyone's come to visit Walter since his funeral. Did many people attend? I could never bring myself to ask Lottie.

God, just thinking her name makes my heart ache. Even after all these months, I love her just as much as I did the last time I laid eyes on her. And now being here, in this town... I knew it would open up old wounds, but I owed it to both my dad and myself to come.

Once I make it to the row of plots, I park my truck and freeze. It takes a couple of deep breaths before I can gather enough strength to get out. After just a few moments, I reach him.

His headstone looks relatively new, having been placed only recently. Just a bit of moss is growing on it, which I brush off when I kneel before him.

"Hey, Dad." I have to choke down a sob, squeeze my eyes shut while I gather myself. "I'm sorry it took me so long to come see you. I've been trying to sort through everything that's happened between us. Not just after we fought, but my entire life. And yours, for that matter." I pause. I thought I'd feel silly, speaking to a stone. But there's something cathartic about saying things out loud. Something big about admitting your feelings.

"I'm sorry, Dad. I... I don't think there are words enough to describe how sorry I am about the time we wasted being apart. I'm sorry for being so immature. It's been about nine months, and I think I've finally completed the five stages of grief, though I gotta say denial stuck with me so damn long I was starting to believe it wasn't what I was experiencing. But I'm sad, Dad. And... And I guess I've accepted that. I guess I've accepted you're gone and, as much as it hurts, I've accepted there's no way we'll ever get that time back. But I loved getting to know you better over the past six months. So thank you for leaving me enough breadcrumbs that I could follow in my journey to do so. Reading your journals was incredibly difficult, but... it was nice. Getting to know you like that. I only wish you'd have known me better. Or maybe not. Maybe you'd be disappointed in me. Who knows?" I sigh and sit back, crossing my legs in front of me on the dewy grass. "I gotta say it was extremely frustrating at times, though, reading your journals and having to admit that you were right more times than you were wrong. It's annoying, actually." I smile to myself and pick a blade of grass from my jeans.

"You were definitely wrong on two counts, though. You were wrong about what you thought would bring me eternal happiness. And I know *you* know you were wrong about my career. Showed you, didn't I, old man? Winning awards left and right." I laugh once, in spite of it all.

"Anyway, I came here to say hi—finally. But also to say goodbye. It's time I figured out what I want now. I don't think... I don't think I want to keep traveling so much. Or maybe I do. But I need to set down roots somewhere. I liked my time in Ceres Cove—though admittedly, much of it had to do with You-Know-Who. So I've been thinking maybe I'll pull a Walter Adams. Maybe I find a quiet town I can get down with and find my place there. Who the hell knows."

I heave myself to my feet, feeling much older than my age. "Goodbye, old man. Love you."

I know it might seem like tempting fate, walking back into the same bar I met her in nine months ago. But I remind myself I shouldn't worry—Lottie's in New York, after all. Although I did forget all about her brother, so when I sit at the bar and he walks up to take my order, Alejandro and I both freeze. "You're—You're back."

Shit.

"Yeah. Hey, man."

"Are you here for…"

I lift a hand. "No, no. Just visiting my dad's grave."

"Oh, yeah?" He glances nervously around the bar, guilt clear on his face. Does he feel like he's betraying his sister talking to me or something? I mean, *she* dumped *me.*

"Yeah."

We fall into an awkward silence—a *painful* one.

"Well, can I—ah—get you something?" His tone is unexpectedly nice, calm. Very our past interactions. Instead of downright antagonism, he's welcoming. The smile on his face is almost kind.

It's disorienting, is what it is.

"Sure," I almost stutter. "IPA would be nice."

He shoots me a genuine smile and a "no problem" before coming back with a frosty bottle. He places it gingerly in front of me, leaning on his forearms to get a better look at me.

"You look… good, man."

I choke on a sip. "Oh. Uh, thanks."

"Are you staying long?"

"No. Like I said, was just visiting my dad's grave on my

way back home. Or I guess to my mom's. I've been traveling for the past six months."

He nods seriously. "That's a long time."

"Yeah. Just having a beer before I hit the road."

"You probably shouldn't drink and drive, then."

Duh. I shrug. "It's just one beer. And I'll eat something before I go."

"Right." He looks away for a beat before turning back with a face-splitting grin. "You know. Today's the grand opening of the new bookstore in town. Where your dad's place used to be."

"Oh, yeah?" I swallow, my heart jumping in my chest.

"You should check it out. From what I heard, they have a really cool cafe in there, too. The new owner bought the space beside it and really opened up the place. Now you can sit there, order coffee and a muffin and read all afternoon. And some nights, they open the wine bar and serve tapas or whatever."

"That actually sounds... kind of incredible. Definitely different from anything this town has seen, right? It sounds like something Lo—" I grimace, catching my slip just in time. "*Lots* of people would enjoy. You know, since there isn't anything really that chill."

"Yeah, they reinstated book club, too. Which, as you know, was a pretty big deal here."

I nod, wanting off the subject. Too close to Lottie. And any topic close to Lottie starts picking at those stitches. What a visual.

"Right."

He gives me a look, as if waiting for me to come to this

magical realization. "How about I give you the flyer? You can go once you're done with this beer." From behind the bar, he pulls out a pink sheet of paper, an illustration of the new storefront under the words GRAND OPENING SATURDAY with the times below.

"Uh, sure. I guess I could check it out."

"Good. Good, yes." And it's that odd look in his eyes plus the unsettling feeling that this man who has historically been so antagonistic towards me but was so welcoming now that leads me to walk the five minutes it takes to the new bookstore in town: Strike a Prose.

I snort at the name, bringing an unexpected smile to my face. "Strike a Prose," I repeat under my breath. "Classic."

Without another thought, I push the door to the book-store open. As soon as I do, I freeze. Because whoever bought this bookstore has turned this place into definitely more than just that. The space has been divided into three clear sections. On the left, the actual bookstore part of the space filled with several bays of books each one containing a wide variety to suit everyone's needs, apparently. On the right, a cafe where I can currently see people lining up, eyeing brownies and other baked goods behind the display case. In the middle, a bar at the far end of the room with a set of couches surrounding a coffee table, where many people are currently enjoying a book. And wherever there seemed to be enough space on the wall, large prints of photographs of the town and of its people.

My photographs.

CHAPTER FORTY-ONE

LOTTIE

I love Ceres Cove.

And I know what you're thinking—*Whoa, what? Since when?* Turns out, since always. I just had to do some work on myself to realize that much of what was happening was internal. It took months of therapy and a lot of introspection to realize I had *a lot* of baggage to deal with. Not just with my divorce and my infertility, but so much about my parents and their loss.

Grief. Such an odd thing. I should've known, especially after speaking about it with Knox on several occasions. At the time, I thought I knew all about grief. But it's shocking how deep the iceberg really is.

Now, as I look around at my wonderful friends and family, at the people of Ceres Cove who have been able to make it to the opening, I feel calm. *Excited*, for sure. But calm. I no longer feel trapped or like there's an elephant on my chest. I no longer feel like a failure. I no longer have these arbitrary expectations on what it means to have "made it" in life. *I* decide what it means to have "made it." No one else. And as I stand in the middle of *my* bookstore, that *I* got off the ground, based off of a concept *I* developed that also helped my community, I know that I have officially *Made It*. Capital M. Capital I.

Sure, it would be great to have the one person I love most by my side. But even if he *had* answered my calls over the past few months, even if he *hadn't* ignored my emails or texts, even if he *had* forgiven me, I'm happy to have done this on my own.

I miss Knox. I miss him on a visceral level. But I'm getting my life together, just getting a business off the ground, taking better care of my physical and mental health. My endo flare-ups have come few and far between since taking this major step in life. And though I'm still going through with the hysterectomy, there's no rush. I'm waiting until the initial excitement from the store comes down.

As for Knox, I hope that maybe one day he will pick up the phone. Maybe one day, when he's less angry at me, he'll answer my calls or emails. Or maybe he'll find the one person that truly makes him happy. And though it's devastating to think that person might not be me, at least there'll be peace in knowing he's happy.

"This is amazing, Lottie. We're so insanely proud of you." Daniel hands me another glass of pink champagne before placing a kiss on my cheek while Brandon places a kiss on my other one. "Seriously, this is incredible."

"Thanks, guys. None of this would've happened without you. There's no way I could've afforded buying the bookstore back *and* the space next door without your loan. I don't know how to thank you enough."

"Stop," Brandon says, taking a sip from his own glass. "We're more than happy to do it. Everyone in town is obsessed, and come summer, it'll be packed with people."

"Hopefully before then, Brandon."

"Yes, that too, of course."

"I want to make this a chill place to hang. I mean, you know I have plans to do watch parties and stuff. Like *The Bachelor* in January and stuff."

"Really? Are we doing fantasy leagues, too?" Daniel's eyes light up.

I laugh at his excitement, giddy that so many other people in town are as happy about my new place as I am. "Absolutely."

"So can you give us a tour of the photos? I've made my own assumption as to where they came from, but I just want to hear it from you."

"They're mine, aren't they?" The familiar voice comes from behind me, sending chills running up and down my spine. Every muscle in my body tenses. My wide eyes flash to Daniel, but his shocked gaze is on someone behind me.

"You're here." I pretend like I don't know who he's talking to, but a whiff of that signature scent weakens my knees, making me have to lean on the nearest shelf for stability.

There's only one person who has that effect on me.

Turn around, I tell myself, but it's like my body won't comply.

Knox clears his throat. "Yeah, I—"

"I'm so glad you got my email." Daniel is beaming, bursting at the seams with happiness.

Email? They've been in contact?

"No, actually. I haven't checked my email or phone in months. Not since the sale went through."

A piece of me unwinds. *He hasn't checked his email or phone in months.* So maybe he wasn't ignoring me. But maybe he just... forgot about me.

"Kinda shut myself off from the rest of humanity, actually."

"Right. Lottie, do you think maybe you could get it together enough to turn around and say hi to Knox? Seeing as somehow he made it to your grand opening?"

Brandon laughs but tries to hide it with a cough.

"*I hate you,*" I mouth to both of them before turning around.

"*Your* grand opening?" Knox asks.

He's just as handsome as ever with his charming scruff, glacier-blue eyes, and broad shoulders. His puffy coat covers his chest and arms, but my memory isn't bad enough that I don't remember the way his muscles look beneath it.

"Yeah," I manage to breathe. "Mine."

"I—I thought you were in New York. Your brother..."

I look around for Daniel, but he and Brandon have secretly wandered off, leaving me and Knox alone.

"Yeah, I did leave. But. But I came back." My pulse quickens, breathing speeds.

"Why's that?"

"None of it felt right. I missed Ceres Cove and I missed... I missed people."

"People, huh?" His infamous lopsided smile makes an appearance, causing my heart to perform some serious acrobatics in my chest. But just as quickly as it pops up, it disappears, breaking my heart just a little more than it already was.

"You wanna show me around? Tell me what my photos are doing all over the place?"

"Sure," I say, turning to face the closest one to us. A gorgeous scene of a pelican by the dock, about to take flight in the cold spring morning air. Below the frame, a small sign with Knox's name. "Daniel found these photos in the SD card you gave him and showed them to me. They were so beautiful... I decided to print some and put them around for sale. I promise I plan to deposit every single cent into your account. Daniel still has your bank info from before. I don't know much about photography, so I had someone come and asses them. So that's how I marked them with those prices. I didn't just arbitrarily pick a number or whatever."

"I don't doubt it."

"But now that I think about it, I realize it could be construed as crossing a huge line. A total breach of trust." *Shit.* My stomach churns. I run my fingers through my hair. "All this time I thought I was doing something good and now I realize it might've actually backfired."

He laughs. He actually laughs, his eyes full of warmth. "Lottie, relax. I gave Daniel the card, and possession is nine tenths of the law, haven't you heard?"

"I can't tell if you're joking or not, but if you are, you kind of suck right now because I'm trying to make things right in any way that I can and—"

"Hey. Relax. I didn't mean to make you feel bad. I didn't want the photos anymore. But I'm glad you liked them. I'm glad they're being enjoyed. And thank you for crediting me and putting them up for sale."

"You're welcome." I want to smile. I want to tell him how happy I am that he's here.

"So if you saw these photos, it means you saw…" His cheeks flush, and suddenly he can't look me in the eye. He scratches the back of his neck, visibly uncomfortable for the first time since seeing each other again.

"I… Yes. I did. I saw the other ones, too." I take a deep breath, everything coming back to me all at once. Coming home from New York in the middle of the night, having an emergency meeting with my siblings, asking Daniel and Brandon for the loan for this store, followed by my brother handing me the two things Knox left behind: his leather jacket and the SD card.

"I think you need to see what's in there, sis. I think you need to see the photos," Daniel said when he handed me the card, his face somber.

I remember going through the pictures, my jaw dropping at the beautiful way in which he captured the town, the people in it. And me. Hundreds and hundreds of pictures of me.

I realized then and there why Knox kept telling me I wasn't ready to see them. Because somehow, without using any words, he had managed to unearth the truth behind this town and present everything that was good and pure about it. And I was too filled with disdain to see it. I rejected my hometown, but most of all, I rejected myself. And here was this man, capturing all kinds of seemingly immaterial moments, representing them in a way that showed their true grandeur and meaning. A group of older women talking on a park bench became an image of decades' long friendship and love. The demolition of shelves in an old bookstore became a symbol of growth and rebirth. And a woman throwing her head back in laughter with sleeprumpled hair became a perfect image of me, utterly in love with the man behind the camera.

There was beauty and truth in so many things I hadn't let myself see. And he was able to capture every second of it. Each photograph became an eye-opening gift. So I felt the need to celebrate them, to have them hung in the place I was making my own.

"So what did you think, then? About... About it all."

"I think they look like a love letter. To the town, of course," I amend.

He scoffs. "And to you. But you know that."

I gnaw on my bottom lip, hoping to keep it from trembling. The familiar stinging behind my eyes grows uncomfortable, so I look away.

"I guess it was." *Past*. Gone. In that moment, we loved each other. But now? Now it's just me, standing in front of a boy, *not* asking him to love her. Because I don't deserve it after everything.

I feel his hand come under my chin, he tilts my face back to his. "Show me the rest of your bookstore?"

I sniffle and nod, smiling as best I can. "Of course."

So I give him a tour, leading him through the crowd, stopping every so often to greet people. I show Knox the punny way I classified each bay ("metaphors be with you" for fantasy, "kiss and tale" for romance, etc), and get a "Holy shit that's genius" from him.

"Thanks," I say with a laugh. "I think one or two people have found it annoying, but most find satisfaction in guessing the genre. I think it keeps the reader engaged."

When I show him the bar and we take a seat, I order us both a mocktail. "And Alejandro isn't pissed at you for having this in your bookstore since he used to own the only bar in town?"

"No," I say before taking a sip of my favorite new drink, Spa Day (cucumber, lime, coconut water, and seltzer on the rocks). "It's a different vibe and he knows it. Ale's bar is great —but for a different audience. What I wanted to create was an all-in-one safe and fun space for women in this town, mostly. For everyone, but I'm filling a particular need Ceres Cove had. No offense to my brother, but going to his bar has never given me the same type of feeling as going to a nicer, chill lounge-type place with the girls. It's just not the same. Don't get me wrong, there's a time and place for going some-where that smells like hops, but it isn't every night. Plus, you can sit here and watch Bravo or other trash reality TV. It's a place for people to get away, while still feeling at home."

"And I'm sure you're less likely to get unwanted attention here than you are at your brother's bar."

I smile at him, barely able to breathe. "I don't know. The last guy who tried to pick me up at his bar wasn't so bad."

He inhales sharply, eyes locked on mine. "I'm glad you feel that way. Wouldn't want you regretting anything. It's not a good way to live your life."

"Do you have any regrets?" The words leave my mouth before I can even think. Tears start to build in my eyes because I realize I've just set myself up to hear something I might not want to hear. But would most definitely deserve.

"About you? None. Maybe that I didn't fight harder, but..."

I sniffle. "Right. But." I look away before I lose it. God, it would just be so typical of me, too. To just start crying in the middle of my grand opening because my ex-boyfriend came back and—

I stop. Take a deep breath. No, we are not doing this. We are going to enjoy today.

"I love it, Lottie. Seriously. I'm so proud of you." He takes my hand in both of his, his eyes locked on mine.

"Thank you, Knox." I wrap my other hand around his. "I'm so happy you made it. I don't know *how* you made it. But I'm happy you're here. It's been... It's been a rough six months."

"It doesn't look like it, though." He smiles, looking around.

"I think you know what I mean."

His expression drops. So do his hands. To his credit, he pulls them away gently. And because I am an absolute masochist, I tell him, "I missed you."

Knox sits up straight in his stool, brow furrowed. "It's cause your aim sucks, kid."

I groan, half thankful for the comic relief, half frustrated with it. "That was a terrible dad joke."

"Says the woman who literally made her bookstore all about puns."

I snort-laugh, spilling some of my drink. He reaches out with his napkin to dab at my chin. But his face grows serious, dropping his napkin in my lap. Knox cups my jaw in his large warm hand, and I can't help but lean into it. His eyes flit to my lips, which he traces with his thumb.

And it's like we're back to that first night. To that spark.

"Knox, I—"

"Hey, sis. Hey, Knox."

I glare at Adriana for interrupting us, seriously considering the whole murder thing again.

"Adri, we were just—"

"I know, but I just had to interrupt you because the guy from the The Maine Courant is here to interview you."

I look back at Knox, conflicted. "I'm so sorry. It's just... They have the third biggest circulation in Maine and—"

He holds a hand up to stop me, a sad smile on his face. "Don't worry about it." Knox slides off his stool and begins to walk away but I stop him just in time, grabbing him by the sleeve of his coat.

"Don't go. *Please*. There's still so much I want to say. So much I *need* to say."

He stares at me for a moment and swallows, considering my plea. After a painful stretch of time, he nods. "Okay. How about I go book a room at the motel and come back when everyone is gone?"

My breath catches in my chest, heart lurching. "R-really? I... Yes. *Yes*, please."

He kisses my cheek while I stand very still, wanting desperately not to ruin this moment.

"Be right back. Enjoy your celebration. You deserve it."

CHAPTER FORTY-TWO

KNOX

Lottie locks the bookstore door with shaking hands, turning off the neon pink *Open* sign hanging by the window. The place is a mess, covered in disposable bamboo plates, cups, and paper napkins. It's... a lot, this mess. So I make a mental note to stay and help pick up, no matter the outcome of this conversation.

After putting some paperwork away behind the counter, Lottie pauses, her back turned to me, taking a few steadying breaths. I don't blame her. As I watch her try to get herself together for us to talk, I do the same thing. Preparing myself to hear whatever it is that she has to say, good or bad. Whatever it may be.

She slowly turns to face me, that full bottom lip caught between her teeth. And, *god*, the need to kiss her, to feel those soft lips on mine... She's so beautiful. So fucking beautiful it hurts to look at her.

I miss her so much.

"Knox." The sound of my name on her lips is something

I've dreamt about every night since leaving this town six months ago. Something I'd sometimes think I'd hear even while I was away. And now that she's here, now that I get to hear her say it, it sounds even more surreal.

Ethereal, almost.

"Lottie."

"Thank you for staying behind. Alejandro stopped by earlier for a bit and mentioned you were on your way home from a long trip, so I appreciate you staying an extra night so we could talk."

I could spend $49 on a motel for one night and get home a day late to get some answers, or I could spend the rest of my life wondering where we went wrong. I need the closure, so I chose the former.

"Of course." *Anything*, I almost tell her. Because despite understanding that she doesn't want me, deep down, I will always love her. I will always want her. I will always do whatever she needs.

I wait patiently for her to speak, but it takes her a while to gather up enough courage. And when she does: "I called you. A lot. But it kept going to voicemail."

Surprised, I take a step back. She called? "Well, you already know I haven't really checked my phone. I was away in Scotland."

She frowns, eyes sad. "Right. But... I mean, you never had access to WiFi?"

I sigh, run my fingers through my hair. "I only turned my phone on a couple of days ago and, frankly, I needed to disconnect. I was going through a lot, between losing you and finding Walter."

"Finding Walter?"

I smile. "That's what I was doing. I went to his hometown after reading more of his journals, speaking to my mom. I went and met his—*my*—family. And slowly, through them and his stories, I got to know my dad more."

Her grin is wide. "Your dad."

"Yeah." I smile. I can't help it. "My *dad.*"

"That's amazing, Knox."

"Yeah. I needed it. We both did, you know? He and I. It was good."

"Good." We fall silent, unsure of what comes next. But I'm not going to be the one to break the silence this time. She ended this. If she wants to talk, then... She should talk.

"I... I made a mistake, Knox. Lots of them. And I pretty much realized it as soon as I got to New York. But I figured, I had already messed things up between us, so." She shrugs, but her eyes begin to water. "I tried giving it a shot, but it didn't feel right. I wanted to apologize— *needed* to apologize. But when I came back to do so, you were gone. You had left."

"You left first."

"I did."

"And now you're back."

"I am." Her voice sounds more determined than I've ever heard it.

"What are you trying to say, Lottie? Because losing you was— I can't even describe it. I felt like you cast me aside so easily—"

"No, Knox. *No.* That's not what it was. I was just..." She sighs. "I was scared and so messed up. And wanted to protect you."

"So what are you trying to say?" I repeat.

"I'm... I'm..." She pauses. Swallows once. "I'm trying to say that I miss you. That I... That I love you. That I messed up—I *know* I messed up. And now you're here. How the hell did that happen? So I'm going to shoot my shot, because I don't know whether I'll ever get a chance like this again. But I was wondering whether you'd be willing to maybe forgive me? Go back?"

"There is nothing I want less than to go back to how we were." My words land harsh and destructive, and I realize how badly they can be misconstrued. "Not because I don't care about you, Lottie. But because I deserve more."

She swipes a tear away and nods. "No, you're right. You do deserve more. I mean, it's why I broke up with you in the first place. The whole kid thing."

I groan. "I told you I never gave a shit about the kid thing. I don't care about having kids. I wanted you more. I just want *you*. But I mean that I don't want to go back to you keeping all these walls between us, hiding stuff from me. I don't want to go back to letting you make all our relationship decisions, not treating me like the partner I was supposed to be. Honestly, no matter how much I love you, nothing sounds worse than being with you but not really having you."

"That's fair. I totally get that. But it wouldn't be that way again. And I know this is all sudden, bringing this back up again after not seeing each other for so long. But I've thought about this a lot and... Well, I am pretty damn sure you're the love of my life, Knox. I don't think there will ever be anyone but you. And if I've messed this up too much... Then, I get it. I didn't handle things well. But I just want you to know that everything I did was because I thought I was doing the best thing for you. I loved you—*love* you—in a way that haunts me. Because it's almost selfish. I want the best for you, so a huge part of me feels like I'd be taking something away from you if you stay with me. Yet at the same time..." She lets the sentence hang before taking a deep breath. "Okay, it's like this: I love you enough to want you to have everything you want in life. Which means that I wouldn't hold it against you if you left me because you wanted kids. But if you love me, too, and you're okay with who I am and what I have to offer, then... then love *me*, Knox. Be with me. Be my partner—I promise I won't keep you at arm's length anymore because I don't want to. I want you to know every inch of me, just like I want to know every inch of you. You're *it.* But if I'm too late and I messed up too much..." She chokes back a sob, so I take a few steps forward, close enough to catch her perfect caramel scent. "If I messed things up too much, then I get it. I'll let you go. Because I just want you to be happy, Knox. It's all I want."

"That's a lot of information." I exhale, wanting so badly to say yes, to pull her in my arms and start this new life together.

"It is. But I wanted to put it all out there. Because there are so many things I need to tell you. *Want* to tell you. And I promise if you give me a chance, I will."

"I want to say yes, Lottie. I do. God, I've dreamed so many times over the past six months of you saying exactly this. But I'm terrified of losing you again because... I just don't think I'll be able to survive it."

She shakes her head vehemently. "I'm not pushing you

away again, Knox. I was holding on by a thread, too. And while I am happy with my bookstore and think that I've created something really special here, I finally realize that I won't ever be satisfied if I don't have my partner by my side. And I don't mean the business kind. I know you have your work and you travel, but I want to be your home base. I want to be the person you come back to after your adventures. So... love me, Knox."

I roll my eyes at her, a smile on my face. "I've always loved you, Lottie. I think I fell for you the second I watched you order a martini from across the bar."

A sharp inhale, a step forward, and suddenly, my arms are around her, pulling her tightly into me.

"I'm s-so sorry," she sobs into my chest. "I really m-messed up."

"I know." I kiss the top of her head, inhaling her scent, letting it heal every broken inch of me. "But it's okay. I may be a sucker for forgiving you so quickly, but I want this, too, Lottie. I love you."

"I promise I'll never keep you out again."

"I should've never let you go." I cup her face, angling it toward mine.

"No," she says between sobs. "I think in a messed up way maybe we needed this. I needed to realize that I wasn't this broken, half-woman for not being able to have kids. I needed to realize that I could have a full life with the man I loved despite everything. And I'm glad you took this time apart to grieve Walter. To get to know your dad and heal that part of yourself."

"Yeah." I grin, pushing her overgrown bangs from her face. "Maybe."

She sniffles once, her beautiful face red and splotchy. She's still the most beautiful woman I've ever seen in my life.

"Can you kiss me? Please."

I don't hesitate for a second. I duck down to kiss her deep and long, to try and make up for lost time. But nothing will ever be enough, because no amount of time with her will ever be enough. I want Lottie. I want her always by my side. And as I sink deeper into this kiss, need building inside, I nearly burst with happiness.

"I never have to let you go, then?" I ask. "You're mine for good?"

She laughs before placing another kiss on my lips. "Yes. If you'll have me. Though I'm older than you, so I'll probably die first, who knows."

My stomach lurches. "Jesus, don't ever say that. I just had to live six months without you—I don't want to think about actually *losing* you."

"You won't. We'll live forever." She kisses me again, her body molding to mine.

"Should we get married now?" The words burst through my lips, completely unchecked. *Shit.* But I don't take them back, even though she's only *just* come back to me. Even though I know this might terrify her.

But Lottie just smiles up at me and shrugs, unbothered. "If you want. Though I don't need a piece of paper to tell me we belong to each other. I'm yours, for good. And if you say you're mine, then I trust you."

"Yes. Partners, then."

"Partners." She reaches up on her tiptoes to kiss me on the nose. "What do you think Walter would have thought about this? About us?"

I throw my head back and laugh. "You're never going to believe this…"

Saturday, February 3rd

It's been three weeks since she started working here, and already I can see a change. Lottie showed up broken and more than a little lost. And if what I've heard around town is right, she has a right to be. But I can see her improving a bit, day by day. You can tell she's far from being happy, but something inside her—maybe an innate work ethic?—has kept her from sliding down into a deep, dark hole of despair.

This town, though. They are so nosy. They keep mentioning setting her up with other men, wanting her to restart her life as if it were as easy as snapping one's fingers.

But I know heartbreak. I know heartbreak well. And only one who has truly suffered through that experience—real loss—can truly understand how deep the sadness goes. Plus, everyone keeps focusing on the man, in this scenario. On the fact that she lost her husband. But does no one see that what she's grieving isn't him? This woman is grieving who she thought she would be. And that's not something that can be solved by going on a date. Certainly not from any of the simpletons here.

Lottie is brilliant. It's no wonder she got so far in her career at such a young age. She just needs to recover on her own time. She reminds me so much of my own son.

Knox.

Maybe that's why I've grown to like her so quickly. Because, in a way, they're so similar.

Young people meant for greatness.

I pray to god she finds peace and happiness one day. I believe she deserves it.

I look up at her and smile, taking the dog-eared journal from her. "He loved you right from the get-go. Just like I did."

She's crying again, so I kiss her cheek before pulling her into my arms.

"Walter," she croaks. "And you've been traveling around with all these journals?"

"Not all," I say, rifling in my duffel for the other journal I want to show her. "But certainly the more influential ones. Now read this." I flip through the dates until I find the one I marked for reference. One of the entries I've reread multiple times over the past several months.

Monday, January 15th

Well, I got my diagnosis today. It doesn't look good. It's clear to my doctors that I do not have much time left here.

I was thinking about what I would like to do until the day comes where I must go, but I'm not too keen on many of the clichés. I don't want to reach out to Knox just because I'm dying. I don't want him to feel obligated to forgive me simply because I've got less than a couple of months to live. I don't want to talk to Melissa again. And I certainly do not want to make a big thing out of it with anyone else in my life.

But one thing is for certain, I won't leave anyone with a mess to clean up after I'm gone. So I've decided to clearly outline what will happen with the bookstore and the rest of my possessions.

The obvious answer, of course, is to leave Knox everything. He is my son, after all. Which is why I called a lawyer today, right after I left the doctor's office, and discussed leaving a detailed will. I figure Knox could get a pretty penny from selling my things, which would perhaps help him in his work. Maybe help with new gear, as I believe photo equipment can get quite expensive.

But as I was thinking about my legacy, I became saddened by how unsatisfactory I find it. Is that really all I'm leaving my son to remember me by? And isn't there anyone else I can help so my death can have a more positive impact?

It's why I've decided to leave him with one last thing before I go: a business partner. The opportunity to meet Lottie, to bond with her. Because I also hate the idea of leaving her alone in this town full of nitwits. And as I've gotten to know her, I've also grown to care for her. And maybe she needs this. Maybe she needs something to bring her back to life. Whether that be by taking on more responsibility in the book- store or whether it's by meeting and bonding with my son. Either way, I've chosen to include her among my list of beneficiaries. Darling girl.

Through her, I hope maybe Knox will get to know me better. Hate me less.

Tomorrow, I meet with Leroy to outline everything in detail.

"He wasn't explicit about it, but I think he meant for this to happen. I think he believed we would be good together. Good for each other. So, yeah. I'm pretty sure he'd be thrilled."

Lottie laughs once, wet and teary. "Yeah. I think we're pretty good together."

EPILOGUE: LOTTIE

FOUR MONTHS LATER

"Ok, so I got you chocolates, obviously. But I also thought we'd go for a little more variety this time," Knox says, his brows furrowed in concentration, so serious. "Salt & vinegar chips, some cookies, *soup*—because even though you're not super feeling it, you do need to eat something that isn't processed or full of chemicals. I also—"

I put my fingers to his lips, stopping him. "You are adorable. Thank you for getting me all this stuff. For taking care of me." I move my hand to cup his face. Knox gives me his trademark lopsided smile, eyes blue and bright as ever. His hand covers mine, holding it to his cheek.

Though my pain had gotten substantially better over the past year, I still decided to go through with the hysterectomy. There's always a chance that it might come back, but it's low. I'm one day post-op and optimistic that this is going to be the first day of the rest of my life. Pain free, with the love of my life by my side.

"I just want to take care of you." His voice is soft, his eyes pleading.

"You are, and you do it so well." My heart is full and I feel lighter than I have in years—and it isn't because of the painkillers they've got me on. It's this knowledge that I'm exactly where I want to be with who I want to be. The knowledge that I am exactly the person I want to be.

I'm not saying that my life is perfect by any means. Knox and I still have arguments, the bookstore is a ton of work, and I still sometimes battle this nagging feeling that I'm not enough.

No, life definitely isn't perfect. But man, is it good.

"Plus, this whole thing is kind of bittersweet. It's the last time we'll be doing this."

I laugh and shake my head before giving him a peck on the lips. I wince a bit, the movement uncomfortable despite the pain killers. "It's bittersweet that I just had a hysterectomy to never have debilitating abdominal pain because it means you'll never get to take care of me like that again?"

"Uh... Yes?" He seems unsure. "I mean, I'm obviously glad you got the surgery. But I secretly enjoyed getting to hold you and bring you whatever you needed while you weren't well. It was our thing."

I roll my eyes at him, attacking a chocolate truffle. "If you want to watch Twilight so bad, just watch it."

"You know that's not what I meant."

I giggle and tug on his hand, pulling him in bed next to me. "You can still take care of me in my old age. Or when I have a cold. And I can take care of you."

He smiles softly and presses his lips to mine. "Okay. We'll take care of each other."

THE END

ACKNOWLEDGMENTS

Thank you, dear reader, for picking up this book. Lottie's journey was a rough one, and I'm so happy I was able to give her a HEA.

Thank you to my incredibly supportive husband for being there every step of this book's way (and more).

Tracey, ILY 4eva.

Cassie—you're an absolute queen. What would I do without you?

Jenissa, thank you for helping me take this book to the next level.

To the real Touching My Shelf peeps. Love you.

To MO. Thank you.

ABOUT THE AUTHOR

Caroline Frank is a Venezuelan indie author and self-proclaimed shoe addict. She currently resides in Philadelphia with her husband, two crazy cats, Señor Kitty and Salem, and her German Shepherd, Tilly.

She spends her days reading, crocheting, crafting, writing, and biking. Her favorite things include the first sip of an iced-cold Coke and using self-deprecating humor to get through the day.

Though she always planned to eventually take over the world, she thinks writing fun stories every day is pretty freaking awesome and plans to continue to do so for the foreseeable future.

ALSO BY CAROLINE FRANK

<u>Seasons of Love Series (Open-Door Romantic Comedy):</u>

Fall Into You (Book 1)

Shall We Dance? (Book 2)

Happily Ever Disaster (Novella - Book 2.5)

Second Chance Snowmance (Book 3)

<u>Tastes Like Summer (Book 4) - Coming Soon</u>

<u>Standalone:</u>

Reply All

Chosen, Eternally